W9-BFI-790

BEDSIDE MANNER

"You could help me sleep," Cole said.

Emy wondered if she really wanted to hear the answer. "How?"

"By joining me in this bed."

Emy shot him a stern look. "Monsieur, you are far too ill to allow wicked thoughts."

"A man can never be too sick for that, darlin'."

"Behave," she warned him. "Go to sleep."

"There's something in my eye," Cole lied. He wanted her closer, much closer, and didn't hesitate to use any trick.

"I don't believe you."

"There is. I swear."

Emy reached for his face, and immediately her hands were captured in his. She laughed. "I knew you were lying."

Cole shook his head. "You suspected me of lying. You didn't know for sure, or you wouldn't have come so close."

He pulled her closer still. Emy felt her heart thump at his smile. With amazing strength for one so ill, he pulled her to lean over him until she plopped hard upon his chest, her hands held wide from her sides.

Her lips were almost touching his, and Cole almost groaned in his anticipation, knowing she was going to allow the kiss.

His hands released hers and came to gently cup rounded cheeks, bringing her mouth within contact of his. He knew it. He knew she would feel like this. He knew her mouth would be this soft, this warm, this sweet. It was the best thing he'd ever known.

His mouth was fire and Emy felt her resistance melt away at the need in his kiss. She groaned, unable to deny either of them this pleasure. Her lips parted to his gentle persuasion. . . .

PATRICIA PELLICANE

NIGHTS OF FIRE

ZEBRA BOOKS
KENSINGTON PUBLISHING CORP.

ZEBRA BOOKS are published by

Kensington Publishing Corp.
475 Park Avenue South
New York, NY 10016

First Printing: July, 1993

Printed in the United States of America

Prologue

The two men waited, hidden in the growing shadows of a tall building, their brows creased into worried frowns, their bodies damp with nervous perspiration. Now that they'd come to this decision, they were impatient to be done with it, for neither had the heart, never mind the expertise, for what was about to come.

As the evening slowly darkened to night, their attention never wavered from the large brick building in the center of Baton Rouge. Traffic of every description, from lone horses and tightly sprung buggies to closed carriages and heavy laboring work wagons, moved slowly down the busy cobblestone street. From an alley they watched as wooden sidewalks groaned beneath the weight of the city's finest and those not quite so fine. Ladies of the night already prowled, even though the gaslights located at each corner were only now being lit. Distinguished from their sisters by heavy face paint and revealing low-cut gowns, they impatiently awaited the approach of their first customer for the night.

Ladies of fashion hurried home from a day spent shopping or visiting to prepare themselves for a night of social festivities, while men and women weary from a long day's work stumbled with the last of their energy toward their dwellings. Both men knew once finished with this chore, they could easily fade into this crowd with no one the wiser.

Today was the last of the month and many of Baton Rouge would bring their hard-earned drafts and credits to the bank to exchange paper for gold. In a few minutes an armored Wells Fargo wagon would be arriving, filled with enough money to see to the city's needs. All these two men wanted was a small part of it. Just enough for Emy and Grandmère to cease their worrying. Just enough so that they would no longer be forced into taking in wash, or sewing dresses for rich ladies until their fingers ached and their eyes were nearly blinded by the strain of working long into the night.

A man didn't feel much like a man when he was forced to depend on his womenfolk for support. Granted, they couldn't be accused of actually supporting their men, for the money earned was barely enough to put food on their table. Still, it was a man's job, his pleasure, in fact, to see to his family's need. It was bitter medicine indeed to find their positions suddenly reversed.

Jacques Du Maurier and his son Anton hadn't felt like men for some time now. For two consecutive years the Mississippi had flooded its banks and robbed them of that distinction. It had risen so high

6

as to overflow the levy and destroy to the last plant the crops upon their land. They were deeply in debt to the bank from last year's devastation, and yet the Lord had seen fit to allow another catastrophe to befall them.

Jacques sighed at his thoughts, knowing no good could come of wallowing in his misfortune. The truth of it was, what was done was done and no amount of prayers or bemoaning the fates would change a thing. It was time to take control of his life. It was time for action.

Not so long ago, father and son each thought of himself as basically good and decent. Now each man wondered if that was truly the case. For they had turned willingly enough to a life of crime when it appeared there was no other way. Perhaps they had never been good, or decent. Not deep down, where it counted, for at the first testing of their character, they failed, and miserably so. But what else was a man to do? Desperate times called for desperate measures. And one wasn't likely to get more desperate than when watching the bank take back your land—land that had been in the family for as long as anyone could remember.

They had been to see Mr. Whitehead, of course. But that fat carpetbagger from New York offered only a sickening façade of a smile meant to imply his supposed sympathy at hearing of their difficulties, all the while professing he had no choice. He had to call the note in.

Jacques shrugged. He, too, had no choice, no choice but to see to the welfare of his family, and if that meant relieving the bank of some of its heaviest burden, so be it.

In their secreted positions, the two lifted their neckerchiefs to cover the lower part of their faces as the guards brought the last of the gold inside the bank. Moments later came the steady, heavy clip-clop of horses' hooves as the Wells Fargo wagon rolled out of sight.

Their heartbeats accelerated, their blood pounded, growing almost deafening as the moment approached, nearly blotting out the sounds of the city around them. It was time.

Jacques and Anton slipped unnoticed into the mahogany-walled room, positioning themselves before the huge, thick double doors. Two enormous desks stood, one at each side of the immense, high-ceiling room, while at the far end, glass and wood cubicles formed a line of semi-private work areas. Behind each of the six partitions stood a young man, one nearly indistinguishable from the other, for they all sported identical spectacles perched low on small noses, slicked-down brown hair, dark jackets, and high, stiff collars. With cheerful smiles they handled the bank's transactions.

Wood had been polished to a high luster, marble floors gleamed, and a huge candlelit chandelier overhead added to the room's overall sense of sedate opulence.

Soft murmurs of polite conversation came from all directions. As the patrons were involved in their own business, none had yet noticed the two masked, armed men standing at the door.

The peace and gentle tranquility that filled the room was about to disappear.

"Ladies and gentlemen." French being Jacques's first language, the words were spoken in an accented, musical tone, one that was wonderfully pleasant to the ear, but in this case hardly above a whisper. One could only identify the attempt to bring attention to himself as altogether lacking confidence, for it brought about no results.

Jacques cleared his throat and tried again. His second attempt brought about exactly the same results.

Anton shifted nervously and frowned, his dark expression not without a touch of amazement. After all, two armed and masked men stood at the bank's door and not one of the patrons within even glanced in their direction. Surely the clientele's lack of reaction left much to be desired and tended to rob a man of a bit of his self-assurance.

Jacques ventured to speak once again, but the moment he opened his mouth his words were cut off by the most god-awful, ear-piercing screech. It seemed a fashionable, delicate-looking lady, finished with her business, had turned toward the door. She was pushing a thick roll of bills into her purse when she noticed the two villainous-looking men. The trouble was, by the time she noticed them, she was nearly upon them. Her proximity and the shock of seeing armed masked men inside a bank caused the woman to faint dead away an instant after her cry of alarm. She fell to the floor before anyone could reach for her. The sickening thud of her head hitting against the marble floor did not go unnoticed.

The patrons of the bank, and those who worked there as well, froze in place, but they were hardly the only ones affected by that cry. It startled both would-be thieves as well, who, in truth, were nervous enough, since this was only their third attempt at robbery, their first at a bank.

Now, after two felonious efforts, one would imagine both men to have gained at least a small measure of self-confidence. Sadly enough, that was not the case, for their previous ventures into larceny had provided them with less than fortunate results. The first time, they had stopped a buggy in the dark of night and Anton had been struck a painful blow to the head by a nearly hysterical would-be victim with the wrong end of a buggy whip before the man made a hasty escape. The second time, both had suffered the disgrace of being forced to walk back home, clothed only in their drawers, as yet another supposed quarry turned out to be of much the same intent as they and decidedly faster with his gun.

"Everyone stand still," Jacques murmured unnecessarily, for not one among the ten customers or eight employees could breathe, never mind bring their temporarily paralyzed bodies from their present positions.

Jacques moved carefully around them. Anton kept watch near the door.

Without another word spoken, a canvas bag was handed to the first teller and then passed to the next and the next while handfuls of money were hastily pushed inside. Within seconds the last man handed the now-full bag to the nervously waiting thief.

Jacques was on his way back to his son's side when a man entered the bank. All might have ended well except for the fact that this was no ordinary man.

Mr. Guillaume was the owner of Baton Rouge's most distinguished gambling house and restaurant and had not once in the past twenty years deprived himself of the vices that plague mankind. Indeed, he had greedily indulged, and so much so that over the years his width had grown profound, the inches around his middle coming perilously close to equaling those in his height, and his height was more than adequate. In any case, both doors were needed to allow him passage into the building.

Had Anton remembered to lock the doors as was the plan, things might have turned out quite differently. The problem was, he hadn't remembered, and to add to that mistake, he was standing just a bit too close to the doors.

When the edge of the door hit him in the back of the head, the force knocked him forward just enough to cause him to stumble off balance and trip over the still-unconscious lady lying all too close to his feet. He almost fell flat on his face.

The rifle that had been aimed with something less than enthusiasm at those inside the bank was now aimed at the ceiling. Inadvertently, Anton's finger tightened on the trigger.

The sound of a discharging gun echoed loudly within the large mostly open room, for a moment deafening those within. But that wasn't the worst of it. Seconds later came an even louder sound, for the lovely chandelier that had been hanging high above them crashed to the floor with a thunderous roar of splintering glass. Miraculously, it fell only inches from Anton's fallen body.

Jacques gasped as he realized the heavy crystal

had fallen with unnerving exactness between father and son. Another inch or so in either direction, and one of them might have been seriously injured or killed.

The sound seemed to jar everyone from their stunned immobility. The place was suddenly bedlam. Men were moving, shouting for the thieves to give up their ill-gotten gains. Two pulled guns that were tied to their hips and careless of further endangering the innocent shot wildly in the outlaws' direction. Women fell to the floor, and finding no cover there, whimpered or screamed their terror of being caught in the midst of a gun battle. Another lady fainted.

Jacques had no doubt that such a ruckus would soon bring the law crashing through those heavy oak doors.

In an effort to help his limping son, for Anton had somehow managed to hurt his leg in the fall, and hurry their exit from the building, Jacques wouldn't realize for some time that he had dropped the bag of money.

Chapter One

Emeline Du Maurier sat at her well-scrubbed kitchen table, her grandmère asleep in the rocker across the small room, her sister, Kit, gone off to bed. Emy forced aside the need to rage at the two subdued men she faced. Castigating their intent would serve no purpose. What was needed here was logic and a cool head. Dark eyes flashed with suppressed anger as she listened to her father's outrageous proposal. She waited long minutes before she was able to trust herself to speak, and when she did, she realized she hadn't waited long enough. *"Mon Dieu!* You cannot be serious," she said, knowing even as she said the words that he was very serious indeed. Still, she couldn't repress the hope. Perhaps he was teasing her, waiting for her to laugh as they had in the old days, in the days before the problems came to plague. "You promised to never . . ."

Jacques waved aside her exclamation, and a frown came to mar his handsome forehead. "I know what I promised, *chérie,* but we have little choice."

Emy muttered a low sound that was an odd mixture of prayer and outrage at her father's unbelievable suggestion. She took a deep, calming breath and began. "Let me get this straight." Her hands came together, but she was unconscious of the fact that they tightened into painful fists as she sought to control her need to rage. "You are planning to rob the paddle steamer *Princess.*"

"What's wrong with that?" Anton returned, noting the touch of ridicule in his sister's soft voice.

Emy turned her attention toward her brother, her dark eyes incredulous at his question, even as her voice remained sweet and liltingly soft, if slightly louder than usual. "You mean beside the fact that stealing is a sin, never mind that the two of you might very well end up in prison or dead?"

"Emy," her father warned as Grandmère Marie stirred from a light doze in her rocker.

"We know it's wrong," Anton threw in, his voice low, hardly above a whisper, meant only for his sister's ears, "but what else can we do?"

"You could find employment," she offered for perhaps the hundredth time.

"Emy"—Jacques's sigh told again his opinion of her suggestion—"you know, even between the two of us, we could never make enough to cover the note. We'll lose the farm if we don't do something."

"Do something?! Is that what you call what you've done so far?" Both men remained silent as Emy gave in at last to her fury. They had been expecting it. The only thing that had surprised them was that Emy had remained calm for so long. "If ever there were two more inept, clumsy fools parading themselves as thieves, I've yet to hear of it." Neither man dared to disagree. "First of all, neither of you has the first notion of how to be a criminal. People are actually laughing at the spectacle you made at the bank."

"And I suppose you could do better?" Anton responded with the snide comment, unable to put aside the shame of yet another failure. They were about to lose their land through no fault of their own, and even though desperate, they couldn't seem to make a success of this, their newly chosen profession. His tone told clearly of his bitterness.

Jacques shot his son a hard look and sought again to ease the tension between all three. "No one knows it was us, *chérie.*"

Emy's dark eyes narrowed with warning. "Give it up, Papa. It is more than obvious that you know nothing about crime." And at the man's stubborn look, she sighed wearily. "How many times have you tried? Have you once accomplished what you've set out to do?

"If it weren't for my prayers, I've no doubt that the two of you would be dead by now." Emy murmured another such rapid prayer and quickly crossed herself.

Jacques smiled at her devout belief. "Thank you, *mon âme.* I feel better knowing you're there, helping us with—"

"Non, you are mistaken if you believe my prayers are aimed toward your success. I'm not helping you! I pray only that neither of you will come to harm."

"Nothing will happen to us," he said as he patted her hand in a condescending fashion.

Emy tore her hand from her father's and shot both men a hard look. "Answer one question, if you please. Discounting the fact that guards no doubt watch over the game room, how are you planning to leave the steamer after you rob its patrons?"

It was obvious from their expression that neither man had thought about guards or their means of escape.

"*Sacrebleu.*" Emy nodded her dark head as a weary sigh slid from full, pink lips. She tightened her mouth as she continued with her questioning. "Will you jump into the Mississippi?" she shrugged, a very Gallic gesture, common to her and her entire family, and waved her hand in a flippant manner. "The river is miles wide at any given point, but I've heard tell that every so often one escapes the currents at its center. I suppose there's a chance you might as well."

Jacques shook his head. His daughter was right. Why hadn't he thought of it before? They couldn't jump into the river, especially not if carrying gold. Gold was heavy. They couldn't carry it and swim at the same time.

Jacques sighed as he watched the lovely woman sitting across from him. His daughter, despite her tender years, was a woman of rare wisdom and forethought. Unlike himself, she wouldn't make foolish mistakes. She wouldn't rush into a situation without thinking the matter through to the end. Sadly enough, he didn't seem to have the intelligence to do as much. He knew enough to be sure that he and Anton would never make a go of this business. If only he could convince her to—

"Emy, if you helped us, we could—"

16

"You know already my answer to that. I cannot stop you, but I will never enter your criminal gang."

"Gang?" Anton laughed aloud. "There are but the two of us."

Through narrowed eyes Emy shot her brother a long, hard look. The sight of those flashing dark eyes and the temper he knew to exist behind it immediately succeeded in stripping away any sign of merriment. Reprimanded by a look, Anton lowered his gaze to the well-worn table, his handsome mouth forming an almost childish pout.

Properly chastised, Emy grunted in satisfaction.

Jacques watched the power play between brother and sister, knowing long before it was finished who would emerge the victor. He leaned back and gently swirled the hot, rich sweet coffee in the mug set before him as he suggested, "Suppose we promise."

Emy snorted a sound of disbelief. She'd heard his promises before.

"A solemn vow," he offered. "Suppose we both give our solemn vow," he reiterated, "that this will be the last of it and that we will never again waver from what we know to be right. Would you help us?"

Emy's eyes widened and her father was once again reminded of her mother, the only woman he'd ever loved. The ache came again, even after all these years, and he knew once more a deep sense of loss and loneliness. "The last time? The very last? Do you swear?"

Jacques nodded while Anton remained silent, his mouth and eyes hard, slightly defiant.

"Do both of you swear?"

It took a moment of glaring, for Anton wasn't

17

happy with the thought that his young sister would be giving the orders. She needed a man, this sister of his. And a strong one at that, for it would take someone of considerable strength to curb that streak of bossiness and make her into the docile creature all women were meant to be. His father had allowed her too much freedom. Why, it was nothing less than a disgrace how she berated the men of this family.

Under Emy's watchful eye Anton shrugged and then sighed, relenting at last. Both men nodded this time.

"And if, despite my help, we fail? What then?"

"Then it is finished. Then we will know for certain it is God's will for us to be done with this life of crime."

Emy nodded, knowing that statement to be nothing less than the truth. Anton and her father were completely out of their element. They were simple men, farmers almost from the moment they learned to walk. What did they know of intrigue, of crime? The truth of the matter was, they knew much about land and crops but nothing at all about planning robberies. Not that she did, of course, but Emy always had a logical streak. There were times, especially of late, when she imagined she was the only one in her entire family to possess that particular characteristic.

"It's up to you, *mon âme*. With your help we will save our land."

Emy bit her lip and prayed she didn't look as guilty as she felt, for she had no intention of helping her father and brother commit yet another felony. To her mind it was a foregone conclusion that they were going to lose the land. And she wasn't going to do a thing to stop it.

Emy gave a mental shrug and sighed at the coming loss. Land was only land, after all. And land could be replaced. But honor once lost was an entirely different matter. How could she go to mass every Sunday and receive the sacraments knowing she lived a lie? She couldn't. No. It didn't matter how badly she felt at this deception, what she was about to do was the only way.

Emy looked at her father and forced a smile. "Tell me again about the plan."

"Anton and I were to take the *Princess* south to New Orleans. Sometime during the trip, probably late into the night, we planned to enter the card room and relieve its patrons of their winnings."

Emy nodded as her mind made instant and subtle adjustments in the original plan. "Suppose instead of you and Anton, a lady went aboard. But suppose she boards at New Orleans and disembarks in Baton Rouge, which would save traveling while in the possession of some incriminating evidence."

The sound of a ridiculing snort interrupted her words. Emy looked at her brother. "Why not share the secret, Anton? I've no doubt that a touch of gaiety would be a welcome reprieve right now."

"I've no secrets, little sister."

"But you laughed."

"Because you don't even know how to hold a gun."

"And why would I need a gun?"

"Do you imagine all men so gullible as to give over their winnings at the sight of your smile?" He

19

chuckled a low, mocking sound. "Perhaps your intent is to flutter your lashes. No doubt that would empty their pockets quickly enough."

Emy took a deep calming breath and put aside the need to respond in kind. "I never said I would rob anyone."

"But you said—" her father reminded her.

"I said I'd help, and I will." She covered her left eye as she felt the lid begin to jerk. It was a physical impossibility for her to lie without that eye rebelling. She never understood why it should be so, but it was. If she lied, her left eyelid always quivered.

She watched her brother for a long moment before she began again. "As I was saying, I'll board the *Princess* in New Orleans. While the steamer moves up the Mississippi, I'll spend all of my time in the card room, paying close attention to the gamblers. When the boat docks in Baton Rouge, the hour will be late. The two of you will be waiting and I will point out the man who has won."

Again her hand came to her eye. Neither man noticed.

Jacques smiled at the simple logic. "And your brother and I will relieve the poor soul of his burdensome weight."

Emy allowed a cheerful smile. Her father did not see that her smile did not quite reach her eyes. "Exactly."

"Mon Dieu." Emy's eyes sparkled with pleasure as she stood before the full-length mirror and held the silver brocade dress against her body, silently

dreaming of the day when she might own such a creation. *"Belle,"* she whispered as she fingered the luxurious fabric.

Jacques didn't miss the pleasure in his daughter's eyes, and despite the fact that he could hardly afford such extravagances, pressed all the bills he had in his pocket into Madame Gautier's small hand.

"See to it that it is ready by tomorrow morning."

Emy came to her senses at the words. *"Non.* We cannot—"

Jacques pulled his daughter from the lady's watchful gaze to a more private corner of the small dress shop. "You cannot expect to board the *Princess* dressed like that."

Emy looked down at her drab gray dress and sighed her disgust. Her father was right, of course. She could never mingle with the *Princess* clientele dressed as she was. Even her Sunday best, a pretty if simple pink cotton, was a far cry from what was needed. But she couldn't allow her father to use the last of their money. "I have fabric at home. I will make something suitable."

"There is no time. We'll be leaving for New Orleans the day after tomorrow."

Emy felt a wave of extreme guilt. No one but she knew nothing would come of this trip. She planned to describe a man, a nonexistent man, a man that would never be found, and her family would not recoup their expenses, never mind find the money needed to save their land.

Emy lowered her gaze to the floor, her dark eyes filled with sadness. She was using the last of the family's funds for a costume she did not need, and yet she had no choice but to allow her father to purchase it. She couldn't have felt more miserable.

Cole Brackston placed his booted feet one atop the other upon the scarred wooden desk, leaned back, and balanced the rickety chair upon its hind legs. With his hands he cupped the back of his head. One corner of a marshal's badge peeked from beneath a black leather vest. His strong mouth was tight with annoyance, stretching his neatly trimmed mustache into a thin line as his gaze fell again to the open telegram. Twice. A pair of bungling crooks had twice accosted the good people of Baton Rouge. Normally Cole wouldn't have become involved in this matter, for the city was miles north of New Orleans and his office, and of course had its own law enforcement, but their last criminal effort had involved the attempted robbery of a bank.

Because he was the marshal, any serious crimes such as bank robbery, or in this case, attempted bank robbery, fell under his jurisdiction.

The problem was, he wasn't taking kindly to the idea of leaving New Orleans at this particular time. It had taken him weeks of dancing attendance upon a certain lady, and he was nearly there. He knew in his gut it wouldn't be much longer before she'd be sharing his bed, and now he was being called away. Damn.

Eleanor Maxwell was five years his senior, but she could hold her own in a town filled with beauties. Her hair was the color of corn silk, her eyes a delicate china blue, but it wasn't hair or eyes that so attracted the dark, handsome marshal. Mrs. Maxwell, a widow of three years, had a figure that could tempt a saint. It didn't matter that her overly lush curves would no doubt grow one day to fat as had her mother's. Her present tempting form and sweet, delicate beauty were enough to turn many a man's head.

Cole figured that at twenty-eight and after five years of being alone, it just might be time to consider settling down, and to settle down with Eleanor would bring about no hardship. The few kisses they'd shared and the softness of her body against his had convinced him of the fact.

Mina was gone. It had taken years to come to grips with his pain and sorrow, but he'd long since accepted his loss. He was alive and it was time, well past time, in fact, for him to start thinking about living again.

Chapter Two

It was late. The boat had pulled from its moorings only a half hour before Emy grew bored at the passing darkness. There wasn't a thing to see but an occasional flicker of light in the distance as they passed a farm or plantation house. With nothing to do, Emy entered the card room.

Emy didn't much care that upon entering the room, she'd brought the notice of every patron to herself. She did mind, however, that thanks to the unseen raised slat of wood flooring, she'd broken the heel from her slipper, ruining the only good pair she owned. Of course there was no means to repair it now. She'd simply have to limp about for the remainder of the trip. Emy sighed, knowing with absolute certainty that to have joined in this fiasco was to court disaster.

Emy's dark gaze rose from her ruined slipper at the decidedly spiteful sound of a snicker. Finding the culprit to be a dark-haired painted woman clinging to the arm of a handsome gambler, Emy couldn't help but wonder why her stumble should have brought about such delight.

The woman whispered something to the man at her side, her red lips almost touching him. But the man seemed unconcerned at the intimacy. He glanced at the woman at his side and then brought his attention to Emy, even as the lady turned again to smile in ridicule at Emy's moment of distress.

But Emy missed her glare of spiteful glee, for her gaze had followed the woman's, and Emy now found her gaze caught in the black eyes of one of the most handsome men she'd ever seen.

He was obviously a gambler, for he wore a gambler's outfit—white shirt, black jacket, vest, and string tie. Only the black of his clothes appeared faded when compared to his hair and eyes. A thin mustache covered his top lip, and Emy felt something flutter deep inside as the man suddenly smiled. The flash of white against darkly tanned skin was a startling sight.

Cole felt as if he'd been poleaxed at the sight of her wide dark eyes. It took him a moment before he was able to regain normal breathing, for he'd never seen anything or anyone lovelier, and Cole had seen more than his share.

She stood at the doorway to the card room alone, appearing slightly unsure of herself. A slight frown creased his forehead. What was she? As far as he could tell, she wore no face paint as did all of the women there. If she wasn't one of them, then what was she doing here? Who was she? And where was her man? Surely a lady knew better than to enter this room unescorted. Cole imagined she had come on deck to join someone, but when no man made an attempt to go to her side, he realized he was wrong.

For a brief moment he felt a surge of unreasonable anger. What did she think she was doing? A woman alone was easy prey, especially upon entering this room. And then he realized the truth of the matter as the woman once again regained her composure. It was a certainty. She wasn't the innocent she appeared. The woman wouldn't be here if she didn't know what she was about.

Cole made a low, soft sound that ridiculed his first impression. She was lovely and apparently alone and in need of assistance. He'd be a fool to allow this opportunity to slip through his fingers.

"Are you all right, miss?"

Emy never heard the steward's anxious question, nor did she notice his offer of assistance as he reached out a supporting hand. "Miss? Are you hurt?"

Emy felt not a little sense of confusion. Something was happening here, something she did not understand. The room faded out of focus as her gaze held to the man across from her, her breathing growing shallow at his gentle smile. Her cheeks grew warm. If she didn't know better, Emy would have sworn she was blushing. An impossibility, of course, for Emy never suffered from the affliction.

Living in a tiny house within the proximity of her earthy family whose male members, her brother in particular, thought nothing of discussing the most intimate and natural details of their lives within her hearing, had long ago cured her of crimson cheeks. She did not blush or simper, nor suffer from the vapors as did the weaker versions of her sex. Not Emy! Emy was the solid strength behind her family. Emy was always in control.

It was at the very least unsettling then to feel that very control begin to slip away. Trying to prevent such a catastrophe from actually happening, Emy began to rationalize her uncharacteristic reaction to the dark-haired, dark-eyed stranger and immediately discounted the glaring truth. He had nothing to do with the sudden breathless and bewildering feelings that were careening through her. No doubt she'd somehow hurt herself in her stumble. Emy disregarded the fact that she had not fallen, for she could imagine no other excuse, but her near accident, to have caused this dizzying weakness.

His skin was dark. She frowned some at the oddity, for she would have imagined a gambler to spend less time in the sun. A white smile flashed again and Emy caught her breath. Lord, but he was a handsome man.

A glass was thrust into her hand. Emy brought it to her lips and emptied its contents in one thoughtless gulp. Now, Emy, being of French ancestry, was accustomed to the taste of wine, for she took a glass, sometimes two, with most every meal. But there were spirits, and then there were spirits, Napoleon brandy being quite a different brew from the delicately flavored wines served at her home. True, she had once sipped of the beverage, but had found the taste unpalatable, its fiery aftereffects so strong as to leave her breathless and gasping. She had never tried to develop a taste for it. And now to find it barreling down her throat with the strength of a roaring inferno, setting afire every molecule of flesh it touched upon, Emy could well understand her inability to breathe.

Her eyes blurred with tears as she tried to draw in breath to no avail. Somehow stuck in the middle, she was unable to draw air in or out. A man stood beside her, a tall man, she knew, but Emy was less conscious of his height than the fact that he was, without her permission, lifting her in his arms. An instant later she was outside the room, standing before the railing, clinging to the thick, smooth wood while withstanding his less than gentle ministrations.

She coughed and took a deep breath, even as she shot the man her most threatening glare. Her back would tingle for an hour from the hard blow he'd delivered between her shoulder blades. How dare he touch her! How dare he lay one finger on her!

"Are you all right?"

For a moment Emy gave careful consideration to the option of ignoring his question altogether and simply walking away. After all, it wasn't as if she'd been in any danger. She hadn't been on the verge of collapse from lack of air. The strong brew had merely and momentarily taken her breath away. There was no need for this brute to create a scene. Emy didn't for a minute appreciate his high-handed manner. She turned on him in an angry tirade.

"Sacrebleu! Are you out of your mind? Whatever possessed you to dare to touch me?"

Cole had lived in New Orleans for a little more than a year. During that time he had picked up a bit of the French spoken there, but as yet had not mastered the language, especially not when the words were spoken in rapid succession. "Excuse me?" Cole looked at the lady before him not without a touch of astonishment. She appeared terribly upset. What he couldn't figure out was why. Nor could he understand why her comment, instead of imparting gratitude, suspiciously resembled an accusation.

"Why did you to do such a thing?"

"What?" Cole asked, unable to hide first his surprise and then his growing annoyance at her show of temper. He had expected the woman to thank him, and to his way of thinking, rightfully so. He had hoped she might have considered showing her thanks in a number of delicious and more intimate ways. But what did he get for his efforts? A woman who appeared so angry as to be on the verge of violence. "What did I do?"

"You made a spectacle of us both." Emy didn't truly care about such things. Why, then, she wondered, was she so angry? Emy shrugged aside her silent questions, unable to explain her odd reaction to his assistance.

Cole bit his lip as his narrowed eyes took in the flashing anger in hers. A fleeting thought came to mind to kiss those tight lips, knowing somehow that it wouldn't take much more than a kiss to transform that anger into quite a different kind of raging passion. A second later, realizing that they were in clear sight of any passerby, he thought better of the notion and remarked with no little sarcasm, "The next time I see you struggling to breathe, I'll be sure to ask your permission before coming to your aid."

"For your information, I had no need of your aid." She shook her head as she remembered the few moments after downing the liquor and blatantly lied. "I often enjoy an after-dinner cognac." Her eyelid began to tick.

"You mean you weren't in distress?"

"Of course not," she insisted, shamelessly continuing the lie.

"Then please accept my apologies, and since I ruined the enjoyment of your drink, allow me to offer you another."

Emy was trapped into a nod.

Cole grinned. The woman couldn't lie worth a damn, but refused to back down when cornered. He enjoyed her spirit, and as his gaze traveled down her body, he noticed again there was more to this woman than spirit that he might enjoy.

Two drinks were ordered from a passing waiter, while Emy cursed her temper and pride. Why couldn't she have simply thanked the man for coming to her aid? Why had she insisted his aid hadn't been needed and why when offered had she agreed to yet another horrible drink? The last one was already softening her resolve to rage at this man. She could feel the warmth in her belly spread in soothing waves into her chest and arms. Soon it would attack her brain and bring a smile to her lips. A smile she did not want. Lord, was she ever going to gain control of her willful tongue?

"It is a beautiful night, don't you think?"

"Très belle," Emy returned with as little feeling as possible. She did not want to share a drink with this man. The look in his dark eyes sent tingles of excitement down her spine, or was it fear? Emy couldn't figure out which. She knew instinctively that he posed a danger. He caused her to feel the most unsettling things, things she couldn't explain. Things she didn't want to try to explain.

"What is your name?"

Emy never thought to lie. "Emeline Du Maurier."

"Cole Brackston, at your service," he said with what was more a nod than the expected bow. Emy thought he needed a lesson in manners. And at his next question she was sure of it. "Are you traveling alone?"

Emy might have been an innocent, having been well chaperoned where men were involved; still, she knew well enough the ways of some men, having watched her brother when involved in an *affaire de coeur.* She knew what was meant by that expectant look in a man's eye and wisely responded, *"Non,* my husband is below in our cabin. He does not much care for the river."

"But you do?"

She shrugged again. "It does not make me ill."

Cole had no doubt that she lied. Not only were her words stilted and unsure, she refused to look him in the eye. A quick glance at her ungloved hand confirmed his doubts. Still, it was possible that the absence of a ring meant only that it had been lost. Cole shook away the notion. She wasn't married. There was an innocence about her that belied the fact and yet there was something . . . something more. Cole shrugged aside the thought, not understanding the things she made him feel.

"Let me see what's keeping our drinks."

Emy never thought to escape now that she had the chance. There was no place to hide, in any event, and no reason to as far as she was concerned.

She laughed aloud at the notion. No doubt looking for the waiter and their ordered drinks was only a ruse. The man wouldn't return.

Emy turned toward the river, and leaning back just a bit, lowered her gaze to below the railing. Eyes wide with excitement, she watched the huge paddles churn through dark waters. She shouldn't stand so close, she knew, for the fragile material of her gown was sure to be ruined by this heavy mist. Still, having never been on anything larger than her father's small boat, and never before having the opportunity to witness the wondrous workings of a paddle steamer, she couldn't resist the sight as the boat moved with apparent effortless ease through dark moon-drenched waters and left behind a wide trail of foaming white suds.

Leaning against the railing, she listened to the sounds of merriment from inside. A man played a piano, another a banjo, while two others attempted to follow the lively tune in voices slightly off key. A woman laughed loud and coarsely. Another hidden in the shadows somewhere close by murmured a sound of apparent enjoyment. Emy might have wondered what was behind the murmuring of that particular sound had not a man suddenly shouted with excitement at the outcome of a turn of the wheel.

Emy thought again of her dilemma and tried to put aside her sense of guilt. It was her father and brother's fault. She shouldn't be the one to suffer like this. But she was. Her father and brother were right now racing back toward Baton Rouge, ready to put her plan into effect. Oh, Lord, if only they could have gone about things more honestly. Emy bit her lip. She was a fine one to talk about honesty. She was playing a cruel hoax on her own family. They would expect her help later that night, help that would never come. But the worst of it was, they had spent the last of their money and she had allowed them to do so with not a prayer of recouping a penny. Emy sighed even as her mind raced on searching for a solution to their problem.

"A lady shouldn't ever sound so sad. Especially a lady as lovely as you."

Lost in thought, Emy started and turned toward the sound. An instant later she almost moaned her disappointment to find the gambler had returned with two glasses in hand.

"Merci." Emy took the glass from his hand and turned back to the water, praying he would correctly discern her lack of interest. The man was handsome enough, to be sure, but tonight was not the night for what he obviously had in mind and she was

definitely not the woman. Even if she'd been so inclined, how could she think of starry nights filled with gaiety and romance while caught in this dilemma?

Cole grinned as she turned her back to him. Without permission he reached into his pocket, pulled out a cheroot, and lit it. Emy ignored the fact that he had not asked if he might smoke. She was praying he'd simply leave her alone.

Cole eyed her straight back through a trail of smoke. So the lady was playing it cool, was she? No doubt to further intrigue. She needn't have bothered, for Cole was already enchanted. He eyed the long, graceful curve of her neck, her small ears, and dark, moon-kissed hair. The honey-gold of her shoulders, and the sweet, inviting mounds of womanly charms, barely covered by the deep neckline of her dress, were enough to make a man's mind swim. This was one sweet piece. Obviously she was experienced and worldly enough to know that those cool glances of hers would only bring him closer to her side.

Cole laughed a low, soft sound that sent chills down Emy's back. She wondered why. Emy had had her share of beaus, but to date had not lost her heart to any one of them. She wondered now why the sound of a man's laughter should cause this unsettling reaction.

Cole liked his women cool and confident. That was probably the only thing that annoyed him about Eleanor. She was forever simpering while seeking his advice, forever asking his opinion, never giving her own, if she had one, always hoping to please, to the point of annoyance, and worst of all, forever searching for compliments.

"You did know that I'd be back, didn't you?"

She shrugged, a delicious and somehow titillating gesture. "How could I possibly know such a thing?"

Cole delighted in the sound of her voice. It was lovely when she wasn't excited or angry. Still, even angry there was something about it, something he couldn't name, but it fascinated him. Accented and soft, it held almost a lilting musical quality. "Since you are alone . . ."

Emy opened her mouth, ready to remind him of her supposed marital status.

". . . At least for the evening." She closed her mouth and again looked once more into the dark waters. "Perhaps you might honor me with your presence during dinner?"

Emy felt her stomach rumble at the mere mention of food. Thank God the paddle wheel was making too much noise for the impolite sound to be heard above her own ears. She would have been mortified if this man even suspected she hadn't eaten since early morning, and then only a chunk of hard bread swallowed with water.

She was greatly tempted, but it was impossible of course to join the man for dinner. A lady would never sit at the same table with a stranger.

Perhaps she could eat though. Her father had given her a dollar, their last dollar, in fact, just in case she needed something. It was tucked inside her low-cut bosom. Emy's conscience and stomach fought a duel. Her conscience won out. No. She wouldn't spend it. It didn't matter how hungry she was, she couldn't use the last of their money to appease her own selfish needs.

"Thank you for the invitation, *monsieur,* but I cannot."

"Why?" The word came startlingly close to her ear. She hadn't realized he'd moved so close and felt a sudden unexplained thudding of her heart. It wasn't excitement, of course, it was surprise. The man was daring in the extreme. He shouldn't have moved so close.

"My husband might need me." The words came softly, without any real resolve, for Emy wasn't a woman to lie easily. "I cannot be from his side for very long."

Cole flicked his smoke into the Mississippi waters, took her arm, and with very little pressure turned her to face him. "We'll leave word with the steward. He will tell you the moment your husband calls."

Lord, but this man was temptation personified. Dark, handsome features, white smile, he stood so close she could smell his own distinct and ever so inviting scent. He towered over her. Emy had never considered herself particularly small, but she couldn't remember a time when she'd felt so delicate, so feminine. He caused her a sense of deep confusion and yet she'd never felt so suddenly sure of herself. What in the world was happening here?

It was dangerous, she knew, to linger in this man's company. The danger increased tenfold when he smiled, but she did so need to eat. Did she dare chance it? Perhaps she could take a meal with him and after a heartfelt thank-you, wish him good night, neither suffering unduly from an hour or so of shared conversation. Emy made up her mind. Of course she could. This was, after all, 1873. Women often dined with men. There was nothing disgraceful in doing so. *But not alone,* came a voice from somewhere in the depths of her consciousness. *We won't be alone,* a silent voice returned.

Dinner was a delicious affair and conversation flowed almost as easily as the wine. Emy enjoyed herself. Feeling free and slightly wicked, she smiled and teased, surprising herself at her outrageous flirting. She finished the last of her butter-drenched shrimp and rice as Cole refilled her glass for the third time.

"What do your friends call you?"

Emy smiled at the question, her gaze wicked with suppressed laughter. She never realized how that look enticed. "My friends call me Emy, but you, Mr. Brackston, may call me, Mademoiselle—" Emy caught herself, remembering her lie almost in time. "Madame Du Maurier." It was too late. Cole noticed the slip but said nothing, feeling only relief that his suspicions of her martial status were true.

"Why were you in New Orleans?"

"Visiting friends," she answered with only the slightest hesitation. "My husband and I love to visit our friends." Emy almost laughed aloud at how easily the lie came to her lips. If she'd thought about it, she might have been shocked at her inclination to blatantly disregard the truth. But she wasn't thinking. Two glasses of brandy and two of wine had relieved her of that tendency. Emy reasoned away all logical thoughts, promising herself that a little lie didn't matter. This was a time for fantasy. Tonight wasn't real. Nothing here was real, and there was no need to tell the truth. Her eye hardly twitched at all.

"Where do you live in Baton Rouge?"

"North of the city, in a lovely home." A smile touched her lips again as she silently corrected herself: *Well, a home, anyway.*

Dinner was over sooner than either would have liked. Cole found some surprise at the thought of delaying the finish of their meal, for he wanted this woman in his bed. He hadn't been able to think of much else beside bedding her since first laying eyes on her. Still, she had been a delightful companion and he had enjoyed himself more than he had in a very long time.

Emy found herself walking beside him. Outside the main rooms the deck was quite dark. She stumbled a bit, but Emy put her lack of balance to the rocking of the boat and her missing heel. They said little, the silence beginning to grow thicker, filled with some unnamed tension. It sent chills down her spine, and Emy understood she had the choice of continuing this walk and perhaps finding herself pressed into a darker corner in a dangerously romantic interlude or thanking the man for a lovely dinner and escaping his company with her dignity intact.

"Thank you, *monsieur,* for a most enjoyable dinner, but I'm afraid I cannot linger. I must return to my husband's side."

Cole nodded. "I will escort you below."

Emy stiffened. The only problem with that suggestion was that there was no cabin below, at least none that was hers. *"Non,* there is no need."

But Cole wasn't taking no for an answer. He knew the games women played. Only this one was one of the best players he'd seen in some time. Those sultry looks she'd shot his way throughout dinner and the accompanying teasing laughter had more than once brought an ache to his middle. Good thing the dining room sported long tablecloths, or he might have embarrassed them both. She was good. Damn good. "Of course there is," Cole returned, a wicked gleam in his dark eye going unnoticed. "A gentleman always escorts his dinner companion home. Besides, your husband would be upset, I think, if I allowed you to go below alone."

Emy grinned at the mention of her husband. She hadn't realized she was so good a liar. She felt a moment's pride at the accomplishment, for the man believed everything she said.

The truth of it was, Cole believed almost nothing she said. Having had more than his share of experience with the opposite sex, Cole knew well enough when a woman was lying. He knew as well the games they played, and for himself, enjoyed every minute of them. The problem was that this woman had that special ability to lie, and yet at the same time appear an innocent. Her blank looks at his occasional not-so-veiled and decidedly wicked allusion to the remainder of this evening were intriguing. He nodded, confirming his thoughts. Intriguing was exactly the right word to describe her, for the combination of worldliness and innocence was the best he'd ever seen. It sent out mixed signals, and mixed signals were the most enticing of all.

It was shadowy below. Candles placed in brass holders were positioned every few feet along the hallway, but the small flame gave off a minimum of light. Emy forgot to hide her lost heel and limped along at his side. She weaved a bit and smiled, blaming it on her uneven heels, but the truth of the matter was, Emy was feeling the effects of one glass of wine too many. She did not realize her inebriated condition, having never before reached such a state, and because of her alcohol consumption paid little attention to the moment of reckoning ahead. For a fleeting moment she imagined the stranger behind the door of cabin number fourteen and what he was going to say when he opened his door to find his "wife" standing before him. Idly she wondered what she would say. Still, the effects of the wine were enough to cause her to forget the thought almost as soon as it came.

She giggled and then bit her lips together, trying to hide the sound.

Cole was aware of every nuance of this lady, particularly the fact that she was biting her lips in order not to laugh. Since he wanted to be the one doing the biting, that act especially did not escape his notice. "Why are you trying not to laugh?"

Emy leaned into him and away as she grinned. "'Cause."

Cole joined her in soft laughter. "'Cause why?"

"'Cause I don't know."

Cole thought her adorable and couldn't wait to get her into his room. He knocked on the cabin door while Emy continued to sway a bit at his side. She lost her balance once more, and never realized how intimately she touched him in order to right herself again.

Her hand pressed boldly and, had she been in a more sober state, she would have realized, quite shockingly, against his belly. It took some effort on Cole's part to keep his mind on this sweet diversion, for he wanted nothing more than to pull her into his arms and crush that luscious mouth beneath his.

She smiled as he glanced in her direction at the prolonged silence. Cole knew the room to be empty, for when Emy had gone on the supposed task of asking a steward to look out for her husband, Cole had booked that very room for himself. Still, he played along with her game. "Your husband must have gone up on deck for some air."

"Oh, thank God," Emy breathed unknowingly and not quite silently. She turned, ready to return to the deck above. "I'll go find . . ." She forgot what she'd been about to say. What in the world was the matter with her? The wine. Lord, but she really shouldn't have drunk so much. She was terribly dizzy, and she couldn't seem to think very clearly at all.

Cole grinned at her obvious relief and easily turned her back to face him. "Perhaps you could use your key and wait inside for his return."

If I had a key, I might, she silently returned, while thinking the whole situation hilarious and having a time of it controlling the urge to giggle. This was a great joke she was playing. Emy couldn't remember the last time she'd so enjoyed herself. She leaned against him again, continually off balance due to the combination of wine and her missing heel, and whispered conspiratorially and with great care, "I lost it."

"Here it is. You must have dropped it," Cole said as he bent down and retrieved a key that had magically appeared from out of nowhere, on the carpeted floor.

Emy blinked and shot him a look of confusion. She certainly knew she hadn't dropped it, didn't she? Of course she hadn't. She'd never had a key to this room, so dropping it would naturally be out of the question. Then where had it come from? Emy was ushered inside before she could figure out an answer to her last question. She turned, wobbling only slightly, and watched him close the door behind them.

She frowned as she watched his grin. Something wasn't right, but for the moment Emy couldn't understand what. "You are a beautiful lady."

Emy's hand reached for her perfectly coiffed curls and mussed them in her efforts to smooth them. A heavy lock of black hair fell to her shoulder. "Thank you."

She was enchanting. Limping, her hair mussed and falling from its pins, her dress slipping from one shoulder—Cole couldn't remember the last time he'd seen so delectable a sight. "Would you like another glass of wine?"

She shook her head, the movement making the room swim around her. Cole reached out to steady her. "I've had enough wine tonight."

"Good." His voice dropped to an oddly thrilling and dangerous husk. Emy blinked and wondered how a man could sound dangerous. She'd heard of looking dangerous, of acting dangerous, but sounding dangerous? She shrugged away the illogical thought, promising herself she'd look into it later. "I have better things in mind than drinking."

Emy, despite her temporary infirmity, understood clearly the sound if not the meaning behind those words. She thought for just a second she'd be safer to extricate herself from his company. "On second thought, perhaps we could . . ."

His hands at her waist tugged her gently forward and at the feel of him suddenly against her, Emy forgot her intent. "Why are you traveling alone?"

Emy never bothered to reinstate her lie. She'd already forgotten it. "I can't tell you," she whispered, unable to prevent a soft giggle.

"Why not?"

"It's a plan," she continued in the same vein.

Cole had never known a woman quite so delightfully enchanting. Silently he vowed to get to know her a damn sight better. His eyes darkened as he allowed the thoughts of exactly how he'd go about such a task. "Mysterious women are fascinating."

"Are they?" She sighed with honest disappointment as she leaned against him again. Emy did not embarrass easily, but she would have been mortified if she realized how provocatively she was behaving. "Too bad, then, that I'm not in the least mysterious."

She was weaving against him and then away. God, the feel of her against him was delicious. "Yes, you are."

Emy's eyes widened with surprise at this unexpected piece of news. No one had ever told her she was mysterious before. Emy thought she quite liked the notion. "Really?"

"How much did you drink tonight?"

"I don't know." She grinned, and then with her elbow against his chest, and her hand supporting her chin, she asked as if his question had been a riddle of some sort, "How much?"

Cole grinned. He removed her arm and placed her hand on his chest. "I'm going to kiss you." His breath was clean and deliciously warm as it brushed against her lips. The feel of it made her more dizzy than ever.

Emy giggled again. "Surely not, *mon âme.*" She never realized the endearment.

"Have you never been kissed before?"

"Bien sûr." She smiled again while noting the laughter in his eyes. It was enjoyable in the extreme to tease with this man. What Emy couldn't understand was why she hadn't done this before? "Many, many times."

Cole thought it odd that that bit of information should cause him a feeling of unease. No, not unease exactly, it was more like . . . He shrugged the ridiculous thought away. There was no way he could be jealous of this woman's past. The mere thought of jealousy was pure and utter nonsense. "Then you wouldn't mind if I kissed you, would you?"

Emy laughed at what she considered a most absurd question. *"Oui,* certainly I'd mind."

"Would you really? Or is this another part of the game?" came the gravelly toned, teasing inquiry.

Emy shivered at both the sound and feel of his words against her lips. She knew by then that she had taken too much wine and was drunk, perhaps very drunk. What she didn't realize was the liberties she was allowing this man. All she knew for certain was that it felt good, standing there in his arms. She tried to block out anything else. Still, that voice in the back of her mind reminded her again of the danger. "Mr. Brackston." She tried to step back, but her feet wouldn't obey the commands of her mind. "I don't think . . ."

"It's very wise of you not to," he breathed as he closed the short distance between them.

45

Chapter Three

"Mon Dieu." Emy never realized she uttered the exclamation as she leaned weakly into his strength. Already dizzy, her infirmity increased tenfold as he purposely dragged his lips from hers with slow, aching, tantalizing expertise, the parting of lips perhaps more sensuous than the kiss itself, for the kiss had demanded nothing of her but the wonder of touching his mouth to hers. It was tender, gentle, an exquisite sampling of his texture, a total delight.

When he released her lips at last, he allowed only enough space between their mouths to breathe. "I knew you would feel like this."

Emy didn't hear the words, or if she did, they didn't register in her reeling mind. All she knew was the sound of his gravelly voice was nearly as overpowering as the touch of his mouth on hers. Caught in the magic of the moment, her hands rested upon his chest, her fingers curling into the dark material of his jacket, urging him closer.

Emy hadn't known that a kiss could be so

enchanting, so overpowering—that the coming together of two mouths could tremble a woman to the depths of her soul, that toes could actually curl, that chills would run down her spine. Lost in the wizardry of his touch and scent, she didn't recognize the danger and felt not a glimmer of fear. So it was that she didn't think to question the wisdom of being there, of allowing his kisses, of wanting more.

Yes, she'd known the feel of a man's lips on hers, but those few passionless kisses had been only gentle moments of shared tenderness. Nothing had ever prepared her for this man's expertise and gentle mastery. And to add to that mastery the overindulgence of alcohol was asking too much of Emy's natural reserve. She raised her mouth to his, not in the least satisfied at the meager sampling so far granted. She wanted more. Much more.

Cole smiled at her act of innocence, at the barely restrained eagerness, watching as she allowed just enough impatience to show. He ran the tip of his tongue along her offered lips. The action brought Emy's eyes wide with surprise. Cole felt her stiffen and almost laughed aloud at her playacting. The woman was good, damn good. Better than any he'd been with before. He felt a moment of assurance. He was going to enjoy this night as he hadn't enjoyed a woman in years.

"What are you doing?"

Cole grinned at the question. She was exquisite. "Kissing you."

"You licked me."

"I know." His tongue was investigating the

delicate shape of her ear, when he whispered his response.

She moaned softly at the whispered words and the somehow intriguing feel of his tongue in her ear. Who would have thought that so odd, indeed almost shocking an action could prove to be so very delightful? "You shouldn't."

For just a moment his dark eyes registered puzzlement. Could it be that she was the innocent she portrayed? He smiled at the thought, his chest twisting, heavy with an endearing tenderness not felt in five years. "Don't you like it?"

"I don't think it's right."

"Don't you? Why?"

Emy had no answer for that. She could have told him the feel of his tongue did strange things to her stomach, but that was ridiculous. It was her lips and ear he touched. Why would that affect any other part of her body? She sighed, not wanting to, but knowing she'd have to go. "I shouldn't be here."

Cole realized he'd allowed her time enough to collect herself. A mistake on his part. He wasn't interested in conversation. What he wanted needed no words. He kissed her again, only this kiss was hotter, wilder, and wetter than anything Emy could have imagined. It totally disintegrated the strength in her knees. She felt them buckle, and before she had a chance to do more than hold on, his arms wrapped around her, keeping her in place, bringing her tighter to his hard, long length.

"Mmmm," she murmured as he pulled her closer still, spreading his thighs, creating a tiny haven for her slim form between their powerful strength. He

48

cradled her softness against him, and ran his hands down her back as his mouth left hers and spread a dozen whisper-soft kisses over her temple, eyes, cheeks, and jaw.

She moaned a soft sound and dropped her forehead to his shoulder, leaning heavily against him as she whispered again, "I shouldn't be here." She knew that much, at least. What she didn't know was how she was going to tear herself from this delight, or if she really wanted to. Her head was beginning to clear. It helped quite a bit that his mouth no longer held to hers.

Cole took heart in the repeated statement, knowing had she truly wanted to leave, she would have done so by now. "Why?"

"Because you are much too forward."

"Am I?" He almost laughed. Damn, but this woman constantly threw him off guard. Allowing him to see just a trace of the passion she held in check and then the pretence at innocence. It was an intoxicating combination.

She nodded even as she allowed herself this wicked moment of intimacy. "A gentleman would never kiss a lady without her permission."

"I had your permission."

"Oh." Emy couldn't remember giving her permission. Then again, she couldn't remember too much about this last hour or so.

"Don't you like this?" His mouth grazed the side of her face, and as she tilted it back for more, he sank his lips into her throat with a low groan.

"Well, it's not that I don't like it, exactly. It's more that . . ."

"What?" he asked after a moment of silence as she forgot her objection and found herself sliding again into that world of pure sensation where words were superfluous.

He was licking her again. Emy had never imagined that such an action could be quite so enjoyable. His mouth came up the length of her throat at the sound of her soft moan, but he only breathed against her lips, taunting the ache for the feel of them against hers. She knew he wanted to kiss her, and at this moment Emy couldn't think of anything she wanted more.

"Tell me," he said, the words low, almost ragged as he sought control.

"Tell you what?"

Her eyes were closed, her head tilted back, waiting for yet another delicious sampling. "Tell me," he repeated, his lips against her mouth, and then they were gone. "Tell me what you want."

"Kiss me," she answered honestly, without a thought to the consequences. "I want you to kiss me again."

Emy didn't know what she was asking for, for this kiss was deeper and more thrilling than any so far experienced. She felt a startled moment of surprise at the hunger. It might have been her mouth that he kissed, but she felt that kiss in every cell of her being. It went on and on until the pressure of his mouth forced her lips apart and he was licking her again. To her amazement, Emy found herself relishing the feel of his hot, rough yet smooth tongue against and just inside her lips very much indeed.

He crushed her more tightly to him, eager for the

next step in this game, but forced himself to linger, knowing it would be all the better for the waiting.

She couldn't breathe, but never thought to complain. It was wonderful. She hadn't realized it was possible to kiss like this, to so enjoy the taste and feel of a man's mouth against her own.

Long fingers threaded through her hair, holding her mouth to his. Pins fell to the floor unnoticed as he dragged his mouth against hers again and again, pulling at her lips with gentle suction, easing them further apart.

He was trembling as if a youngster as he teased her mouth, urging her lips wider apart. When was the last time a woman had so excited him? When had a woman caused such need?

He was drowning in her taste, her scent. Everything about her was delightful captivation, delicious and sweetly sensual. Cole forced aside the aching need to see to a hurried and urgent culmination of this act. This lovely woman deserved a gentle hand, a sweet leisurely enjoyment. They both did. As long as he kept a tight rein on his control, they'd both know a night of pure enchantment.

"Sweetheart," he murmured as he tore his mouth from hers and breathed with heavy ragged gasps into the warmth of her neck. She never noticed the buttons of her dress coming undone. Dazed from his kisses, she allowed the hot, moist lingering of ecstatic caresses at her neck and shoulder. She was oblivious of the slow, purposeful seduction of her mind and senses as he lowered his mouth to graze over the gentle mounds of flesh newly uncovered. Emy managed a small whimper of sound and then another delight as he sucked the tip of one bared breast into a furnace of heat.

She was beyond thought now. It never entered her mind to bring this intimacy to a close. The burning touch of his mouth upon her was an ecstasy she'd never known existed, and she wanted more.

Emy's hands slid from his chest and circled his neck. Moments later they cupped the back of his head as she, with a half-muffled cry, wantonly arched her back and brought his mouth tighter to her. The room swam around her, and Emy knew she could no longer blame the wine for this wild moment of blissful exhilaration.

Her dress was lowered over her arms and she was helpless but to allow it. Her plain cotton chemise followed. She was naked now to the waist, held tightly to her lover by unsteady arms.

The silence of the room was broken only by the rasping of his breathing. Emy never realized her breathing easily matched his labored sounds. He brought her away from him, just far enough so he might see the delights his mouth had known. For a long moment he simply stared.

Emy knew by the look in his eyes that he thought her beautiful. She smiled as with one hand he arranged her fallen hair about her shoulders.

Emy had given little thought to the happenings between a man and a woman. Still, she'd imagined her first time with a man, every time, for that matter, would come under the cover of darkness. She wasn't ashamed of her body, just naturally modest. Therefore she felt some surprise at standing proudly before this man and allowing him not only to look his fill, but to touch as well. Even in her limited experience, she knew she was beautiful in his eyes and felt a moment's pride to be the cause of the pleasure she saw there.

Cole felt the breath rush from his lungs. "My God, you're so . . . so beautiful. If I could only tell you . . ." His gaze ran the length of her from the creamy flawlessness of her shoulders to a waist so small he could almost span it in his hands. Her skin was smooth, a dusty honey-gold, her breasts full and firm, the lustrous dark tips budded into hard nubs of desire and beckoning for his touch. He never realized that he reached out. He was touching her softness, cupping her loveliness in the palm of his hand, running his thumb over the tips, before he thought of it.

"Combien?" She wanted to hear more. She wanted to know everything that was on his mind. Emy never realized the thoughtlessly murmured words would be misinterpreted, that they would change everything.

It took a moment, for Cole was engrossed in this most delightful study, but the softly whispered words finally penetrated his dazed mind. At her question, Cole's gaze rose from the sight of her exquisite beauty. Her eyes were closed, her lips parted, her head thrown back, her black hair falling down her back in loose curls. She was trembling as if she savored his caress above all else. She looked every inch the sultry courtesan, and at her question of *how much?* Cole knew her moans and sighs for the performance it was.

He felt a wave of almost crushing disillusionment,

a disappointment so strong as to momentarily steal his breath, and then he nearly laughed aloud at the imagined notion. What the hell did he care? Of course she was a woman of some experience, he'd known that from the first despite her portrayal of innocence. Still, he hadn't realized till that minute the exact extent of that experience.

A wry, almost sardonic smile touched the corners of his mouth. He was a fool to have somehow imagined her different from the others. Face paint or no, there was no question as to what she was the moment she entered the card room unescorted.

He shrugged. What the hell difference did it make? Tonight would be just like old times. As a kid, he'd spent enough hours in the company of whores to know most of them were damn good. Being raised in a bordello had its moments; he grinned at the thought. His mother, busy with her own customers, hadn't cared how he busied himself as long as no one knew he was her son.

Cole frowned. Odd that he hadn't been sure about this one from the first. The thing was, it had been a long time since those days when his taste had run to whores. This one was more beautiful than most, and her techniques a hell of a lot more subtle. He swore he didn't care what she was. She was a beauty, and now that he knew the truth, he could hardly wait to lie between her creamy smooth thighs.

"Anything you want, darlin'. Name your price."

The harshness of his tone slowly edged away the haze of desire that had held her in its grip. When she opened her eyes, Emy blinked at his angry stance, the savage look in his eyes, the hard, humorless curve of his mouth. Emy could only wonder what she might have done to cause him to look at her with such hatred.

It hardly mattered. The fact of the matter was, she had almost—Emy shivered at the realization at what she had almost done. How could it have happened? How could she, a woman who believed in morality, who lived those beliefs, have so easily succumbed to this man? To almost have lost her innocence! She shuddered at the thought. Good God, what was she doing? What could she be thinking to allow this? Emy frowned as she tried to understand.

The truth was, tonight's misadventure could have come about only because Emy was exactly the innocent she portrayed. Had she been another, perhaps one of slightly more experience, she would have recognized the danger sooner and taken steps to ensure her safety.

Emy backed away from his hard glare, noting for the first time with a clear mind her nakedness and his cool control, the way his dark eyes moved over her with almost insulting interest. She trembled, instantly suffused with nearly debilitating shame.

Humiliated to the core of her being, she fumbled in her attempt to cover herself. It felt like forever, but took hardly a moment to bring her dress back into place, and as she struggled to reach the buttons down her back, she limped toward the door. Cold sober now, she shivered at his glare of disgust and could only thank the Almighty that this man had shown his true nature in time. She trembled with horror as she imagined what might have happened if these heated, insane moments had been allowed to go on.

"I'm sorry." She shook her head. "I can't do this. I simply can't," she mumbled, loathing to meet his gaze, knowing she'd never again live through a moment more shattering, more horrifying.

"Can't you? Why not?" Cole felt another surge of disgust. Did she mean to raise a price not yet agreed upon by this sudden act of embarrassed reluctance?

Her eyes widened and the pulse he had felt against his lips only moments before visibly throbbed in her throat. "I have to go."

She was afraid. No, she wasn't, fool. She was merely a good actress. There was no need to feel this sudden surge of protective tenderness. "You're not going anywhere."

Emy, not being one to take orders lightly, felt her back stiffen at the flatly stated challenge. She grunted a derisive sound and sneered her response to that. "And how, exactly, will you stop me, monsieur?"

"I'll stop you," Cole said with all confidence, never expounding on the unequivocal remark. The moment the words came, he felt a stunning measure of amazement. Christ, he was a lawman. What the hell did he think he was doing? He knew better than to force a woman. What he had in mind was nothing less than a criminal offense. And then he grinned as he realized he was taking the game too seriously. He wouldn't be forcing this one. Her display of reluctance was simply another ploy meant to drive him mad with wanting her.

"Do you mean to keep me a prisoner?"

Cole merely grinned at the question as he backed

her toward the door.

"I'll scream," she warned, never realizing the low husky sound of her threat only further enticed.

He laughed, the sound silky and terribly dangerous. "No, you won't. Ladies of your profession don't like to cause too much of a fuss. You wouldn't want the steward to report our little business venture to the captain."

In truth, Emy would have liked nothing more than to report this man to the captain. This man was a monster who belonged in irons for forcing his attentions on a woman. But what did he mean about a business venture? What was he talking about? Emy knew she was on the edge of a full-blown case of hysterics, for she couldn't seem to understand his meaning. Focusing on his words proved less than useless, for they managed only to confuse her further and somehow cause her greater fear. As if palsied, her entire body trembled with the emotion, but Emy forced aside the numbing fright. She had to keep her wits about her if she expected to win here.

Her voice shook only slightly as she managed to ask, "What are you talking about?"

"I'm talking about the way you were laying all over me, darlin'."

Her response came in French, a sudden rush of expletives, words a lady would never use, all incoherent and beyond Cole's understanding. Cole grinned and Emy raised her hand at his blatant and insulting disregard of her obvious distress. Just before it contacted his cheek, Cole caught her wrist and yanked her against him. The movement knocked the breath from her, but not her will to escape. Still, it took only a blink of an eye to pin her hands behind her back.

Cole laughed at how easily he managed to subdue her, imagining she fought him with the most meager of strength. The fact of the matter was, Emy was not nearly as strong in body as she was in mind, and was naught but a flame in a windstorm against this man's superior strength.

Cole, believing her to be a woman of considerable experience, was blissfully unaware of her fear. He imagined her supposed change of heart was meant to intrigue. He laughed. So, she wanted it rough, did she? Cole shrugged, knowing he would have preferred a slow, luscious few hours, but the woman was obviously of a different mind. No doubt she had others awaiting her ministrations tonight.

Emy continued her struggles, trying to free herself from his hold, but they were as nothing compared to the man's strength. She didn't have a clue as to what he was talking about and swore she'd bite off her tongue before she asked. "I hate you!" came out in a grunt. He felt her shift and knew she was about to raise her knee. For a big man, Cole could move with amazing agility.

Up to this point Cole thought her antics most enjoyable, if a bit prolonged, but the thought of the pain she could have easily brought about was not in the least amusing. Cole instantly took her up into his arms, and despite her kicking, clawing and curses, carried her to the narrow bed and dumped her upon its hard surface.

"You're carrying the act too far."

Emy's eyes widened with fear. She knew a

moment of panic and might have screamed, but her scream would have been lost in the furor that suddenly took hold of the entire ship.

Bells were suddenly ringing everywhere. Along with the bells, loud, shrill whistles permeated the air even as the ship's horn joined its sound to the racket. Something was obviously the matter.

Cole cursed. Had he not been aware of the impossibility, he might have blamed the lady for yet a further delaying of the evening's finale.

He walked to the door and nearly wrenched it from its hinges in his frustration. People in every state of dress and near-dress ran from their cabins toward the steps leading to the deck above. What the hell was going on?

Cole stepped into the foray and reached a hand to a man's shoulder only to have it shaken off as the man ignored him and almost trampled the lady before him in his efforts to escape.

Cole didn't have to wait long for an answer to his so-far-unvoiced question. A second later, between the clanging bells came the sound of a man calling from above, "Fire. Fire!"

Cole cursed and turned back to his room and the woman that was supposed to be occupying his bed, only to find the bed empty. He frowned and for just a second wondered if he hadn't imagined the whole thing. How the hell had she disappeared?

Cole moved quickly into the room. No doubt the fool thought to tease him further by hiding, but a quick glance under the bed proved she was gone. There was nowhere else to hide. She was definitely gone. No doubt she'd managed the chore while he'd been trying to find out what was going on.

Odd that he hadn't seen her pass him by.

In truth, it wasn't odd at all. Emy had instantly come from the bed and was behind him when he opened the door. She took the first opportunity offered and lost herself in the many passengers trying to reach the stairs as Cole tried unsuccessfully to interrupt the man's hurried escape. Quickly she had stepped before a large woman, all the while praying that Cole would not notice her absence until it was too late. On this score her prayers were answered.

The fire had started in the kitchen and soon spread to one of the dining rooms. It took nearly an hour for the blaze to come under control and information to be filtered down from passenger to passenger. The captain expected the fire to be out within minutes.

All breathed a sigh of relief, for to abandon ship in these dark waters would surely find many hurt, or worse.

Emy knew her own sense of relief. Hidden in the shadows of the boat, behind the stairwell that led to the top floor, she listened to dozens of people, all telling of their particular circumstances when the bells had sent out the first alarm.

Emy alone knew the factual reason behind the fire. She silently thanked the Almighty for this great favor, for providing her with the means of escape even as she swore to never do anything so foolhardy again.

It was easy enough to offer a quick prayer of thanks, but far less easy to let go of the night's unfortunate happenings. She wished she could offer yet another prayer and never have to think of it again. But Emy knew differently. It would take a long time, perhaps even longer than a long time, before she could forget her foolish actions on this night. No doubt she'd never stop remembering the way his mouth had felt on hers.

Oh, Lord, it was so shameful. She had allowed him to touch her where no man had ever touched her before. She had allowed him to look at her, lost in some sinful haze, standing almost proudly before him. She shuddered at the memory.

He had seen her! Emy's cheeks blazed with heat. He had seen her and in her wickedness she'd wanted him to see even more. He had kissed her in shameful places, places where only a baby would one day touch, would one day suckle.

She hadn't thought that a man would find so much pleasure by touching her there. She hadn't thought that she would find at least equal pleasure in the ghastly episode, the mortal sin.

Cole searched for her everywhere. He'd even dared, despite the obvious shock of two ladies, to enter the ladies' facilities on the pretext of looking for his little girl who had somehow become lost in the confusion. She wasn't there. She wasn't anywhere. Dammit, where had she gone? The ladies, unsuspecting of his true intent, offered to help him find his daughter. Cole found himself forced into giving them a description of an imaginary little girl as he hurried to look elsewhere.

An hour went by, and still he found not a trace of her. By this time, most all of the passengers were very mellow indeed, thanks to orders from the captain that the crew should serve free drinks to anyone interested in the partaking, and there were many. Cole presumed he was trying to make amends for his passengers' forced discomfort and ease away any lingering fears. It worked.

Cole only wished his fears could be so easily stilled. No one had seen a trace of her. It was impossible, of course, and yet a fact. The passengers had not been allowed to go below again. Cole discounted the possibility that she might have done so without anyone's knowledge. She couldn't have gotten past the guards.

So where was she, then? Why had everyone he'd so far approached professed not to have seen the lady? Cole shot the man before him a hard look. He was weaving just a bit from overindulgence, and smiled, while not hesitating to tell Cole he wished he had seen her. The truth being, he could go for a piece right about now.

Cole forced his hands to remain at his sides. Maybe he didn't understand exactly why, but he suddenly knew he would have liked nothing better than to sink his fists into the leering man's face.

The lights of the city loomed ahead. Baton Rouge appeared to silently await their arrival, while the minutes ticked by and Cole desperately increased his efforts. Once the boat docked . . .

Cole was suddenly hit with the realization and

smiled as relief washed over him. Once the boat docked, he'd find her. There was but one way on and off. She'd have to pass by him or remain on board. Cole smiled as he accepted a drink from a passing waiter. Why the hell hadn't he thought of that before? He'd just wasted more than an hour searching for her like some madman, when he had only to stand by the railing and watch for her eventual appearance.

Cole knew a sense of real confidence. Before this night was through, he'd have her with him again. More than that, he'd have her in his bed.

At least four times, Emy watched him pass no more than ten feet from where she stood. Four times that she knew of, at least. What in the world was he doing?

It looked as if he were searching for someone. Her dark eyes widened with fear at the thought. It couldn't be that he was looking for her, could it? And then she remembered how it had been seconds before they had been interrupted. He had imagined that she was something other than what she truly was. She couldn't fault him on that score. She had acted the fool tonight, flirting, allowing herself to drink too much, to lead him on, so to speak. Obviously the man had come to some erroneous conclusions.

He passed by again. Oh, Lord, no! She didn't want to face him again. She *couldn't* face him again. Not after the things they had done. Not after what had almost happened between them.

*   *   *

The lights of Baton Rouge came into view and Emy pressed herself more firmly into the shadows. Once the ship was tied securely in place against the wharf, they would open the gates, and she'd be forced to expose herself. She prayed that he'd position himself elsewhere, but knew deep inside the truth of it. He'd be standing at the gate, waiting for her to pass him by.

Emy racked her brain trying to think what to do. Nothing came to mind but either imminent capture or jumping into the river to avoid detection.

She could swim, so it wasn't water she feared, it was being seen while jumping. Everyone would no doubt think she was trying to kill herself. Men would probably jump in after her. In any case, it would create yet another scene that could only lead to discovery.

She waited as the steamer closed the distance to the shore. It was very late, probably sometime after midnight. Her father and brother were awaiting her arrival, eager for the fruition of their plans.

Emy fought back the sudden urge to cry. Lord, but she'd done her family a dreadful disservice. Had she been half the woman she'd supposed, she would never have pretended to give in to her father's plea, never pretended to go along with this ridiculous and now-disastrous venture.

She knew it was with a disgusting sense of righteous indignation that she'd thought to show them the folly of their ways, but Emy had learned instead that she could be just as foolhardy, just as weak. And now that it was far too late, she'd accomplished nothing but the terrible wasting of the last money they had. Worse yet, she had somehow become involved with a man, a strange man, and had come closer than she'd like to remember to lying with him! Good Lord, what was happening to her? Had she lost all sense and reason? If only she could take back these last hours. If only she could start again. A weary sigh accompanied wry laughter at her own idiocy. It was a bit late for if onlys now.

The liberal dosing of those who would indulge turned out to be a blessing in disguise for Emy, another disruption of his plans for Cole, and a mistake for the captain and his crew. Three fights, all within seconds of each other, began on deck.

Cole, careful to mind his own business, was gently elbowing his way beyond the combatants and screaming, terrified women, toward the gates when one man, who was an active participant in one of the contests, thought Cole's gentle touch but a contribution of his own efforts. He turned and swung a meaty fist into Cole's eye. Cole never saw the blow coming and stood suddenly stunned by the vicious attack.

Cole was a peaceful sort, but hardly the kind to take such an offering and give nothing in return; still, he might have put aside any need for retribution, at least temporarily, his interest on more important matters at present, but the man seemed disinclined to allow Cole an option. He hit him again.

Cole was in the midst of watching the man go down after landing his third punch, when the boat docked and with two dozen or more people separating them, he watched with a sinking sense of despair as Emy walked through the gates, down the gangplank, and out of his life, perhaps forever.

She breathed a weary sigh as the *Princess* pulled up to its moorings. Eager to be gone from there, she watched with nervous interest as the men jumped to the dock and secured the steamer. Her father was out there, waiting. She had no choice but to face him. But facing him was indeed the lesser of two evils.

The gangplank was set in place, and Emy was one of the first to leave the ship. A small crowd accompanied her ashore. Emy didn't notice her brother, even though he was waving wildly in her direction, for her thoughts had been caught up again in the man she had spent most of this disastrous night with. The unfortunate incident had done something to her. She couldn't explain what it was, but she was different. Everything was different because of it.

"What's the matter with you?"

"What?" Emy asked, surprised, although she'd been expecting to see him. She felt a rush of guilt as she watched her father and brother take in her appearance. Could they know what she'd been about? Could they imagine the disgraceful things she had done on this night? "What do you mean?"

"Why are you limping? Are you hurt?"

Emy almost laughed aloud in relief. Thank God for the dark. Neither man had noticed her wrinkled dress. She'd brought along no purse, therefore had no comb to smooth her tousled hair. It was pulled back, the few pins found clinging to the mass of curls barely holding it in place. Neither could see her swollen lips, or the guilt she couldn't hide. "No. I broke the heel to my shoe."

Anton didn't ask how; his mind was set on other matters. "Which one?"

"What?"

Anton breathed a sigh of disgust. What was the matter with her tonight? Where was her mind? She knew, well enough, what he was about. Why was she playing at stupidity? To delay the inevitable, of course. So, she was getting cold feet at the last minute, was she? Too damn bad and way too late. After her little plan, they had no money left. This was their last chance. Damn her, he'd shake it out of her if he had to. Anton took her arm in his large hand. His fingers bit into the soft flesh, but Emy didn't notice. "What does he look like, Emy?"

"He was tall," she answered absentmindedly.

"And?" he asked anxiously.

"And dark." She'd meant to say light, blond, in fact, but somehow the word had just slipped out. "I mean blond. He was blond."

"Make up your mind. Which was he dark or blond?"

"Blond," Emy insisted, never realizing the darkness of the night and the fact that Cole would be wearing a hat and the color of his hair would never enter into the matter.

"What was he wearing?"

"I don't know." She racked her brain, trying to think.

"What do you mean, you don't know? What was he wearing?"

"A suit." Emy breathed a sigh. She was safe in saying a suit, she thought. Only she wasn't. There weren't nearly so many men who were tall and wearing a suit.

"And . . ." Anton said expectantly.

"And tie."

The plan was to describe some fictitious winner of great fortune, a man who would never turn up, simply because he did not exist. She went about the chore, inadvertently describing only too well the man who refused to leave her thoughts.

"Is he big?"

"Oui," she said, and realizing she'd done it again amended with a sharp, *"Non!"*

Anton, who was nervously anticipating the fortuitous outcome of tonight's activity, found himself fast losing patience. He glared at her. "Well, which is it?"

"He is bigger than me, that's all." Emy breathed a sigh and thanked God for a quick mind.

Anton nodded at her whispered description and then brought her to the alley where their horses stood, tied. He left her there as both her father and brother moved closer to the boat.

Alone in the dark, Emy petted her horse, feeling no sense of fear. She was fast and nimble on her feet and had a scream loud enough to raise the dead, or so she'd been told. She chuckled at the notion and her horse as well as he welcomed her attention with a whinny and a playful nudge of his head.

She mounted the stallion with a great sigh. She

was tired. It had been a long day and night and the rush of emotions she'd suffered throughout had left her strangely depleted. It would be another hour yet before they would reach their home and the comfort of her bed. An hour, that is, if they left now. What in the world was the delay? Surely all had left the boat by now. What could her father and brother be waiting for?

Emy chuckled at her thoughts, remembering her description. A tall, but not so tall dark, blond stranger wearing black. A man with a mustache. A thin mustache.

Emy gasped, her entire body tense as her eyes went wide with alarm. Suppose, just suppose? Her horse noticed her tension and stirred uneasily. What had she done? Good God, she couldn't think about what she'd done! She was supposed to have described a fictitious winner, a man who did not exist, but had come dangerously close to giving the exact description of the very man she'd been with for most of the night! God, how could this have happened?

She thought for a moment, trying to steady her heart while silently praying for the safety of all involved. It would be all right. She had to believe that. Please, God, make it all right.

But despite her desperate prayers, Emy couldn't deny the deep sense of imminent disaster that seemed to overpower all rational thought. Would her father and brother imagine Cole as the man she described? No, she thought, trying for a sense of well-being she couldn't seem to grasp. She'd left them with a confusing picture of the imagined quarry, hadn't she? Oh, please, God, hadn't she?

She trembled at the very thought of either her father or brother accosting Cole. Mr. Brackston was a man too sure of himself not to handle any situation with ease. She knew instinctively that he was hardly the sort to take kindly to being robbed. Worse of all, the man wore his gun low on his hip! Lord, why hadn't she noticed that at the time?

She was off the horse and running back toward the docks when she heard the shot. Emy almost crumpled to the cobblestone street at the sound, for she knew without a doubt that one of them was dead. A sob tore itself from her throat, and although blinded with tears, she forced herself to go on. It was all her fault. Oh, God, everything was her fault.

Chapter Four

Cole watched her go with an odd tightening somewhere around his heart. No, dammit! Not his heart. His heart didn't have anything to do with this.

And then a surge of anger came to assault. Cole welcomed the emotion with greedy acceptance, for it took from his mind thoughts that might have terrified a lesser man.

Just what the hell did she think she was doing? Didn't she realize that it wasn't safe for a woman to wander the streets of a city alone, especially in the dark? Anything might happen to her, and she was too damn trusting for her own good.

Or was she? Was it her plan to leave him with this confusion, to never know the truth of the matter?

No, he realized after some thought. It was amazing how clear things appeared when a sexual haze was no longer in evidence. She wasn't at all what he'd first imagined. A woman of experience would never have left him. She might have played the game of innocence but in the end would have

71

gotten all she wanted and then some. Besides, had she been merely a prostitute, she would have looked for the culmination of the act in order to gain her monetary rewards. Even now she would have been at his side, eager that he find them a moment of privacy.

What she was was a damn fool. Her disappearance and hurried escape had proven that much.

Cole felt a sense of panic. He might not know it all, but he knew one thing, the woman was an innocent and in her innocence was bound to trust the wrong man. Hadn't he taken advantage of that trust with hardly any effort at all? Well, perhaps he hadn't taken advantage, exactly, but another might. A vile curse slipped from his lips as he shoved a man aside while working his way through the hostile crowd. If given the opportunity, another most certainly would.

It wasn't as if he felt anything for her, of course. Well, perhaps he did feel something, but it was only a small sense of concern. Any decent man would have felt as much.

She was such a little thing, after all. Well, maybe not so little as simply innocent. It didn't matter that he'd introduced her to passion. Nothing had come of it but the most luscious teasing of the senses. The woman was an innocent. And then, of course, there were her eyes. Dark, fathomless, mysterious, and yet trusting. Damn her and those eyes.

Cole put aside his thoughts and hurried from the boat. His eye was killing him. Damn that man, he hoped he suffered equally as much. Still, he couldn't think about the damage he'd inflicted now. All he

72

could think about was her. It wasn't that he wanted her in his life. No, he wasn't going after her because he wanted her. He was simply worried for her welfare.

Cole's gaze searched the dimly lit street as he disembarked the steamer. Where was she? It hadn't been but a few minutes since she left. Where could she have gone?

The hotel! Of course. Cole felt a wave of relief at the thought and then wondered why he'd known an almost debilitating sense of panic. She might be an innocent, but Emy was far from stupid. The first thing she'd do would be to head for the hotel.

Cole grinned as he imagined knocking on her door and after apologizing for his actions, for his suppositions, and maybe, just maybe . . . If things worked out as he hoped, he wouldn't leave until morning. But not until he was certain she was safe.

Cole imagined her surprise as she answered his knock. Only his vivid imagination went a step further. Suppose she wasn't alone? Suppose someone had been awaiting her arrival? Suppose . . . Cole couldn't believe it. He wouldn't, for a minute, allow himself to believe it.

The smells of the city accosted him one block into its midst. Horses, garbage, wood and coal smoke, cooking, and unwashed bodies. The same smells of every city he'd ever visited in the five years since leaving his home in Glory. A streetlight flickered, giving off a minimum of illumination. Beneath the light stood a woman. Cole hardly noticed her, for his mind was on another and the things they'd be doing within minutes.

It wasn't until she reached out for him, placing her hand on his arm while telling him in the most coarse and vulgar terms exactly what she could do for him if he met her price, that Cole realized her existence. He shook her hand off and glared at a face that might have been pretty if some of the paint were removed. His nostrils filled with the scent of cheap perfume; the strong smell mingled with flesh that had not known soap and water for a considerable time.

Cole found himself comparing this pathetic soul to Emy. Vacant eyes to ones dark and shining with passion. Hair colored to a brassy red tint to rich, dark tresses that felt like silk against his skin. A whiny plea to low, seductive laughter, laughter that carried him to near madness in his pleasure. His top lip curled with revulsion as he turned from her.

Cole's gaze held to the cobblestone sidewalk as his mind raged on. Damn her! He was going to wring her neck the minute he laid eyes on her. How dare she endanger herself by walking these streets alone? Didn't she know the things that could happen to her? Didn't she know that most men wouldn't care if she was an innocent or not? That one look at her beautiful face could cause even the few who might have cared to forget their sense of decency. Was she out of her mind?

Cole neatly put from his own mind his involvement, his own disregard of her innocence, and swore he'd kill any man who laid a finger on her, any man who even thought of it.

Cole, deep in thought, never noticed the two masked men as they came from an alley. It was dark.

Even had his thoughts been a bit less occupied, he might not have noticed. Not until it was too late. He saw the barrel of a gun aimed at his chest and knew it already was.

The two had moved out of the darkness with guns drawn, giving Cole no option but to leave his six-shooter where it was, tied to his hip. Cole looked quickly around. They were alone, no help in sight. On both sides of the street, empty shops were closed for the night. A light flickered farther down the street, but offered no illumination to the immediate area. In the distance the tinny sounds of music and raucous laughter flowed into the night. A man, obviously drunk, lurched from a swinging door and staggered down the street away from where they stood.

The man who had stopped him was clearly nervous. The gun, as well as the hand that held it, shook. Cole knew better than to offer any objections. It went against the grain to give in to these thieves, but to do otherwise would surely end in disaster. A nervous thief was a dangerous thief. Very dangerous indeed.

"Empty your pockets."

The words were accented in French. The reports he'd read had stated that the thieves were French or of French descent, which had narrowed the list of suspects down to a few hundred thousand, for most who lived in this area were of French descent. Cole wondered if these culprits were the very ones he'd come to find. He almost grinned at the irony, for it had taken very little effort on his part. They had found him.

Very slowly and very carefully Cole reached into his coat and drew out a small roll of bills. They were instantly snatched from his open palm.

"The rest of it."

Cole looked at the two with something like confusion creasing his brow. What rest? How much did they think he had?

"The winnings. Hand them over."

"What winnings?"

"In the card room. You won . . ."

Cole realized then that they had watched him leave the steamer. Obviously they had not been aboard, or they would have known better than to believe him a winner. That was their first mistake. The second was to pick him to rob out of all those who were aboard. He narrowed his gaze, trying to make out the pair in the dark, trying to memorize the little he could see. "I wasn't in the card room for more than a few minutes. I didn't—"

"Hand it over."

Cole was beginning to feel more than a bit annoyed. These two bumbling crooks imagined he was the winner of some huge sum. How was he supposed to convince them otherwise? "If you don't believe me, search my pockets." He only prayed they would agree to his offer. If he could just get one of them close enough . . .

One of the men moved almost within reach but came to a stop at the other's warning. "Don't go near him. It might be a trick."

To Cole, the apparent leader of the two said, "Open your coat and turn your pockets out."

Cole reluctantly did as he was told. A pocket

knife, a comb, a packet of papers, and a leather wallet soon fell to the sidewalk and lay at Cole's feet.

Jacques scowled. Emy had described this one, hadn't she? Perhaps not. Her description had been vague at best, confusing if truth be told.

Had they made a mistake? Perhaps not. Still, if not, where was the money? Where had he hidden it?

His boots. Of course. He should have thought of that before. He was wasting too much time. Any minute now, someone might come upon them.

Just in case of such a happening, Jacques waved his gun, edging Cole closer to the alley's opening and then ordered, "Take off your boots."

Cole glared at the two. He bit his lip, wishing above all else that he could get his hands on them. They were stupid enough and, Cole imagined, would be easy enough to beat, for neither had thought to relieve him of his gun. If he could . . . Cole bent in half, in apparent obedience to the order, but his hand didn't reach for his boot. It reached, instead, for the Colt that lay holstered to his leg. In an instant he had it drawn and pointed at the two.

"Hold it right there," he said, but the last word was barely spoken when Jacques noticed the gun and without another thought almost reflexively pulled the trigger of his own.

The sound of a firing gun was loud, but not nearly so out of place in this town of late-night fights than might be imagined. It brought no surge of inquisitive people to investigate. Nothing but an eerie silence was heard to echo in the stunning all too quiet aftermath.

Jacques and Anton, so caught up in what they had

done, stood frozen in place. The sounds of their own pounding hearts blotted out the running footsteps.

Emy came upon their dazed, motionless forms, breathless with fear. A soft cry escaped her lips as she came abreast of their position. It was only then that she realized it was Cole who had been hit.

A wave of emotion assaulted her at the sight. She was at once thankful that her father and brother were unharmed, but horrified to see the man she had been romantically involved with crumpled and bleeding at their feet. Blood rushed from a head wound in sickening, pulsating spurts. Emy choked back the nausea that slammed into her stomach and averted her gaze. She couldn't look lest the churning in her stomach take hold.

"Mon Dieu! What have you done?"

"He pulled a gun. I didn't mean to . . ."

Emy glared at her father, disgusted at the whining sound that told so clearly of his helplessness. She couldn't think of the fear he had to know. There was no time. A man was bleeding at her feet. She didn't dare think of how seriously he was hurt. She heard a low, pain-filled moan. He was alive. Thank God! He was alive, but in desperate need of help, and all her father and brother managed to do was stand there and watch the man bleed to death. "Do something."

"What can I do?"

Emy knew again the heavy weight of responsibility that her father and brother all too often avoided. She reached under her skirt and tore a ruffle from her cotton petticoat. "Wrap this around his head," she said to her brother. She glared again at her father and ordered in a clipped tone, "Get the horses."

The two men were more than happy to see to her bidding. Neither had ever killed before. Neither had ever shot a gun except at targets or while hunting food, and this happening was quite beyond their ability to comprehend. If asked, neither would have been able to say what to do next.

"Put him on your horse," she ordered her father the moment he reappeared with three horses in tow.

"But Emy, *chérie,* where . . . ?"

"Just do it!"

Moments later the three rode out of town. With Cole slung across Jacques's saddle, it was slow going, but they made their home, fifteen miles north of Baton Rouge, less than two hours later.

It was almost morning. The house was quiet, for all but Emy slept. She sat at Cole's side in the rocker her grandmère often used and in the silence of the night listened to the even sounds of his breathing. He had lost a great deal of blood, but Emy imagined a man of his size and obvious strength could live with the loss. What she feared now was the likelihood of fever. In truth, Cole appeared healthy enough, but fever had been known to steal the strength from the most hardy of souls and bring them to the brink of death. Once there, little but prayer could stop a man from plunging over the edge.

She bit her lip and forced aside that particularly abhorrent image, while wondering why the thought of his dying should bring a sense of discomfort to her chest. It wasn't that she cared for the man, well, no more so than she would for any living creature. It

79

was guilt, of course, guilt that she should have been the cause of his suffering. His possible death.

And then, of course, there was the fear of reckoning, for she had no doubt an explanation would be demanded the minute he awoke.

Supposing he lived, what could she say that would keep her father and brother out of prison? Could she plead their cause and win? Emy shook her head. No, not with this man. Instinctively she knew no amount of begging on their behalf would suffice.

Her eyes filled with hope as her thoughts went on. Their faces had been covered. Cole couldn't have seen much more than vague shadows in the darkness. Could she pretend that they had, all three, come across him after the shooting? Could she get away with such a story? She doubted he'd believe her. Still, he wouldn't have much choice if in the end she stuck to her story.

He was a marshal. Emy remembered back to her first sight of him. She had imagined him to be a gambler, dressed as he was in a black suit, white shirt and string tie, but his face had been tan. She remembered now wondering at the peculiarity of a gambler spending so much time in the sun.

Of course she hadn't known he was a marshal until they had gotten him home and Anton and her father had gone through the few things emptied from his pockets. He was a marshal and had, in his papers, a warrant for the arrest of her father and brother. There were empty places where the names should have been, but all three of them knew the warrant had been issued for the arrest of the Du Maurier men.

Lord, what a mess. If only she hadn't been thinking of him at the time. If only she hadn't been fool enough to have thoughtlessly given a description that fit so few men aboard. Why hadn't she told her brother and father that the man was fat? That he was short? That he was anything but like the man on her mind?

But all wasn't lost yet. If she could concoct a good story and get this man to believe it, all might yet be saved.

Kit and her father and brother had helped, but it had taken hours before her grandmère had retired to the room the three women shared. Upon arriving home, a makeshift bed had been brought in from the barn. Discarded feather mattresses and thick quilts had been piled one upon the other and covered with clean bedding to provide for the injured man.

Thank God, grandmère had come from her usually forgetful, slightly dazed state and in rapidly spoken French had taken control. Before an hour had passed, Cole was lying on the bed before the fire in the kitchen, his wound cleaned and stitched closed. A medicinal salve containing some particularly nasty-smelling ingredient was placed upon the wound in the hope of preventing any festering, and then a clean bandage was wrapped around his dark hair.

There was nothing to do now but wait and allow his body time to heal.

Horrified at what they had done, her father and brother had sworn this was the end of their unlawful ways. Never again would they resort to criminal means to save their farm. They had left the small house barely an hour before, heading south toward the bayou. They had taken Emy's horse to sell for the traps and supplies. They'd set those traps in the bayou, and with any luck at all, they would return in less than a month with enough money to satisfy that fat carpetbagger.

Cole moaned and Emy leaned close, the cool rag in her hand replacing the one already upon his forehead. "Easy, now, *chéri*. Go to sleep," she said in French. Emy never noticed the endearment. Cole never heard it.

"I wish he'd get on with it and die," Catherine Du Maurier muttered in a disgruntled fashion as she anxiously paced the length of their dilapidated porch while Emy sat in sunshine allowed by a gaping hole in the porch roof, sewing the last touches to a dress Mrs. Kingsly had ordered to be ready by the end of this week. They had both been banished from the house, for being unmarried ladies, their grand-mère could not permit them inside while she bathed her patient. Emy, of course, did not mention the fact that she had seen this particular man before, had touched him, in fact, and he her, in the most intimate manner imaginable. Her cheeks grew warm just thinking about it, but she forced her thoughts back to her sister's grumbling. "I hate living like this. It's our house and we can't talk above a whisper. It's been almost a week since any of my beaus have been allowed to visit."

Emy shot her selfish sister a look that promised untold suffering. As usual, her threatening glare went unnoticed.

"You know I'm right, Emy. We have enough to worry about." Kit never mentioned the fact that she had not worried in the least about anything but her hair, dress, or next beau in the last two years.

"It's been exactly three days, Kit. I understand your being upset about the lack of visitors, but to wish someone dead . . ." Emy shook her head in dismay.

"Oh, you know I don't mean that. I wouldn't care if he got well instead. It's just that he's so big and that stupid bed takes up the whole room."

The bed was big, but not nearly big enough to take up an entire room. Emy decided against correcting her sister of the exaggeration. "He'll be better soon. Grandmère says it won't be long before the fever passes."

Kit snorted a disparaging sound. "When she remembers what fever and who has it, you mean. Besides, how could she possibly know when he'll be better?"

Emy had been nine when her mother died while birthing Kit. She could remember the pretty woman in the faded picture her father kept upon his chest of drawers. But she remembered most her grand-mother, soothing away her tears, caring for scrapes, hugging her close to her side when a storm came, sleeping cuddled against the woman's softness as a child. Emy wasn't about to allow anyone to talk about the woman in a disrespectful fashion. Grand-mère was close to seventy, and if she at times forgot things, her nasty little sister could well accept the slight failing or answer to Emy why she should not.

"Kit, you are the most selfish, insolent brat. And if I ever hear you talk like that about grandmère again, I'll, I'll . . ." Emy couldn't think of a punishment severe enough. "When Father returns, I will, of course, bring up the subject again of the convent."

Kit made a dramatic sweep of her arm as if brushing aside the ridiculous thought.

"If not a convent, then a husband. You need a man who wouldn't hesitate to pound some sense into you."

Kit ignored the threat, knowing full well she could talk her father into or out of anything. She had no fear of convents or forced marriages. No, she'd marry when she pleased, and she'd marry whomever she pleased. Someone tall and dark, perhaps. Someone rich. Laughter sparkled in her dark eyes. "That one"—she nodded to her right, in the direction of the house—"I wouldn't mind if he did the pounding. I could even show him where . . ."

"Kit!" Emy couldn't believe her ears. Her sister was only fifteen. How in the world did she come by such thoughts?

Kit laughed at her sister's shocked expression. Kit imagined herself, at fifteen, a woman of the world. She knew quite a bit about men, all learned, she was sorry to admit, from whispered conversations with her friends at school. But Kit was determined to learn firsthand what it was like to be with a man, and she wasn't about to wait much longer. "Why don't we put him in Papa's room? It's empty."

Emy grunted at the suggestion. "You want him in Papa's room, go ahead and put him there." Emy smiled at the thought of any of the three women carrying the delirious man into the next room. She knew for a fact that he was as heavy as the wash bucket filled with water and clothes. Hadn't she twice struggled to raise his shoulders so he might drink? He'd squash any one of them, or all three, flatter than one of grandmère's delicious crepes.

Kit moaned her disgust. "I don't want to. Tell grandmère to do it."

Emy shot her sister a look of amazement. "Tell an old woman to bring in wood while your arms appear perfectly capable of the chore?" Emy looked in the old woman's direction and smiled at the sight of her asleep in the rocker.

Kit shot her sister a look of disgust. "Well, I'm all dressed up. Pierre will be here any minute."

"Then sit here and watch him. I'll do it myself."

Emy was struggling with the doorknob, her arms filled with wood. It took some doing, but she finally managed to open the door without dropping the armful of wood on her toes. "Thanks for your help," she muttered as she added to the small pile of wood stacked near the stove.

"He really is quite good-looking, don't you think?"

Emy turned to scowl at her sister. She'd never in her life imagined that a fifteen-year-old could be so brazen. The girl needed a husband badly, and the sooner the better. "I wouldn't waste my time mooning over Mr. Brackston, Kit. The man is much too old for you."

"Oh, I don't know. Older men are so much more

interesting and attractive than—"

"Pierre will be here in a minute," Emy interrupted. "Why don't you wait outside for him."

For once, Kit gladly did her sister's bidding.

"Don't leave the porch." Emy sighed as she watched the door shut tightly behind her sister, having no hope that the girl would obey her last suggestion. Perhaps it would be better if she did leave the safety of the porch and venture into the darkness with her beau. Perhaps, if Kit found herself with child, despite the scandal it would cause, she'd at least be forced to marry. Once Kit was a married lady, she would be her husband's problem and Emy could finally stop worrying.

She was pumping water into a pot for coffee when she heard the low masculine chuckle. Emy almost dropped the pot at the sound. She turned to find Cole's dark eyes open, his bright, feverish gaze upon her. "Is she always that willful?"

Emy forgot the question, for this was the first time in almost a week that the man had put together two intelligible words and done it while appearing wide awake. "How are you feeling?" she asked, not at all sure he wasn't again suffering from some feverish delusion.

"Weak." Cole watched the pretty woman brush back a thick lock of black hair that had come loose of its pins and wondered who the hell she was and what the hell was he doing there.

"Would you like some water?"

Cole nodded and then groaned at the movement. His head was killing him. Why? Cole reached a shaky hand to his forehead and knew no little surprise upon finding it bandaged. "Was I in an accident?"

Emy nodded in return, her dark eyes puzzled at the odd question. Didn't he remember how he'd gotten hurt? She felt a glimmer of hope as the weariness, the fear, the anxiety she'd known for the last week, eased from her shoulders. A tentative smile curved her sweet lips. "You were in an accident."

"What kind?" he asked as she struggled to lift him to a half-sitting position.

With a grunt Emy slid behind him at last. Trapped between his body and the wall, she had no choice but to allow him to lean against her. "I'm not sure. All I know is that my father found you." Emy prayed the shaking in her voice would go unnoticed. At least she didn't have to face him and lie. Her eye would have twitched like mad. She almost shrugged at the thought, knowing he wouldn't have understood the meaning behind it. "He brought you home."

Cole, as ill as he was, was not ignorant of the fact that the woman was as soft as she was pretty. He languished for a moment in the pleasure of leaning against that softness as her hand reached for the glass of water upon the low table and brought the glass to his lips.

His body ached. He wondered if he'd been in a fight. Considering the throbbing in his head, he was sure it had to have been one hell of a battle. Odd that he couldn't seem to remember it, though. No matter, he reasoned. He'd think about it later. He'd remember then. Right now his mind wandered to other, more delicious matters, like who was this woman with the dark, mysterious, and yet somehow familiar eyes, and why was she taking care of him?

Cole drank his fill and then rested his head against her softness. Damn, but this felt good. For just a minute he tried to think of an excuse to stay in her arms. But the effort grew too taxing, and despite his intentions he soon found himself drifting off to sleep again. "Thank you, ma'am," he murmured just before his mind eased into the healing blackness.

Emy was overjoyed by the knowledge. He didn't remember anything, not even her. That last thought brought a tiny surge of disappointment, but Emy soon put it all into proper perspective. It was best, of course, that he didn't remember. Thank God for it, in fact.

She trembled at the thought of the few moments spent in his room, spent together, the disgraceful, wicked things they'd done. How could she have found the courage to face the man if he'd remembered?

Cole slept peacefully for the remainder of the evening. It wasn't until late that night, after Kit's beau had gone and she and grandmère were in bed, that Emy was brought from her light doze by the sounds of his mumbles and cries. He was thrashing about, twisting his legs in the sheet that covered him, throwing aside his pillow, groaning at the ache in his head that had somehow penetrated beyond his feverish dreams into his consciousness.

"My head," he moaned.

"Lay still, *chéri,*" Emy whispered above him.

"Hot." He tore the sheet away. "Hot. God, I'm so hot."

Despite the fact that the man was dreadfully ill,

Emy felt a sudden flush of warmth at the sight of his near nakedness. Her grandmère would never permit her patient to be totally unclothed, of course, so he'd been left to wear a pair of drawers, form-fitting drawers that came to his knees. Still, the undergarment hardly went far toward disguising his shockingly aroused state. Emy couldn't imagine why or how that should be. Certainly she'd done nothing to bring on this happening. No. She wasn't at fault here. Then why? Emy couldn't help but give the matter some thought, but came at last to no conclusion. Finally she managed to shrug the entire matter aside while cursing her ignorance of the human body, whether that body be male or female. There was simply no help for it. No doubt she'd never know the answers to her silent questions.

"Here." Emy squeezed another towel from the bucket of water near her feet and replaced the hot, almost dry one that covered his forehead. Again she wet the cloth, and refusing to look at anything below the waist, she moved the towel over his feverish chest and neck. "This will make you feel better."

Cole shoved aside her ministrations, for the feel of cool water against his feverish skin was comparable to an Arctic blast. "No."

"Lay still," she said again as she covered him once more with the sheet. Emy dared to sit on the bed at his side. It gave her an odd feeling to sit this close, their hips touching, but it was awkward, indeed, to reach for him from the rocker.

"Jesus, it's as hot as hell in here. Open a window."

"Listen to me. You have a fever. I have to keep this towel on you."

89

"It hurts, dammit!"

"I know, but there's no other way."

Cole muttered a few choice words as he struggled to fight off her help.

Emy was to the point where she was ready to awaken her grandmother, when Cole suddenly quieted. A few minutes later he dozed again, never realizing the efforts of the woman at his side.

He was dreaming the most delicious dream. A lady, a dark-haired lady with the most beautiful eyes, was there. She was whispering something to him, something low and deliciously provocative, something he couldn't understand. But he understood well enough the look in her eyes. He knew what she wanted from him. And he was more than willing to oblige.

He smiled as she moved close to him and then away. She was teasing him, taunting him with a smile, with the softness of her body, with a look in those dark eyes, daring him to reach for her.

He knew her, but for some reason couldn't remember her name. It didn't matter. Names weren't important when a man wanted a woman.

He touched her, pulling her close against him. His mouth lowered and his lips were almost upon hers when he heard the laugh. Jesus, it was his mother! Cole shivered his disgust. He'd almost kissed his own mother. Disgust or not, for just a weak moment he wanted to pull her close, to feel her soft arms wrap around him, to shelter him from the sorrow. But it didn't happen. Instead, he felt again the old pain, the revulsion for what she was. He shoved her back and watched as her lips contorted in hatred. "You," she said with venom. "It was because of you that he left."

Cole had heard that complaint enough times in his life not to care anymore. She was yelling something, cursing probably, for the woman rarely spoke without using vulgarities. She didn't want him there. She was telling him to get out. Worried about her customers, no doubt. Cole shrugged. He didn't care what she wanted. He was only a kid, but he wasn't going to let her see the hurt. He wouldn't cry. And then he was sixteen, and still he didn't cry, not even when she died.

Suddenly Mina was there. How could that be? Mina was dead. Oh, God, not the dream again. He didn't want this dream. He didn't want to feel the old pain again.

But Cole had no control. He tried, but he couldn't wake up. The ache came, familiar, almost soothing in his sorrow. It didn't matter that it had been five years. The ache grew suddenly stronger than ever as he watched her wave good-bye. "Don't," he muttered, straining to reach her waving hand. She was slipping away. "Don't leave me!"

"I won't, *chéri,*" came the low, sensual voice above him.

But she did. "Goddammit! Where are you going?"

That intoxicating voice again, whispered close to his ear, *"Non, chéri.* I'm here. I will stay."

Cole sighed, feeling a staggering sense of relief. She'd stay. She said she would, she'd promised, and he believed her. His feverish mind never put together the fact that Mina couldn't speak a word of French.

Chapter Five

Cole felt the cool touch of her hand skim lightly over his face. He knew she moved closer, for the bed dipped slightly beneath her weight and caused him to roll just a bit toward her. The movement brought their hips within contact.

He was sick, sicker than he'd ever been in his life. He burned with fever, his body ached of it, his mind grew numb with it, his senses swam in a sea of dullness. And yet, despite the fever, Cole knew it was a woman who cared for him. Through the haze of illness he heard her talk to him. Most of the time he couldn't understand her, but it didn't matter. Understanding wasn't necessary. He knew she was there to comfort and soothe, and he found himself eagerly accepting that comfort, his body aching for her gentle touch.

Something cold was placed upon his forehead. The shock of it against raging heat brought Cole suddenly awake. He blinked at the angelic vision before him and wondered for an instant if he hadn't died. Cole discounted the notion. If he were dead, it wouldn't be angels that visited his side. "Who are you?" he asked as clearly as if he suffered not at all.

Emy bit her lip, suddenly reluctant to tell him her name. Would it bring a light of recognition to his eyes? Would it bring back a memory better off lost? And if he remembered who she was, would he then suspect her involvement with what had later occurred?

Emy knew she had no choice in the matter, for to appear reluctant to answer so simple a question would only stir the man's suspicions, thereby causing more questions. "Emy. My name is Emy."

"Do I know you?"

Emy felt only blessed relief. Her name had stirred no memory. Thank God, his memory appeared lost. Emy prayed it would stay that way forever. *"Non."*

Emy. Where had he heard that name before? He smiled a heart-stopping flash of white teeth against dark stubble. "I knew a woman named Emy once."

His eyes were glazed with fever. They shone like black diamonds. Emy wondered if he'd have any recollection of this conversation upon awakening, for this wasn't the first time he'd asked who she was. "Did you?"

Cole nodded, never noticing, or, for that matter, realizing the reason behind her discomfort. His gaze had moved to her mouth and was studying the delicious way her small teeth worried her bottom lip.

"Where are we?" he asked, his gaze never moving from her mouth.

"About fifteen miles north of Baton Rouge."

"How did I get here?"

"My father found you and brought you here."

"I was hurt?" Cole wanted to ask her a hundred questions, not the least of which was why the hell he couldn't remember anything.

Emy touched the bandage that nearly covered his entire head, and nodded. "Your wound is healing nicely."

Cole pushed aside a sense of panic, somehow knowing to give in to the emotion would bring about no satisfactory results and asked as calmly as he could manage, "Why can't I remember?"

"You will, monsieur. Do you know who you are?"

"Cole Brackston," Cole said with some relief. At least he remembered that much. He knew his name and quite a bit more. What he couldn't remember was the immediate past.

Emy smiled as she nodded. "It will all come back. Do not worry."

Cole wasn't sure if it was simply a matter of wanting to believe her, but he realized he did, and because he did, he felt himself relax.

"Does it bother you?"

"What?" she asked, her eyes narrowing with fear at the question. She wondered if he hadn't been playing a trick on her all along. Had he remembered from the first? Was he hinting at an aching conscience? Was he simply waiting for her to blurt out the truth?

"Your lip."

"My lip?" Emy's dark eyes darkened further still, confused at the sudden change of subject.

"Does it itch?"

"No. Why?"

"Because you keep biting it."

"Do I?" She shrugged. "I often do that when I'm nervous," Emy remarked without thinking.

"Do I make you nervous?"

"Certainly not." She bit her lip again. "I meant, I often bite it. I don't have to be nervous. Sometimes I bite it when I'm worried." She touched his forehead and remarked, "You're very warm. You must rest."

Cole smiled. She was biting her lip again. Somehow Cole knew the action had little to do with his fever.

Emy figured it was best not to dwell on lips. The subject only brought to mind the feel of his against her mouth and the things they'd done to each other after his mouth had caused her to lose all sense of reason. She knew better than to think about that.

"You could make me better."

"I'm doing everything I can, monsieur."

"There's one thing you haven't done."

Emy was immediately suspect. Over and above the fever there was a distinct twinkle in his dark eyes. She couldn't imagine what might have caused it. "Sleep will take care of it, I think."

"You could help me to sleep."

Even as she asked, Emy wondered if she really wanted to hear the answer. "How?"

"By joining me in this bed."

Emy shot him a stern look. Now she had no doubt what that twinkle meant. Her gaze became as prim and proper as a spinster schoolmarm. "Monsieur, you are far too ill to allow wicked thoughts."

Cole smiled. "A man can never be too sick for that, darlin'."

"Behave," she warned him in a threatening tone. "Grandmère will hear you."

Cole frowned. He had no idea that they weren't alone. His gaze moved over the small room, taking in with one sweep the simple furnishings, the fire, the wood-beamed ceiling, and the two doors leading off the main room. No doubt her grandmother slept behind one of them. "She couldn't hear if you kissed me."

Emy smiled at the hopeful note in his voice. "She couldn't hear if you stopped this nonsense altogether. Now, go to sleep."

"There's something in my eye." Cole felt no twinge of conscience at the bold lie. He wanted her closer, much closer, and didn't hesitate to use any trick in order to gain his ends.

Emy's look was filled with doubt. "I don't believe you."

"There is." And at her continued disbelief, he dropped his tone to a breathless plea. "I swear."

Emy reached for his face. She was about to open the eye in question, when her hands were captured in his. Emy laughed at the look of victory he shot her way. "I knew you were lying."

Very gently, in order not to dislodge something that was no doubt on the very edge of being loose, or he wouldn't have this pounding headache, Cole shook his head and allowed Emy a glimpse of his most charming grin. "You suspected me of lying. You didn't know for sure, or you wouldn't have come so close."

As he spoke, he was pulling her closer still. Emy felt her heart thump hard against the walls of her chest at his smile. She chuckled a low, oddly familiar sound. Had she laughed before? Had he, in his delirium, heard it? Is that why it seemed so familiar?

Cole figured that particular question could wait until later. She was off balance as he, with amazing strength for someone so ill, pulled her to lean over him. He tugged once more and Emy plopped hard upon his chest, her hands held wide from her sides.

Her lips were almost touching his, and Cole almost groaned in his anticipation, knowing she was going to allow the kiss.

His hands released hers and came to gently cup rounded cheeks, bringing her mouth within contact of his. He knew it. He knew she would feel like this. He knew her mouth would be this soft, this warm, this sweet. It was the best thing he'd ever known.

His mouth was fire and Emy felt her resistance melt away at the need in his kiss. She groaned, unable to deny either of them this pleasure. Her lips parted to his gentle persuasion, only his tongue didn't penetrate her mouth as expected. Instead, his lips appeared to grow lax, soft, as if they had somehow forgotten their intent.

His hands fell away.

Emy pulled her mouth from his and with a puzzled frown searched his flushed face. His eyes were closed and his breathing regular. Too regular. Not at all like hers.

Emy grunted as she gained her balance and came to her feet. She glared at the sleeping man. One of two things had just occurred. Either her kiss was so powerful, which she doubted, that the man had lost consciousness because of it, or so boring that he'd found it impossible to stay awake.

Emy shook her head at the nonsensical thought and fought to regain her composure. Her cheeks grew warm at the liberties she'd just allowed. Whatever was the matter with her? Why had she no will against this particular man?

She began to pace her small kitchen while wondering how she could have allowed yet another kiss. Especially in delirium. Hadn't she learned her lesson the last time their mouths had come together?

Emy groaned. She'd never suspected this flaw in her character, this weakness when near this man. How was it that it had never surfaced before? She hadn't lived twenty-four years without knowing the feel of a man's mouth upon hers, but never until this man had she imagined the exquisite delight gained in touching her lips to another's.

Emy felt a sense of utter confusion. She wished she could talk to someone. Her thoughts turned at once to her grandmother and her never-failing wisdom. Grandmère could help her understand this weakness. But in order to do so, Emy would have to confess all. She couldn't. She absolutely could not. It had been bad enough when telling the priest. But at least in the sanctity of the church, cloaked in the darkness of a confessional, she had been granted a measure of anonymity. The mere thought of admitting to her indiscretions and doing it in the light of day was too mortifying to bear.

Emy tore her mind from the man and her most recent encounter. She wouldn't think about it. She *couldn't* think about it. He was burning with fever and needed her care. Later she'd try to understand. Later she'd think.

Cole groaned against the pain in his head. It pounded like a hammer behind his eyes, causing him to gasp at its intensity. He dared not move lest the pain increase.

Lying very still, he tried to think why his head should hurt so badly. It took a moment, but he finally realized it wasn't only his head, but his entire body that ached. He felt as if he'd been caught in the midst of a stampeding herd of horses. Jesus, he was sore. What he couldn't figure out was why.

A frown creased his brow as his mind searched for an answer. Nothing. What the hell was the matter with him? Why couldn't he remember what had happened?

Cole opened his eyes to the glare of morning and stared at the ceiling overhead. At first he thought he might be in a barroom, but quickly dismissed the thought. No such establishment boasted of a ceiling this clean.

Where the hell was he?

Cole's gaze moved to the walls painted an identical white, stopping at a picture of some saint. Below the picture stood a table, upon which sat a small prayer book and a flickering candle. Framed needlepoint hung on the walls, bringing a warm homeyness to the room.

Despite the pain it caused, he forced his gaze to follow the wall, noting the door that obviously led outside. To his right, a huge stone fireplace took up

99

most of one wall. Between him and the fireplace stood a plain, well-worn table and six mismatched chairs. A lady's rocker and small table were positioned close to his bed.

Cole closed his eyes and tried to will himself the needed strength to come to a sitting position. Damn, but he was weak. What was the matter with him? Why couldn't he remember?

A small sound came from his right. Cole opened his eyes to find, much to his surprise, a pretty young girl peering down at him.

"So, you are awake at last." Her eyes sparkled with bold mischief and Cole felt a responding grin curve his lips.

"How long have I been asleep?"

The girl shrugged. Her dark curls bounced with the movement. Cole figured she'd practiced that movement a number of times, until attaining the effect she wanted. Despite her tender years, there was a worldliness to her. It shone in dark eyes that were perhaps a shade wiser than they should have been.

Cole could tell at a glance that this one was a daring sort, one who wouldn't allow an exciting opportunity to pass her by. He knew he'd never seen her before, and wondered why she seemed so familiar. There was something about her, something he couldn't place.

"More than a week," she returned as she made a fuss of adjusting and smoothing the sheet that covered him.

Twice she touched him, "by accident," her fingers lingering upon his chest long enough for Cole to realize what this girl wanted. Cole might have laughed at her less than discreet attempts at seduction, but considering her tender years, he frowned instead. This one needed a strong hand, or she'd soon find herself a piece of used baggage.

And then he realized her response. More than a week! Lord, he must have been in bad shape for his head to hurt still.

And then it came back. The night, the men, nervous and jittery, trying to rob him. Christ, one of them had shot him! Apparently in the head. No wonder his head hurt like it did.

"My name is Kit. You know, like a kitten. Soft and purring, especially when I get what I want."

Kit's supposedly seductive remark was completely lost on Cole, for his mind was filled only with questions. He'd been shot. How had he come to be here? And where the hell was here? Cole didn't remember having asked in his delirium much the same question of another beauty. One that was a bit older and far more appealing in her innocence. "What happened? How did . . . ?"

Kit shrugged again, and again those pretty, dark curls bounced. "All I know is that Papa found you in the city." Her eyes sparkled. "And that you were badly hurt. Grandmère and I have been taking care of you." Kit discounted the lie, knowing it would cause no harm if this handsome man felt a degree of indebtedness.

"I don't remember." Cole closed his eyes, forcing both his body and mind to relax. He couldn't remember a thing after he'd been shot, except perhaps for the sound of a scream. Had he imagined

101

it? Had he screamed? Had the men who attacked him? No, the scream had been higher-pitched, not of a man, but of a woman.

How had her father come upon him? How had he managed to bring him here? Judging by the pain in his head, he'd been hurt pretty badly. He'd probably been unconscious for much of the time. No wonder he couldn't remember it all.

Cole lay still for a moment, trying to put his thoughts together. He took a deep breath and felt nothing but relief that the memories were still there. He remembered Glory and his family living there yet. He rememberd Mina and her death five years ago. He remembered the traveling, the restlessness, the searching for something he'd never know again, the job he'd finally found in New Orleans, the fact that he was the marshal. He breathed another sigh, knowing his memory was intact.

"Where am I?"

"On our farm north of Baton Rouge."

Cole frowned, there was something missing, a memory he couldn't quite grasp. The sound of a soft voice, the feel of cool fingers brushing against his skin. But it hadn't been her. Cole couldn't say how he knew, but he did. She wasn't the one who had cared for him, the one who had reached out cooling fingers to brush against feverish skin. "Who else lives here?"

"Well"—Kit smiled, trying her best to hold this man's attention—"there's father and Anton, my brother, and Grandmère and, of course, myself." Kit didn't mention her sister. She figured there was no need for him to wonder about another woman when she was right here. "Would you like to sit up?"

"I don't think I can."

"I'll help you." Kit grinned, delighted at the opportunity of being able to touch him. "Just put your arms around me and I'll pull you up."

She really was a brazen little thing. If Cole's head hadn't been threatening to burst open, he might have been tempted to do one of two things. Either take her up on her obvious offer or paddle her backside. Cole almost grinned at realizing it was indeed possible to do both.

"Here"—she fluffed a pillow—"I'll put these behind you and help you slide up."

Cole didn't have much choice, considering his complete lack of strength, but to do as he was told. She put her hands around his neck and pulled. With a soft exclamation she suddenly and "accidentally" fell full-length upon him.

The feel of her body, her soft breasts pressing into his chest, might have been a welcomed sensation. No doubt at any other time it would have been, but in falling, the little twit had knocked her head into his nose. Now, because of her clumsiness, he had yet another ache to contend with.

Cole groaned.

"Oh, I'm sorry," the girl murmured with false sweetness while extricating herself as slowly as possible from the bed.

Damn little brat. If she was sorry, then he was Genghis Khan. "It's all right. You're not strong enough."

"But I am. Let's try again."

Cole managed to lift himself this time. He wasn't

103

about to take another blow to his already aching head. A groan of pain slid from his lips at the effort it took.

"Here," Kit offered, "Emy always gives you this when you sound like you're in pain."

Cole took the offered glass and downed its contents in two greedy gulps. It wasn't until the glass was empty that he almost choked on the taste. What the hell was that? He'd expected whiskey and had taken instead some noxious-tasting brew. Cole shivered at the tang that remained in his mouth. He needed bourbon. A whole bottle of the stuff. That could guarantee any man to forget the worst pain.

Cole handed back the glass, his gaze on the girl who had made herself comfortable on his bed. "Who's Emy?" Jesus! Could it be? Could it be that the woman he searched for had been taking care of him? How? How had she managed to come upon him when he was in his most need?

"Emy? Did I say Emy? I meant Grandmère, of course."

"Who's Emy?" Cole asked again, knowing instinctively that the girl was lying. His heart thudded as the memories of that night on the boat came crashing over him. If he was a man who believed in praying, he'd pray now that this was the Emy he'd been looking for.

"Oh, Emy." Kit smiled prettily. "She's just my sister. My spinster sister." She tried to change the subject. "Are you hungry?"

Cole grinned. He was feeling better. Whatever it was that had filled that glass was easing the pain enough for him to enjoy the girl's antics. It was obvious that this little would-be hussy wanted to change the subject. Cole thought this one could use a lesson in manners and deliberately refused to let it go. "A spinster?" It was her. He knew it was her. It had to be. He remembered the whispered words heard in fever. The sound of her voice, the feel of her hands. It was her.

Kit nodded. "She's old."

"How old?"

Again the girl shrugged. "Well, I guess she's about twenty-four."

Cole chuckled, and instantly thought of his own twenty-eight years. "That old, eh?"

Kit nodded enthusiastically. "You might think she's sort of pretty, but Emy doesn't like men." Kit whispered the last comment as if she were telling of some dreadful family secret.

Cole grinned at her dramatics and knew if the absent sister was the very same Emy he'd romanced just before being shot, she liked men, all right. At least she seemed to like him. And if she was whom he suspected, he wondered why she wasn't anything like her younger sibling. Cole shrugged aside the thought. It didn't matter. The only thing that mattered was that he'd found Emy.

Kit's hip pressed up against his leg. Cole moved, only to find her hip again butting against him.

"You didn't answer me before. Are you hungry?"

"I could do with a little somethin', I reckon." Lord, but that was an understatement. Cole felt like he hadn't eaten in a month. He was starving.

"A little what?" she asked, and Cole knew for a fact that this girl had better get married and fast. She was a hot little piece, begging for trouble. As she spoke, her voice lowered to a deliberate seductive husk while she ran her fingertip over his chest.

Just as she lowered it to where the sheet covered his waist, the door opened. Cole realized he was holding his breath as he waited for someone to enter. A sigh of relief whispered from between his teeth at the sight of Emy.

His fever broke that morning. It wasn't the first time, but Emy prayed it was the last. He was terribly weak. And as far as she could tell, since it would have been out of the question to give his body more than a perfunctory glance, he'd lost a great deal of weight. Even the dark bristles of his beard couldn't hide cheeks that had grown gaunt.

No doubt he'd sleep for many days, but at least the danger was gone. To Emy's relief, Grandmère, at the crack of dawn, had announced Mr. Brackston would live.

Emy couldn't imagine why that knowledge should have put her in such a good mood. It hadn't, of course. Emy was characteristically a cheerful woman and often in such a mood. Still, today she might have been just a bit more cheerful than usual. She hadn't complained that Kit, the lazy girl, had forgotten to bring in the eggs. After milking their one cow and seeing to it and the calf's feeding, Emy went about that chore. Sometimes it was simply easier to do things herself rather than nag at Kit.

Her small basket was full as she entered the house again, her mind on the delicious desserts Grandmère would concoct from these eggs and the blueberries that had been put up last season.

Cole was siting up in bed, his back pillowed from the hardness of the wall, when she came in. The fact that her lazy sister was sitting on the bed with him, her finger tracing boldly over his chest as she teased him to laughter, had absolutely no effect on her at all.

"Would you like a bath?"

"You figure you're old enough to give a man a bath, darlin'?" Cole caught her hand and removed it from his belly. Still the light of laughter in his eyes did not waver. It was easy enough to see that the man was enjoying himself. Of course his all-so-obvious enjoyment of her sister didn't matter in the least to Emy. The only reason she broke at least six precious eggs was that the stupid basket had slipped from her hand to the table. She hadn't slammed it down.

The fact was, Cole's obvious good mood had nothing at all to do with Emy's sister, but with the woman herself. True, he'd answered the girl's silly comment, but with hardly a thought. All he could do was stare at Emy. All he could think about was his good fortune to find himself there.

Emy muttered a word she had no business knowing. The sound and its accompanying glare brought Kit from the bed. "Our patient is better this morning."

Our patient? Now he was ours, when only a few days ago her sister had wished he'd die? "So I see." Emy refused to look at the man. He could grin from now until forever and move that dark gaze over her until his eyes fell from his head and it would make no difference to her. "You forgot the eggs."

"We were talking." Kit gave a charming, if helpless shrug.

"Do your talking after your chores, lady," Grand-mère said as she came from the bedroom. "There's laundry to be done."

Emy never realized her good mood had completely disappeared. Not, that is, until she was gently reminded by her grandmother that the banging of the pots could hardly do the poor man's head a bit of good.

Silently Emy wondered how much good it would do if she hit him over the head with one of these pots. Emy felt a jolt of surprise at the thought. What in the world had come over her? She was obviously upset, but couldn't for the life of her figure out why.

Of course she wasn't disturbed because her sister and Cole had been teasing each other. She didn't care who Kit batted her lashes at. And she cared even less that Cole seemed to find the girl's attentions a pleasant diversion.

It didn't matter to her, of course. Why, a line of women a mile long could be waiting to see him, to talk to him, to touch him, and she wouldn't have cared.

"Good morning," Cole said to the beautiful lady with the flashing eyes, standing across the room. He couldn't believe his good luck. He'd been searching for her when accosted and now she was there. He was delighted at the thought of accepting her care. "Am I your patient?"

"*Oui,* monsieur, our Emy cares much for you."

Emy shot her grandmother a sharp look, for the

words said in broken English took on a completely different connotation from what was meant. "What grandmère means is, I as well as she took care of you."

Cole watched her honey skin darken in embarrassment as she explained her grandmother's statement. Her sister, at least he supposed the young girl to be her sister, had been mildly amusing, a lovely surprise to any man upon awakening. The girl was far too forward, of course, but delightful in her eagerness to please.

But this one. Cole felt an absurd ache begin somewhere in the pit of his belly. Oddly enough, it seemed to grow in strength the longer he allowed his gaze to linger upon the woman. Nonsense. He was hungry. There could be no other reason for the ache. Idly he wondered how much longer it would be before he could eat.

"Did I give you a hard time?" Cole had been told that he wasn't a good patient. He'd rarely been ill, but according to his sister-in-law, who was a doctor of sorts, he was the worst.

"Excuse me?" the woman returned, busy mixing a bowl of batter her grandmother had handed her.

Lord, but she was beautiful. He hadn't remembered until then just how beautiful. Dark hair was pulled back and tied with a green ribbon. Her lashes were half moons of black against her soft pink cheeks. Her lips were full, but not too full to suit him. Cole's mouth watered as he remembered the taste of those lips.

Her **body** was perfect. Turned from him, she permitted **him** now to view her only from the side, but he remembered the luscious sight of her coming through that door, and more. He remembered what she looked like with her dress brought to her waist, exposing to his view her sweet beauty. Her body was slender, her breasts full, even now pressing tightly against her gray dress. God, but he wished he could see them again.

He watched her hands move. Her fingers were long and tapered, the nails short and clean. He couldn't help but remember how they felt against his skin. He knew she must have touched him while he was ill, but it wasn't those memories that stirred him now. There was a time when her touch had been shy, deliciously captivating. All he could think was for her to touch him again.

Cole raised one leg. His thoughts were doing some peculiar things to his body, things he wouldn't be happy to have the old woman see.

"Was I a good patient?"

"Very good," Emy returned while keeping her gaze averted, her concentration on what she was doing.

"And I didn't give you any trouble?" he asked, his voice clearly telling his amazement.

"Non."

She was lying. She could tell by the faint flush of her cheek and the way she quickly changed the subject as she spoke in French to her grandmother.

Cole could only hope he hadn't struck out at her. A little thing like this one could be easily hurt.

Cole felt his eyelids droop and smothered a yawn while wondering why he was so tired. Kit had told him he'd been asleep for more than a week. Surely a week's worth of sleep was enough for any man. But apparently not enough for him.

The next thing he knew, Cole was being gently shaken awake. The beautiful lady he'd been admiring before he'd fallen asleep was leaning over him.

"I was looking for you," he said as his hands came to reach for her. "Where did you go?"

She moved back, out of his reach, and said something in French. Cole understood a smattering of the language, but Emy spoke too fast and he couldn't understand her words.

"What?"

"I said, are you hungry? Breakfast is ready."

Apparently he was to wait for his answers. Cole didn't mind. He had her within his grasp. He'd wait for however long it took.

Chapter Six

Cole downed the last of a huge stack of fluffy pancakes that were drenched in fresh butter and covered with sweet blueberries, knowing he'd never tasted anything so good in his entire life. He sighed his pleasure as he sipped a cup of coffee liberally laced with thick sweet cream, and watched the woman across the room.

She'd just about ignored him since she'd shaken him from his nap. Except for one glance in his direction, he might have been invisible.

Oddly enough, Cole felt himself growing annoyed. The funny thing was, he couldn't figure out why. It wasn't like him to insist on a woman's attention. At least, it had never been like him before. From as far back as he could remember, women had never been all that important. Of course they were necessary at times, but easy enough to put aside and forget once his needs were met. But most important, if a woman found him not to her liking, it never took much effort to find another who did.

Why then did he feel this growing irritation at being ignored? He knew the reason behind her act. It was obvious that she didn't want her family to know of their first meeting. He could understand that. Still, why did he feel this need to be the center of her attention? Cole had no answers to the curious questions that plagued him, and figured maybe he was in worse shape than he'd first imagined. The fever had likely made his mind as well as his body go soft. Once he was himself again, he probably wouldn't give the woman more than an indifferent glance.

Even as the thought came to mind, Cole knew it for the lie it was. She was a beautiful woman, and once himself again, he was apt to do more than glance in her direction. But more than beauty, she had something he found himself struggling to name. Intrigue. Cole gave a mental nod of agreement as the word came to mind. She intrigued, all right. Even now, sitting at the table, talking to her family and ignoring his dark gaze, she intrigued.

Cole's gaze moved over her shapely form, noting the smooth line of her back, the gentle curve of a full breast, the clean profile, and lips that he remembered to be soft and sweet. Silently he promised himself that before he left this place he'd sample those lips again, and if given half the chance, he'd sample a hell of a lot more.

The three women spoke in rapid French. Cole caught only a word here and there. Apparently the youngest of the three wasn't taking kindly to the others' opinion of her earlier conduct.

Cole watched Emy sigh her vexation as she pushed back a stray wisp of black hair that had come

113

from its confines and lay curled against her cheek. Her hair was beautiful. He could remember the silkiness of it between his fingers. Too bad she hid its loveliness by pulling it back from her face.

Cole wondered how long it would take before he saw it loose again.

Despite the strong coffee, Cole felt his eyelids grow heavy once more. Idly he wondered what was in that glass he'd earlier emptied. Whatever it was, it had pretty much dulled his pains and aches. The only problem was, his mind was somewhat dulled as well, and he couldn't fight this overwhelming need to sleep.

It was late when he awoke again. The sun had already set. The old woman slept in the rocker now positioned near the fire. The house was silent but for the crackle of a fire and the old lady's occasional snores. Cole must have made a sound, because Emy was suddenly at his side, leaning over him, concern showing clearly in her fathomless eyes, eyes that had haunted his dreams. Eyes he wasn't ever likely to forget.

"Is it bad?"

Cole realized she was referring to his discomfort. "No."

"It is. Take this," she said, offering him a glass probably containing the same dreadful concoction he'd taken that morning.

"No. I don't want it. The stuff puts me to sleep."

Emy smiled. "The more you sleep, the faster you will heal."

"Will I? Heal, I mean?" At the moment Cole was so uncomfortable that he couldn't be sure.

114

Emy nodded, and as if it were gospel truth remarked simply, "Grandmère said so."

Having no choice in his weakened condition, Cole drank from the glass pressed to his lips. The moment he finished the appalling liquid, he gasped a word Emy did not recognize and then felt the effects of the brew take almost immediate hold.

For three more days Cole slept, awakening only when the need for water and an occasional meal brought him from the depth of drugged sleep. The old lady helped when he needed to use the commode. She bathed him, fed him, and dosed him again with the drug.

Kit eyed the basket filled with scraps of silver-gray material with some real longing and then frowned, unable to understand why Emy would all but destroy the beautiful garment. It would have looked wonderful on her. But no. Seam by seam Emy had taken it apart, professing the need to repair some unseen damage, never stopping until the poor garment resembled little more than a pile of expensive rags. Kit fussed at the thought. One would think that if Emy had taken such a dislike to the gown, she might have given it to her younger sister rather than destroy it. Kit had complained, in the most unkind terms, of the selfishness of her sister's actions, especially since Kit had only one change of clothes. Like Emy, she owned only one pretty dress, which was reserved solely for guests and, of course, Sundays, when the small family climbed aboard the springless wagon for the more than ten-mile drive to church.

It was Friday. The night before, Kit had worked for hours attaching a wide trim of black lace to the modest neckline of her pink silk dress. The added frill emphasized already full breasts and the accentuating of that attribute caused her small waist to appear even smaller. Kit couldn't prevent a sense of satisfaction as she viewed the result. Well, almost. The truth of it was, she longed to lower the too-high neckline, but dared not. At fifteen, she was very much under the guidance and control of both her sister and grandmother and as yet had not the courage to defy either woman to that extreme, or face what promised to be near-violent tempers.

She smoothed back a curl that insisted on ruining her sleek, sophisticated hairstyle as she admired her lush form. A smile curved her lips even as a wicked light entered her eyes. Pierre would have a time of it keeping his hands to himself tonight. So far Kit had feigned reluctance in Pierre's arms. She knew most men preferred their women less than eager. Still, she was nearly obsessed with the thought of experiencing the pleasure she knew awaited her there. She was tired of being a young innocent. She wanted to be a woman. And tonight Pierre was going to show her exactly what being a woman meant.

Of course, Pierre wasn't her first choice, but Kit could hardly seduce the man she really wanted, what with either Grandmère or Emy constantly hovering at his side. Why, they hardly allowed the poor man a minute's solitude. Kit had thought to outsmart them this Sunday past by feigning a headache in order to remain home while the two had gone off to mass. But her efforts had proven less than useless, for the stupid man had slept through what might have been the greatest moment of his life. No matter how she prodded and poked, or whispered her urgency, she couldn't bring him awake and the fool never knew of the opportunity missed.

Kit shrugged. It didn't matter. She was confident that the day would come when she'd know the man's touch. In the meantime there was Pierre, her newest and richest beau to date. No one of her acquaintance had ever owned so much. He had his own horse and buggy. And after his mother and father died, he'd inherit a farm that was triple the size of hers. A farm that actually made money. Not that she wished his parents dead, or course. At least not in the immediate future. She might marry Pierre, but certainly not until she was ready. Kit's intent, now that she was fifteen, was to enjoy these few short years before marriage. Getting married now was definitely not part of her plan.

Her friends were gathering at the Bonats' tonight, under the watchful eye of both parents. Intent on an affair far more personal, she had little interest in the gathering of her peers. After an hour or so, perhaps a half hour or so, in their company, she'd claim a headache. Pierre would then take her home. On the way the real excitement of the evening would begin. She'd ask him to stop his closed buggy, for she'd feel a weakness in the extreme and the sudden need of fresh air. Kit laughed aloud. After that, nature would take its course and Kit would know at last the mysteries she could only now dream of.

Emy brushed back an errant wisp of black hair as she leaned over her patient. Having cleaned and ministered to his wound, she was wrapping a smaller bandage around his dark hair. "The injury heals nicely," she said. "Is the pain better?"

Cole had been without the aid of medicine for almost the entire day and his headache, merely a vague thudding behind his eyes, had grown no worse. "Much better."

"Do you need something to help you sleep?"

Cole, careful of any abrupt movement lest the agonizing pain return, slowly shook his head. "Maybe later." At the moment he wasn't the least bit interested in sleep, not when this beauty leaned so close. Her breasts were in direct line of his vision as she lifted his head from the pillow. He needed only to raise himself an inch or so in order to nuzzle his face against her lush softness. For just a moment he wondered if he could get away with such outrageous conduct and then forced back the urge, knowing disaster lay in store, should he dare. He dared not touch her until her grandmother and sister were out of the house. Still, he couldn't dispel the intriguing thought, especially when every movement brought her warm, sweet scent to invade his senses.

God, but he wanted her. It was beyond his ability, despite his weakness, or perhaps because of that weakness, to do more than to allow the thought to linger. All he could think about was the passion he'd known in her arms. He wanted to taste that passion again, and this time he wouldn't stop until he knew every inch of her.

Still, but for an occasional glance that spoke of the fire within, Emy had behaved in the most proper of fashions. It was easy enough to see that she would not be happy if he allowed his needs to surface, especially not with her family nearby. She told him with more than one look that she was not one a man could easily trifle with. Later, he promised himself. Later, after the old woman had gone off to bed and they were alone. Then he'd pretend a need that would bring her close again and once within reach, initiate the beginnings of a gentle seduction that would eventually end in the most exquisite pleasure. Soon, he promised himself, soon they'd take up again where they had once left off.

Emy frowned when she saw her sister enter the kitchen. "What did you do to your dress?"

"I made it prettier. Don't you agree?" Kit said while eyeing the man still in bed. She pushed out her chest, hoping to offer him an enticing view. Cole hardly noticed, but Emy did. For some unexplained reason, she felt angered, most particularly at her, in this case, innocent patient. Her movements suddenly became less gentle as she finished her chore, and Cole groaned as she dropped his head back to the pillow. His groan went unnoticed.

"Black lace is not for the young. Take it off."

"I cannot. The dress would be ruined. The needle marks will show."

"You should have thought of that before you began."

"Emy, for once in your life, stop acting like an old woman and let me be."

As the sisters argued, grandmère had walked to Kit and inspected the garment. "She is right, *chérie*. The marks will show."

Emy shot her sister an angry glare. "What are

119

your plans tonight?" she asked suspiciously.

"I told you. The party at the Bonats'."

"Chaperoned, of course."

"Of course."

Emy sighed. If only she could convince her father to marry off his youngest daughter, she might feel some assurance of her welfare as well as the safe-guarding of the family name against scandal. As it was, Papa thought that Kit was still a child, his baby in fact, and believed there was time enough before such an event should occur.

The two women sat at the table, sipping from cups of hot, strong coffee. Cole held his cup in his hands and lay propped up by pillows, relaxed against the wall as all three conversed.

It seemed a fox was determined to enjoy what little was left in the way of their chickens. Having sampled one of the dozen or so, his obvious intent was to have yet another. Twice this week Emy had gone out to investigate the uproar of squawking and shrieking caused by the scent of the lurking animal, only to see his orange-red tail disappear in the moonlight as he took off for the woods. Both times she fired the shotgun, but had no hope of doing the predator any real harm, for he was fast and agile, evading her aim with apparent ease.

Since his arrival, Emy had made sure that the chickens were locked up in their little shed at night. This took some doing, for the creatures were allowed freedom during the day and had to be chased down for their own protection.

She had just returned from the chore. Her eyes sparkled with pleasure at accomplishing this less-than-simple feat. Her face was flushed, her hair in disarray. Cole figured she was probably the most beautiful creature he'd ever seen. "I did it," she breathed on a sigh. In deference to their company, both women spoke in English. "Let's see if that wily old fox won't try another farm after tonight."

Grandmère said suddenly and completely out of context, completely out of sense, for that matter, "The beef feels good tonight. Grandpère always loves a cup before bed. I wonder what is keeping him?"

Emy realized her grandmother was confused again. Apparently she was talking about the coffee, which was laced with a few precious drops of vanilla, but couldn't form the correct words. This happened now and then. At first it had nearly paralyzed Emy with fear. Now she managed to take these moments in stride, having come to accept her grandmother's confusion as nothing more than the effects of age. Still, her first instinct was to protect. In doing so, she shot Cole a look that dared him to critize the old lady's comment.

Cole might have known a moment of confusion, but it passed in an instant at the sight of Emy's uneasy glare. "The coffee is good," he agreed, imagining that was the woman's meaning. "Everything you make is delicious."

Emy felt an enormous sense of relief as well as a softening somewhere deep in her heart at his kindness. And then came a jolt of surprise at Grandmère Marie's smile. If she didn't know better,

121

Emy would have sworn that her grandmother, her own grandmother, was reacting in the most absurd fashion to this man. "Thank you, monsieur."

Lord, was no one immune to the man's charm? First Kit and now Grandmère? Emy could have laughed as her grandmother's cheeks gained a bit of color and she shyly lowered her lashes. Emy, for the first time in her life, realized the woman hadn't always been old. She could easily see how pretty she must have been in her youth. Her thoughts went a step further. There had to have been a time when she flirted with a man, when she loved, when she laughed in the arms of her husband.

Her grandfather had died before Emy was born and Emy was suddenly struck with the waste. Why hadn't her grandmother remarried? Why had she, as a young woman, taken herself from the pleasure life had to offer?

Emy shot Cole a soft look of appreciation and Cole felt something tighten in his chest.

He couldn't stop himself from going on, in the hope of securing yet another gentle look. "The soup tonight and the biscuits"—he shook his head and remarked with feeling—"I've never tasted anything so good. As soon as I'm better, I'll hunt for meat."

Emy felt another jolt of surprise. As soon as he was better? How long did he intend to stay? Emy wasn't exactly sure what would happen if this man lingered overlong, but she did know every day that he put off leaving only chanced disaster. He couldn't stay. It was possible that one day he would put together the events on that disastrous night. What would happen to them, to her father and brother, if he realized the truth?

"Your family will worry if you do not return."

Cole shook his head. "My family lives far from here. No one will worry."

"No one?" Emy frowned, unable to believe that anyone lived totally alone. Had he no one to care for him? No friends?

"My deputy. As soon as I'm able, I'll ride to town and send him a wire."

Emy shrugged, avoiding the warmth in his dark eyes. She knew by his last comment that there were no women in his life. At least none of any importance. Emy wondered why that information should bring a jolt of happiness to her soul.

She didn't want him there. Cole would have had to be deaf and blind not to realize that fact. He wondered why. Could it be that she was afraid of the things she felt? Could it be that his presence made her remember the moments they had shared? Could she be suffering from much the same affliction as he?

Cole figured he'd find out soon enough. Another day or so and he'd be out of this bed. Once he was on his feet, he'd find out her feelings.

Kit was sorely disappointed. Pierre might have come to her home alone to visit for the evening, but he hadn't come alone tonight, and they weren't alone now. How stupid of her not to realize that he'd never leave a party with her unescorted. It simply wasn't done. Of course another woman, in this case Mrs. Bonat herself, would be called upon to accompany them to Kit's home.

So she not only missed a party, but missed as well the promise she read in Pierre's eyes.

God, but she was tired of constantly being chaperoned. Why couldn't the older generation allow the younger a taste of the freedom they enjoyed? Her plans were ruined. It had taken her half the night to sew the lace upon her bodice and it had all been for naught. Granted Pierre had remarked upon her dress, telling her she was lovely, but what good had it accomplished?

She was sick of it all. You cannot do this, you must not do that. She wanted freedom and the chance to do exactly what she wanted for a change.

Chapter Seven

Cole sighed with relief as he entered the house and leaned weakly against the door. Thank God he was strong enough, just barely, to make the trip to the outhouse. There were but a few things that could cause a man to feel less than a man, and an old woman seeing to his most personal needs surely topped the list.

The house was quiet. All within slept. Cole smiled, for the old woman's snores penetrated the thin walls. In the flickering light of the fire, he eyed his bed, and wondered if he had the strength to make it without falling on his face. From the corner of his eye he saw movement.

"What are you doing out of bed?" The words were whispered lest her grandmother awaken.

"I needed to step outside for a minute."

Emy was about to argue the wisdom of such an action, when she realized to what he referred. She nodded and lowered her gaze to the floor, her cheeks staining a delicious shade of pink. It was one thing to discuss or remark upon such matters with members of her family, but quite another to hint upon such things with a virtual stranger. And no matter her foolish actions in regard to this man—he was a stranger.

Cole, with some effort, could probably have made it to his bed on his own, but eyeing this lovely lady, with her hair down around her shoulders, dressed in a robe and sleeping gown, thought better of the notion. There was no sense in being overly brave, after all. He had nothing to gain by chancing a fall and perhaps much more. Purposely he allowed a low moan.

Emy's gaze lifted from the floor. "Are you all right?" she asked, and then immediately looked at the polished wood floor again.

She was nervous, he could tell, for she was biting her lip again. He was naked to the waist, having only slipped on his trousers before stepping outside, and the sight of a man's chest was obviously upsetting. Good. He hoped he upset her plenty, 'cause he was finding it harder every day to be in her company without doing the things he wanted to do to her. She didn't know it yet, but she was going to help him to the bed. Cole could only imagine the feel of her pressed tightly to him. He could hardly wait. "I could use some help getting back into bed."

Emy, never suspecting him of ulterior motives, moved close to his side. "Put your arm around my shoulders."

Cole smiled. He stood a good foot over her and probably outweighed her by close to a hundred pounds. Did she think she could so easily manage his weight?

Cole did as she asked, hugging her tightly to him in the process and groaning again, this time from the feel of her softness against him.

His arm around her shoulders brought her face nearly against his chest. True, her lips weren't actually touching him, but it hardly mattered. The warm scent of his body filled her senses, causing her mind to reel. The wave of dizziness grew in strength until Emy found herself holding on. Vaguely she wondered which of them would end up helping the other. "Uh, I don't think this will work," Emy whispered in a shaken voice. She had to move away. She had to stop breathing his scent, relishing the warmth of his arms before disaster took hold.

"No. Don't go." He tightened his hold and leaned just a bit of his weight upon her.

"I'll get grandmère to help."

"Don't wake her," he whispered, his breath brushing soft and warm against her cheek. Emy had no defense against his allure. She never realized she leaned close, far closer than necessary. "We can do it."

His arms were around her slight form, pressing her tightly to his naked chest as they stumbled toward the bed. Cole was weak, but he figured he'd have to be dead before giving up such an opportunity.

Once they covered the distance, he managed to position them so that they were sitting side by side. His arms were around her still, her face pressed to his chest.

She tried to wiggle free, but Cole had waited too long to allow this moment a quick demise. He moaned again. "Wait," he said, satisfied that he sounded a bit breathless.

"Are you all right?" she asked while wondering if her pounding heart would ever again find its normal rhythm.

"Dizzy," he said as he breathed in the sweet scent of her hair.

Emy nodded as she pulled away and pushed him to lie down. "You've been very ill. It will take time to get your strength back."

Unless he was willing to wrestle her to the bed, there was nothing he could do but allow her to escape his hold. Nothing, that is, but lie. Cole figured a man never had a greater cause and wasn't about to let what little he had of a conscience get in the way of enjoying this woman. "My shoulders and back hurt."

Emy nodded in understanding. "Turn over," she ordered easily, "and I'll rub some of the stiffness away." She bit her lip and almost groaned aloud as she heard the words. For just an instant she wondered what fool could have said them. Lord, what could she be thinking? What in the world had ever possessed her to make such an offer? Surely she knew nothing could be more dangerous than touching this man.

On his stomach he lay very still, awaiting her ministrations. He'd done as she asked. Unless she was willing to admit what touching him was likely to do to her senses, it was too late to back out now.

God, but he couldn't have asked for anything

better. Well, maybe he could have asked for one thing, but that would have to wait a bit.

Her hands were small, delicate, and slender; still, they possessed amazing strength. Cole hadn't imagined her capable of such strength. He groaned in delight as she pressed her palms deep into the hardness of his back. It was heaven.

He wasn't a brawny man, but tall and sleek with rippling muscles gained from days spent in a saddle. Emy trembled as her hands slid over warm, smooth skin. This was definitely a mistake. Surely he could hear the pounding of her heart, magnified to a thunderous roar in this thick silence. What to do? How could she get out of this? Emy racked her brain thinking of a way to make a graceful exit, even as her hands continued what was to Cole's mind a delicious bone-melting assault.

Her manner was far from suggestive. She did not touch him in any way but with the palms of her hands and her hands did not linger sensuously, but pressed hard into firm flesh. It didn't matter. Cole couldn't stop his body from responding. He groaned as the ache came to take hold. Thank God he was on his stomach, or she'd surely be frightened at his aroused state.

A log slipped in the fireplace, sending hundreds of sparks up the chimney. The sound seemed to break the spell of touching him, and Emy found herself able to pull her hands away at last.

"Better?" she asked, her voice a soft, low husk of raw emotion. It was only then that Cole realized she was suffering from the same need as himself. It wasn't the right time, or place, but, God help him, he couldn't resist.

Cole turned and sat up. Emy took a step back at the abrupt movement. "Come here."

In the light of the fire her skin appeared flushed and her eyes glowed with a need that easily matched his own. Cole felt something tighten in his chest and trembled against the raging need that threatened his control.

For a long moment they simply looked at each other.

Emy's lips parted as she struggled for every breath. She didn't think what was happening to her. Emy was beyond the point of thinking. She'd known this would happen the moment she'd left her room and saw him standing against the door. She knew it and yet had done nothing to stop it. Why? Because she wanted this as much as he did. More, perhaps, for the ecstasy had haunted her awake and asleep. She wanted to feel again the touch of his hands on her body, breathe again his special scent, lose herself in his strength, his tenderness, and forget that it was wrong, this pleasure he'd once shown her.

Her eyes were glassy and held just a touch of fear. Her body trembled with the need to do as he asked, even as she shook her head and begged for reprieve. "Cole, please."

Cole hooked a finger into the belt of her cotton robe and gently pulled her toward him. He exerted almost no pressure and she almost no reluctance. "I won't hurt you, Emy."

Emy almost laughed at the softly spoken pledge, knowing it to be a lie. Should he find out, should he one day come to know the depth of her deception, she'd know nothing but hurt. God, if only she could take back that entire night.

At last came the moment when she stood at the edge of the bed, nestled within the warmth of his thighs. His body ached to possess hers, but he wouldn't give in to that need. There would come a better time, a better place. For now, he'd find contentment in simply holding her against him.

"Emy," he whispered as he pulled her close and rested his face at last upon her softness. He knew without a doubt that no woman had ever felt this good before.

Emy had no will. She felt her body shudder and whimpered a sound that reminded him of a trapped animal. "Don't be afraid," he said as his arms tightened just a fraction. "I swear to God, I won't hurt you."

Emy made another sound, this one something closer to a groan, knowing she had no will but to endure this slow, purposeful attack upon her senses. His warmth, his scent, the feel of his arms pulling her body forward as he nuzzled his face to her breasts— it was more than she could bear. Emy fought to keep her hands at her sides, but no matter her silent insistence, they rose to touch him. Long, slender fingers curled over his shoulders and then around his neck and into thick, dark hair.

She was burning up, and yet his mouth was burning hot against her. Emy hadn't felt the sly movements. She didn't think how he had opened the bows. All she knew was the sudden heat as his mouth took her bared flesh deep within a furnace. It was like the last time, only better. She was no longer

131

totally innocent, ignorant of the goings-on between a man and a woman. She knew the pleasure of his touch, how his mouth had felt on her, and, God help her, she wanted it again. She wanted this and more.

"Mon Dieu," came the soft exclamation as her fingers threaded into his hair, gripping him tightly, holding his hot, hungry mouth to her smooth warmth.

Cole groaned at the phrase. She'd whispered like this the first time. The only time. It was enough to drive a man mad with yearning, with the need to know all of her. His body trembled with the desire to experience the delicious torture of touching her, of discovering again the sweet secrets held from him.

Emy knew this was sheer insanity, and yet she couldn't resist. In the back of her mind came the thought that grandmère could come upon them, and that Kit might return, and still her hands refused to fall to her sides, her legs to move her quivering body from his arms. Her mouth fell to his head and she breathed in his scent. It ended the last of her thoughts. All she could do was hold his hungry mouth to her flesh. All she knew was a need for more of this most exquisite of tastings. All she wanted was this man, and if her soul was lost in the process, she couldn't find the will to care.

The night to some is but an empty, dark, and silent void, but for the two would-be lovers, this night became a myriad of seductive sound, of daring excitement, of pending, eager discovery. Soft moans of pleasure, gasping, desperate breaths, pounding hearts, and gentle caresses drew each into the mindless search for the aching magic that hovered

132

just beyond their reach.

His hand slid down the length of her gown and then under the soft cotton to the silkiness of warm, womanly flesh. God, but she felt good. Cole couldn't remember the last time a woman had felt so warm, so sweetly inviting.

He felt her tremble, realized her weakness, realized the acquiescence in that weakness and brought her to his lap. Emy moaned yet another sound of pleasure as he leaned her back, his hand again finding its way beneath her gown, his mouth so desperately hungry for the taste and feel of her softness, it almost bruised.

It was too much to bear, and Cole shuddered, wondering if he had the strength to stop something he never wanted to end, when he heard the sound, and the magic slid out of reach.

"Emy sweetheart," he said, a tender smile touching the corners of his mouth as he brushed her hair from her face. "Your sister's home."

For a moment Emy made no attempt to move. Cole thought perhaps she was still lost in the throes of her pleasure and hadn't heard his whispered warning. The truth of the matter was, she'd heard him well enough. The reason she couldn't seem to move was because of the absolute shock of her own sinful behavior. Good God Almighty! How could she have allowed this to happen yet again?

Cole was about to repeat the warning, when she grunted and literally threw him to his back as she scrambled from the bed. He grinned at her sudden burst of strength, for once gaining her feet, she was hardly able to keep her footing. With shaking fingers

133

she righted her clothing and staggered off to her room without another word.

Cole moved quickly beneath his covers, feigning a sleep he couldn't hope to know on this night. He closed his eyes just as the door opened and forced his breathing to grow shallow and even as the unsuspecting girl walked by his bed.

A moment later he heard the door to the bedroom open and close. Cole lay there until the sun broke through the dusk of morning, gripping the pillow to his chest, pressing his body into the feather tick, willing the ache to ease even as he realized the impossibility, for his mind couldn't stop imagining the pleasure that lay in store.

She was missing! Emy fought back the panic that assailed her. Grandmother was gone, and she couldn't find her in any of the usual places.

She entered the house again, the third time in less than a half hour, her face white to her lips. A shudder of fear rippled through her slender body as she desperately tried to control her voice. "I can't find her, Kit!"

Kit, being a selfish, self-centered girl, merely shrugged at the news as she studied her face in a small mirror at the kitchen table. Apparently she'd been brushing her hair, no doubt for Cole Brackston's benefit. Emy felt little annoyance at her sister's flagrant disregard of propriety. Right now she didn't have the time to think about her sister's outrageous actions. She didn't have the time to think about anything but her grandmother.

Kit never glanced away from the mirror. "She's done this before. Why are you so worried?"

"Because every time she has, I've found her within a few minutes. She's not at the grave, she's not in the barn or any of the other outbuildings." Emy's fear was slowly growing to panic. She bit her lip, her eyes growing larger in her terror as every second went by. "Where could she be?"

Cole, lying in bed, listened to the conversation. Most of it was spoken in French; still, he caught a word here and there and soon realized the problem. "How long has she been gone?"

Emy seemed to suddenly remember her patient. She glanced sharply to her right, never realizing the pleading in her eyes. "I'm not sure. An hour perhaps."

It was obvious to Cole that this woman was in some real need. There was no way that he could simply lie in bed. Despite his weakness, he had to help. "Get me my pants."

Emy shook her head. "You're not well enough. You can't—"

"I'll be fine, just do it."

Emy ran to her father's room and retrieved Cole's clothes. She dumped them on the bed and turned her back. A second later, to Emy's dismay, she realized that Kit was watching with real interest as Cole slipped his legs into his pants. "Kit!" she admonished her.

"What?"

"Step outside."

Kit shot her sister a look of defiance. "You're in here."

"At least turn around." Emy breathed a silent sigh as Kit reluctantly did as she was told, while Cole pushed his feet into his boots. Concentrating on the effort it took, he paid no attention to the sisters' conversation. The truth was, neither could have seen anything but a man in his drawers, not so evil a fact, considering the dire circumstances at the moment. He came to his feet and moaned a low sound at the dizziness that resulted.

Emy swung around at the sound and came to his side at his obvious swaying. "I told you you were too ill."

"I'm not. Get me a stick. I'll be fine if I can lean into something."

Emy did as she was told. She returned a minute later with the pole of their largest broom.

Cole was buttoning up his shirt and nodded as he took the pole from her hand and followed her outside. "Tell me where you've already looked."

"In the barn, down by the river, in all the outbuildings."

"That's all?"

"No, I looked by the graves too. She goes there sometimes to talk to my grandfather."

Cole nodded. "Let's go there first."

"But . . ." It took all of Emy's control not to rage at the man. Perhaps he hadn't understood that she'd already looked there.

"Maybe she went to pick flowers. You might have just missed her."

They walked together toward the graves, over the small hill behind the farmhouse, just to the edge of the woods. "Does she do this often?"

"What?" Emy couldn't think about his words just then. The panic she knew disallowed any conversation.

"I said, does she do this often?"

"Do what often?"

"Disappear."

Emy nodded. *"Oui,* but she's never been gone this long."

They reached the top of the gracefully flowing hill. From here they could see the small graveyard. The small, empty graveyard.

Emy made a sound. She was clearly panicked and was at a loss as to what to do next.

"Let's look in the woods. If she went for flowers, we'll find her there."

"And if she didn't?" All Emy could think about was the river. Suppose her grandmother had walked to the edge of the water and somehow had fallen in. Suppose the strong currents swept her out to the river's center. Suppose . . . She shuddered, terrified, and was unable to think any further on the matter.

"Then we'll know for sure."

Emy followed Cole's suggestion. At the edge of the woods they separated, each taking a different path. Cole hadn't taken five steps before he heard Emy calling out to her grandmother.

Hardly ten minutes later he saw the edge of a white petticoat. Above the white cloth was the brown skirt she always wore. She was sitting on the ground, leaning against the tree behind her, sound asleep. To her right was a small bunch of wildflowers. Cole smiled, knowing he'd been right.

"Mrs. Du Maurier," Cole said gently but to no avail.

He touched her shoulder and then smiled as he watched her stir. "Mrs. Du Maurier," he said again, only to see the old woman start a bit and then glance his way with a puzzled frown. "Are you all right?"

"Who are you?" The words were in French, but the phrase was short and spoken clearly enough for Cole to understand.

"Cole Brackston, ma'am. Remember?"

"Are you one of my husband's friends?"

Cole knew something was wrong. The woman had been caring for him for more than a week and yet had not recognized him. "Emy is looking for you."

"Emy?" The woman frowned and looked as if she had no notion of who Emy could be.

Cole nodded. "I'll call her." He shouted in the direction where he'd last heard her calling out. "Emy. I've found her."

Less than ten seconds went by before he heard the rustling of underbrush and Emy, breathless and flushed, ran into the tiny clearing. "Oh, Grandmère," she said as she nearly flung herself at the tiny woman. "You had me so frightened."

"What happened?" the old lady asked. "Why were you afraid?"

"I couldn't find you."

"I wasn't lost, Emy. I took a nap."

"I know, Grandmère, but you didn't tell me, and you know how I worry." The note of censure in her voice could not be denied.

"I'm sorry, Emy. I was tired."

"That's all right, sweetheart." Emy smiled at the

138

old lady with dark eyes shining with love.

Cole felt an odd fluttering in his chest at the sight of that love and wondered . . . What? Nothing, that's what. He didn't for a minute long for her to look at him in the same way. To do so would have been ridiculous. Yes, he had ideas for them, ideas that concerned a certain amount of willingness on her part, but that didn't have anything to do with love. A man didn't need love in order to want a woman. For that matter, a woman didn't need love to do the same. What the hell could he be thinking of?

"Come along now. I'll help you back to the house."

Cole followed the two women. He made it to the front porch of the house before his legs gave way. He figured he'd sit out there for a time. The fact was, he needed a little fresh air and sunshine. All that lying around in bed was hardly helping him regain his strength.

Emy soon had her grandmother comfortably ensconced in bed. As soon as the old woman drifted off to sleep again, Emy left her side and came out to the porch. Cole was still there, the lines that bracketed his mouth deep, his skin pale and damp with weakness. "Are you all right?"

"Fine," he said, enjoying immensely the fact that she had come to him and was even now pressing her hand to his forehead.

"You shouldn't be out of bed. I don't want to see the fever return."

"The fever was from injury, not an illness. I'll be fine."

Emy nodded and sat across from him in a rocking chair. She fidgeted a moment, for this was the first time they had sat opposite each other and quite alone. Conversation was needed here and Emy didn't know where to begin. "It's not very warm today."

"What's the matter with her?"

Emy glanced quickly in his direction, her eyes round with fear. "What do you mean?"

"I mean, she didn't know me."

"Oh." Emy sighed and then smiled gently. "She gets confused, is all." Emy shrugged. "You saw it the other night."

Cole nodded.

"I suppose it happens to most of us when we get old."

Cole nodded again as he realized the truth of it.

"You have a pretty place here," Cole said as his gaze moved over the farm all the way to the water's edge. "How long will your father and brother be gone?"

Emy shrugged at the question. "They'll be back soon."

"Kit said it was your father that found me."

Emy nodded. She avoided his eyes, not at all happy that their conversation had taken this route.

"I owe him a debt of gratitude."

Emy almost groaned at the statement, the fact of the matter being Cole owed her father nothing but retaliation for his suffering. "It was nothing."

"Nothing? He saved my life." Cole smiled. "I hope that's worth more than nothing."

"I mean, he would have done as much for anyone."

"I'd like to thank him in person."

Emy nodded and gave her familiar shrug. "He won't be back before the end of the month."

"I might be gone before then."

Please God, she prayed he'd be gone before then. "You could leave him a note."

Cole smiled. "You wouldn't be eager to see me on my way, would you?" As far as Cole was concerned, they had some unfinished business to attend to and he wasn't leaving until they finished it together.

"Of course not." Her eyelid twitched.

"I didn't think so." Cole laughed, knowing she lied.

Emy didn't like the sound of that laugh, or perhaps she liked it a bit too much. At the moment she was afraid to think which. All she knew for a fact was his eyes had darkened with a fire. She knew he was remembering three nights before, when she had helped him back to bed. She knew she was remembering it. She only wished she could forget it had ever happened.

"Why were you traveling alone?"

The question startled her. She'd been waiting for this moment of reckoning and yet had been startled nonetheless. "I went to see friends." Her eye twitched.

"Why?"

"To try to borrow money." Emy sighed with relief. She'd been practicing her answer for weeks. The lie sounded perfectly reasonable to her way of thinking. She thought there should be no reason that he wouldn't believe her.

"Why didn't your father go?"

"It was my friend."

Cole nodded as he watched her nervous fingers smooth her already smooth skirt. She was lying. He'd been a lawman long enough to know when someone lied.

"They were waiting for me when the steamer docked. I was in no danger."

"You might have been if I hadn't found you. It was a damn stupid thing to do. Do you realize how easily a man could have taken advantage of you, alone and unprotected?"

Emy's eyes widened as she remembered the night and Cole's apparent and quite convenient loss of memory, for he had done exactly what he'd accused others of wanting to do. "Surely not," Emy professed with some exaggerated shock. "A man would have to be less than a gentleman to do such a thing, don't you agree?"

Cole felt uncomfortable. Too late he realized he shouldn't have brought the subject up, for his answer could only put him in an unfavorable light. He changed the subject. "Why did you need money?"

"To save our farm." She lowered her gaze, obviously embarrassed. "We're behind in the payments."

Cole nodded again and watched as she bit her lip and her eye twitched. "Is something the matter?"

"*Non.* What could be the matter?"

"Are you nervous?"

"Not at all. Why?"

"You're biting your lip."

Emy made a conscious effort to keep her teeth from doing it again.

"We should talk about it."

There was no reason for him to explain his comment. She'd been wondering when he would get around to bringing up the subject. Emy knew well enough the way of his thoughts. It took only a glance in his direction to know. She shook her head. "We should definitely not talk about it. It was a mistake."

"Was that night aboard the steamer also a mistake?"

Emy felt her cheeks grow warm at the memory of what she'd allowed him to see, to touch. It took all her strength to return his look and say, *"Oui.* Definitely."

"There's nothing wrong with a man and woman enjoying themselves, Emy. You shouldn't feel guilty about it."

"Mr. Brackston, I'm indeed sorry if I gave you a false impression of what you might expect from me."

"I know exactly what to expect, Emy. I remember how you lost yourself in my—"

"Enough!" she said, coming quickly to her feet. "I have chores. You can make it back to bed on your own, *non?"*

Emy did not wait for his answer, but was off the porch and walking toward the barn before he had the chance to respond. Cole watched the gentle sway of her skirt as she moved quickly away from him. He smiled, knowing this woman might deny the things she wanted from him, but she couldn't deny them for long. The moment he got his strength back, he'd see to that.

Chapter Eight

Cole leaned against the side of the barn, breathing heavily. It was hardly two hours past dawn and already the early morning sun burned dry the dancing clouds of mist that clung low to the ground on both sides of the Mississippi. It was hot. Sweat ran from his throat down his chest. It dampened his back and caused his trousers to cling to his thick thighs.

The sun on his naked back and chest felt good. Being able to swing an ax again felt even better.

Right now the ax was deeply imbedded in a log a few feet from where he stood. Grandmère was, of course, too old, and Kit too spoiled to even consider chopping the wood. That left Emy. It didn't matter the cost, Cole wasn't about to let Emy perform that task. Not as long as he could crawl from his bed. He'd been up and about for a few days now. It was time for him to do his share.

The trouble was, he'd been working for less than a half hour and his legs and arms already trembled with weakness. When the hell would his stamina return?

According to Emy, he had lost a good deal of blood. She said her father found him lying in a puddle of it. Cole remembered again the blast of sound that had left nothing but blackness in his wake. He shouldn't have pulled his gun. He should have known better than to startle a man so nervous.

Cole shook his head in disgust at his own stupidity. Had he allowed the thieves to take what they wanted, he never would have gotten himself hurt in the first place. A grin touched the corners of his mouth. If he hadn't done as he had, he might not have found Emy again. He laughed softly, knowing his weeks of suffering to be worth every damn ache and pain he'd gone through.

From the corner of his eye he saw a flash of skirt, knew an instant of hope, and then sighed his disappointment. It was her sister who had brought him a drink, not the woman who had occupied his thoughts since the first moment he laid eyes on her. Why was she keeping her distance? What was she so damn afraid of? It took only his presence to find her scurrying off to see to some chore. They were never alone. No intimacy had come between them. Not since that night almost a week earlier. And Cole was getting damn sick of watching her run.

After those few moments of pleasure, Cole thought her reserve was broken down. He thought they'd enjoy many days and nights in each other's company, going further each time as each discovered new and wonderful ways to pleasure the other.

He knew by their short conversation a few days after the happening that she'd been embarrassed by the things she'd allowed him to do. He knew she was a religious woman. She never missed church on Sunday and often lit candles before the picture of the saint in her home. No doubt that was the problem. Her strict moral beliefs and the things she wanted were at odds with one another. It caused her some confusion, no doubt. He had to talk to her again. He had to make her see that there was nothing wrong in what they had done so far. That there was nothing wrong with a man and woman enjoying each other.

"Thank you," he said as he reached for the offered jug. Cole drank his fill and then poured a goodly amount over his head, hoping the cool water would revive his energies.

Kit made a soft hissing sound as she watched water run in sleek rivulets down his face and into his beard. Cole no longer sported a thin mustache. His facial hair had grown during the weeks of fever. Since recuperating, he had left the new growth, unaware that his good looks were emphasized a hundredfold by the dark, beautifully formed beard, a beard that struck both of the Du Maurier sisters as devastating. Kit's blue eyes followed the water's path over the firm muscles of his throat and naked chest, down his thick arms. *"Mon Dieu!* You are so strong." She reached out to touch his arm. Cole stepped away. Only Kit wasn't the kind of young woman who noticed rejection. She simply moved closer. Her long, dark lashes fluttered in what she hoped was an irresistible sight. "I've never known a man so big, or one so strong."

Cole grimaced. First of all, he wasn't the least bit strong, and second, this one needed a good paddling. If he was her father, her rear would be glowing what with the antics she'd pulled so far. Yesterday she'd cornered him in the barn and rubbed her body against his. Cole felt a deep sense of disgust. It was her sister he desperately wanted, and yet he could still feel the heat of this one against him. He could still smell her musky sexual scent. He could still feel his body's momentary and definitely unwanted response.

The day before, it had been the river. Thank God he had finished his bath before she'd come upon him. There was no telling what the girl might have done if she'd caught him in the water with his drawers hanging on a nearby branch.

He couldn't remember knowing a girl so forward. Even the whores he'd grown up with knew when to keep their hands to themselves. They knew when a man was interested and most certainly when he was not.

"Don't you have something to do?"

Kit grinned as her gaze moved over his chest. He could see the hunger and cursed as he felt an unwanted response. Christ, he needed a woman badly, but not this woman. "I can think of many things to do."

"Stop it, Kit."

"Stop what?"

Cole shot her a hard look.

"What harm could it bring?" Kit grinned and then shrugged. "I've never had a man before." That fool Pierre had refused her offer, and she wasn't about to make him another. "I want you to be my first."

Cole frowned, his mouth growing tight at the thought. If her sister heard this, there was no telling what might happen. "Meaning there'll be others after me?"

"Of course, *chéri*. I know you feel no tenderness for me." Kit tried to act the sophisticate. The last thing she wanted was for this man to think of her as a child. "What I want needs no emotion."

Cole looked at the young girl for a silent moment, never realizing his glance held more than its share of pity. He almost felt sorry for her. To want as a man wanted, simply because of a physical urge, would see her suffer in the end. He had known his share of women. Many, in fact, who had satisfied the needs of a hungry male. He could remember the emotionless takings, the cravings for satisfaction and the haunting glimmer of emptiness upon achieving release. If it weren't for Emy, he might have taken this young girl just to ease the primitive needs of his body. But no. The thought of yet another indifferent sampling, no matter how lushly tempting her body, left him cold. She wasn't the one he wanted. His body might be starved for sex, but she wasn't the one. "What you want is better when emotion is involved."

"Have you never taken a woman you didn't love?"

Damn her to hell. Cole had been too long without a woman, period. If she kept this up, there was no telling where it might end. "Go back to the house, Kit."

Kit laughed. "Why?"

God Almighty. She knew she was getting to him,

and her knowledge made her braver than ever. Cole took a deep breath, while wondering what more he could say to cool this little hot piece of her wants. An instant later she was up against him, her arms wrapped around his neck, her face, her mouth inches from his.

Cole reached around his neck for her hands and then groaned as her sister chose just that moment to step around the corner of the barn.

"Kit!"

Kit gave an elaborate sigh of annoyance, not the least bit embarrassed at being found in a man's arms. "Go away, I'm busy."

Emy felt a searing pain grow to life somewhere inside her chest, and then instantly denied the agony. No. This scene did not cause her pain. She felt only rage that this man had been about to take advantage of her young sister. She almost laughed at the thought. Even shock and anger couldn't persuade Emy to believe the absurdity of that particular notion. Emy knew well enough where the fault lay. He wasn't taking advantage of Kit. Kit was taking advantage of him. The problem was, the beast obviously enjoyed all too well her advances.

Emy's eyes flashed fire, her lips were tight, barely moving when she finally trusted her voice enough to say, "So I see. Grandmère wants you in the house."

It took a bit of effort, especially since Cole tried not to hurt her, but he managed to break Kit's hold and finally stepped back.

Kit murmured her annoyance only half under her breath as she turned away and stalked angrily toward the house. Neither Cole nor Emy noticed.

Their gazes locked in a heated accusing duel. Damn you, she silently railed as the pain came again, nearly stealing her ability to breathe in its blinding intensity. Fool, she silently berated herself. How could you think there was something special in this man? How could you have been influenced by those dark, hungry looks? How could you have imagined it was only you he wanted?

Kit was a beautiful girl. An all-too-available beautiful girl. Emy was old enough to understand the lust a man could know, the temptation he could feel. The trouble was, she'd thought this man better than most. She thought he was different. Emy sighed her disappointment.

Even while these thoughts careened through her mind, Cole silently accused her; *You. It's you. If you hadn't run. If you hadn't lied about your wants, it would have been you in my arms. It should have been you in my arms!*

"I think you are well enough to leave us, monsieur. I want you gone from here before dark." She spun on her heel, gone with a flash of skirt.

It took a moment before her words registered. By that time she had already turned the corner of the barn. She was running again, denying again the things they both wanted. God damn her!

Cole moved quickly after her. "Wait!" He grabbed her arm, bringing her to an abrupt stop. "It's not what you think."

"Isn't it?" She turned to glare at him again, trying to shake loose his hold. "You bastard," she raged, unable to hold back her fury. "I know what she's like, but you." Her eyes narrowed in censure. "I thought better of you. I thought you could control your needs. She's only fifteen."

"I did, Emy. I swear to God, I did." The moment he said the words, Cole realized how they condemned him. They weren't what he meant. He hadn't felt any need to control himself with Kit. Well, maybe he had, but that was because he wanted this woman so damn much, he could taste it. He couldn't remember when he hadn't wanted her. He ran his free hand through his dark hair in frustration, wondering how he was supposed to put the blame on her sister and yet remain in a favorable light.

It was more than Emy could take. Did he think her so stupid as to not believe her own eyes? Emy sneered a ferocious sound, bared her teeth, and swung at him. Had Cole been a fraction slower, for the next few days he would have sported a black eye. As it was, he caught her hand only an inch from its target. "Emy, calm down and listen to me."

"Let me go," she snarled between clenched teeth. Her dark eyes grew almost black as they narrowed with her next words. "I'm going to kill you."

His hands took both of hers and held them behind her back. This was obviously getting them nowhere. Still, he had to try. "I'll let you go if you promise to listen."

It took a moment before Emy gave the slightest nod. She hated to give, even that much, but realized this brute wasn't about to let her go until she agreed. And the last thing she wanted was to be held in his arms. Cole released her.

She refused to look at him, but kept her gaze to

the ground, waiting for whatever lies that were sure to come.

Cole felt a surge of desperation and wondered if he had any chance at all of making her understand. He took a deep breath and began. "I have no interest in your sister, Emy. She's just a kid." Cole shrugged. There was no way that he was going to explain any further, no way that he could tell this woman what her fifteen-year-old sister wanted from him. She was already furious. All he had to do was tell the truth and Emy *would* probably kill him.

Cole listened as she turned a laugh into a snarl. "You weren't holding her like she was 'just a kid.'"

"I wasn't holding her at all."

"And you weren't the least bit tempted?"

Cole forgot his pledge to keep the truth of it to himself, and blurted out, "Christ! What the hell do you want? I'm a man, and she was rubbing herself all over me. If you didn't insist on hiding from me—"

"Oh? So now it's my fault?"

Cole sighed. "Emy, it's nobody's fault. Nothing happened."

"Right. And I'm Joan of Arc. I want—"

He cut her off with an angry and less-than-gentle shake. "I'm telling you the truth!"

"And what truth might that be?"

Cole gave a mental groan at the question. If he told her the whole of it, he'd sound every inch the villain. If he said nothing, his silence would only confirm her suspicions.

"I just thought you were different." Emy shrugged and plastered a wide smile to her lips. The problem was, the smile never reached her eyes. "No need to explain."

She was terminating their relationship before it had a chance to begin. He could hear it in her voice, see it in her careless shrug. There was no way that Cole was going to allow that. The best defense being a good offense, Cole plunged in with "Oh, no, lady, you're not getting away that easily."

Emy was slightly taken aback at his change of tactics and found herself asking, "Get away with what?"

"You want me out of your life? Then have the guts to say so. Don't try to use your sister."

"The trouble is, *you* were trying to use my sister."

In his frustration, Cole said exactly what he'd sworn not to say. "The hell I was. If I wanted her, I could have had her a dozen times in this last week alone."

In Emy's present mood, it was probably the worst thing he could have said. She longed to scratch his eyes out and amazed herself at her ability to not only control the need, but speak with perfect calm. "If you are here at sundown, I will shoot you."

Cole did the only thing he could do, considering the woman had just ordered him out of her life forever. He grabbed her and held her close against him, praying he could somehow manage to make her calm down and listen.

Cole wasn't sure, his French not being what it might have been, but he thought he heard the words "cow dung" mingled in with a curse that laid low the next five generations of his loins.

She broke loose just enough to kick his shin.

153

"Goddamn it, woman!" Cole grunted as he pulled her more firmly against him. She struggled furiously, but even in his weakened condition her strength was no match for his. Cole took her flailing hands in his and brought them again to her back. He gave her a not-too-gentle shake. "Listen to me!"

Emy stopped struggling. The only thing her movements managed to do was to rub their bodies together anyway. It was bad enough being held so close to him. She didn't want to feel every sinew and bulge of muscle against her. Especially she didn't want to feel the growing thickness against her belly, gaining in hardness with every minute he held her close. Her heart thundered in her chest, and Emy thought she just might swoon being held so close in his arms. Still, Emy fought against the weakness. She wouldn't let him affect her. She held her breath, refusing to breathe his scent. She wouldn't let their closeness bother her one whit.

"You know it's not your sister."

Emy refused to listen. She tried to block out the sound of his voice, tried to think of a rhyme, the latest gossip she'd heard about the Taylor twins, something, anything that would prevent the lying words from penetrating her mind.

"It's you, dammit!" He shook her again. "It's you I want."

Emy felt something twist in her chest. Yes, she'd been aware of his looks, his obvious interest, but to be told so bluntly, so easily, of his feelings, left her suddenly speechless.

But what of his feelings, Emy? He didn't say he loved you. He said he wanted you.

Love and wanting were two different things. Emy knew it, but at the moment she couldn't get her mind to accept the difference.

Emy had been haunted by the night almost a week before, a night that left her with a mortifying awareness that she had no sense, no control once in this man's arms. Up until then she had done an excellent job of putting from her mind their first meeting and the sinful evening that followed. Now she couldn't think of anything but that night and the desperate longing she knew to press her body close to his again. His words hardly mattered. She couldn't resist the feel of him against her. With a will of its own her mouth offered itself, eagerly awaiting his response.

His mouth came slowly toward hers. His movements were torturously slow, until at last he touched her. Emy moaned a soft whimper of terrifying need and almost instantly lost her ability to stand. Her knees wobbled and grew useless. His arms raised her from the ground, holding her tightly against him.

There was no tentative probing here. Their mouths came together with a hunger born of anger, jealousy, and frustration, a hunger the depths of which neither had ever suspected. Her hands came to his cheeks, threading through his silken beard, holding his face to hers. He tasted so good, better than she remembered. God, she had waited so long to taste him again.

"God, oh, God," he moaned into her mouth. He couldn't stop kissing her, couldn't stop his hands from reaching for the soft lushness of her body. "Emy, my God."

His hand pressed against her belly and then lower to the aching softness. He heard her hushed cry of pleasure. It was only then that Cole realized they were standing beside the barn, within sight of the river and the road that ran alongside it. Anyone who happened by could see them. He released her even as a torturous groan was torn from his throat. His body was on fire and trembling with need. "Jesus, God, we have to stop."

Emy stumbled back; she shivered and wobbled a bit. A low sound of distress escaped her throat. Having no idea that Emy wanted only that this moment never stop, Cole thought he had gone too far and had shocked her. A muffled, unnoticed curse slid from his lips as he took her gently into his arms and brought her just inside the doorway of the barn. There, with considerably more privacy, he lowered her to the ground. "Are you all right?"

Emy's arms were around his neck. She couldn't tear herself from the feel of him, the scent of manly sweat, the moist heat of his chest. If God could grant her but one wish, she'd ask to always stay in his arms.

When she didn't immediately respond, he whispered into her hair as he brushed a stray curl behind her ear, "I'm sorry, Emy. I didn't mean to scare you. I was too rough."

Cole felt an overpowering urge to shelter, to shield this woman from the pain of the world. He couldn't remember feeling like this before. Not even with his wife had he felt the need, for this woman had a delicacy about her that brought out a man's protective instincts. This woman wasn't the kind a man could use as he pleased. This woman needed a gentle handling, a tenderness and restraint that he'd find somewhere, God help him.

Emy breathed in the scent of him and groaned, the sound unnoticed to her ears as she absorbed his strength, his scent, the touch of his chest against her cheek, the curling hairs that tickled and yet somehow excited her skin. Cole smiled above her, knowing the effects his nearness was having on her usual self-control. He felt her soften against him, and his heart lurched as her hand, of its own accord, came from his shoulder to caress his chest.

Her face rose to his. In the dim light of the barn her skin appeared flushed and her eyes glowed with a need that easily matched his own. Cole felt something tighten in his chest and trembled against the raging need that threatened his control.

For a moment they simply looked at each other.

Emy's lips parted as she struggled for every breath. She whimpered a soft sound of longing as he touched his mouth to hers. His lips grazed hers again and again, dragging back and forth, bringing her to the edge of madness. She needed him to complete the kiss to show her again the magic.

Her hands reached for his face, bringing his mouth more firmly against hers. At his slightest prodding, Emy parted her lips. She was under no alcoholic influence now. She couldn't blame her reaction on strong brew. She was doing what she'd been aching to do for days. He'd taunted her senses from the moment he'd awakened. She'd tried to keep her feelings hidden; she'd tried to ignore the need. She'd tried not to show the desire that never subsided, but he'd seen it in her eyes. And she'd known he'd seen it, no matter her efforts to hide.

She'd watched his long, hot gazes, the silent communication of souls when she had no will to deny. He'd seen the longing, the fire there. He'd seen it and known she would be his.

Cole's arms pulled her closer. God, but she was lovely. Delicate, innocent, and sweeter than any woman he could ever remember. His hand reached for her hair. His fingers slid into its silky, thick blackness as he held her closer still.

"Emy," he murmured on a gasping breath as his mouth and tongue discovered the exquisite taste of her. Warm and clean, her scent rivaled the most exotic flower. It took his breath away as his mouth traveled the length of her neck and then back again to those soft, delicious lips.

"Chéri," she murmured as her hands slid to his cheeks, her fingers threading through soft black hair. *"Chéri,"* she said again, and Cole wondered if he had the strength to resist the longing he heard in her voice. He wouldn't take her now. He couldn't. Not there, in a barn, where her grandmother or sister could come upon them.

Still, despite his best intentions, Cole found himself unable to resist a further sampling. Just a touch, he promised himself. A touch and he'd stop. He gathered her against him again and moved into the privacy of a stall. Gently he lowered her to the clean straw and reached for the buttons of her gown. Within seconds her soft flesh fell free of the garment and filled his hands. He groaned into her mouth and she whimpered a helpless plea for more.

He wanted to touch her everywhere, kiss her everywhere. He tore his mouth from hers, intent on discovering still more of the pleasure.

Fire, molten liquid fire. Emy couldn't hold back her cry of delight as his mouth took her flesh deep into the heat. She was lying back, his body half covering hers, his hand sliding down the length of her midriff, hip, and thigh, searching for the hem of her gown. Emy trembled, knowing what was to come. Knowing the touch of his fingers upon her could bring her to the edge of delirium and then perhaps over the edge into a mindless, beckoning pit of madness.

Her low moans and the slightly impatient movement of her hips told him of her willingness to experience more. Cole refused to chance discovery and her subsequent embarrassment, but he would show her a small portion of the magic that existed between a man and a woman. He would show her things she never, in her innocence, imagined of her own body.

His hand found the hem of her gown at last and slid up the length of her leg. His heart was thunder in his chest, his breathing almost an impossibility as fingers slid beneath the cotton drawers, over the warmth of her thigh, and then found at last the hot, eager wetness that begged for his touch.

It took no effort to part her thighs, for she was a willing captive in this pleasure. And then as his fingers moved over her moist, sensitive skin, her soft, husky cries of pleasure were lost in his mouth.

It was as she had imagined. No, it was better than she imagined. It was better than anything, ever.

Emy groaned as his fingers expertly massaged her. Gentle and then slightly rough and then gentle again, driving her insane with the need for more. Her hips arched toward his hand even as her head pressed back into the straw-covered floor. Her body grew stiff, her belly tight, and then tighter still.

Her blood pounded in her ears, deafening her to all sound. Her eyes half closed and she moaned again and again, almost unable to bear the mastery. It was more than any human being could take, and she wondered how she managed. But she wondered for only a second, because she was soon so far into the magic that she was unable to think or know anything but the feel of his fingers moving against her body.

She murmured a fearful sound of approaching pain and arched her hips higher into his hands, her own coming to clutch his shoulders as her eyes begged for mercy, for release from this rapture.

Enthralled at her abandoned murmurs of delight, Cole could only smile, knowing he was the cause of this pleasure. She was nearly at her limit. Her head twisted back and forth, her hair, free of pins, wild around her face. Her eyes grew wide, dazed with feeling, filled with longing, with need, her lips parted, her mouth open as she tried to say something. But whatever it was was lost in the sudden crashing euphoria of release.

Cole instantly covered her mouth with his, muffling the cries of pleasure that went on and on.

It took some time before Emy's senses returned. And when they did, Emy knew yet again a mortifying sense of embarrassment. God Almighty, how could she have allowed this? What was lacking in her character that permitted such intimacy? She couldn't look at him. She couldn't ever look at him again.

But Emy's embarrassment didn't last long. She found herself shocked from the emotion with a whispered "Marry me?"

Cole breathed into her hair. "Oh, God, please, marry me, Emy?"

Emy pulled back, her eyes wide with shock, and almost laughed aloud as she realized no one was more shocked than the man who had just proposed. She bit her lip as she tried to control the sudden burst of merriment. It wouldn't do at all to laugh at a man's proposal no matter that it was said without thought and in a moment of extreme emotion. "Cole, we cannot marry. Not now."

"Why not?" Cole couldn't deny the sense of relief he felt at her softly spoken words. And yet oddly enough, he found himself ready to argue the point.

It was impossible. She and her family were responsible for this man's injury. How could she marry the very man she had laid low? What would happen when the day came that he realized as much? And most importantly, how could she begin a life based on lies? No, despite the feelings of tenderness she knew for him, the idea of marriage was quite out of the question. "Because my family needs me now."

"I could help you."

Emy came to a sitting position and adjusted her gown. "Cole, you're a marshal. You won't be staying on here once you've found the men you've come for."

161

"Come back with me, then."

Emy shook her head. "I can't leave them."

"Is it the farm?"

"It's that and more. Someone has to watch my grandmother."

"Will there ever come a time when you can leave?"

Emy shrugged. "Perhaps." *Perhaps I'm out of my mind to allow even this conversation, never mind what just happened.* Emy lowered her gaze to the ground as she remembered her disgraceful response to this man. She couldn't stop the shudder that rippled through her, nor the low groan of approaching doom. *Oh, God, Emy, keep away from him. This can only end in disaster.* There was no way she could marry this man. The thought of what she had done to him filled her with guilt. And because of that guilt, no matter how much her body might long for his, they could never marry.

Cole sighed, knowing he had no choice but to agree with her decision. For now.

Chapter Nine

Emy came from the wagon and tied the horse to the hitching post. With nervous fingers she smoothed imaginary wrinkles from her dress and adjusted her bonnet. Her throat was dry. She longed for a cool drink or the more lasting effects of a peppermint stick, but a glance toward the general store brought only a shake of her head. She'd accomplish little by delaying this meeting. Nothing would be gained but a prolonging of the anxiety, the fear of the unknown. Mr. Whitehead had sent a note. With her father and brother out of town, Emy had no choice but to answer his summons.

"You want me to go in with you?" Cole asked.

Emy shook her head. "No. It's better, I think, if I go alone." A moment later she bit her lip and with shoulders straight walked into the cool interior of the bank.

Cole watched her walk away from him. Once she entered the building, he headed for the telegraph office. It was necessary to notify Hawk that he had arrived in Baton Rouge and all was well. His deputy would no doubt be anxious, not having heard from him for so long, but a wire should put the man's mind to rest.

Cole had no intention of returning to New Orleans any time in the near future. The fact was, he had no definite plans as to when he'd be going back. All he knew for sure was he wouldn't be going back alone.

A young man sat at a desk just outside the bank president's office, engrossed in the papers spread out before him. Emy cleared her throat and was immediately rewarded with a smile of admiration along with the man's full attention. "May I help you?"

"I'd like to see Mr. Whitehead, please."

"Have you an appointment?"

"No." Mr. Whitehead's note had asked her father to come. No particular time was mentioned. Last night she'd made her decision to come in his place. She thought perhaps if she talked to the man, if she begged for an extension on their loan, maybe, just maybe, the man might allow them more time. She'd left the farm almost at the crack of dawn for this one purpose. "Tell him Miss Du Maurier is here to see him."

The young man smiled again, stood, and entered the room behind him.

A moment later he came to the door and with another smile ushered her inside.

Mr. Whitehead came from around his desk, his

hand extended toward her. Emy had no choice but to allow him to bring her hand to his thick lips. "My dear Miss Du Maurier. It is indeed a pleasure to see you. You must tell me if I can be of some assistance."

Emy forced back the need to shudder. Her smile was stiff. She did not like this man. She didn't like his obvious condescension in regard to her and her family.

Mr. Elridge Whitehead, formerly of New York City, was the president of the Baton Rouge Bank, the very bank that held the mortgage to Emy's home. He was a big man, and to Emy's way of thinking, a particularly rough and coarse sort who masked those less-than-admirable attributes behind a façade of supposed civility. He had the most unappealing way of looking at a woman, as if he had had personal and carnal knowledge of her body.

This wasn't the first time she felt vulnerable in his presence, but it might have been the worst. How did he cause her to feel naked with one look? Again she repressed a shudder and forced a smile.

Whitehead's lips widened into a knowing grin at her look of annoyance even as his ever-present cigar protruded from between stained teeth. Emy thought him brash and arrogant to the point of disbelief when she allowed herself to think of him at all. During those brief moments she could only wonder why. As far as she could see, the man had little to be arrogant about. His money, perhaps? She shrugged aside the thought, imagining it a sad state of affairs when money appeared to be the man's only redeeming quality.

"I came in response to your note."

"The note was sent to your father."

"I know, but my father is out of town."

"Please, sit down, my dear."

Emy sat and knew some surprise when Mr. Whitehead took the chair at her side rather than returning to the opposite side of his desk.

He waited until she was settled before he spoke again. "I'm afraid you've made the trip for nothing. You see, my dear, I can hardly conduct business with a girl. I have to talk to your father."

If he called her "my dear," one more time, Emy thought she just might explode. Her gaze lowered to her hands as she forced her fingers into a relaxed position.

"Mr. Whitehead, I've come in my father's place, to talk to you about an extension of our loan."

"Most people believe it unseemly for a woman to discuss money."

"Perhaps, but with my father out of town, I must."

Mr. Whitehead sighed in apparent gloom. Emy was under no false impression that he cared a whit about her dilemma. His next words only confirmed her belief. "I'm afraid there's nothing I can do about extending the loan. After all, I have others I must answer to."

"I thought you owned the bank."

"I do, but there are investors involved. You know how it is."

Emy didn't have the vaguest notion as to how it was. All she knew was, she couldn't let her family be put into the street. Her father and Anton had tried, perhaps not in the best way possible, but they had tried. And now they were trying again. Emy had no real hope that this last-ditch effort would succeed. Not at this late date.

"There must be some way, Mr. Whitehead. There must be something I could do." She felt as if she were groveling, but it didn't matter. Emy would have done anything to see her family safe.

Whitehead's smile was evil incarnate. Had Emy looked to her left, she would have known what the man was about before the first word was spoken. "As a matter of fact, there is something you could do."

She looked at him then and asked, "What?"

"Take off your clothes."

From the first, Emy had taken no pleasure in this man's company. Somehow she'd known him for the lowlife he was. Still, she couldn't imagine that he had actually told her to undress with all the emotion of ordering a cup of coffee. Emy almost laughed at the thought. She must have misunderstood. "Excuse me?"

"You heard me. Take off your clothes."

Emy might have known some real dislike for this man, but she hadn't expected even him of such perversion. "You cannot be serious!"

"But I am, dear. I'm very serious." He shrugged and leaned back in his chair as he allowed a leering smile. "As a businessman, I'm a man ready to bargain."

"What do you mean?"

"It's very simple, my dear. You have something I want. I've been known at times to be very generous to my ladies."

"When you get what you want, you mean?"

"Of course." He smiled again. Emy didn't bother to hide her disgust. "It's possible that I could even forgive the entire note. What would you say to that?"

Emy came to her feet. "I'd say that you should be ashamed, Mr. Whitehead."

Whitehead laughed and also came to his feet. The man was enormous, half as wide as he was tall, and he was indeed tall. Emy was a small woman, but standing before him she felt almost dwarfed. She took a step back, wondering if it was possible to reach the door before something terrible happened. His hands were on her before she took her second step.

She tried to no avail to squirm from his hold. "I'll tell your wife," she warned, her whole body stiff with dread.

Whitehead's thick lips twisted into a lascivious smile. His pale eyes glittered with the knowledge that this small, beautiful woman was his for the taking. No one would come in here. No one would dare interrupt what he had in mind. After he had her the first time, he might even be persuaded to keep her as his mistress. Ann was becoming a bore. It was long past the time to replace her. She was good only for one thing, and now every time she did it, he had to give her a trinket. Lately she was getting more and more greedy. He shrugged. "That, of course, is your prerogative. But you might as well know that Harriet is aware of my indiscretions and has the sense to overlook them."

Emy was suddenly crushed against his body, his arms like bands of steel. "Let me go, or I'll scream."

"You won't scream," he said with quiet assurance. "Everyone will know what's happening if you scream."

Emy struggled, but to no avail. The man was far her superior in strength.

He laughed as he lowered them both to the floor. His hand slid beneath the hem of her dress. Emy fought like a madwoman at the touch of his thick, meaty palm just above her ankle. "I'll kill you!" A moment later her nails raked four clean lines down one side of his face, and the room filled with the most vile curses.

Emy never saw the coming blow. She simply and suddenly felt the impossibly hard jolt, and along with it an accompanying array of sparkling, shining lights, and then knew only peace as the dense blackness closed in around her.

She never heard the opening of the door. She never saw the big man step inside and pause, momentarily unable to comprehend what he was seeing. She never saw Cole's smile turn to a grimace of horrifying rage. She never heard his whispered curse, nor realized the moment Mr. Whitehead was pulled off her body. She never heard the man's cries of pain as fist after fist was embedded into his soft, quivering flesh.

It was many blows later that Cole realized he'd come as close as he cared to think to actually killing the man. Not once had the fat man tried to defend himself. Cole never realized that after the third blow, defense was an impossibility. He stood before the unconscious form, trembling with rage. What the hell had Emy been thinking to come in here alone with this piece of filth? And how the hell was he going to get her out without half the city knowing what had happened? What had almost happened, he silently corrected himself, knowing only relief that he'd lost his patience and entered the office the moment the young man outside the door had left his desk.

Suddenly he realized that along one wall stood a door to the alley behind the bank. It took less than a minute to bring her horse and wagon around. Before Mr. Whitehead inched his way back to consciousness, before he even moaned, Cole was guiding her lazy horse out of town.

He held her to his side, pressing her face to his chest, hoping to hide her identity from curious glances. The truth was, most folks were busy with their chores and didn't even notice the slow-moving wagon and the pretty lady held a bit too close to the big man beside her. A few men observed the woman with the luscious shape reclining real comfortable-like against the lucky bastard. They grinned until they saw that Cole's expression came as close as they cared to see to a promise of death. Who could blame them when they turned quickly away and pretended not to notice?

The wagon was two miles outside the city before Emy moaned. Cole pulled to the side of the dirt road and stopped. "Are you all right?"

"Mmm," she murmured against his neck, and then moaned again. "My head is killing me. What happened?"

"That bastard, Whitehead, must have hit you."

Emy brought her hand to the side of her face and

groaned at the pain of touching an eye that was already swelling. "How many times?"

"I don't know." Cole gathered her into his lap, his arms holding her securely to his chest. He felt his body's response and cursed at his insensibility. Jesus, couldn't he control himself just this once? Couldn't he hold this woman in his arms without wanting to take her body? Cole forced aside the everlasting need and focused his mind on her injury. "When I opened the door, you were already out cold and that—"

"Shush," Emy murmured. "Don't talk so loud."

"I'm not talking loud, sweetheart. You're leaning your ear against my chest."

Emy sat up straighter. God Almighty, he wished she wouldn't move like that in his lap. Slowly she moved her head to the left and then the right. "Where are we?"

"On the road home."

Emy nodded and then winced at the movement. Only it wouldn't be her home much longer. Not unless a miracle happened and Papa and Anton got the money they needed. She sighed her despair even as she promised herself she would worry of it no more. From this moment on, it was all in God's hands. His will be done.

It was all well and good to allow God's will to be done, but when you came right down to it, God helped those who helped themselves. And as long as Emy was able to walk and work, she would help herself and her family survive this low point in their lives. There was a very slim chance, perhaps, but still a chance, that her father and brother would manage the impossible and get the money they needed for the mortgage. But just in case things did not work out as she hoped and they did in fact lose their home, Emy already planned for their future. She would bring her family into town. For the time being, or perhaps longer, they would rent a small apartment and between the laundry she took in and her sewing, plus the odd jobs her father and brother might find, they would manage just fine.

In the meantime she would wait and do her waiting without fear.

Emy looked into the empty stall and shot Cole a puzzled glance. "I'm sure the hammer is in the kitchen."

"I left it in here."

"I don't see it."

The stray puppy, found sleeping in the barn just the day before, tugged at her skirt. Emy picked up the furry little creature and laughed as it licked her face, never noticing how Cole expertly managed to move her farther into the stall. "He is happy, yes?" she asked as she tipped her head to one side and leveled her dark eyes on the silent man leaning his back against the now-closed door.

It never failed. Just standing this close caused a powerful response in his body. His breathing grew labored, his heart a pounding hammer in his chest. How much longer could he sample her charms and still deny himself the taking of her body? "I reckon anyone would be happy when allowed to kiss you."

Emy knew she shouldn't allow this, but she was powerless to resist. She couldn't fight both their needs. All she could do was enjoy the sweet innocence of these moments. Soon enough they would come to an end. Soon enough she and her family would be forced to pay for the wrong they had done, for the terrible deceit perpetrated against Cole.

Emy put aside all thoughts of the coming misery. There would be time enough to suffer, time enough to bemoan her foolishness. For now she couldn't keep the flash of laughter from her eyes, nor the deviltry from her smile. "Then I must make you very happy, monsieur." For almost two weeks, since the day he'd asked her to marry him, Cole had kissed her whenever and wherever he pleased, except, of course, if Grandmère or Kit were about.

Cole grinned at the sassy remark, his dark eyes narrowing, filled with longing. "You wouldn't be complainin', would you, darlin'?"

Emy's eyes twinkled with laughter, and both of them knew she lied when she said, "Maybe just a little."

"Come over here." The words were little more than a husky drawl.

She shook her head. "A lady should never be alone with a man."

"You should have thought of that a few weeks back."

He moved toward her then, and to her squeals of delight grabbed her as she tried to scurry past him to the door. He rolled them both to the straw-covered ground. The puppy barked excitedly as he joined these two humans in play. "Now you have to pay."

The puppy jumped on his head and fell to the opposite side of them, trying to squeeze his face between theirs.

Emy smiled at his antics. *"Non.* I've already paid. You kissed me this morning."

"Darlin', that was no kiss. This," he said as his lips brushed enticingly over hers, promising pleasure almost beyond bearing, "this is a kiss."

Cole groaned as he tore his mouth from her plump sweetness. The ache in his belly was almost unbearable. God, he couldn't remember the last time he'd suffered like this. How much longer before his body could claim hers? How much longer was he to bear the torture?

He was gasping, hardly able to speak, his fingers lingering overlong on her soft, giving flesh, bringing them both closer to the madness, as he reluctantly brought the bodice of her dress back into place. "Damn, but it's getting harder every time."

"What?" she asked dreamily, her arms around his neck, her mouth nuzzling his ear, her body moving sensually against his.

"Covering you up. I want to see you. I can't wait to see you, and all I seem to do is cover you."

"You cover only me because you uncover me first."

Cole smiled. "One of these days, your sister or your grandmother is going to walk in on us. Then you'll have to marry me."

Emy smiled, content for the moment to enjoy the fantasy. She couldn't marry him, of course. She could never marry him and yet it was lovely to imagine the possibility.

"I know a place where we could be alone." Emy felt a jolt of surprise at her own words. Was that her? Was she boldly planning a rendezvous for the sole purpose of loving this man?

Cole stiffened, imagining the luxury of privacy, of being able to touch her, hold her, love her. There was nothing in the world he wanted more. "Where?"

"It's a small cabin. No one lives there."

"Tell me where."

"About an hour's walk from here."

"Let's go now."

"We can't. I promised Grandmère that I would help her in the kitchen. Tomorrow. We'll leave early."

Emy reached over the edge of the roof, and while holding tightly to its thick ledge slid the slats of wood and nails forward. Cole was doing a few repairs around the house. Emy wondered why he bothered, since it was more than likely that they would soon be dispossessed. Still, Cole had insisted, claiming he needed to keep busy. "You're not going to fix anything else, are you?"

Cole glanced at her expression, full of hope. Tendrils of black hair clung to damp, creamy skin. Her face and neck glistened with sweat, she having just left the kitchen. Cole could smell the delicious scent of bread baking. What he wanted to smell was her, but that would have to wait until tomorrow.

She was standing on the ladder, her head and shoulders just visible over the porch roof, upon which Cole sat. "Why?"

"Because I'm exhausted."

"I'm the one who's doin' the fixin' and you're exhausted?"

Emy's laughter was pure disdain. *"Oui.* You fixed the barn door, strengthened the support beam of this roof, replaced two slats of wood on the front steps, but I'm the one who had to find the hammer, nails, and wood. I'm the one who had to bring you water when you got thirsty. I'm the one who bandaged your thumb and has to leave my kitchen every time you call."

"All right, all right." Cole laughed and brought his brows up and down in quick succession. "But if I remember right, we looked for the hammer together."

Emy shot him a knowing look. "And that made me even more tired."

"Darlin, if you told me where everything was, I wouldn't have to bother you."

Emy scowled and gave a dismissive wave of a slender hand. "And when I tell you, do you believe me?"

"Sure I believe you."

"Then why did we spend nearly an hour looking in the barn for the hammer and nails, when I told you they were in the kitchen?"

Cole's eyes darkened with pleasure. A slow, very lazy smile tugged at one corner of his mouth, allowing a flash of white teeth against a black beard and mustache. Emy felt her breath catch in her throat. Lord, but the man was beautiful. "If you think we were lookin' for a hammer in the barn, then I'm doin' something wrong."

Emy's cheeks darkened with soft color, and she lowered her gaze from his smile, feeling something squeeze at her chest. He was dangerous, almost as dangerous as the ridiculous situation she had somehow found herself in. If she wasn't careful, if she didn't keep a tight guard on her emotions, she might find herself in love. Emy shuddered at the thought. God help her if she ever loved this man.

Emy shrugged aside the thought and then responded to his daring comment with a low, sexy laugh as she remembered the lovely time spent in the stall that very morning.

"That laugh tells me you're getting sassy again. And you know what I do to sassy ladies?"

Emy's dark eyes flashed with warning. "It had better not be kissing. I had chores to do and wasted almost the entire morning kissing you instead."

"Emy, you're mistaken if you think kissing is a waste of time." Cole looked up from repairing the hole in the roof at the sound of an approaching rider. "You expectin' somebody?"

Emy turned to see Mr. Whitehead trot his horse toward the house. Her lips tightened in obvious displeasure. "It's Mr. Whitehead."

"Go into the house. I'll take care of him."

"No. I don't want any trouble. Besides, he won't try anything with you here."

A slight breeze ruffled the hem of her long gray

skirt, allowing the approaching man to catch a glimpse of the ruffled edge of her cotton petticoat. Emy quickly descended the ladder lest the breeze pick up and more than a ruffle be exposed.

"'Morning, my dear," Whitehead said as he pulled his horse to a stop before her home. His pale gray eyes swept leisurely over her trim form, and he obviously liked what he saw. He glanced at Cole, who was just coming down the ladder. "You hire on a new hand since I stopped by last?"

Emy barely hid her disgust as Whitehead dismounted and came to stand before her. Her eye still slightly discolored, Emy wondered at the man's gall in coming here. How did he dare after what had happened in his office? She couldn't stop the shudder. Lord, she could still feel the slobber of his wet mouth upon her cheek and his pawing, thick fingers edging up her leg.

"Mr. Brackston is staying with us until Papa and Anton's return."

Whitehead didn't recognize Cole as the madman who had come into his office at a most inopportune time. He had, after all, been engrossed in another matter and hadn't noticed the intrusion at all, not, that is, until he saw the flash of blinding light and felt the first mind-numbing blow. After Cole's first punch, Whitehead hadn't seen much of anything. He shot Cole a dismissive glance. "So, my dear, I take it your menfolks have yet to return."

Emy glared at the man. "The note is not due until the end of this month."

Whitehead's laugh was pure condescension. "Will a few days make that much difference?"

178

Emy prayed it would, but in truth held out little hope. It would take nothing less than a miracle for her father and brother to trap enough animals in one month's time in order to pay what was needed.

"It may, Mr. Whitehead."

"Have you considered my offer?"

Emy shook her head and glared her hatred. "I'm afraid your offer was not worth considering."

"You say that now, but what will you say when your home is gone?"

"My answer will always be the same."

Whitehead glanced at Cole, annoyed at his hovering presence, and scowled. "I'd like to speak to Miss Emy in private, if you don't mind."

Cole narrowed his gaze as he hooked his thumbs into his belt. His smile was ice. It was directed at Whitehead and yet Emy shivered at the cold hatred found there. "Fact is, Mr. Du Maurier left the ladies in my care." Cole had never met the man, at least not so as he could remember, but figured embellishing on the truth in this instance wouldn't hurt. "I reckon that means keeping an eye on them when a gentleman calls."

Emy smiled and jeered with considerably more courage than had she been alone, "Mr. Whitehead is no gentleman."

"You don't say." The threat in Cole's dark eyes was not to be denied. His arm slid around Emy's waist in a protective as well as possessive fashion. Whitehead didn't miss the movement and frowned. "What would a man who's no gentleman be wantin' here?"

Whitehead glanced at Cole. It was easy enough to

see his presence was not a welcome sight. "And you are?"

"Cole Brackston."

Whitehead's eyes widened with surprise. "Cole Brackston? The marshal from New Orleans?"

Cole nodded.

"Everyone is looking for you. Your deputy is in town right now, asking everyone if they've seen you."

Cole grunted a low sound. Apparently Hawk had already been on his way north when Cole sent the wire. "I had some trouble. The Du Mauriers were kind enough to take me in.

"You could do me a favor and tell my deputy that I'll be in town later tonight."

After gaining knowledge of the stranger's identity, Whitehead seemed to lose all interest in the eldest Du Maurier daughter and within seconds took his leave.

Emy kept her gaze averted from the man beside her. Cole knew something was wrong. "What's the matter?"

"Nothing."

"Something is, what?"

"You'll be leaving now."

"No, I won't."

"But your deputy is here."

"So? He probably came looking for me before my wire got there. After I talk to him, he'll go back."

Emy kept her gaze on the small patch of dirt to the right of her front door, a patch that would allow nothing to grow, no matter how hard she tried to cultivate it.

Cole teased, "If you're afraid that I'll leave, you'd

better marry me while you have the chance."

Emy laughed and allowed Cole to wrap his arms around her waist. She knew she shouldn't permit the intimacy. Still, it was beyond her power to deny this man, or herself, these last few moments of happiness. He'd leave, she was sure. Deep in her heart, she knew it was all for the best.

Chapter Ten

Silent, both men were lost in their own misery. Jacques watched his son guide the flat boat through the still waters of the bayou with a long pole. Around them, leafless trees grew out of the murky depths. A crane flew overhead and landed on one of the thick, bare branches. In the distance came an eerie croak of an unseen animal, and a splash as yet another plunged into the water's obscure stillness. A gator missed nothing as it watched, with a sinister smile, the forms of life around it. Waiting for the right moment to make its move, it lay as still as the log it imitated, its hungry, beady eyes just above the dark water's surface.

Jacques winced as his gaze fell to the pile of furs at his feet. He almost laughed aloud his thoughts, for to call the measly few they'd managed to trap a pile was an exaggeration in the extreme.

Jacques sighed. Sorrow mingled with overwhelming despair brought an ache to his chest. He felt almost physically ill. He hadn't been able to do it.

Perhaps if he'd started sooner, he might have had a chance, but no, there hadn't been enough time. He'd stayed as long as he could, praying for a windfall of furs to somehow come his way. At last he'd been forced into the realization that there was no chance, no way he could save his home.

Jacques had always believed that things turned out for the best, only he couldn't find a best in this situation. Perhaps the Lord had more in mind for Jacques and his small family, more than owning and working his little farm.

Jacques shook his head. It didn't matter what the Lord had in mind. He wasn't the kind of man who waited for the Lord to make His plans known. Jacques was a man to take matters into his own hands.

He hated to do it, but as each smooth, silent mile covered brought them closer to home and the sad disappointment he was sure to see in Emy's eyes, Jacques grew more positive that his decision was correct, the only decision possible. He'd promised, no, more than a promise, he'd vowed before God and the saints never to turn to crime again. But it was time to break that vow. He'd tried his best, hadn't he? He'd tried and gained nothing for his efforts. Just one more time, he silently promised. Just one more time and he'd never do it again.

Jacques thought of Emy and knew his daughter was a force to be reckoned with. Emy would understand an honest try, but she would not understand or approve of what he was about to do. He was sorry about that, but wondered which in the end was truly the greater disappointment. Was it better to hold to honor and lose everything? Jacques shook his head at the thought, knowing honor could only come in a weak second to his family's welfare.

Jacques and Anton sold the furs and boat to the first trapper they came across. Almost a month's worth of work and they'd managed only to eke out enough to buy a sack of flour and perhaps a few pounds of coffee. It was less than Emy made in one week of sewing.

Jacques couldn't remember when he'd felt less a man and vowed it was long past the time for that to end.

Jacques and Anton paid for the feed and care of their horses while they'd been gone and were on the road, heading north and home before either spoke of their failure.

"What are we going to do?" Anton couldn't hide his panic. The note was due in less than two weeks and they hadn't managed to get even a small portion of what was needed.

"We won't lose the farm."

"What, then?"

"We will pay it." Jacques's dark eyes darkened further as they filled with determination. "We will pay it."

It took a day of hard riding before they entered Baton Rouge. The moon was full, casting its silvery light upon the city. Jacques would have felt better if the sky was overcast. He shrugged, knowing there was no help for it. They would do what had to be done.

Jacques and Anton stood within the shadows of an alley that ran between the bank and general store, and watched the pedestrian traffic. They waited, waited as their anxiety grew. Waited until the dinner hour was upon them, when most were in their homes, enjoying a hearty meal and the warmth of family. Waited for one particular lone passerby.

"You're going into the city?" Kit asked with obvious excitement. She could count on one hand the number of times she'd been to Baton Rouge and wished above all that she could leave this stupid farm and move into the city forever.

"Cole has business to see to and I have two dresses to deliver to Mrs. Williams."

"Can I go with you?"

Emy glanced at her sister as she restored the kitchen to its usual order. Grandmère couldn't be left alone. Emy wanted no repeat of the last time she'd wandered off. Either one of them had to stay, or . . .

Fifteen minutes later Cole walked into the kitchen. He'd just washed up. His hair was wet, his arms as well. He was rolling his sleeves to his wrists. "What do you mean, your sister's going?" Cole said, sounding none too pleased at the thought.

Emy glanced in Cole's direction and realized Kit had told him she was going to town.

Kit took just that moment to enter the house. Emy thought she was still in her room and knew a moment's surprise to find her wearing her fanciest dress. She had tugged the modest neckline as low as it would go without ripping the fabric, revealing far more than she should of lush, youthful charms. Cole sighed unhappily and shot Emy a pleading look. Apparently he thought Emy was going to let Kit go in her place. Emy only smiled and said, "I mean we're all going.

"Kit, help me with Grandmère."

"But we'll be late getting back. Should Grandmère be out so late?"

Kit had never showed her grandmother the slightest bit of consideration before. One might have thought it odd that she should now, only Emy was no fool. She knew well enough her sister's intent. She knew Kit would like nothing more than to get Cole alone. She shot Kit a look of warning. "We'll take a room at the hotel for the night."

Cole breathed a sigh of relief. The last thing he wanted or needed was that little brat all over him.

It seemed they waited forever, but the traffic began to thin at last. On each corner the city's gaslights were lit. Down the street came the sound of music and laughter. The evening's entertainment was about to begin.

Someone called out "Good night, Mr. Whitehead" just before a door closed and a jingle of keys could be heard. With a nod toward his son, both men drew their guns. The man was fat, and neither Jacques nor his son expected any resistance.

The pounding of hearts blotted out all sound. They waited, never noticing the soft sound of footsteps was accompanied by a distinct jingling of spurs. Had he noticed the jingling sound, Jacques would have imagined a cowhand to be walking either directly before or after their intended victim. It wouldn't have stopped them in their intent.

The trouble was, the jingle of spurs represented no cowhand, but the deputy marshal.

With masks pulled into place, both men stepped out of the alley. Jacques felt a moment's surprise. Whitehead was tall but hardly trim, and the man who stood suddenly before him was every inch hard, rugged, menacing male.

Whitehead cried out in fright and ran as fast as his fat legs could carry his obese form, while the deputy, and Jacques knew it was a deputy, for the man's badge glittered in the soft moonlit night, stood stock-still, awaiting their next move.

Jeremiah Hawk, Cole's deputy, glared at the two masked men facing him, glared because these were probably the very same two whom Cole had come to find, glared because there was no way he could reach for his gun, glared because they were probably going to get away again.

Jacques cursed rapidly in French as he watched the fat man run down the street.

Jeremiah grinned at the dilemma these two faced. They had lost their pigeon and were left, instead, with a man who made thirty dollars a month, a man hardly worth robbing.

"Why don't you give it up? You can't hope to get away with this forever." Jeremiah was sure these two were the bumbling pair every lawman in the state had been looking for. He imagined they weren't hardened criminals, just two men down on their luck, perhaps at their wits' end over some catastrophe. The problem was, one of these days someone was going to kill them, for if all the reports were correct, neither of them seemed capable of handling a gun with any precision, nor did they possess any of the intelligence or luck needed to succeed in their chosen line of work.

"It won't be forever. I only need two hundred dollars and then we'll never do it again."

The man's statement merely confirmed Jeremiah's suspicions. "Why not go to the bank and borrow it?"

Jacques had all his life been an honest man. It was only sheer desperation that had driven him to these lengths. So he never realized his mistake when he blurted out, *"Oui,* the bank. It's the bank I have to pay. That bastard is the reason I've been forced to do this."

From the real anger in his voice, Jeremiah hadn't a doubt that the man spoke the truth. He knew as well that the safest and most expedient way of putting an end to this would be to give the man two hundred dollars and then wait at the bank, when he made his payment. The problem was he didn't have that kind of money.

Jacques was of the same mind. He thought it probable the man, being a deputy marshal, would have less than what was needed. Still, something was better than nothing. "Your money, monsieur," Jacques said, his tone low and he hoped filled with just enough threat to keep this big man from arguing the point.

Jeremiah reached into his pocket and withdrew a

few bills, even as he watched, from the corner of his eye, the slow progress of a wagon that had just turned the corner onto the main street. It was coming toward them. If he could for just a second divert the attention of these two, he might be able to . . .

Cole snapped the reins, trying to hurry the lazy horse along. A frown creased his brow at the effort it took. He'd left his own horse in New Orleans, thinking to rent another once he'd arrived in the city. Perhaps he'd do just that before returning to Emy's farm.

It was dark, but the moon bathed the city in silvery light. It lent a festive atmosphere to ordinarily drab cobblestone streets and darkened storefront windows.

Cole urged the horse forward with another snap of the reins and a muttered command. Apparently the horse was of a mind to do as it pleased, for no matter Cole's insistence, it only meandered along, having a tendency to visit every trough they'd passed so far. Cole grumbled his disgust, just as, from the corner of his eye, he noticed three figures in the shadow of an alley.

One man held both hands up in surrender, while the other two stood before him with guns drawn. It didn't take an instant for Cole to understand what was happening. And it took less than that for the memories of the night he'd been shot to come crashing back.

The three women in the wagon gasped as Cole, with no warning, appeared to be suddenly flung from the seat. The wagon rolled to a stop and the horse was allowed to drink his fill at last, just as Cole landed atop one of the men, knocking both himself and the thief to the cobblestone sidewalk. Cole came effortlessly to his feet and glanced at his adversary. The man was out cold. He turned then, his intent to see to the other, but Jeremiah had been coiled and ready to strike at the first opportunity offered and had not allowed the moment to pass him by. Anton was already face down, his hands held behind his back as Jeremiah cursed the lack of a rope.

Cole ran to the wagon. In the back lay more than enough rope to see to both men.

Emy sat in the wagon; the shock of watching Cole fly from the wagon had yet to fade as she listened to the sounds of a scuffle. A man cried out in French as a meaty fist was delivered with excruciating precision to his jaw. Emy watched as the man along with her heart crumpled to the ground.

It was dark. The men had been standing in shadows, but Emy knew well enough who they were. *Anton, you fool,* she silently bemoaned. *You promised. You swore before the saints!* It couldn't be, but, God in heaven, it was. Her father and brother had just tried to rob someone. They had promised this would never happen again and yet there they were, Anton moaning his discomfort while his hands were tied behind his back and her father lay unconscious on the ground. Soon they would be carted off to jail.

Mon Dieu, how could they have gone back on their word? How could they have lied so blatantly? Fool that she was, she had believed them when they said they were going to trap for furs and all along they were robbing again. She was filled with rage and swore they deserved whatever punishment lay in store. And she hoped they suffered mightily for their misdeeds. Emy sighed in her misery. She knew they deserved to suffer, but they were her family. How in God's name could she stand by and allow it? She couldn't let them go to prison. She had to do something. But what?

Cole threw the rope at his deputy and Jeremiah quickly bound the man's hands. It was only when he finished the job that he noticed the man who had come to his aid was Cole. Suddenly he snapped, "Where the hell were you? I waited for almost a month, and nothing."

"I had an accident," Cole said as he checked the other man, noting his unconscious state.

"So? You couldn't let me know?"

"I sent a wire a few days ago. You must have left before it arrived."

Jeremiah nodded as he digested this information. "You all right now?"

"Fine.

"Let's get these two down to the sheriff's office."

"I'll be with you in a minute," Cole said as he nodded toward the wagon and the three wide-eyed women waiting in terrified silence. He walked to the wagon and stood there a moment, stunned into silence as a distant and yet distinct memory came to assault him. Silvery light shone upon dark hair and the face of an angel whose eyes were round with fear and guilt. And Cole was suddenly flooded with the memory of the night he'd been shot. And then, as if it were written out plainly before him, he knew.

Without a word spoken between them, he knew it was her scream he'd heard that night. And somehow he knew as well that she'd not only known all along, but had actually been part of the gang!

Cole was filled with a variety of emotions, not the least of which was feeling very much the fool. And when a man feels the fool, a woman's best bet is to run.

God damn her! She had played the innocent virgin to perfection. Why? What had she hoped to gain by the performance?

Cole suffered under no delusion that a woman of morals would have worked with thieves. She wasn't at all what she appeared to be, and before this night was through, Cole vowed he'd know exactly who Emeline Du Maurier was.

He watched her face for a moment, his eyes dark with growing condemnation. He hadn't pushed, but respected her supposed morals, and she had, in return, toyed with his affections. God Almighty, he had actually asked the conniving little bitch to marry him!

Cole knew he wouldn't easily forgive her for the treachery, for the suffering she'd caused. He didn't speak until he was sure she was aware that he knew the truth of the matter at last. He watched as her eyes filled with fear and then color touched her cheeks before her gaze lowered to her lap. He nodded in satisfaction and finally said, "Go to the hotel. I'll be along shortly."

Through eyes narrowed into glimmering slits, he watched as the wagon drove off. She hadn't been able to hide her guilt. Cole swore she'd know a reckoning for her crimes on this night.

Cole shook aside the thought. He didn't have the time right now to think about how he was going to make her suffer. Right now he had work to do.

Kit couldn't stop talking about the scene they had just witnessed. Had she ever seen a man so capable, so strong, so wonderful? Wasn't he just like the heroes of the penny novels she sometimes read? How exciting! And then, "What was that all about?" Kit asked as Emy urged the horse down the street.

"What was what all about?" Emy returned, knowing exactly what her sister was talking about, exactly what Cole's dark, dangerous look had been about. He knew! Emy shivered as she remembered the condemnation and promise of retaliation in his eyes. Oh, God, she'd known this would someday happen. Why had she allowed the relationship? Why had she chanced living a lie?

"You know what I mean. The way he looked at you."

The wagon came to a stop some hundred feet down the street in front of the hotel. "Kit, I haven't the slightest idea as to what you are talking about," Emy lied as she jumped to the ground and helped her grandmother from the wagon.

Emy settled her grandmother in their room. The elderly lady was tired. The ride from the farm was slow going and uncomfortable in the springless wagon. Emy went about the chore of seeing to her care with mindless proficiency. Grandmère was almost asleep when Emy slipped her shawl over her shoulders. That she was leaving was obvious.

"Where are you going?" Kit asked as she preened

before a mirror, twisting her black curls this way and that.

"I have to see Cole."

"He said he'd be along shortly."

"I know, but I have to see him now."

"I don't want to stay here," Kit whined. "I want to go downstairs." What good did it do to go to the city when one was cooped up in a room for the entire night? She might as well be back on their farm.

Emy couldn't help but know the girl's intent. The spacious downstairs consisted of not only a lobby but a restaurant on one side and a barroom on the other. As they passed through the lobby, Emy had noticed at least a dozen men congregating at the bar, each in varying degrees of intoxication. Emy tightened her lips and shot Kit a look of warning. "I have to go. Don't you dare leave this room."

Kit was still muttering her disgust as Emy slipped into the hallway. She stood for a moment at the top of the stairs, watching the doings below. A young couple was heading toward her. At any second Cole might walk in the door. Emy shivered at the thought. She couldn't chance it. She might have said she was going to see him, but the truth of the matter was, he was the last man she wanted to see. From the look in his eyes, Emy understood that he knew she was involved in his mishap. She could no longer deny her responsibility. All she could do was delay the inevitable confrontation until other matters were seen to.

Emy used the stairs that led to the back door of the hotel. Five minutes later she stood half hidden behind a wooden crate, alone in the shadowy alley. She pressed her back against the wall of one building as she watched the sheriff's office across the street.

Through the window, Cole was clearly visible. He leaned his hip upon the desk as he conversed with two men. A man she supposed to be the sheriff sat behind the desk. Another man, perhaps the one Cole had helped, leaned against the wall by the door. His back was to her, and all Emy could see of the man was a low-slung gun at his hip, and the darkly tanned skin of one hand.

Emy had no clear-cut plan in mind. All she knew was she was going to get her father and brother out of that jail. She didn't know how. She didn't know when, but she knew she had no choice but to do whatever needed to be done.

Inside, Jeremiah and Cole spoke. "What are you doing here?"

"I thought you were dead. Came to find your body," Jeremiah said, and then asked, "So, what happened?"

Cole touched the side of his head and nodded toward the back of the room, where the two men sat in a small cell. "One of them shot me when I tried to disarm the other."

"You mean they tried to rob you too?"

Cole nodded. "I think they're the same two. Their faces were masked, but they're about the same size and they sound the same." He shrugged. "It doesn't matter. They tried to rob you."

"So how come you happened to be at the right place at the right time tonight?"

"Lucky, I guess. I heard you were in town. When I

saw the three of you standing by the alley, it was like a replay of what happened to me."

"They're not very experienced."

"Or smart. I reckon it don't matter none." All three men silently agreed.

"You want to question them?"

Cole shook his head. "You do it. There's someone I've got to see."

Emy watched as Cole left the sheriff's office. An hour passed and then another, and still she waited. The evening's damp chill had long ago spread into her bones. She shivered constantly now. Tightening her shawl around her shoulders no longer brought comfort.

Her teeth chattered and she bit down until her jaw ached, forcing aside her discomfort. She longed for the comfort of the hotel, for the warmth of a soft, clean bed, but she wouldn't leave. Not until she could do something to help her father and brother.

She breathed a sigh of relief as the other man left the building at last. The sheriff was alone but for his prisoners. Emy moved across the street.

When she entered, she refused to look toward the barred cells at the back of the room. Her gaze was solely for the gentleman behind the desk. She allowed her prettiest smile. "Excuse me, monsieur."

Jack Hendricks had been thinking about the boredom of this job, when to his amazement a vision, no, an angel entered his office. His jaw dropped almost to his chest, for Jack couldn't imagine what a woman who looked like this one could be doing out at this time of night. "Ma'am," he said as he came to his feet.

Emy motioned that he should sit, and breathed a sigh of relief as she took a seat as well.

"How can I help you?"

"It's my husband."

So she had a husband, Jack mentally groaned. Lucky bastard. "What about him?"

"He has disappeared."

"What do you mean?"

Emy lowered her gaze to the desk and tried to look as shy and virginal as it was possible to look. The truth was, it took very little acting on her part. Emy might, for the moment, be involved in matters that were a shade less than honest. Still, her motives were unselfish, and her heart innocent. Her look did not belie the fact. "We were only just married." Her eye twitched. Luckily for her, the man had no reason to suspect the meaning behind that twitching eye. "He left our room to find us a bottle of wine"—Emy glanced at the sheriff and shrugged—"you know, to celebrate our marriage. He never came back."

"How long ago did he leave?"

"Three hours."

Jack Hendricks knew the women who worked downstairs at the bar. Each of them was a beauty, but none, not even all of them together, could compare to this one. A man would have to be out of his mind or dead to leave a woman who looked like her on their wedding night. Jack figured there had been trouble.

He stood. "Let's go see if anyone has seen him."

"Oh, no! I couldn't. I'm afraid he'd be upset. I don't think he'd take kindly to his wife in a barroom."

Jack frowned, wondered what kind of a man this woman had married. "All right, you wait here."

"Thank you, sheriff. I was praying you could help."

Jack figured one of two things had happened. The newlywed had either gotten himself into trouble, or had partaken of one too many drinks in celebrating his good fortune and was probably fast asleep at the back of the barroom. Perhaps he had even found his way back to his room by now.

Jack was at the door when he remembered to ask, "What's your husband's name? And your room number?"

Emy wasn't sure how many rooms the hotel had, so she said, "Number three." It was the room directly across from her own. "My husband's name is John Luke," she said, taking the names from the gospel.

"Luke your last name?"

She nodded. Poor thing, he could see she was scared to death.

The sheriff was right on that score. Emy had never been so terrified in her entire life. She shuddered at her deliberate lies and wondered if she wouldn't lose her soul to this deception.

No sooner had the door closed behind the sheriff than Emy jumped from her seat and ran to the back of the jail. There was no sense wasting time venting her anger on the two terrified men who faced her. That could wait until later. Now she had to find the key and she had to find it now!

"The key! Where is it?"

"He had it on his belt."

Emy moaned a low sound of despair. No, it

couldn't be. She hadn't stood outside for hours and lied as she had for nothing!

"There might be another set," Jacques said hopefully while Anton nodded his head in vigorous agreement. "Look in the desk. Hurry!"

Emy opened each drawer, but to her disappointment and rising panic she found nothing. She slammed the last one shut and heard the jingle of keys in the drawer. They shook against each other when she'd slammed it shut.

It took only another minute and all three were out the back door of the jail. "Where are your horses?"

"We left them by the bank. The sheriff must have brought them to the stable."

"Then run. Just get out of here!"

"What about you?"

"I'll be all right." Emy doubted the truth of that statement. Once she came face-to-face with Cole, she figured she'd never be all right again. "Just hurry."

Cole watched from the shadows as the woman and two men came out the back door of the jail. He'd searched this town for the last three hours, his anger growing as each second ticked by. She wasn't in her room. She wasn't anywhere. When he'd walked by the sheriff's office and found her making eyes at the poor fool behind the desk, he'd almost collapsed in relief.

He might have entered the office then, but for some reason decided to wait and watch. The sheriff left. Cole's eyes widened and his heart began to pound as Emy rose instantly from her chair and ran to the back of the room. He watched as she exchanged a few words with the two held there. He watched as she came back and searched through the desk drawers. He watched as his heart shriveled up and died.

She was helping the two escape. Cole knew it didn't matter, for they were a harmless, foolish pair and could be picked up again in a matter of days. After all, he knew what they looked like now. A cold smile twisted his lips into a sneer. If only she were half as harmless. If only she weren't the lying, conniving bitch that had brought him from the brink of death, only to kill him more surely than any gun could.

He could have loved this woman. He could have easily loved her. Cole almost laughed in ridicule. Could have?

As the two turned the corner of an alley and disappeared from sight, Emy breathed a sigh of relief. It was then that the menacing whisper came. Emy stiffened with dread, for she instantly recognized the thread of danger that lay behind those seemingly innocent words. "Taking in a bit of air, Emy?" Cole asked, coming suddenly and silently upon her.

Emy spun around, her big eyes glittering in the moonlight, glittering with both surprise and fear.

Cole cursed. So she was afraid of him, was she? He almost laughed at the thought, wondering when he'd last met a woman with her considerable acting ability. "You're not afraid of me, are you, Emy?"

"Of course not."

Cole's grin was sly. It reminded her of a wolf ready to pounce upon his helpless victim. She shivered as he took her hand in his and without a word spoken

200

simply headed toward the hotel. Emy had little opportunity to do more than follow, or be dragged along. His hand almost crushed hers, and Emy knew for a fact that all was lost when she heard his whispered remark. "Trouble is, lady, you should be. I swear to God, you should be."

Chapter Eleven

Cole could hardly contain the rage that filled his being. It tightened his throat and caused him an ache deep in his chest. Jesus, God! He'd watched her break two men out of jail!

The woman he thought to be a sweet innocent had actually put herself above the law. Why?

Cole was having a time of it putting his thoughts in order. His mouth twisted into a grim, ridiculing smile. How stupid to believe she was an innocent.

Cole had thought himself considerably more worldly than the innocent she had pretended to be. Now, of course, he knew the truth of it. She had been sent out as bait, that night aboard the boat, a part of a gang of criminals, and he had been the stupid son of a bitch that had willingly succumbed to her magic.

What a laugh they must have gotten out of that. Only Cole was going to laugh when it counted most. He was going to laugh last.

Cole's hand held hers captive as they walked into the hotel lobby. He asked for a room. Even as he signed the register, his free hand held firmly to hers. There was no way she was going to escape his wrath.

Emy didn't miss a knowing, licentious look from the clerk. Apparently the man had remembered her as taking a room with her grandmother and sister. Now it was obvious that she was joining the marshal for an evening of scandalous pleasure. She could feel her cheeks burn, and cursed both the silent and presumably all-knowing clerk, as well as the fool at her side, for Cole was oblivious of the entire incident.

His room was a floor above the one she, Kit, and her grandmother had taken. Emy, nearly dragged up the stairs, was almost flung inside. Cole watched her for a silent moment before he finally shrugged and then turned to the door. She felt her heart jump at the sound of the bolt sliding into place.

Emy didn't know what exactly, but she knew he had at that moment made up his mind about something. The problem was she didn't know what his thoughts were. All she knew for sure was she had every right to be afraid. Her heart thundered in her chest, partly from exertion, partly from fear of his obvious anger. His movements were carefully controlled, as if he had to move slowly or lose all control. He pocketed the key.

The room was hot, almost airless. The heat added to his anger and his anger intensified the ache. The need was stronger than anything he'd ever known. Cole felt the sweat dampen his shirt and knew before this night was out that the two of them would sip of each other's moisture. A pulse throbbed in his throat.

"Cole." She bit her bottom lip. Unable to face the glaring condemnation in his eyes, she kept her gaze on the faded red carpet. "I know this looks bad, but I can explain."

"I was sure you could." His voice was little more than a husky whisper, as if he couldn't quite gain the power of speech over the anger he knew. Emy raised her gaze from the floor. His eyes glittered. The man was on the verge of . . . what? Violence? Madness? "After all, you've had a few hours, four, in fact, to come up with something."

"No." She shook her head. "It's not like that."

"No?" His voice, silky-smooth now, sent shivers down her back. "What is it like, then?"

She sighed. There was no help for it. She had but one alternative, and that was to throw herself on this man's mercy. "I might as well start at the beginning."

The sound of his hard laugh snapped her gaze to his, and Emy knew the outcome before she began. No matter her pleas for mercy, she and her family would suffer greatly from this man's self-righteous rage. The look in his eyes was almost cruel, and Emy cringed, knowing he wasn't about to listen to anything she might say. But Emy was wrong. Cole found himself oddly curious. What, he wondered, would she give as an excuse? He almost couldn't wait to hear the next installment of lies. "Might you? Do you think you might also add the truth this time?"

"I've never lied to you."

"Haven't you?"

His hard gaze forced her to reconsider. And Emy knew she was going to have a time of it trying to convince this man of her motives. "Well, perhaps I have, but I didn't lie for me. I lied for—"

He cut her off. "Emy, in case you haven't noticed, you've been found out. Stop trying to portray the innocent."

"I'm not." Emy couldn't profess her innocence, for she believed in her heart that knowing what her family had been about proved her as guilty as they. "I'm just trying to explain."

Cole hung his jacket on a hook behind the door, his gun belt on the bedpost. He sat in one of the room's two chairs and pulled off his boots. "Explain away," he said as if he couldn't care less, for he wasn't about to believe a word of it. His grin was hard. Emy couldn't help but wonder how a smile could hold such hate. Hate and something more, something she couldn't name.

"What are you doing?"

"I'm getting ready for bed."

"Now? Here?" Emy felt a chill of apprehension. The fact of the matter was, Emy had never suspected his motives in bringing her there. She'd thought that Cole had taken this room in order to sort out the evening's happenings and the meaning behind them, to berate her for her involvement, to gain the truth at last.

"Of course now. What the hell do you think we're doing here?"

Emy pressed her lips together. She knew he thought the worst of her. She wasn't about to add *fool* to the list. Now she understood the look in his eyes. "After all that's happened, do you expect me to simply join you in that bed?"

"After all that's happened, I expect you have no choice."

"Meaning?"

"Meaning, if you don't get your ass in that bed before I'm finished undressing, I'm going to personally see to it that you're put behind bars forever."

"You're threatening me?"

Cole laughed with some amazement. "I never thought I had it in me. I've always known that some women could bring out certain qualities in a man. You just happen to bring out the worst."

Emy's heart thudded, almost closing off her ability to breathe. How could he be so cold? How could he even think to force her into submission? Didn't he realize that anything they did now would serve no purpose? That no pleasure could be found, if it were against her will? "How do I know that you won't put me in jail anyway?"

"You don't."

"Cole, please."

Cole had had enough of her innocent act. For weeks he had treated her like a lady, only to find that he'd been duped. How his gentle care and self-imposed restraint must have amused her. He shuddered at the thought of proposing marriage. God, he could only imagine the laugh she must have gotten out of that. "Take off your clothes."

Emy wasn't about to accommodate that particular order. He'd chosen the wrong woman if he expected docile submission. He might be bigger and stronger, but she knew he wouldn't hurt her, at least not physically. She felt some trepidation, to be sure, but he stirred no fear in her heart. Emy breathed a great sigh, imagining herself strong enough to bear the worst of what he might offer. "Can I tell you something?"

Cole shrugged. "If you feel the need, but you might as well know, it won't make any difference."

Emy went ahead anyway. As far as she could see, she had much to lose and nothing to gain by keeping the truth to herself. "We were about to lose our farm. They did it only because they were desperate. Mr. Whitehead wouldn't give us an extension."

Whatever she was talking about was lost on Cole. All he could see was a tiny woman standing at the other end of the room, her hands twisting nervously before her. All he could think of was the creaminess of her skin. He felt a surge of fury and then lust explode in his belly as he remembered every time he'd touched her and the agony he knew at holding back. Idly he wondered how he had managed to wait. Well, the waiting was at an end. Tonight he'd claim her body for his pleasure. "Who are they?"

"My father and brother."

He frowned at that. "What do you mean?"

Emy took a deep breath, praying for strength, for courage, for the grace to escape his cold intent. "It was my father and brother that I—"

A light dawned and Cole suddenly knew. Had he ever felt more the fool? "—broke out of jail?" he finished for her. His eyes were wide with amazement and then came a touch of humor. The corner of his mouth lifted with a genuine smile. Suddenly a low chuckle escaped his throat as he realized the joke. Moments later that chuckle grew into a roar of laughter. "Damn, but that's something, isn't it? Your father and brother shoot me and bring me home for you to take care of." He'd known for the past few hours that it was her voice he'd heard after being shot. It was her cries of horror. Cole shook his head. No, not horror. He'd probably hallucinated that. She wouldn't have cried for him. She wouldn't have cared. "It was your voice. I thought, I wondered, but it was . . ." He laughed again. "Sounds a bit odd, but I guess it takes all kinds."

Emy shook her head. "No. You don't understand. Shooting you was an accident. We couldn't leave you to die. We had to take you home."

"We?" Cole knew she'd been there. But he hadn't known until that minute how deep was her involvement. Judging by the control she seemed to have over her family, she was probably the mastermind behind all of it. No doubt she had been standing just out of sight, watching the holdup. "Meaning you were a part of that too," he said, his words a statement of fact.

"No. I was just—"

"The bait."

Was that sorrow she heard in his voice?

Damn, why couldn't he forget what had happened between them? Why should it have meant so much to him? It was only part of the game she played. It meant nothing to her, then or now. "I understand."

"You don't understand a thing." She watched as he threw his shirt to the floor. She glanced at the bed and twisted her fingers until they grew white. How could she think? How could she tell him the whole of it while he stood there half naked, his chest gleaming, damp with perspiration, while thoughts of

208

what he had in mind loomed before her? "Why can't we talk about this like civilized human beings? Why do we have to go to bed?"

Emy imagined a man couldn't look more ruthless, less understanding of her dilemma. His eyes were hard, his mouth harder still as he almost casually remarked, "Because I want to go to bed. For weeks we've been doing what you want. Now it's my turn."

"Cole, I didn't mean for you to get hurt."

"What you mean is, you didn't give a damn if I got hurt or not."

"No. I was thinking of you and the things we had done"—her voice lowered almost to a whisper—"that night on the boat." Her face colored at the mention of it.

Cole marveled at her ability to blush on command. He wondered if she knew how difficult that was for most women.

"I was upset. I'd never done anything like that before. The plan was to describe someone to them, and I don't know how it happened, but I must have given them the impression that you were—" She couldn't seem to go on. She couldn't find the right words.

"Meaning you couldn't get me off your mind?" he asked in obvious ridicule. And then he laughed almost happily as she nodded. "You're very good, you know. If I didn't know better, I could almost believe you." His voice lowered to a dangerous husk. "The trouble is, after watching what you did tonight, I can't see how it's possible to believe a thing you say."

Emy felt an almost debilitating sense of hopelessness. It weighed heavily upon her heart. She'd ruined everything. If only she would have told him from the first . . . But no. She couldn't have done that. There was no way she could ever have told him. A huge tear welled up and slipped from one eye.

Cole grunted as he watched the tear roll over a smooth cheek. He shook his head, almost in disappointment. "Emy, I would have thought you were beyond using that kind of trick."

He walked toward her. She backed up as far as she could go. Her back pressed hard against the wall, her dark eyes darted to the left and right, but there was nowhere to run, nowhere to hide. He pulled her hard against him. His arms were like steel—hard, almost bruising, and as unyielding as his heart. Emy knew there was no way she was going to leave the room unscathed. Still, it wasn't in her to simply submit, not without trying again. She knew he'd never forgive her, but clung to the hope that at least she could try to make him understand. "Cole, I swear, I never meant for any of this to happen."

He chuckled a low, wicked sound of victory. "I'm sure you didn't, sweetheart," he said just before he lifted her into his arms and walked toward the bed.

He was using her body for his own pleasure. She refused to enjoy this. Emy knew she'd have to be demented to enjoy even a minute of it. He didn't love her. He didn't even care for her and showed his contempt and hatred with every look, every muttered sound he made. And she detested every stroke of his hand, every lingering kiss that never actually managed to reach her mouth.

That was fine with her. She didn't want him to kiss her. Kissing meant more to her than the coming together of two sets of lips. Kissing meant caring; sometimes kissing meant the beginnings of love. She lay still, waiting for him to complete the act. Perhaps then she could talk to him. Perhaps then he would listen.

"If you want to save your skin, you'd better put more into this than lying there like a dead fish."

Emy had never been so blatantly insulted. Granted, she was much of what he believed her to be. Untrustworthy, at the very least. A liar and probably more, everything but a whore, and she wasn't about to use her body, not even if it meant she would go to prison for the rest of her life.

The sound of a slap seemed to echo on and on in the aftermath of heavy stunned silence.

Cole cursed and roughly pulled her hands above her head. Holding them tightly in one hand, he sneered his disgust and for just a second wondered how it was possible to gain such pleasure with a woman he hated so desperately. What he really wanted to do was return the favor. What he really wanted to do was beat her until he was too tired to ever lift his hands again. He felt ready to explode, on the verge of insanity with the need, and then thankfully the rage began to ease. He shivered at the extent of emotion he'd just suffered. Never in his life had he struck a woman. Never in his life had he come so close to losing control.

Her face was pinched, her eyes and mouth tightly closed, anticipating the coming blow. He knew she was afraid and yet her lips compressed even further, forcing back a plea for mercy. She wouldn't beg for leniency.

Cole felt something stir deep in his chest even as he instantly denied the emotion. He wasn't feeling sorry for her. He'd have to be a damn fool to feel pity. This one knew what she was about. She was good, better than he'd ever suspected, better than he'd ever known. Even with all his experience, Cole felt out of his league. Somehow he knew no matter how she might suffer, he could never best this woman.

He felt an almost doomed sense of despair. Damn, was there no limit to what she could do to a man? To him in particular?

"Open your eyes, Emy. I'm not going to hit you."

A few seconds ticked by before one eye opened. Emy felt some amazement at his gentle smile. "What the hell am I going to do with you?" he asked, never realizing he spoke the words aloud.

"For one thing, you might listen to me and then let me go."

He chuckled a low sound, finding a good deal of humor in her suggestion. "I've been a fool for long enough," he said as his mouth lowered to hers and Emy, despite her wishes, despite her wants, despite the stiffening of her body knew she couldn't long fight his gentleness. It didn't matter that there was nothing behind his touch, his kiss, his words. Nothing but pure animal instinct, nothing but pure physical need.

Had he been rough, she could have fought him and won. But it was the gentleness she couldn't fight.

212

It was his gentleness she couldn't hope to win out against.

Her hands, stretched over her head, were still bound in his. With one last effort to escape she bucked her hips and used her legs to try to throw him off.

Cole groaned at the delicious feel of her moving beneath him. It didn't matter her reasons, it mattered only that her movements excited him almost to the limit of his control. He adjusted his weight lest she bring to a close all too soon this night of pleasure.

"I'm not going to make it easy," she gasped, for his weight made it less than easy to breathe. "I'm not going to let you . . ."

Cole would never have thought to take a woman, any woman, without her consent. Not until now. Not until this woman. Only he knew it wouldn't be without her consent. Soon now her mouth would soften. Soon her body would as well. Soon they'd both know the delights of each other. "You don't have a choice." And then silently came the most damning, the most terrifying words of all. *And neither do I.*

It was beyond his power to resist that mouth. There was no sense in fighting it. It was evil filled with lies and deception, but he loved the taste, the feel, the warmth he found there as he never had with any other. No, he tried to reason. Not loved. He liked the feel of her mouth. He liked the taste of her, the delicious warmth. There was no room for love here. There never could be.

He was simply going to use her, not in the same

fashion, perhaps, but with much the same intent as she had used him. Emotions were not involved. It meant nothing but the coming together of two bodies. It meant less than nothing.

He felt the soft groan bubble from his throat at contact. Her lips were thin, stiff, and unyielding, but Cole knew her passions would soon win out. He knew she hadn't the strength to fight this longing any more than he. He knew she couldn't long resist.

Cole's lips curved into a smile as he listened to her soft moan of despair. "I hate you," she said even as her lips softened and returned his kiss. Despite the harsh words, the kiss took on a greediness he'd never before known. He almost sighed with relief knowing she was a willing partner in this pleasure.

His mind swam, delighting in the deliciousness of her. Had a woman ever tasted like this? He deepened the kiss, satisfied at her soft whimper of pleasure, delighting further still as her mouth grew wet and hot and then wetter and hotter. Cole, already lost in the scent and feel of her, couldn't think but to have more.

His fingers reached between their bodies and unbuttoned her dress. He released her arms. She gave no resistance, but eagerly helped him ease her dress from her shoulders and down her hips. Her mouth still beneath his, taking and giving of the pleasure, she never thought but to allow her petticoats to follow the garment to the floor. Next her shoes and chemise were discarded, and she leaned up on one arm. Gazes locked, she purposely rubbed her chest against his.

Both moaned in delight as softness brushed

against hard muscle, as smooth silk grazed a hair-covered chest. Eyes held, lost in the feel, the scent, the texture.

His hands moved down the length of her, beneath her drawers. She raised her hips, helping him. Emy watched his eyes. He couldn't, wouldn't look away. Unable to fight his superior strength, or her weakness against his allure, she fought him now in subtle, more devastating ways. She taunted him, silently daring him to take what was offered, to take her without the emotion he swore was dead.

He sucked in a lungful of air, wondering how he was going to find the strength to drag out this moment. His body screamed to take hers, and Cole shuddered at the intensity of that need. He'd never wanted like this, never felt the ache to possess so impossibly strong.

He came from the bed and slid his trousers down his legs. She lay there, propped up on her elbows still, one knee raised, her eyes half closed, the most seductive creature he'd ever seen. For a moment he stood watching as her passionate gaze moved over the length of him. He could see in her eyes the need to touch him. His body trembled, silently begging that she would. He felt his sex stir, harden, thicken, pulse with blood, with the need to bury himself deep inside her warmth.

She reached out and Cole closed his eyes, wondering if he would live through this delicious torment. Her fingers trailed a blazing path up his thigh. Higher, higher. He couldn't breathe. His hips pressed forward in a silent plea, begging for more, begging for the one thing that could destroy him.

And then she touched him and his world exploded into a thousand fragments of shining lights.

Her fingers moved over his erection tentatively, unsure, but moving nonetheless, moving, moving him to madness. He was thicker, harder than he could ever remember. Her finger touched upon the tiny drop of moisture at the tip and spread the dew over the engorged, throbbing flesh. He'd never known pleasure such as this. He'd never imagined anything this good.

With a groan he tore himself from her touch. It couldn't go on lest she bring to a premature end the pleasure he ached to endure.

On the bed again, he knelt between her legs, his upper body supported by unsteady arms. His gaze delighted in the soft, creamy flesh exposed to his view. He couldn't hold back his low moan of pleasure as his mouth took the rosy tip of her breast deep into its heat.

Gently his hands cupped her fullness and brought the sweet globes of perfection together. He ran his beard over her then, smiling as he listened to her cries of delight, sensitizing already exquisitely sensitive flesh.

His tongue flicked out, delighting in the taste and feel of her. "Soft," he murmured against her flesh. "My God, you're so soft."

She arched her back, engulfed in pleasure as he pulled her deeper into the maddening flames. The nails of one hand bit into his shoulder, his back, and she silently urged him on, silently begging that he take what was offered, that he never stop giving in return.

Her heart thundered as his mouth moved down the length of her. She trembled almost violently, unable to fight this. Despite the hatred he felt for her, she knew one thing. She'd wanted for so long, so incredibly long.

Her hips rose from the bed as she awaited the final, most intimate of all acts. Cole's gaze moved over her incredible loveliness. He shook his head, knowing he hadn't the strength to resist this sweet invitation into madness. It might have started as an act of revenge, but it was more than that now. It was more than anything he'd ever known in his life.

The scent of her, the touch of her, assaulted more than his senses. It attacked his heart and Cole hadn't the strength but to allow its sweet invasion.

She became everything in his world. He knew nothing but her taste and feel. He wanted nothing but to love her to eternity.

Cole felt an aching jolt at the last thought and strove to reason it away. It wasn't true. He didn't want her for all time. It was only now that the need raged. After he sampled her charms, after he knew her body at last, he'd do what had to be done. He swore the day would come when he'd forget this night. Like all the others, the day would surely come when he wouldn't remember her name.

Emy groaned and arched her back, eager to feel again the magic of his mouth on her. His lips brushed over her, teasing her to madness as they plucked at the sensitive flesh of her midriff and stomach. Emy's moans turned into low cries, incoherent whimpers that pleaded for him to show her more of this ecstasy.

He was drowning in torment, unable to remember a time when a woman had shown such desperate need. His gaze swept over the length of her, and he found himself unable to resist her allure.

His mouth lowered again, leaving behind the sweet intoxication of one temptation, intent on furthering his discovery. Over her gently rounded belly and down one leg, he watched her response in fascination.

She groaned as his mouth touched the back of her knee, the arch of her foot, sending chills to race up her spine and an ache to grow into unbearable strength somewhere in the pit of her stomach, and then up her leg again to the magic that awaited them both.

Emy felt dazed at the overpowering sensations. How could it be that a man knew so much? How did he imagine the sensitivity of her legs, her feet, when she hadn't known herself?

Closer and closer he came to the heart of her passion. Emy felt her breath close off as her mind screamed for him to hurry, to touch her as no other ever had, to love her this one time as no one would again.

Between clenched teeth she sucked in her breath and then moaned a low sound that spoke of exquisite torment. He was killing her, killing her. He'd once promised her pleasure, but this was so much more.

The ache began in earnest now, now that he moved his tongue over her, now that he spread burning kisses to places she hadn't known existed. He grunted his approval and whispered against the damp flesh of her loveliness. It was her imagination, of course. Nothing could be this good.

But it was. It was better than good. It was good beyond bearing.

Emy groaned again, whimpering sounds of pleasure as the ache grew in strength. What was he doing? What was happening? How did the movement of his tongue cause her an ache that only demanded more?

Her feet came flat upon the bed and she raised her hips to allow his mouth greater access. She fell back upon the bed. Urging him closer, her hands slid into the thickness of his hair and then she raised her head and watched the artistry of his mouth.

Her body tightened, the ache growing out of control, consuming her entire being, and she whimpered for release of a pleasure that bordered on agony even as her hands pressed him closer to her warmth.

"Cole," she gasped as the ache grew to overpowering proportions. It threatened to tear her asunder, and she found herself eager for the pain. "Please. Cole, *mon Dieu.*"

"Easy, darlin'," came his muffled response. "Let it come. Easy."

Emy didn't understand his words, nor would she have known their meaning had they been spoken more clearly. But she did understand the tone. The trouble was, it was far too late for her to take anything easily. Her body ached in its need. He had once shown her the pleasure, but it hadn't been like this. She wanted so desperately, longed to know it all, and only he could help her. Only he, for he alone

219

caused the pain.

Her hands moved to his shoulders, trying at the last minute to push him away. She couldn't take any more. She couldn't and survive.

But Cole knew what she was about. He knew the suffering she endured and wasn't about to witness less than her deepest pleasure.

He felt her stiffen to the breaking point and knew the time had come. Even as his mouth continued its delicious assault, his gaze rose to her face and he watched in fascination as her hands tore at the sheet, her eyes rolled back, and she breathed a near-silent gasp of breath as she greedily accepted the shattering pleasure.

It crashed upon her then, the ripping waves of ecstasy, twisting and churning at her stomach, tightening and then bursting free into almost unbearable sweetness, softening her body, causing a helplessness that could only allow his further mastery.

Cole felt the jolting, squeezing waves of pleasure against his tongue and listened to her softly spoken if slightly incoherent words of bliss. He knew he'd never feel more like a man than when bringing this woman such delight.

He was over her, holding himself above her, entering her body with the greatest tenderness. He closed his eyes against the intensity of the pleasure as her body squeezed around his, drawing from him the last of his will.

Hold on, dammit! Hold on. This is all you'll ever have. Remember this night for always.

Cole listened to the sweet sounds of her enjoyment

as he allowed his body to slide deeper into heaven. She was so incredibly hot and tight. He couldn't imagine anything that might compare. No pleasure like this existed on earth.

And then he felt the obstruction and knew the truth. She was an innocent. Innocent, at least, in the ways of men. God, how could she have done the things she had and remain an innocent? Cole shook his head. He couldn't think about it now. In truth, he didn't care. All that mattered now was that she was his.

Her eyes were glazed, filled with the wonder of these past few minutes. She had no idea that there was more to come. Cole smiled as passion-filled eyes focused again. He couldn't wait to show her the extent of the rapture. He pulled back just a bit and gently lowered himself beyond the obstruction. He felt her body stiffen and saw the flash of pain in her eyes, but his mouth was on hers again. It took only a minute and she began to soften once more, another minute and she began to urge him toward further bliss.

He refused her silent, anxious plea for more, but waited for her body to accept his width, his length, before he began to move. Incredible pleasure. There were no words to describe the sensations as his hands guided her hips into the rhythm. Mindless euphoria tempted, but he resisted its lure for fear he lose the last of his control. He had to bring her completely back, to ride with him to ecstasy. He had to show her the limitless pleasure, for only together would they know its existence.

Cole groaned, forcing aside his need, knowing he

was closer than ever to finding release. He rolled to his back, easily bringing her pliant form with him. Gently he showed her how she could sit. His hands on her hips, he guided her to the rhythm.

Warm hands moved over her lustrous skin, gently cupping swaying flesh, teasing the tips to hardness again, rolling them gently between his fingers to nubs of aching sensation. His hand slid lower even as he kept up the assault, and one dexterous finger slid to where their bodies joined.

Emy started, jumping ever so slightly as his finger touched upon overly sensitive flesh. She wiggled away, but his hands prevented her total escape and merely brought her back to him.

It hurt. No. Yes. She moaned a soft sound and knew it didn't matter, for to know this man's touch was enough to cause her to forget the slight discomfort. And then the discomfort was gone and the need came again. Stronger this time in its intensity, for she knew the promise of what lay ahead. She knew what she wanted.

Cole groaned with the ecstasy, knowing he'd learn every inch of this woman or die from the trying. His thumb rotated the tiny nub of flesh his mouth had gloried upon, and within seconds she was moaning with the pleasure, pressing herself more tightly to him.

It was too much for any mortal to withstand. She could easily imagine dying from pleasure, for pleasure such as this couldn't be meant for earthlings.

"Cole," she groaned as he drove into her, the combination of his moving finger and thrusting body almost too much to bear. "Cole, *mon Dieu. Mon Dieu.*"

She was dizzy, unable to remain upright. "Cole," she groaned again as her head fell back and her long hair grazed his thighs.

He was breathing hard, harder than ever, her whimpers of delight almost lost in the sound of his pounding heart. He couldn't believe the feel of her. God, nothing had ever felt like this. No woman had ever loved like this. He couldn't manage a word of praise, sucked as he was into the sensation of this purest of pleasures, and he knew he couldn't hold back much longer.

"Jesus, God, Emy," he muttered as he rolled her to her back again. It was too late. He couldn't hold back any longer. He had to take her now.

Cole drove hard into her pliant softness, praying his movements would cause her no harm. She was purely delicious. God help him, he couldn't resist. He felt her tightening around him, her body straining forward. Bodies locked together in bliss, their eyes, their hands, their minds, their very souls.

Oh, the feeling. Lord, she had thought the first time to be all she could ever want. But she was wrong. This was beyond imagining.

He sighed with delight. Flesh against flesh, hard against soft, smooth against rough.

He took her body then, took her before her magic could deepen the spell. Took her before he lost what was left of his mind. He heard her cry of delight, heard it even as he tried to block the pleasure. It wasn't this good. Nothing was this good. He'd wanted her for too long. Wanted her almost to obsession. It was only that wanting that made it seem this good.

He felt the tightening of her body squeeze around his swollen sex. Spasms of agonizing release, groans of pleasure, only it wasn't pleasure, it was pain. Pain because it could never be. Pain because he had somehow lost his soul.

He was still gasping for breath as he rolled away from her softness. Cole lay beside her, knowing he lacked the courage to allow their bodies contact. Cole, who had faced down the most hardened criminals, who had killed his wife's murderer with hardly a blink of an eye, almost shivered in fear at the thought of cuddling this fragile woman to his side, for he knew in his heart that this one had the power to ruin him forever. Perhaps she already had.

He wanted her again. He cursed the truth of it, for his body hadn't yet recuperated from the taking and still he ached for more. Idly he wondered how many times his body would have to take hers before it would ease this incredible lust.

Cole frowned as a vague sense of emptiness assailed. Where was the expected euphoria? Where was the peace, the contentment? He'd taken her body, used it, enjoyed it, and yet had found something oddly lacking. Cole shook aside the thought. He wouldn't allow himself to think about it. It didn't matter anyway. He wanted no more from her than release from this all-consuming need.

He heard her sigh and swore he wouldn't reach for her.

"Cole," she said, her gaze holding to the ceiling. Emy lay beside him, unashamed of her nakedness,

MORE PASSION AND ADVENTURE AWAIT... YOUR TRIP TO A BIG ADVENTUROUS WORLD BEGINS WHEN YOU ACCEPT YOUR FIRST 4 NOVELS ABSOLUTELY *FREE* (AN $18.00 VALUE)

Accept your Free gift and start to experience more of the passion and adventure you like in a historical romance novel. Each Zebra novel is filled with proud men, spirited women and tempestuous love that you'll remember long after you turn the last page.

Zebra Historical Romances are the finest novels of their kind. They are written by authors who really know how to weave tales of romance and adventure in the historical settings you love. You'll feel like you've actually gone back in time with the thrilling stories that each Zebra novel offers.

GET YOUR FREE GIFT WITH THE START OF YOUR HOME SUBSCRIPTION

Our readers tell us that these books sell out very fast in book stores and often they miss the newest titles. So Zebra has made arrangements for you to receive the four newest novels published each month.

You'll be guaranteed that you'll never miss a title, and home delivery is so convenient. And to show you just how easy it is to get Zebra Historical Romances, we'll send you your first 4 books absolutely FREE! Our gift to you just for trying our home subscription service.

BIG SAVINGS AND FREE HOME DELIVERY

Each month, you'll receive the four newest titles as soon as they are published. You'll probably receive them even before the bookstores do. What's more, you may preview these exciting novels free for 10 days. If you like them as much as we think you will, just pay the low preferred subscriber's price of just $3.75 each. *You'll save $3.00 each month off the publisher's price.* AND, your savings are even greater because there are never any shipping, handling or other hidden charges—FREE Home Delivery. Of course you can return any shipment within 10 days for full credit, no questions asked. There is no minimum number of books you must buy.

4 FREE BOOKS

TO GET YOUR 4 FREE BOOKS WORTH $18.00 — MAIL IN THE FREE BOOK CERTIFICATE T O D A Y

Fill in the Free Book Certificate below, and we'll send your FREE BOOKS to you as soon as we receive it.

If the certificate is missing below, write to: Zebra Home Subscription Service, Inc., P.O. Box 5214, 120 Brighton Road, Clifton, New Jersey 07015-5214.

FREE BOOK CERTIFICATE

4 FREE BOOKS

ZEBRA HOME SUBSCRIPTION SERVICE, INC.

YES! Please start my subscription to Zebra Historical Romances and send me my first 4 books absolutely FREE. I understand that each month I may preview four new Zebra Historical Romances free for 10 days. If I'm not satisfied with them, I may return the four books within 10 days and owe nothing. Otherwise, I will pay the low preferred subscriber's price of just $3.75 each; a total of $15.00, *a savings off the publisher's price of $3.00.* I may return any shipment and I may cancel this subscription at any time. There is no obligation to buy any shipment and there are no shipping, handling or other hidden charges. Regardless of what I decide, the four free books are mine to keep.

NAME

ADDRESS   APT

CITY   STATE   ZIP

(   )
TELEPHONE

SIGNATURE   (if under 18, parent or guardian must sign)

Terms, offer and prices subject to change without notice. Subscription subject to acceptance by Zebra Books. Zebra Books reserves the right to reject any order or cancel any subscription.

ZB0793

GET
FOUR
FREE
BOOKS
(AN $18.00 VALUE)

ZEBRA HOME SUBSCRIPTION
SERVICE, INC.
120 BRIGHTON ROAD
P.O. Box 5214
CLIFTON, NEW JERSEY 07015-5214

her dazed mind hardly recovered from the trauma, only moments before, suffered in his arms. Still, she knew it was long past time to talk, to explain why. Now, in the quiet aftermath of loving, she had to use this chance to tell him the truth. "Can we talk?"

Cole breathed a long, deliberate sigh meant to relate an absolute indifference he did not feel. "I'm not interested in anything you have to say."

"I'm going to tell you anyway."

He shrugged and then came from the bed and walked to where he had thrown his shirt. Standing there naked, he reached into his pocket and took out the makings of a smoke. He was rolling a cigarette when he spoke again. "I reckon I can't stop you, but you might as well know, I won't believe anything you say."

Emy pressed her lips together and forced back the ridiculous urge to cry. She waited until she was sure her voice wouldn't waver before she began. "Two years in a row the river overflowed its shores and washed out our crops. Except for my sewing, we had nothing.

"Mr. Whitehead refused to extend our mortgage loan. In two weeks the note comes due."

Cole shot her a look that told clearly he was far from impressed at her sad tale. "I wonder how many people have lost their homes and yet remained honest citizens?"

"I didn't say what they did was right. All I'm trying to do is explain why they did it."

Cole's gaze turned harder, and if possible even more condemning. It raked the length of her as if drawn against his will. Cole wondered which of them disgusted him more, her, for her deceit, or him for wanting her despite all she had done. "They? Meaning you had no part in it?"

At his look, Emy realized her nakedness and pulled a sheet from the bottom of the bed to cover herself. "Not until the last. Not until . . . Cole, I begged them to stop, but Father was desperate. Can't you understand? He couldn't see his family be put in the street."

Cole looked at her for a silent moment before he finally shrugged again. "Go on."

Emy couldn't help but take hope. She could only pray her words would matter. "You have to know they were the worst. They never succeeded at robbing anyone."

"They won't serve time for failing or succeeding. They'll go to prison for the attempt."

His eyes held to hers, demanding she speak the truth just this once. "If you weren't with them, why . . ."

"I was terrified that they were going to get killed. So I came up with a plan."

Cole's lips lifted at one corner into a sneer. Another lie. He should have known.

Unable to face his obvious disbelief, Emy lowered her gaze to the sheet and continued as she mindlessly smoothed the fabric across the bed. "They had asked me to join them a number of times, but I always refused."

"How admirable of you."

Emy ignored his sarcasm and went on. "I thought I could put a stop to it if I promised to help. I finally did, on the one condition that no matter the outcome, they would never do it again."

Cole snorted a sound of disbelief.

"They promised. They swore they would give up this life of crime." Emy bit her lip, knowing he was far from convinced. Still, she was determined to try. "I came up with a plan. I would travel on the *Princess* from New Orleans to Baton Rouge. While on board I was supposed to watch for a winner in the card room."

"But you found something a bit more pleasant to occupy your time."

Emy shook her head, her cheeks ablaze with color at his casual reminder of the first of her sins. "I only told them that. I wasn't going to do it, in any case."

"Right," he said, unconvinced.

"The truth of the matter is, I had too much to drink and got caught up in something I was hardly prepared for. I guess I was preoccupied when I left the boat, and when my father asked for a description, I inadvertently described you."

Cole laughed. "Not bad. Not at all bad. It explains some things but hardly excuses them or you for what happened."

"I never said it would. I only wanted to explain the reasons behind what happened."

"All three of you are going to spend a long time behind bars." Cole wondered why the thought brought no pleasure. It should have. After her lies and treachery, he should be delighted at the thought of her spending a good many years in prison.

Emy nodded. She'd known from the first that any explanation on her part would prove fruitless, that this man's sense of right and wrong was resolute, that he had no forgiveness in his soul.

She came from the bed.

"Where do you think you're going?"

"I'm getting dressed." The words were flat, said in absolute calm, and Cole frowned, wondering why she hadn't begged for mercy. Didn't she know he had the power to destroy her? Didn't she know one word from him and the three of them would spend years behind bars? Cole shook his head in wonder, unable to imagine a woman in more control. She might be standing there, wrapped only in a sheet, but she didn't seem to notice the disadvantage. "I may be going to jail, but I won't be going naked."

"You're not finished yet. Tell me about the games you played afterward."

Her gaze snapped to his, her confusion obvious. "After what?"

"After I recuperated from being shot."

"I wasn't playing a game, Cole."

"And you expect me to believe that, of course."

What was the use? He wasn't about to believe a word she said. Her voice hardened. "I don't care what you believe."

"Did you have yourself a good laugh when I proposed? Was it part of the plan to bring me under your spell?"

Emy realized at last the root of his anger. He thought she played him for a fool. The problem was, she didn't have an inkling as to how to persuade him otherwise. "I had no plan but to keep my family out of prison."

"No matter what it took?"

"What do you want me to say? Will it make you

228

feel better to know that I was playing with your affections?"

"Supposing I had any, you mean?"

"I wasn't, Cole." She looked him right in the eye when she said it, and Cole cursed. It was so damn easy to believe her. If he wasn't careful she might . . . Cole shook away the thought. He wouldn't weaken. She was a liar. He wasn't about to forget that. "I knew the day would come when you'd find out. I tried to stay away from you. I couldn't."

"Now you're going to tell me I was irresistible."

"You were."

He laughed in ridicule. "If I'm so irresistible, get back in that bed."

"You've gotten what you wanted from me. It's time to go."

"It's time to go when I say so. And I've hardly begun to get what I want from you."

"Cole"—her dark gaze pleaded with him to end this now—"it won't mean anything."

"It doesn't have to." He threw his cigarette into the commode and walked toward her. She couldn't take her gaze from his body. He was a beautiful man. The sight of his hard, muscled strength brought chills of longing down her spine, but it was his smile, a smile that was hardly more than a sinister curving of his lips that brought the most chills of all. She shivered as she backed up. "My body wants yours. Right now, that's all that matters.

"You were good. Really good." He nodded in agreement at the thought. "Those shy looks were perfection. And the prayers before the saint, when you lit the candle every day, an exquisite performance." He backed her toward the bed. "My body screamed for yours, but I wouldn't take you." He grunted a short, humorless laugh. "You were a lady, a very moral lady, and no matter how I suffered, I vowed to wait." Cole laughed again in self-disgust. "God, a man can really be stupid where a woman is concerned." He yanked the sheet from around her and dropped it to the floor. His hands moved to her throat and exerted just enough pressure to bring her gaze to his. "Did you laugh at my stupidity, Emy? Did you and your grandmère and Kit, another little bitch, did you laugh good and hard?"

There was nothing she could say, nothing he would believe.

He grunted in satisfaction at her refusal to respond. "I hope so, 'cause it might be your last laugh for a very long time."

He cared for her. He might not love her, but he cared, or he wouldn't be half so angry. She hadn't deceived him when it came to their relationship. The truth was, she was as close to loving him as she was ever likely to get. But if she told him the truth of her feelings, he'd only accuse her of yet another lie. There was no way to soften his heart and no way that she was going to allow further abuse without a fight.

"No, I didn't laugh." Her dark gaze clung to his even as she struggled to free herself from his arms. "I didn't laugh, because you weren't any more stupid than I was. We wanted each other. I wanted everything you could give me . . . do to me. But it doesn't make it right. It makes us, both of us, no better than beasts."

Cole cursed as he crushed her against him. She was like some dark death he couldn't escape. He wanted her like he'd never wanted a woman in his life. She was poison and he knew it, but knowing it didn't stop the wanting.

"It doesn't matter."

"It does. It does matter."

"Tell me you don't want this."

He couldn't hold back the need. He couldn't stop, or deny the insanity that invaded his soul. Not when his body touched on the heat of hers.

His hand reached between her legs, splaying the moist flesh there. A low groan, a groan that bordered on torture, slid from her throat as his mouth touched upon hers. It shouldn't be this easy. She hated herself for the weakness. All that was needed was a touch, a smile, a look, and that prim-and-proper miss turned into an immoral creature, someone she couldn't recognize.

Of course he wouldn't believe her. How could he believe her when she said one thing and did quite another? Only it was too late to worry about believing or not. She couldn't fight her body's reaction to this man's touch, to his kisses.

Under his spell, ruled only by passion and the need he had created, she raised her hands to his face and cupped his cheeks. Lord, but his beard felt luscious and soft against her skin. She hadn't imagined a man could use a beard in the exquisite ways he had. She hadn't imagined the feel of it over her entire body and what it would do to her mind. God help her, she wanted to feel it again.

Cole frowned almost as if in pain as her mouth

moved beneath his. He couldn't remember that she had ever kissed him before. He would have remembered, he was sure. She hadn't ever kissed him before. Returned his kisses, yes, but not this, never this.

Cole felt his strength ebb slowly away. He was a fool and there was nothing he could do about it except mindlessly beg for further hurt. He loved her. Damn his soul to hell, he loved her. Even knowing what she was, and that if given the chance she'd destroy him, he loved her.

Still the memory lingered of their times together. Of the sweet playful innocence. She had been a virgin then; now he knew that for a fact. Maybe some of what she said was true. Maybe he could work something out. Maybe he could . . . Cole forgot his thoughts as her mouth, her deliciously sweet mouth, ravaged his. And then she pulled away and her lips, those soft, luscious lips, slid down the length of his throat and over his chest. His eyelids fluttered closed. Weak and as helpless as a newborn, he stood in place and allowed her loving. He knew she didn't love him, but it felt like loving. God, but it did.

His knees felt about as strong as jam, but through sheer force of will he managed to hold himself from crumpling to the floor. Her hands . . . oh, God, her hands. She was driving him mad with her gentle touch, her sweet, inquisitive touch. He'd never known it could be like this. Even with a wife he had adored, it hadn't been like this.

Her mouth lowered and his heart threatened to explode. Did she know what she was doing?

He couldn't stand. Knowing he was bound to

232

break the mood, he couldn't stop his body from nearly falling upon the bed. But the movement didn't stop her. Cole could only groan with pleasure as her mouth came to him again and continued down his body.

Down his chest, over his belly, and lower still. His heart was thunder. Cole thought he would surely die. His body had never felt so hard, so tight, so sensitive to every sensation. He was on fire. The heat of her mouth burned a path of torture down the length of him. He groaned at the hot, delicious wetness of her darting tongue.

His breath got caught in his throat as her lips tentatively grazed his erection, kissing him ever so gently, driving him beyond madness. He must have made a sound, for she pulled instantly away. Her dark eyes were wide and filled with concern as she asked, "Did I hurt you?"

Cole's eyes met hers, and at that moment there was no doubt in his mind that she hadn't an inkling of a man's needs. Cole knew no matter what she was, no matter how he might suffer for it, there was nothing he wouldn't do for her, nothing.

Chapter Twelve

"Get dressed," Cole said as he rolled from the bed. Again he hadn't cuddled her against him. Again he hadn't dared, lest he lose himself forever to her magic.

Emy moaned and snuggled her face into the pillow. Lord, had she ever known this degree of exhaustion? She couldn't imagine moving from the bed, never mind getting dressed. Not today, not tomorrow. Perhaps not even next . . .

Impatient with her lack of response, Cole shook her shoulder.

"I can't," she moaned sleepily. What was the matter with him now? Why couldn't the vile beast leave her alone? All she wanted was to sleep. "I'm too tired."

"If you want me to carry you, just say so."

"Where?" Emy wondered why she bothered to ask. They both knew she was going to jail. What was the hurry? "God," came a muffled groan, "can't you let me sleep for a minute?"

"No. Get up."

Emy blinked open one eye. There wasn't a soul on earth she hated more than this fiend. Her top lip curled into a sneer as flashing pictures of the last hour came to haunt her. The monster had forced her to admit aloud that she loved the things she was doing, that she loved the things he was doing. She hated him more than anything.

From the corner of her eye she saw movement. She lay perfectly still. She wouldn't look at him, wouldn't acknowledge his presence, wouldn't watch his knowing grin. The madman was getting dressed. Thank God. Apparently sated, he was eager to cart her off to jail. She didn't care. All she wanted was that he never touch her again.

Her head was turned toward the far wall. Cole watched her for a moment before he came to the only decision possible. He wouldn't be sending this woman to prison. To do so would only cause untold suffering. His, most of all. There wasn't a doubt in his mind that he'd forever be haunted by those huge, dark eyes, by the remembered whispers in the night, by her sweetly hesitant and yet somehow eager touchings. The damn woman had ruined him for any other. He wanted to curse her for that, and would have but for the knowledge that he'd done as much.

After this night, both of them would always compare, and find others to be lacking. Except she wasn't going to get the chance. His eyes narrowed and his mouth tightened into a thin line at the thought of her with another. She was going to be his wife, and he'd kill any man who dared to touch her.

Cole shrugged aside the intensity of his thoughts.

He couldn't feel so much so soon. It wasn't possible, especially not with knowing her for what she was. Besides, he was marrying her only so he could watch both her and her family. After the wedding it would be easier to make sure all of them lived according to the law. Cole almost laughed aloud, for his sorry excuses were bound to fool no one, least of all himself. He knew why he was doing this. Even though the marriage would surely deepen his suffering, he couldn't leave things as they were. He had to have her, to keep her with him always. Only he didn't have to tell her why. He didn't have to give anyone a reason. To say he wanted her was enough.

"I would have thought that you'd be excited."

Emy's smooth brow furrowed into a frown. She groaned again as she rolled to her side, her back to him. "About what?"

"About getting married."

She gave a lusty yawn. "Who's getting married?"

"Us."

Emy almost strangled on a laugh. "Us? As in you and me?" The thought of living with this beast gave her a surge of energy. She came to a sitting position, careful to hold the sheet against her body. Only she didn't notice how the material hugged her lush curves.

Cole wished he hadn't noticed either. He should feel drained, knowing only a deep sense of satisfaction, but one look at this woman and he felt again the familiar stirrings of lust. He recognized the weakness in himself and cursed her for the temptress she was. His voice was hard when he asked, "Something funny?"

She shot him a look that might have cowed a lesser man. "Marry a beast like you? I'd die first."

It was Cole's turn to laugh. The sound might have been a bit less than merry, his eyes hard with hurt, but Emy never noticed. Cole would have gladly suffered the ravages of hell before admitting to the gnawing pain somewhere in his chest. "You might hate me, sweetheart, but no more than I hate you." It was an out-and-out lie, but she didn't have to know it. Cole vowed she'd never know the power she held over him.

"If you hate me, then why . . . ?"

"We like well enough what we do to each other in bed."

He was vile. No other word fit quite so perfectly. He was an odious fiend who cared only for his own wants. She shot his grin a dark look that told clearly her thoughts. "We don't have to marry for that. Besides, there are others who, better than I, can satisfy your lust."

"Fact is, darlin', at the moment I don't want another, and we do have to marry for that. I can't very well get what I want from you if you're in prison."

At the moment? Did that mean his wants were likely to change in the near future? Emy could only pray it was so. She longed for the day when she'd see the last of him. Then why did those words bring a dull ache to her chest? She was upset. And who wouldn't be upset after the night she'd just experienced? The man didn't have the power to hurt her. She shot him a look of loathing. "You are disgusting."

He shrugged, apparently not concerned with her opinion. "Probably, but it's either marry or go to jail. You choose."

"I won't do it."

"I think you will." He pulled his watch from his jacket pocket and checked the time. "You will, or find yourself behind bars before this night is through."

Her laugh was pure defiance. "You can't blackmail me. Faced with the choice, I'd like nothing better than to go to jail. Anything rather than marry you."

"Maybe, but what about your family?"

"What about them? You've already made up your mind to—"

"Actually, I haven't."

Emy came to her knees and impatiently shoved her long, dark hair from her face. The sheet gathered between her legs. She held it firmly against her nakedness. It almost covered her. Cole couldn't take his eyes from the seductive sight. She was breathtaking, all warm and mussed, her skin glowing pink from being well loved. Her hair was a mass of unruly curls falling down her back and over one shoulder. She was the most delicious woman he'd ever known. He wondered if the day would ever come when he'd have enough of her.

"What does that mean?"

"Exactly what I said."

She shrugged and then snapped, "Which is nothing."

"Which is"—he hesitated for a meaningful moment before finishing with a wicked smile—"I'm open to suggestions."

Emy knew well enough at what he hinted. His sly innuendos only confirmed the lascivious glitter in his eyes. He leaned against the bedpost, his arms folded across his chest, waiting for her to whore for him. No matter that they had spent the last two hours in this bed, the truth was, she hadn't been able to resist the pleasure in his arms. Still, she'd die before she deliberately used her body for gain. "You're lower than dirt."

Cole laughed at the insult. "Which is what? A step higher than you?"

"Drop dead."

"Sweetheart, I'd love nothing better than to stand here trading insults, but I figure you're almost out of time."

"I've made my decision," she said stubbornly.

"Fine. Let's hope you won't be sorry."

"I won't be." Emy swore she'd rather rot in jail for the rest of her life than ever see this animal again.

"What's the number of your grandmother's room?" Cole was already aware of the room number. It had been the first place he'd looked for her last night.

Emy's gaze snapped to his. "Why?"

"While you're getting dressed, I could take care of business."

"What kind of business?"

"Arresting her and your sister."

Emy's mouth dropped open with shock. "You can't be serious!"

The fact of the matter was, Cole was going to have this woman with or without her agreement, and if

239

that meant using any means necessary, so be it. Of course, his threat was an empty one. He knew the old lady wasn't involved in her family's criminal activities. He knew as well that this was one way, perhaps the only way, to get Emy to see to his way of thinking.

"She's part of your family, isn't she? Far as I can tell, that makes her just as guilty as the rest of you."

"But she's not. I swear she's not."

Cole shrugged, and Emy knew a crushing sense of defeat. This man wouldn't be satisfied until he saw her grovel. Well, for her grandmother she would. She'd do that and more.

"Cole, please listen. I deserve to be punished. But she doesn't. She's good. She never hurt anyone. Not once in her whole life."

Cole wasn't about to make this easy for her. She had to give in. There was no other way except that he win. Except that they both win. "You should have thought of that before."

Her gaze fell upon the gun belt hanging on the bedpost. She muttered something in French as she dropped the sheet and lunged for it. But Cole saw the direction of her gaze and in an instant knew her intent. He was on her in a heartbeat.

Her teeth clenched together in frustrated rage as he easily wrestled the gun from her grasp and then pushed her back upon the bed. He threw the gun into the chair across the room and held her in place with the weight of his body. Her arms were trapped between them. She was totally helpless and knew it. The knowledge only caused her to hate him all the more. "I never believed it possible to hate someone quite so much."

"Maybe, but I reckon it don't matter what either of us feels."

"It matters only that you find a receptacle for your lust," she taunted him.

"I already found her."

If Emy had any doubts, his last words assured her of his total disregard. She could only wonder why it was so important that he use her body. Surely there were other women, others far more agreeable. "I'll hate you forever for this."

"As long as you warm my bed, you can hate me all you want." Cole silently congratulated himself on the lie. He wondered if the day would ever come when he could tell her his feelings.

His mouth hovered above hers and he seemed to give some careful consideration to sampling those sweet lips again. Suddenly he apparently thought better of the notion. Emy silently cursed as she watched him leave the bed. She was happy that he hadn't kissed her again, wasn't she? Then why was she suffering this absurd sense of dissatisfaction?

She sat up, not caring that she was naked to his view. "What do you want me to do?"

Cole almost said, *Love me.* Damn, but he had to guard himself against this one. She was the most dangerous woman he'd ever known. Their relationship promised to be a constant battle, one that assured equal pain with every moment of bliss, but he couldn't give in. He couldn't ever let her go. "For now, I want you to get dressed. We'll talk about the rest later."

Emy mumbled a few words barely beneath her

breath. She hated him. God, how she hated him. "I should have let you die."

Cole laughed again as he sat in a chair and enjoyed the luxury of watching her. She slid her legs into her drawers and glared at his obvious pleasure. "Turn around."

She stood there, naked to her waist. "As your husband, I'll have the right to do more than just look."

"You're not my husband yet."

Cole made no move to do as she asked, so she turned instead. She reached for her shift and was just about to pull it over her head when he was suddenly behind her, his hands sliding around her and pulling her to lean back against his chest.

Gently he played with the soft, adored flesh as he nuzzled his face into the sweet warmth of her neck. "We should make a pact, I think."

Her heartbeat accelerated. Was he giving her an out? Could she somehow convince him to see to the error of his ways? "What kind?"

"That you won't ever hide your body from me."

Emy wanted to scratch his eyes out. The man only had to touch her to set her body on fire. What was the matter with her? She hated him as she had no other. How could it be that she loved his hands on her? "A pact is usually two-sided. What do I get in return?"

"Me." He laughed as he felt her stiffen.

"Oh-la, you."

"And anything you want to do to me."

"Not anything, surely."

Cole chuckled a deep, delicious sound as he

cupped her soft flesh and felt the pink tips grow hard. He couldn't remember a woman ever this responsive, this passionate. "Anything, except murder."

Her sarcasm was obvious even if her voice was a bit breathless. "I'm not sure I could stand the joy of it."

He released her seconds before she would have made a total fool of herself, and turned in his arms. Thank God. Instantly she pulled the shift over her head.

Emy had no intention of marrying him. Somehow, some way, she was going to escape his evil clutches and take her grandmother from harm's way. Emy was buttoning the bodice of her dress as she remarked, "Why do we have to get married? Surely we could be together and not say the words."

Cole grinned again. "Marrying you will guarantee that I won't be able to testify."

"Against me. But what about my father and brother? Do you honestly think I could marry and then stay with the very man who sends them to prison?"

"They won't be going to prison. All of us are leaving Baton Rouge. In New Orleans I'll be able to keep a close eye on them. And they had better not—" He shook his head, his mouth tight with barely controlled anger. "If you know what's good for you, you'll make sure of it."

"What do you mean, you don't know where she is?" The panic in Emy's voice was more than apparent, and Cole felt an ache of compassion grow to life in his chest.

"I mean, I went out for only a minute. When I got back, she was gone."

"When did you get back?"

"About an hour ago."

It was nine o'clock in the morning and she just got back an hour ago? Emy shuddered, only too aware of what the girl had been up to all night. She moaned and then felt the comforting warmth of her husband's arms come around her as she was cradled gently against him.

"Don't worry, sweetheart. We'll find her."

Emy made a soft sound of despair. Her grandmother had disappeared before, but those times had been on their farm. Emy had always found her, of course. Sometimes she had been in the barn, others strolling through the woods that surrounded their farm, and still others sitting at her husband's grave, talking to him as if he were truly there. The last time had been the most frightening, but Cole had found her. Yes, she had disappeared before, but never had she been lost in a city.

She shuddered at the thought. Anything could happen to an old lady wandering the streets alone. She could be run down by accident. She could be robbed and murdered and her body dumped into an alley.

God only knew how long she'd been out there, and she was so old. It had rained last night. Had she remembered or even thought to find shelter? Or was she even now suffering the beginnings of a fever? Emy murmured a prayer that they find her soon and that they find her well.

She held to no real hope that it would be so.

"I promise," he whispered for his wife's ears alone, and then shot his new sister-in-law a look that had cowed more than one brave man. "Stay here. If I find out that you left this room, you'll be sorrier than you can imagine."

Kit knew better than to disobey. She might have shot his departing back a defiant glare, but she sat herself upon the bed, knowing she'd stay right there until told to leave. There was no way that she was going to argue over his right to tell her anything, not a man that angry.

Emy was almost beside herself with worry. No matter Cole's attempts to calm her, the panic she knew could not be repressed. She couldn't control the rising panic and felt as close to hysteria as she was ever likely to come. "Oh, Cole, where is she?" she asked for the dozenth time as they came out of one alley and down another.

"We'll find her, Emy. Don't worry so. I promise we will."

They had been looking for more than two hours before Emy saw her. She almost swooned with relief at the sight of her sitting unharmed upon a chair outside the general store.

"Thank God," she murmured. She leaned into Cole's strength as his arm came around her waist. She'd never known such debilitating weakness, such relief, and it took a moment before she was able to calm herself enough to simply stand on her own feet.

"Grandmère," she said gently as they came to

stand before the exhausted woman, "where have you been?"

"I've been looking for my shoes, Emy. Did you find them?"

Cole glanced at the bottom of her long skirt and frowned. What did she mean? Her shoes were on her feet.

"No, sweetheart." Emy couldn't get her heart to stop pounding. Now that she'd finally found her, she felt none of the relief she should have known. The woman had been outside for a good part of the night. Outside and alone. Had that affected more than her body? Might it have added to the confusion in her mind as well? Her eyes misted at the fear she knew. Her grandmother had always been a bit forgetful. Perhaps more so lately. Had she, because of last night worsened? Emy could only pray not. "Are you hungry, dear?"

"A little, but I have to find my shoes."

Emy turned to Cole and explained in a very soft voice, "She's confused. She's not used to being away from home. Help me get her back to the room?"

Cole nodded as he helped the woman to her feet.

"Are we going to get them, Emy?"

"Yes, dear. Your shoes are in your room."

"What are you going to tell your father?"

They were in her kitchen. Emy had left both her grandmother and Kit in the city, under the watchful if temporary care of Mrs. Simmons, the lady who owned a boardinghouse a block from the center of town. She was measuring coffee into a pot as they waited for her father and brother's return. Emy had thought she would find them already at home. Apparently it had taken them longer than she expected to walk the ten miles or so from the city.

"About marrying you?"

He nodded.

"I'll think of something."

"How about the truth? It would be a novelty for this family, don't you think?"

Emy shot him a look of aggravation. "I'm not going to tell him that I was forced into marrying you."

"Why not? He should know what his actions brought about."

"Because he'll probably kill you."

Cole grinned, not in the least worried at the possibility. "And make you a grieving widow so soon?"

She ignored his comment. "And then he'd hang for murder."

Cole smiled. He wasn't sure why. All he knew was that he'd been smiling ever since they had stood before the judge.

Emy shot him another nasty look. "Do you find something particularly amusing?"

"No. Why?"

She stated the obvious. "You're laughing." *And why wouldn't he laugh, Emy? The man has managed to get everything he wanted. Especially everything he's wanted from you.*

"I wasn't laughing. I was smiling. It just so happens that I'm a happy fellow."

Emy's lower lip twisted at one corner with disbelief. "Odd, but I never noticed you particularly happy before."

"Didn't you? I wonder how you could have missed it."

Emy's sigh held a touch of despair as she brushed an errant curl from her cheek. "How indeed?"

"I'll have it annulled." They were standing in her kitchen, her father's face almost purple with rage. Jacques knew the moment he entered the house that Emy's efforts had been for nought. All was lost. Hadn't he awakened last night in the cell with this very man looming over him?

"It's too late for annulments," Cole returned, his voice equally as hard as his father-in-law's.

Emy knew it wasn't. She and Cole had not returned to his room after the words spoken at the crack of dawn before the sleepy judge. They had gone instead into the hotel's restaurant and oddly enough enjoyed a different kind of intimacy over a long, leisurely breakfast. It was after breakfast that she'd gone to check on her grandmother. They had not as yet consummated the marriage. Emy figured it was best to keep that information to herself.

Jacques was no fool. He knew the reason behind the marriage, or thought he did. The thought that his daughter would sacrifice her happiness for her family's safety was a bit more than any father could take. "I'm the one who shot you," he confessed. "Emy didn't have anything to do with it."

Cole shook his head. "I know you shot me. As far as Emy not having anything to do with it . . ." He shrugged, his doubts apparent. "Well, it hardly matters, since she's my wife." He shot the smaller man a long, hard look, daring him to disagree as he declared, "And she's going to stay my wife for as long as I live."

Emy's gaze moved to her husband. Cole couldn't hold back his grin at her thoughtful look. His tender gaze sent a shiver up her spine as he promised, "And I expect to live for a very long time."

Cole knew a moment's surprise as Emy turned into his arms. His gaze was filled with laughter as she whispered for his ears alone, "No doubt, just to spite me."

Jacques's dark eyes narrowed as he watched the two. Unable to hold back his suspicions, he blurted out, "She's a good girl."

Cole felt Emy stiffen at his side, heard her stifled moan. "Papa, don't," she said in French, her face coloring in embarrassment.

"Did you tell him that?" Jacques asked angrily. "Did he listen?"

Cole answered for his wife, hoping to spare her any further embarrassment. "If she wasn't a good girl, I never would have married her."

Emy wondered how much, if any, of that statement was true. He didn't seem to particularly favor goodness once he had her in bed. As a matter of fact, he seemed to like it when she was as far from good as possible.

"You were married, *oui,* but not in the eyes of God."

"According to the law."

"It means nothing," he said.

"It means you'll stay out of jail," Emy snarled, suddenly having her fill of this conversation. She felt it was just a bit much that her father should suddenly grow so protective. He hadn't seemed to mind putting her in danger in the first place. Lord, but she'd had quite enough of men and their inconsistencies.

"What do you mean?"

"I mean Cole has promised neither you nor Anton will go to prison."

"Is that why you married him?"

Emy realized she had touched upon pride here. She felt Cole's fingers bite into her waist in warning. "No. It's not why I married him."

"You love him, then?" Being French, Jacques believed much could be forgiven in the name of love.

Emy nodded. "I love him, Papa."

He sighed, apparently satisfied with her answer. "I would have liked to see my daughter married," Jacques said in a great rush of disappointment.

Emy figured his anger was due mostly to stubborn pride at not being consulted. She soothed hurt feelings with "When we marry in the church."

Jacques grunted and accepted what could not be changed. He kissed his daughter, wishing her happiness.

"We'll be leaving for New Orleans in a day or so."

Jacques nodded, looking suddenly and terribly saddened. His gaze took in his neat little home. Nothing had worked out the way he'd hoped. He'd lost his home and his daughter as well. How could he care for his youngest and Grandmère without his one sensible daughter? "I will miss you, *chérie.*"

"No, you won't," Cole countered. "You're coming to New Orleans with us."

"But—"

"There are rooms over the carriage house. I reckon you'll be comfortable there."

Emy glanced at her husband, her look filled with tender gratitude. Cole silently cursed the fact that one look could nearly steal his ability to breathe.

Jacques laughed at the unbelievably good news. Not only had he and his son been saved from prison, his family would not be put into the street after all. He couldn't have felt more fortunate and wished all manner of blessings upon his new son-in-law. A moment later he left the kitchen to find Anton and tell him the news.

Emy began to gather the kitchen things together when Cole asked, "When is that going to be?"

Emy glanced in his direction, her dark gaze filled with supposed confusion, for she knew full well what her husband spoke of. "When is what going to be?"

"When are we going to marry in the church?"

She smiled her sweetest smile, fluttered her lashes, and then said, "Never."

Cole grinned, forcing aside the need to kiss that sassy mouth. They'd been married only one day. Cole figured he should give himself some time. He was sure this startling rush of emotion would soon wear off. At least he hoped to hell it would. "Why?"

"Because that marriage would mean forever."

"And this one doesn't?"

"There's a trunk in the barn. Would you bring it in? I'd like to pack some linens."

251

"And this one doesn't?" he repeated, insisting on an answer.

"What do you think?"

"You told your father you loved me."

"I lied."

Cole narrowed his gaze as he silently promised himself the day wasn't far off when he'd hear her say the words and mean them. "But you love the things I do to you."

She shot him a look of shock that he would dare to say such a thing. Suppose her father or Anton had walked in? Her cheeks grew warm with color. "The days are longer than the nights."

"Meaning sex is only a small part of loving?"

Her voice was little more than a whisper. "Meaning sex is sex. It hasn't got anything to do with love."

Cole turned her to face him, his arms draped loosely around her waist. He wasn't unaware of the fact that he didn't have to force her to lean against him. "The best sex does."

Her hands came to his shoulders and she smoothed his shirt in an absentminded and, Cole thought, very wifely fashion. "Then you'll have to settle for second best."

He smiled at her remark and released her. "The trunk's in the barn?" he asked, and watched her answering nod. Cole was standing at the door when he casually delivered the most confusing comment of all. "You might as well know, Emy," he said, his dark eyes glittering with what looked like determination. "I never settle for anything."

Their eyes held for a moment before he turned

away. Emy didn't answer him. She couldn't think of a thing to say. All she could do was wonder what in the world he meant.

"My wife, Emeline Brackston."

"Ma'am." Jeremiah Hawk smiled, a brilliant flash of straight white teeth against dark skin, and offered his hand as he acknowledged the introduction. A moment later he accepted Cole's invitation and settled himself at the restaurant's table.

Emy's whole family was present for a late dinner, in celebration of this morning's wedding.

Emy's dark eyes widened. Cole's deputy was obviously a full-blood Indian. His skin was the color of deep bronze. His hair was straight and almost blue-black. His eyes were darker than pitch. With high cheekbones and thin lips, Emy thought he was one of the most startlingly handsome men she'd ever seen. Emy glanced at her sister and nearly groaned aloud.

Kit couldn't take her eyes off him and, Lord, that could only mean trouble.

Emy shot Cole a plea for help, but Cole only knew a sense of relief that someone else had become the center of the girl's attention. He squeezed his wife's hand, silently assuring her there was nothing to worry about.

Jeremiah was a good fifteen years older than Kit and a man who knew how to take care of himself. It didn't matter that the little hussy would try to seduce him. Jeremiah was a man of honor and wouldn't be swayed.

Two hours later, from the corner of her eye, Emy watched Cole come from the tub and after drying himself quickly, wrap the towel around his waist. She, too, had bathed. She had only just pulled her nightdress over her head when Cole had entered the room. Thankfully, she had been allowed a few moments of privacy while Cole spoke with his deputy.

Normally Cole wouldn't have bothered with a towel, but he knew, even though she tried to hide it, that his wife was watching his every movement. He figured he wouldn't shock her unduly. He almost chuckled aloud at the thought. At least not on their wedding night. His back to her, he lathered his face before a mirror, a straight razor on the dry sink, ready to dispose of his beard.

For just a second the picture of his bearded face moving over her body came to mind. Emy wondered at the oddity that she should feel regret that he was shaving it off, and then ridiculed the notion that she should feel anything at all. What did she care if he shaved or not? What difference could it possibly make to her?

Her gaze moved over the length of him. Above the towel she watched the muscles of his back shift with every movement of his arms. Odd that she should feel such admiration for a man's body. Before tonight, no, before meeting this man, she hadn't thought there was anything pleasing about a man's body. She shook her head at the thought. Ridiculous. It wasn't admiration she felt at all. She simply wasn't used to seeing a man nearly naked. What normal woman wouldn't look? What normal woman wouldn't feel this slight catch of breath in her throat?

"Cole."

"What?" he returned as he rinsed his hands free of soap.

"Did you notice, at dinner, the way Kit looked at Mr. Hawk?" Emy bit her lip, obviously embarrassed at her sister's total disregard of propriety.

"Why doesn't your father do something?"

"My father cannot see Kit's faults. Kit is his baby. In his eyes she can do no wrong."

Cole only snorted for an answer.

"I . . . I was wondering if you could . . ." She bit her lip again.

Cole knew well enough what his wife was about. "Emy, it's best, I think, if I don't get involved. Jeremiah won't take kindly to my interference."

"She's not a bad girl, Cole."

Cole, having had to warn the girl away more than once, figured he knew better, but decided to keep those facts to himself.

"She's a bit wild, but she's not bad."

"If she were my daughter, her . . ." He took a deep breath as he restructured the wording. "Let's just say she wouldn't be able to sit for a month."

He came to her, the tenderness he felt obvious in a gentle smile as he sat at her side. He took her hand in his. "Perhaps I could warn Jeremiah." Cole felt a jolt of surprise at his reaction to her smile. His heart thundered in his chest even as an ache grew to life, an ache of longing that she should always look at him thus. God, but she was the loveliest creature. "Promise me, Emy, when we have a daughter . . ."

Emy gasped at the thought. Her eyes widened in shock. A daughter? God, what was the matter with her? Why hadn't she thought of that?

Cole chuckled softly at her obvious surprise. "You do realize that it's possible, even probable, after what we did last night?"

Her cheeks colored, and she couldn't meet his smiling eyes. "I hadn't thought about it."

"It's a good thing we didn't get that far the first time." Cole didn't take kindly to the thought that she could have found herself in a family way and unmarried. He didn't want to think of the heartache and shame she'd likely have known.

Emy didn't respond. Except for the color staining her cheeks, Cole would have thought she hadn't heard. "Being pregnant and unmarried would have . . ."

The word *pregnant* was hardly used in polite society. Hearing it spoken now didn't go far toward making Emy feel comfortable. She cut him off with, "Lord, do we have to talk about this?"

"About what? Having babies?"

"Oui. About babies."

"Don't you want them?"

She shrugged. "I haven't given it any thought."

His eyes grew hard, his voice harder still at what he saw as further rejection. "What you mean is, babies will tie you to me, and you don't want that."

"Can you blame me?" she shot back. "I didn't want this marriage."

Cole remembered her stiff, obviously unwilling

responses that morning as they stood before the judge. He knew well her reluctance. His mouth tightened with displeasure even as he wondered why her wants should matter. The truth of it was, they didn't matter. All that mattered was that this woman should belong to him. His voice was low, heavy with irritation as he remarked, "So you've said, a number of times, in fact. Still, there is a definite possibility that you're already pregnant."

A low moan of horror escaped her throat. Not at the thought of having a baby so much as actually saying so unsavory a word. There was no way she could talk about this. It didn't matter if the man was her husband or not. She simply couldn't.

Cole, realizing her discomfort, gentled his tone even as he reached for a heavy lock of her hair and watched as it curled around his finger. "Do you truly hate the idea, Emy?"

That was better, at least. She could answer a question as simple as that. She shook her head. "No."

Cole wondered at the conflicting emotions that assailed him. Just looking at this woman could bring about a rush of tenderness, but that tenderness was marred with grave distrust. She appeared so innocent and yet he knew firsthand the depth of her passion and, more important, her deceit. How could one woman be so complicated? Over the years he'd known many, but he'd always been able to categorize them into good and bad. A man married a good woman even if he might long for the bad. Impossible though it may be, this woman appeared to be both. And the thought left him more than a little confused.

Cole shrugged aside the emotion. It was best, he thought, not to dwell too long on what made this woman so different from the rest. What he had to do was never forget the things she'd done. To do so would make him double the fool. To do so might even see him pulled under her magical spell. To do so might, in the end, jeopardize his heart.

No. Cole sighed as he came to his feet and returned to his shaving. He might love her, but she'd never know it. She wasn't to be trusted. He couldn't allow himself the luxury, the weakness. He couldn't ever allow it.

Chapter Thirteen

Emy sighed as the last of their belongings were loaded onto the wagon. Everything from beds, a rocking chair, mattresses, and pillows to a few farm tools, pots, linens, and seedlings were packed and ready for the long drive to New Orleans. Emy scowled at her sister. Had she ever known anyone half so selfish? The girl was just about bubbling with joy, unconcerned at the loss her family suffered.

Her father could hardly talk as he fought to control the need to cry. Anton looked dazed, as if in shock, and her grandmère, so overwhelmed at the thought of leaving the only home she'd ever known, had grown more confused than ever. Somehow the old woman had successfully put the whole matter from her mind and had come up with the notion that they were traveling to meet her husband. And there stood Kit, unable to contain her excitement at the thought of living in a big city. Nothing else meant half so much to her.

Emy wished for the hundredth time that Kit were

married, for it was indeed plausible that she'd never know a minute's peace with this girl let loose upon a poor, unsuspecting city.

Moments before the wagon was due to pull out, Kit and Emy looked through the empty rooms, making sure nothing was left behind. Kit whined for perhaps the dozenth time, "Emy, I don't want to go with Father. The trip is bound to take days, and I'll be a mess when we get into New Orleans."

Cole had been wonderful in suggesting that Grandmère take the paddle steamer, knowing the trip to New Orleans by wagon would unduly tax the old woman's strength. Anton would be accompanying her. The two of them would be staying in Baton Rouge for an extra day, ensuring that their arrival in New Orleans would coincide with the rest of the family's. Emy wasn't about to ask more than that of him. She shot her sister a look of disgust. "And the city will be eagerly awaiting your arrival, I'm sure."

"Why can't I take the steamer?" came a childish whine.

"You can if you have the fare."

Cole smiled as he stepped inside. His wife and sister-in-law were talking in the bedroom. The door had been left open. Neither realized their conversation could be easily overheard. And, because they spoke in English, just as easily understood.

"I'll ask Cole for the money."

"You'll do no such a thing." Emy would have had to be blind to have missed the determination in her sister's eyes. "Kit, I swear, if you . . ."

"God, Emy," Kit said in exasperation, "one would have imagined that getting married would have put you in a better frame of mind. Spending the night in Cole's bed would have done a lot for my sense of humor."

Cole shook his head, decidedly unhappy at the girl's bawdy comment. It seemed he was a bit premature in his conviction that since meeting Hawk, Kit might have redirected her attentions. He turned, about to leave the house, when the sound of a slap stopped him.

Emy felt her cheeks grow warm as she was reminded of last night's loving, warmer still as she realized her sister was thinking about the things she and Cole had done. It was almost an invasion of privacy, an invasion Emy would never allow. She hardly gave it a moment's thought before her hand swung out and slapped her sister's face.

"Ow!" Kit's eyes widened with surprise. This was the first time in her life she'd ever been hit. She couldn't believe anyone had actually struck her. Huge tears came to startled eyes, ready with her next blink to roll over smooth cheeks.

The pretty sight was lost on Emy. "Don't you ever make such a comment again. Get your mind off Cole. Don't think about him, don't even look at him. Understand?" Emy glared, daring her sister to disobey her order. And at Kit's nod, she continued. "Under no circumstances will you ask my husband for money. Have I made myself clear?"

Cole felt an odd fluttering in his chest and thought he rather liked the way she said those two words. *My husband.* Who would have thought anything could sound so agreeable? But what he liked even more was the sound of that slap. If he knew anything about women, and Cole figured he knew a thing or two, Emy was jealous. Damn, but he couldn't remember ever knowing such happiness at another's annoyance.

He stepped into the room. His hat in his hands, he watched as the two women glanced in his direction. "It's time to go."

Kit ran past him while Emy placed her hands on her hips and glared. "How much of that did you hear?"

"All of it, I think." He shrugged and then explained, "Sorry, but the house is empty and your voices carried all the way to the porch."

Emy was beginning to know a great deal of remorse. Except for the one time she'd hit Cole, she'd never struck anyone in her life. That she'd been reduced to hitting her sister did not sit at all well. "I see you think it mildly amusing."

"Which part?"

Emy frowned. "What do you mean, which part? I just hit my sister."

"Oh." He nodded in agreement. "I figure she deserved that and more. I thought maybe you were talking about being jealous."

"Jealous! Who is jealous?"

"You."

Emy's mouth dropped open with surprise just before she snapped, "And what would I be jealous about?"

"The fact that your sister is thinking about the things we're doing in bed."

Emy tried for a ridiculing laugh. She didn't quite make it. "I didn't hit her because I was jealous. I hit her because I was disgusted."

"You're jealous. Admit it." Cole knew a delicious sense of happiness as he moved toward her and watched as she backed against a wall. She should have dismissed his accusation as nonsense, but instead she'd grown annoyed again, far more silent and annoyed than she should have been, especially if falsely accused. No, her denials only assured him of the truth. Her dark eyes flashed fire and silently warned him of continuing on in this vein. God, but this woman intrigued him. He marveled at her every expression, found himself enchanted by a smile or frown as if such a feat were indeed a marvelous act, never before undertaken. She could set his heart to pounding with a simple look. The soft, low sound of her laughter never failed to bring a smile to his lips. Excitement flowed through his veins at even her most innocent touch. He wondered if it would always be so.

Emy watched his mouth. He bit his lower lip and smiled; the smile tipped his mustache into a charming angle. He'd shaved the rest away last night, but thankfully had left a mustache. It was thicker than the one he'd worn when they'd first met and felt wonderful against her skin. Emy was suddenly assaulted with flashing pictures of the things he'd done with that mustache just the previous night. She shivered and brought her mind to the present and his nonsensical accusation.

Emy was not the jealous type, had never been, would never be. She'd have to feel something for a man in order to suffer that emotion. And Emy could have told him she felt nothing, nothing at all. "If you need to believe that, go right ahead."

Cole chuckled at her denial. "If it makes you feel any better, I'd probably kill a man for thinking as much about you."

Emy knew a fluttering sensation in the pit of her stomach and grew slightly breathless. The man was far too big, too dark, too handsome. He shouldn't be allowed to smile, to look at a woman like that. Her voice held hardly any strength at all when she asked, "You mean you'd be jealous?"

Cole allowed a deliciously low, sexy chuckle. "I reckon you'd be safe in assuming that."

"Why?"

He put his hat on, freeing his hands in order to reach for her waist. Slowly he raised her from the floor until their mouths were almost even. "You belong to me. I don't share my wife. Not even in someone's mind."

These weren't exactly the words she longed to hear. The truth of the matter was, Emy wasn't sure what it was she longed to hear. But his statement of ownership was definitely not it.

Her dark eyes only narrowed further. "Don't think you own me, Cole. Don't ever think you own me."

"But I do."

"You don't," she insisted. "I'm not a horse or a farm animal. No one can ever own me."

"You're my wife," he said as if that simple statement were enough to convince her to his way of thinking.

The tip of her boot contacted smartly with his shin. Cole cursed as he pushed her hard against the

264

wall, blocking any further movement with the pressure of his body. "Why, you little . . ."

His hands tightened threateningly, his lips twisted into a sneer as he readied himself to deliver an almost endless reserve of profanity.

Emy figured she'd made her point. To further insist would serve no purpose. It was best, she thought, to go on to other matters. The first being to thank him for his generosity.

Cole's eyes widened as her tight lips softened into a sweet smile. An instant later she touched his mustache in, if Cole wasn't mistaken, a loving caress. And then, as if his leg weren't smarting like hell, she ran her finger over his lip, her eyes holding to his mouth and said, "Cole, I wanted to thank you for what you're doing for my grandmother. She would have suffered greatly if she'd been forced to ride."

And before Cole could come back with an answer, she kissed him. God Almighty, she kissed him like she'd never kissed him before.

Cole didn't know what the hell to think. He doubted a woman lived who could twist him into more knots. First she kicked him in his shin, the next minute she kissed him senseless and with enough heat to sizzle a side of beef. The whole thing was just a bit much for him to take. Could it be she was merely showing her gratitude? Or was she simply using this moment to her best advantage? To gain a measure of control? Cole didn't want to think how much he wanted this kiss to come from her heart. God, but she was enough to make a man crazy.

Cole groaned as her mouth took possession of his.

Her tongue was hot, burning hot as it slipped into his mouth, to tease and flirt with his. He never noticed that they slid down the wall, that he turned, that he sat, that she sat as well, her legs straddling his thighs. He was lost in the feel of her freely given kiss, so lost, in fact, that Cole never remembered that they were far from alone. That this was hardly the time or place to so indulge.

One hand slipped inside the bodice of her dress while the other traveled beneath her skirt, up the length of her thigh, and they both moaned at the delight found in his touch.

A discreet clearing of a throat brought him from the sudden blaze of heat. Cole's eyes were slightly glazed over as he looked up to see his brother-in-law loosen his collar and turn away from the intimate sight. "Sorry. It's time to go."

Cole nodded, and Anton moved quickly out of sight. "Sweetheart."

Emy murmured her answer, a wordless moan of enjoyment as she pressed herself against his hands and kissed the side of his throat.

Cole smiled, luxuriating in her kisses, kisses that could so easily rob a man of his mind. Reluctantly he took his hands from her sweet softness, holding her loosely around her waist, forcing himself to bring to a close this delicious moment. "Sweetheart," he said again. "It's time to go. They're waiting for us."

Five seconds ticked by before Emy suddenly pulled sharply, abruptly, away. She stared with wide-eyed shock for a moment. Her cheeks grew warm as she realized what she'd been about. That she could have lost herself in the feel and taste of this man and done it without the least bit of coercion on his part was just about beyond insanity. It couldn't have happened, of course, not with an innocent thank-you kiss, not in broad daylight. An instant later Emy convinced herself that it certainly had not happened. "So?" she snapped nastily. "What are you telling me for? Am I stopping you?"

Cole thought better of reminding her of what she'd been about only a moment ago. After all, there were other things she could kick, things much more sensitive than a shin, and he wasn't taking any chances. "I didn't say anything. Did I say anything? All I said was it's time to go."

"Fine." Emy scrambled to her feet.

"Fine," he returned even as he breathed a sigh of relief, thankful to see her run off without a backward glance, knowing had she seen his smile, he would have only suffered further punishment.

The road ran along the edge of the river. Because of the levy, the Mississippi appeared more like a huge almost-endless hill rather than a river. She glanced to her left at the beautiful plantation homes, gleaming white in a sea of lush greenery, with live oaks stretching fifty feet and more across manicured lawns that reached the road's edge. The trouble was, unlike these folks, her family didn't have the money it took to protect themselves from the often-flooding waters. If they had, she wouldn't now be Mrs. Cole Brackston, heading for New Orleans and her new home.

Emy glanced toward her sister, who rode up

267

ahead in the wagon their father drove. Emy couldn't imagine how she managed it, but Kit's breasts were practically falling out of her dress and her skirt had somehow raised itself to mid-shin. It was more than obvious that her father noticed nothing. It was just as obvious that Mr. Hawk missed nothing. Emy watched as he licked his lips and grinned at her sister. The sight brought a moan of embarrassment and yet another scowl, a scowl she somehow transferred to the man who rode at her side.

Cole didn't miss her angry look. "What's the matter? What did I do now?"

"You said you'd talk to Mr. Hawk."

"Dammit!" The truth was, Cole had forgotten all about Kit and her possible interest in Hawk. Only he wasn't dumb enough to tell his wife the truth. "I didn't get a chance."

"You have the chance now," she said with more than a touch of bossy arrogance.

Cole hesitated. It was true that he wanted to make every favorable impression on this woman, but it came to him then that he wouldn't be serving any purpose by jumping like a trained monkey at her every order. He shook his head, knowing nothing could happen that couldn't be brought to an instant stop the moment Hawk discovered Kit's age. If his wife wanted his help, she'd have to do a better job of asking. Much better.

"Please, Cole," she asked when she realized his cold, silent look. It occurred to her then that she might gain much if she softened her demand into a gentle plea. "Please do something."

He glanced at her then, knowing he didn't have it

in him to deny this woman anything. All he could do was pray she wouldn't abuse what he took to be his greatest and perhaps only weakness. Without another word he dug his spurs into the animal's sides and trotted off to ride beside Hawk. "Ride up ahead with me a bit, will you?"

Jeremiah figured Cole wanted to talk to him about the fact that the charges against the two men had been dropped. He figured he knew well enough the reason behind Cole's actions. Had he a woman like Cole's, he would have done at least as much to keep her happy. Jeremiah nodded and brought his horse to a faster pace.

They were thirty feet ahead of the wagon when they slowed down to a trot. "What's up?"

"Ah, listen. I don't like to interfere, but . . ."

Jeremiah frowned. "But what?"

"The girl just turned fifteen."

Hawk shot Cole a look of disbelief. "You're full of shi—"

"Fifteen," Cole insisted. "Most figure that's old enough to marry. I'm sure her father would agree."

"Jesus, she's got a set on her that could drive a man . . . She don't look at a man like she's fifteen." Hawk was a quiet, private man but a man who knew how to please a woman if only to gain the best from her in return. But at thirty-one his taste ran to older, more experienced ladies. In his eyes, Kit, no matter her lush body, was only a girl, a girl at a very marriageable age of fifteen, and he definitely wasn't interested either in her or the holy state.

"I know. I thought the same thing the first time I saw her."

Hawk shook his head, and Cole grinned, knowing exactly the disappointment a man could feel.

"My wife's a bit worried about her. She thinks Kit is a good girl."

Hawk shot Cole a sharp look. "If your wife thinks Kit is a good girl, she has a lot to worry about."

Cole breathed a disheartened sigh, knowing his wife's worries were his as well. "I know."

The barn was warm, filled with the scent of horse, leather, and hay. Hawk was brushing down his horse when the peaceful silence was interrupted by soft steps. He turned at the sound and then returned to his work with a scowl.

"What's the matter with you?"

"You talkin' to me, kid?"

"Don't call me kid. You weren't looking at a kid this morning."

"Yes, I was. I just didn't know it."

"Cole told you my age," she said, her voice filled with disgust.

"Yup."

"So what difference does it make?"

"It makes every difference. You're too young to know what you want."

"But you're not and I bet you want these enough"—she opened the buttons of her bodice, almost exposing her breasts to his view—"to take them no matter how old I am."

"Damn," Hawk muttered as he allowed himself the luxury of looking over her tempting, partially exposed flesh. A girl shouldn't look that good that young. He felt his body's automatic response, and cursed even as he wondered if the barmaid had a free hour or so later on. There was no way he was going to touch this one, no way he was going to get trapped into marrying this little whore.

"You're wasting your time."

"I don't think so." Kit smiled as she moved closer and parted the material just a bit more. "You want to touch me, don't you?"

Hawk's voice was tight. "I'm not interested."

Kit laughed at his obvious discomfort. She took another step forward. "Aren't you?"

"You're looking at the wrong man if you want marriage."

"Marriage? Who wants to get married?"

Hawk sighed with relief at her vehement response. Still, her agreeing with him did not lessen the strain of the moment. She was only a kid. Even if she didn't know it, he did. It was going to take some effort to stop what she had in mind.

"You're too young."

Kit shrugged and Hawk almost groaned aloud as her breasts swayed with the movement. No matter how this night turned out, he wasn't likely to be happy about it. "I've got to start sometime."

"Start? You mean you haven't been with a man before?"

Kit narrowed her gaze as she studied his face. That the man wanted her was obvious. She imagined her virginity to be the reason for his hesitation. She'd gone through this before and wasn't about to be rejected again simply because she was technically a virgin. Technically because that fool she was with

271

last night had been too drunk to do much of anything. "Of course I've been with a man. But if you'd rather I was a virgin, we could always pretend."

"Kit, I can't." Hawk wondered if he sounded as sorry as he felt.

"Fine," she said as she moved closer still. "If you don't want it, I'll find someone who does."

"Kit! For God's sake," he said as she rubbed her body seductively against his. She threw back her head and laughed at the hardness she found between his legs.

Hawk's pulse hammered in his throat. The damn piece was enough to drive a man crazy. Jesus, where did she learn this? He groaned, unable to stop his hips from pressing against her. She moaned a soft sound of enjoyment at the feel of him.

"Once I saw two horses," she whispered into his throat. "It was the most exciting thing I've ever seen." Her palm cupped his erection, sliding gently up and down its length. "I can't wait to be mounted like that. I can't wait to scream when you hurt me."

Christ! Hawk shuddered at the need this little temptress instilled even as he put her away from him.

Cole watched from the barn's doorway. He couldn't blame Hawk for being tempted. He wouldn't have blamed the man for giving the little bitch exactly what they both wanted. Nothing had changed since Adam and Eve. Certain women could still drive a man, even if disgusted, to madness.

"Kit." Cole spoke into the barn's dimness. "Your sister is looking for you."

Hawk groaned as she only stepped toward him

once more, pressing herself even more tightly against him. Despite the interruption, her hand moved between their bodies again. Hawk blinked his surprise at her daring. Didn't she care who saw her? Damn, but he couldn't remember ever knowing a woman more eager.

"Tell Kit you couldn't find me."

"I don't think so. If you two want to be alone, I'll wait outside until you're finished, but I'm not going back without you."

"Fine, wait, then."

Hawk shook his head as he put her from him, this time more firmly. The little hussy wasn't the least bit embarrassed at being found with her dress undone and pressed up against a man who should have known better. He shot his friend a sheepish grin as he asked, "Are you sure she's only fifteen?"

Cole nodded. "Positive." And to Kit he said, "Cover yourself."

Kit was fed up. She was old enough to know what she wanted and more than annoyed to find she couldn't take a man without all kinds of interference. After all, she was fifteen, old enough to be married, old enough to know her own mind. And whose business was it, anyway? "If you're that interested, all three of us could go into a stall."

Cole's mouth tightened with disgust. He couldn't believe what he was hearing. It was as if her young body were possessed by a worldly if tasteless courtesan. How the hell had a girl her age even imagined such things? "I'm married to your sister."

Kit laughed low and dirty. "She wouldn't mind. We're all family."

"We were." All three turned toward the door and the small woman who stood glaring at the girl. "I suggest you do as my husband says and cover yourself."

Kit did as she was told even as she backed up at her sister's approach. Emy was livid and her softly spoken command dangerous enough to cause even Cole a moment's pause.

Kit had redone the buttons of her dress and was inching behind Hawk when she warned, "If you hit me again, I'll run away."

"Which would do all of our hearts some good, I'm sure." Emy smiled at her husband and then nodded toward Mr. Hawk, not having quite enough courage to meet his eyes. She was mortified that this wayward girl was her sister. Whatever must the man think of her family? Even in this light her blush of embarrassment could not be missed. She reached for her sister's hand, ignoring the startled cry of pain. "Gentlemen, you will excuse us, won't you?"

With less than a gentle yank Kit was escorted from the barn.

Both men sighed in relief to see the last of the little harlot, even as each wondered about the trouble she was sure to cause in the future.

Hawk was the first to break the silence. "Your wife is an interesting woman."

"I think so."

"She was embarrassed."

Cole nodded.

"Tell her there's no need to be."

"I'll tell her."

He shot his friend a grin. "I find I'm a bit partial to beautiful women."

"Most of us are."

"Too bad I didn't see her first."

Cole returned with some real determination and the slightest shake of his head, "It wouldn't have mattered."

"That bad, huh?"

Cole nodded. "Worse."

Inside the inn, Kit was nearly thrown into her father's room the moment he opened the door. Emy was almost gasping for breath as she faced the startled man. "I am so angry, I can hardly speak."

"What happened?"

"I found your daughter in the barn, offering her services to both my husband and Mr. Hawk."

Jacques's eyes widened with shock. "There must be some mistake." He shook his head. "Perhaps you misunderstood."

"There's no mistake, Papa." She shot her sister a killing look. "And it's not the first time. But if it happens again, I will personally see to it that she is put from my husband's home into the street."

"Emy, she's your sister."

"She should have thought of that before she suggested that Cole and Mr. Hawk join her in a stall."

Cole stepped into their room to find his wife sitting fully dressed in a corner chair. He looked at her tightly held mouth, the distress in her eyes, and asked, "What's the matter?"

"What's the matter? How can you ask me that?"

He closed the door and locked it. "Emy, you're not responsible for Kit and her actions."

"How many times has she done this?" And at his shrug, she insisted, "How many, Cole?"

"A few."

"Two? Three? Has she exposed herself to you before?"

"No."

Emy placed her hands together, her elbows resting on the arms of the chair, her fingertips grazing her chin. "I wonder what you think of us. You and Mr. Hawk both have been robbed, and in your case injured, and then my sister tries to seduce the two of you." She sighed in misery. "Six months ago we were poor, but we had pride. At least I had pride."

Cole sat on the edge of the bed and took off his boots. "Hawk said to tell you there's no need for you to be embarrassed."

The statement only caused her cheeks to burn. She couldn't look at him when she asked, "And what do you say?"

It was too soon. Cole couldn't tell her what he really wanted to say. He looked at her for a moment before he came to her side and reached beneath her, easily bringing her into his arms. He walked to the bed and sat, cuddling her in his lap, wishing he knew the words that would wipe away her distress.

Gently he pushed an errant curl behind her ear. "I say it doesn't matter what your sister does. I say we're each responsible only for our own actions."

For a moment their gazes held, each reading the openness and honesty of the other. Yes, honesty. He hadn't wanted to trust her, but even during the worst of it, he'd known deep in his heart that whatever she'd done she'd done only under pressure, under misguided concern for her eccentric family.

His first impression hadn't been wrong. Circumstances had only temporarily confused the issue. This was a good woman, a moral woman, who, thank God, matched him in his passions.

It wasn't time yet for full disclosures. They both understood it was too soon. It was enough to let their eyes tell of what they felt. And each knew only satisfaction at what they saw.

It was hours later. Cole's arms were wrapped securely around his sleeping wife, holding her close to his chest. A floor above, Hawk had just succumbed to the joyful charms of a serving wench. It was then, in that moment of intense silence known only to those who awaken at night, that both men heard the sounds of sobbing.

Each smiled with satisfaction and snuggled closer to the warmth of the woman at their sides as they drifted off to sleep.

Chapter Fourteen

The sun was beginning its descent in a clear blue sky by the time Cole pulled his horse up. The wagon rolled to a stop behind him. The house was nearly hidden behind a maze of thick shrubbery and high stone walls. It was set within walking distance of both the city and the often equally as crowded docks. Just outside the bustling hub of activity, it stood as if a retreat from the pressures of city life, on a quiet street lined with thickly branched trees. Just like home, these trees sported long, drifting lengths of Spanish moss that floated like a veil of fine lace in the soft summer breeze.

On two sides, a high stone wall and wooden gate cordoned off into a neat square a cobblestone courtyard that boasted at its center a magnificent flowering oleander. The tree stood ten feet above the second floor of the house. Beneath its clusters of fragrant rose-colored flowers and thick shade, a small iron table and two matching chairs sat protected from the heat of the day. Ivy grew in abundance, almost disguising the soft white of the house as it crawled upward from cool, shaded depths toward the warmth of the sun. Potted plants lined all the walls and iron-railed verandas. There were no windows, but French doors in every room that stood open to the cool dampness of the courtyard. Stone steps led to both the first and second floors.

Cole helped his wife from her horse. It had been hours since he touched her last. Who could blame him if he took this opportunity now offered? Nothing compared to the feel of her sliding down the length of his body. Well, almost nothing, and he found himself hard put to release her now that his arms had circled her waist. He held her to him for a moment before he opened the gate.

Emy took no notice of his apparent reluctance to release her, but continued on in a complimentary fashion her one-sided conversation about the quiet, shady street. The moment the gate swung open, her words came to a sudden and abrupt halt, while amazement rounded her dark eyes. It was easy enough to see that the woman had not expected this degree of lush, quiet beauty.

Cole placed one finger under her jaw and with just a bit of pressure closed her mouth. "I take it you're impressed?"

Her gaze moved to his. "You own this?"

Years ago, after his first wife died, Cole had sold his share of the ranch to his partner and brother. At first he'd traveled some, never caring all that much where he bedded down, until he came across this house. He hadn't left Nevada with much, but it had taken every cent he had left to buy this place. Now, with his wife at his side, positively enthralled, he'd never been happier that he'd made that particular decision.

"Would you like to see inside?"

"I can't believe it," Emy said, apparently unaware that she'd spoken aloud.

"Why not? Where did you think I lived?"

She glanced in his direction. "What?"

"Why can't you believe it?"

Emy frowned as she looked at him again, her dark eyes wary. "Are you rich?"

"Would it matter if I was?"

"It might." If there was one word that suited Emy to perfection, the word was *lady*. But Emy was a lady because of her gentle nature, her caring and generosity, her deep religious beliefs. The title had nothing to do with the size of her purse or the advantages of birth. She was unused to mingling with the well-to-do and felt distinctly uneasy at the thought. "If we have to associate with . . ." she said almost to herself, and then turned to him with, "Are you?"

"No."

Emy breathed a sigh of obvious relief. "Good."

Cole laughed. "I don't think I've ever met a woman who was so relieved to find her husband poor."

Emy smiled.

A black man with close-cropped almost pure

white hair, dressed impeccably in a dark gray suit, black string tie, and white shirt came from the house. A huge grin split wide lips. The flash of white teeth against a black face was a charming and welcome sight. Cole and the black man shook hands and then were suddenly hugging each other and smacking each other on the back. "Well, it took you long enough. Thought you were dead till Hawk sent the wire. Did you get them?"

"Afraid not."

"You should have taken a real man with you."

Emy realized immediately that this man, although obviously a servant, was far more than that. She shot her husband a look of surprise at the informal greeting and ensuing dialogue.

Cole turned to his wife and smiled at her amazed expression. "It might take a while, but you'll get used to Jason. All you have to do is understand that his one goal in life is to make mine miserable by regularly butting into my business."

Jason rolled his eyes toward the heavens. "Why do I take this abuse? Mrs. Cunningham is dying to have me come work for her."

"So go. Who's stopping you?"

"Don't tell me what to do. I'll work wherever I want."

Cole muttered almost beneath his breath, "It was a sad day when Lincoln freed the slaves."

"Don't pay him no mind, ma'am. He gets ornery when he's tired."

Emy didn't quite know what to make of this oddity. She'd been only a child when the South had slaves. Her family hadn't been rich enough to afford them. After the war, they had been equally as poor and had never hired any hands to help out. The few blacks she'd known had always been submissive. Hardly ever did one meet your eyes when speaking. She'd certainly never heard a black man talk like this before. "I take it you and my husband are friends?"

"Friends? Lord, but I've got better sense than count that one as a friend." And then as if he'd just realized what she said, he asked, "Your husband?"

He turned to Cole with an enormous grin. "So you finally got married? It's about time."

"This is Emy. You may call her Mrs. Brackston."

Jason immediately went about ignoring the suggestion. "Hello, Emy. I hope you'll be happy here."

Cole sighed in mock disgust, and all three laughed.

"Just because he saved my life, he thinks he can—"

"The biggest mistake of my life. I should have let them hang you."

Cole glanced toward his wife. Emy's laughter had turned into a stiff smile while, if he wasn't mistaken, fear filled her big dark eyes. "It's a long story, sweetheart. I'll tell you later.

"There's a wagon outside the gate that needs unloading. Have the boys bring the stuff to the rooms above the carriage house."

"Jessie." Jason suddenly turned and called out toward the open door. "Get some of the boys and follow me."

"Come inside," Cole said as he took her hand in

his. "I want to show you . . ."

Emy shook her head. "Grandmère is exhausted, Cole. Before I do anything, she should be settled first."

Cole glanced at the four who had come from the wagon and now stood behind them, taking in the scene with mouths agape.

Within the wall opposite the house stood a narrow gate. Beyond the gate was a long drive that led to a lovely carriage house. Cole ushered the small group toward their new home.

The rooms were clean, large, and empty. The apartment boasted of four rooms, three bedrooms, and sitting room. French doors led to a small but private terrace off the sitting room. Emy couldn't believe the size of the place. It was so big. Each individual room measured a good half of their entire farmhouse.

Cole leaned against one wall and watched as servants brought the family's meager possessions up the flight of stairs that was steep enough to disallow the old lady everyday use of them. He made a mental note to see to their replacement.

Grandmère sat in her rocker, her face gray, her lips white with exhaustion as Emy, with Jason's help, directed the placement of every trunk, table, chair, and bed. "Do you think Papa will be along soon?" the old lady asked tiredly.

"Very soon," Emy returned gently.

"You haven't forgotten my shoes, have you, dear?"

"I didn't forget."

Soon the elderly lady was in bed, the sounds of her gentle snores endearing to Emy's heart. Emy smiled as she set the sitting room in order. Finally, at Cole's insistence, she left Kit with a servant to see to the rest of the unpacking.

Emy and Cole stepped outside and around the back of the carriage house to the privacy of a garden that had been allowed to run a bit wild. Emy imagined her grandmother's delight at being able to cultivate the tiny piece of land. "It's lovely here. Truly lovely. I never expected anything like this."

Cole smiled. "No? What did you expect? A few rooms above the marshal's office?"

Emy shot him a wicked, playful grin that just about did him in. Without coaxing, she leaned into him and Cole almost moaned at the luxury of feeling her soft body willingly against his. "Perhaps."

Cole's arms came around her. She not only noticed, but if her smile meant anything, she seemed to enjoy the liberty he took as his hands palmed the fullness of her derrière and pulled their hips within contact. "What shoes?"

Emy smiled at the question. "I thought you didn't understand French?"

"I don't when you're cursing me. You talk too fast. But I understood her ask for her shoes. She said the same sort of thing when we found her in the city. What was she talking about?"

Emy shrugged. "She often mentions her shoes." She shook her head. "Something must have happened in her youth, because I can't put it to anything else. Unless she doesn't mean shoes at all." Emy sighed in obvious distress. "Sometimes she says a word but means something else entirely."

"And that bothers you?"

"It's not that it bothers so much as it frightens. I can see her getting older. I don't want to see her go."

"There comes a time when all of us have to go, Emy."

"I know, but . . ."

"You love her."

Emy nodded and breathed another sigh. She looked around them and asked, "Would you mind if Grandmère worked this little piece of land? She loves gardens."

"You don't have to ask me. This is your home as well as mine."

"I don't know how to thank you. She's going to be so happy here."

Cole wanted to ask her if she'd be happy here as well, but somehow couldn't force the words. Deep down inside he knew her answer meant too much and he was almost afraid of the hesitancy he was bound to hear in her voice. So he said instead, "Let me show you the house now."

There was an hour of light left when Emy sat on one corner of the huge bed, fingering the white coverlet, her head spinning, eyes wide with awe. "I'll never be able to find my way around this house. It's too big."

Cole smiled at her.

"What will we do with three sitting rooms?"

"Use them, I expect."

"Did you always live here alone?"

Cole nodded. "I didn't move here until after my wife died."

This was the first that Emy had heard of a wife. She felt the strangest sensation. Was it jealousy? Certainly not. She wasn't the least bit jealous. She was angry. How dare he marry her and never tell her there had been another before her. Emy came from the bed and began to pace the large room, a room so big, it could have easily held the entire house she grew up in.

"What's the matter?"

"Nothing."

"I can see something is. Tell me."

"It's nothing."

"Emy." Her name was spoken in warning.

She glared in his direction, not the least bit intimidated. "Why didn't you tell me?"

"What?"

"That you were married."

"Because it doesn't make any difference."

"Doesn't it? You didn't think I had the right to know?"

"There's no need for you to be jealous."

"I most certainly am not jealous! I'm angry."

"Why?"

"Because . . . because . . ." Emy suddenly realized she didn't have an answer to that question. All she could do was finish with a lame "Because I'm your wife and you should have told me."

Cole came from the armchair and walked toward her. He took her stiff form in his arms. "Should I tell you now?"

"Now I don't want to know."

"Obstinate woman."

Emy glared at his lazy grin. "Was she?"

Cole laughed. "Sweetheart, the two of you couldn't be more opposite."

"Meaning she was sweet and kind?"

"She was."

"And you treated her like some slave, no doubt."

"I treated her very well, thank you."

Emy snorted a sound of disbelief. "I don't believe that for a minute."

"Why? When have I treated you otherwise?"

Emy shot him a knowing look and knew a measure of satisfaction at hearing him admit, "Except for that."

She tried to pull out of his arms. "I don't want to talk about this."

"But you're going to. First I'm going to tell you about Mina, and then I'm going to tell you about you."

He picked her up and in one leap flung the both of them upon the bed. He rolled his body half over hers, his weight holding her in place as he said, "Stop fighting me and listen for a minute."

"I don't want to hear it."

"Yes, you do. Now, be still."

Emy surprised the both of them by doing exactly that.

"The whole thing started when I fell in love with my sister-in-law."

"Cole!" Emy gasped, obviously horrified.

"She wasn't my sister-in-law at the time, and I

287

found out later I wasn't really in love. It was Nora, that's my sister-in-law," he explained, "who pointed out the fact that Mina meant something special to me. It was only then that I really noticed her."

"What do you mean, you noticed her?"

"I mean, her mother was our housekeeper and Mina lived with us since she was a little girl. I never realized that she had grown up. Anyway, once I did, I couldn't stop looking at her. She loved me."

Emy made a little sound, and Cole smiled. "As hard as it is to believe, she did. She was gentle and sweet. There was nothing she wouldn't do for me."

"Poor woman. She wasn't well, yes?"

Cole laughed.

"What happened?"

Cole's expression sobered as he went on. "A man killed her."

Emy gasped. "How?"

His eyes took on a faraway look, suddenly filled with pain, as if he were again seeing the horror. "He kicked her in the stomach when she tried to save my sister-in-law and nephew from being kidnapped. She was going to have a baby. They both died."

Emy murmured a prayer in French. Her eyes were wide with horror when she asked, "What did you do?"

"I killed him."

Emy couldn't hold back her shiver. She knew without being told that Cole had killed the man just as calmly and coldly as he now said the words. *"Mon Dieu."*

Cole allowed a weak smile as he struggled to pull

himself back from the memory. It had been a long time since he'd thought about Mina. Long ago he had laid her memory to rest. It had been years since he'd ached for her gentle touch, years since he loved her. Now he had only fond memories and knew none of the pain that had once plagued him.

"And then?" she prompted him.

"And then I left the ranch and Nevada. I traveled a bit and finally settled down here."

Emy felt compelled to ask, "And she was sweet and kind?"

"Unlike you, she never said an unkind word."

Emy instantly hated the dead woman and then knew a measure of guilt in doing so. She hated the wrong one. It was this man that she should hate. She sneered. "How lovely for you. Too bad you couldn't find another just like her."

"There are no others like her."

Her teeth were clenched together when she said, "Let me up."

Cole merely grinned, ignoring the demand. She looked on the verge of violence. Her eyes flashed fire. She was jealous. She'd never admit to the emotion, he knew, but she was. "While you, on the other hand, are a hot-tempered little witch."

"Who is cursed with a pig for a husband," she said in French.

"What did you say?"

Emy repeated the words slowly and in English.

Cole laughed. "Tell me you're not jealous and you're a liar."

"Tell me you still love her and you're dead," Emy

snapped in return, and then forced back her gasp. Her eyes were wide with shock. How could she have said something so stupid? Now he was sure to imagine all kinds of things, all kinds of erroneous things.

Cole grinned at her statement and then watched as horror filled her eyes. He took hope in her fury. She cared for him, perhaps a lot more than she was willing to admit. "Sweetheart, a little part of me will always love her."

Emy frowned. She didn't understand. Having never loved anyone before she couldn't be expected to understand. "What do you mean? Which part?"

His eyes danced with pleasure. "Not the part you're thinking of."

Emy felt instantly the fool. Now she understood. When he looked at her like that, how could she not? "You're disgusting."

"That part belongs to you."

"Get off me."

"I mean a small part of my heart. She was special to me. Would you prefer I forget her?"

The truth was, Emy would have preferred exactly that, but knew she'd sound terribly selfish if she said so. She shrugged for an answer.

"If I were to die, you wouldn't forget me, would you?"

"Not likely," she said with some real feeling.

Cole was not unaware of the meaning behind those words, but chose to misinterpret them. "That's what I mean. That's all I mean."

Emy breathed a deep sigh as she tried to dislodge

the pain in her chest. It wasn't jealousy she felt. The poor woman was dead. How could she be jealous? Cole was too heavy. That's what caused this discomfort. "Move. You're squashing me."

He remained in place. "Now, as for you."

Her whole body tensed. "I don't want to hear this."

"Too bad, 'cause you're going to. A few weeks ago I woke up to find an angel leaning over my bed."

Emy laughed. "You were delirious. Kit's as far from an angel as anyone can get."

"I was talking about you."

"Me?"

"Yes, sweetheart, you. And as far as I'm concerned, you're about as close to an angel as anyone can get."

Emy felt her heart stumble. She was suddenly breathless and unable to give even the smallest response.

"Let's see now. Where should I begin?" He smiled as his gaze moved over her. "The woman I saw caring for me was gentle and shy, good-natured, generous, loving to her family. An innocent with wicked, flashing eyes that promised unbearable passion. She intrigued more than any woman I've ever known."

"Did she?" Emy's voice was hardly more than a whisper of surprise.

Cole nodded in confirmation.

"And then you discovered what she was really like. You found out about her family and her own criminal activities."

"Yeah, well, that kinda threw me for a bit, but after I got over the shock of it, I understood why she had done it. It only confirmed my original opinion of her. She loved her family a great deal.

"Her grandmother probably most of all. She was willing to sacrifice everything for the love of her."

Emy was unable to look into his eyes, afraid of what she'd find there. Was he teasing her, making fun? Or did he mean the things he said. She bit her bottom lip and examined a nail just as if this weren't the most important moment of her entire life.

"But you married her anyway. I don't understand why."

"Don't you?"

Emy looked at him then and sucked in a deep breath at the dark fire she found in his eyes.

"Should I tell her why?"

Her voice was soft, hesitant, filled with doubt. "You probably should. How else could she know?"

"If I told her that I loved her, what do you think she would say?"

Emy was absolutely speechless. She couldn't think of an answer that wouldn't make her sound like an idiot.

"If I told her I married her because I couldn't bear the thought of her going to prison, because I couldn't bear the thought of living without her, what do you think she would have said?"

"She didn't know you loved her."

"She knew I wanted her."

"Wanting isn't love."

"But love is wanting." He smiled as his words

registered. "What would she say?"

"I don't know."

"What would you say?"

"I'd say I love you."

Cole sighed and closed his eyes at the incredible pleasure in those three perfect words. "Now the question is why? Do you love me because I've saved your family from jail?"

"That's part of it, but I loved you before that."

"Did you?" He smoothed back a curl from her cheek and nuzzled his lips to where it had lain. "When did you know?"

"When you made my grandmother blush with your teasing."

"You mean my kisses didn't do it?" He smiled as his mouth hovered above her own. "I thought they were pretty convincing."

"They might have been, but they were too late. I loved you already."

"Do you still? Even after the way I treated you? The things I did to you?"

"What kind of things?"

"Forcing you to share my bed, to marry me."

Emy nodded. "Well, yes, I was a little upset over that."

"Just a little?"

She shrugged. "As it turned out, it wasn't so bad."

"You little witch." He gave her a shake and smiled at her girlish giggle. "Wasn't so bad?"

Emy laughed. "I found I was strong enough to bear it."

Cole narrowed his gaze. "I suppose you're going

293

to tell me you hated every minute of it."

"I did. I hated you and everything you did."

"No, you didn't."

Emy's dark eyes narrowed. "I hate you for not believing that I hated you."

Cole chuckled a low, sexy sound. Lord, why did the man have to laugh like that? "No, you don't. You love me."

Emy ignored the last of that statement. "I'll probably never forgive you."

"If you really hated it, why didn't you fight me? Why didn't you scratch? Why didn't you scream?"

"Would that have stopped you?"

"I don't know. I wanted you like I've never wanted a woman in my life."

"Lust," she said with a measure of disgust.

"Yes, lust, but more than lust, I loved you.

"Why didn't you scream, Emy?" he asked, and when no answer came forth he smiled and went on. "Should I tell you why?"

Emy couldn't stop her lips from quivering into a smile. "You beast."

"You didn't fight me because you wanted me to make love to you."

"No, I didn't fight you because I was scared."

Cole gave a shout of a laugh in disbelief. "Scared? A little spitfire like you? I'm the one who was scared."

Emy blinked her surprise. "Were you? Why?"

"Didn't you know? Couldn't you tell? I was terrified. I felt under your spell. You had the power to take my soul."

"Cole." Jason knocked on the door to their room. "Hawk says get on down to the office. He needs you for something."

Cole dropped a quick kiss to her soft mouth just before he came from the bed. "We'll finish this later."

Cole didn't miss her look of disappointment. It gladdened his heart like nothing else could. His eyes narrowed in sexy laughter as he taunted her. "If you know what's good for you, I'll find you in that exact position when I get back."

He laughed as she said something in French and threw a pillow at him.

She jumped from the bed. "You shouldn't have said that. Now you'll never find me there."

He was still smiling as he mounted his horse and headed the animal toward the city.

need to believe that, go right ahead."

Cole chuckled at her denial. "If it makes you feel

Chapter Fifteen

Emy spent the rest of the evening becoming
acquainted with her new home. In the style of many
southern homes, the kitchen was separated from the
rest of the house. The dining room and study, plus
three separate sitting rooms, were all on the first
floor.

Upstairs boasted of four bedrooms, Cole's being
the largest, and a bath that actually had running
water. It was something Emy had never seen before,
but so simple she wondered why she hadn't thought
of it. Water was piped in by a long cylinder that was
attached to a tank standing high on a wooden
platform twenty feet from the house. The tank
collected rainwater while the cylinder sloping
downward toward the house brought it to the bath.
Amazing.

Emy wandered through the rooms for the next
hour or so, unable to believe she was there, that her
husband had given her so much. Silently she
promised that he'd never be sorry, that she would be

the perfect wife, that she would make this house into a lovely home and with her skill with a needle, the inside would soon be as lovely as the outside.

It was hours after dark. The house had been quiet for a long time when she heard the sound of a gate opening. She blew out all but one candle.

Emy waited in the dim, quiet room, listening to the sounds of his spurs jingle as he mounted the steps. One candle stood on a table at the room's center, lending the room its only light.

Emy stood behind the open door, waiting for him to enter.

He glanced inside, noticed the romantic setting, the door to the bath open. Bubbles floated upon the water's surface. In the center of the room stood a candlelit table set for two, but the bed was empty. "Emy?" he said softly, wondering where she could have gone.

"Here," she whispered, her voice coming from behind the door. "Step inside and close the door."

Cole did as he was told even as he wondered what she was about.

A moment later he was pushed up against the door, a hard object pressing into his back. "Emy, what the hell . . . ?"

"Don't talk. You're under arrest."

Cole might have laughed if it weren't for the gun pushing into his back. "Emy, don't play games with guns. It could go off."

"It's not a gun, it's my finger. And I'm not playing a game."

He chuckled a low, delighted sound.

She pressed harder. "This isn't funny."

Cole bit his lips together and forced back his laughter.

"What do you think about my becoming one of your deputies?" she asked as she pressed her body against the back of his. "I got the drop on you easy enough."

"Got the drop on? Where did you hear . . ."

"I read it once in a penny novel. That's how cowboys talk, isn't it?"

Cole was having a time of it keeping his laughter at bay. "Some, I reckon."

"So, what do you think?"

He shook his head. "It would never work."

"Why?"

"Because every man in this city would break the law just so you could arrest him like this."

"Don't give me any trouble," she said in what she thought to be a tough-guy tone of voice.

Cole loved it. "I wouldn't think of it."

"Put your arms up and lean against the wall. I'll have to search you."

"Oh, God," he said, just the thought of it brought him to instant arousal.

She kept her finger against his back as she reached up and kissed his neck. "Tell me what you're thinking."

"I'm thinking I'm probably the luckiest man alive."

"I have you under arrest. You're not supposed to enjoy it so much."

"I can't help it. I love it.

"What are the charges?"

It took a long moment before Emy managed the

298

courage, but she finally blurted out the truth. "You stole my heart." And went on in a higher tone with, "And for that, you'll have to pay."

Cole closed his eyes and took a deep breath. What had he ever done to deserve this? "You stole mine as well."

"You can arrest me for that later."

He laughed, but the laughter was choked with emotion.

Emy gave up any pretense of holding a gun. Her arms circled his hips and her fingers quickly disposed of his gun belt. "Don't drop it."

"I won't. Just don't move," she warned as she left him for the time it took to put the gun and belt on a chair.

Cole was only too happy to obey.

Again behind him, she moved her hands up his back to his shoulder and then under his arms. "Am I doing it right?"

"What?" he could hardly breathe.

"Searching you. I've never done it before. Am I doing it right?"

"Righter than you know."

Around his waist, over his chest, his flat stomach, his hips, down his thighs. He couldn't hold back the moan. And then her hands came to linger for endless moments at his arousal. "There's something here. Do you have a gun in your pants?"

Cole leaned his head against the wall, able only to mutter a groan that mingled ecstasy and torture.

"There's no help for it, I'm going to have to take your clothes off."

Again another sound that wordlessly begged for

further investigation.

"I think you have something there."

His voice was rusty at best. "You might be right."

"Trouble is"—she was back to her tough-guy talk—"you want me to take your clothes off. There's no fun in that."

"Actually, there could be a lot of fun in it."

"Should I try it and see?"

"Emy."

"All right, all right. Nag, nag, nag. Take my clothes off, take your clothes off. Did anyone ever tell you you have a one-track mind?"

Cole smiled. Taking off their clothes was certainly on his mind, but he hadn't mentioned it at all.

"Don't move," she said again as she created some space between their bodies. A moment later came the swishing sound of moving material, and from the corner of his eye Cole saw her nightdress float to the floor.

He almost turned. "I told you, don't move." Her finger was again at his back.

Cole knew she was naked, and the thought of her standing there just about drove him mad. "I won't." He shuddered at the effort it took to remain in place. "Jesus, I swear I won't."

"Well, maybe you could move just a little. I'll let you know when."

He laughed. "You're driving me crazy, lady."

"Good. Criminals like you should be driven crazy."

She unbuttoned his shirt and found no resistance when she pulled it down his arms. She dropped it to the floor and she rubbed her chest against his back. Cole thought maybe he had died and gone to heaven.

She kissed him over and over, from his shoulder to his waist and then side to side. How could he be this blessed? He shuddered again as she dragged her tongue over the smooth muscles. "Do all criminals taste this good?"

"You'll never know."

"Maybe, just for the sake of justice, I should find out."

"Maybe for the sake of my sanity you should take that thought out of your mind forever."

Emy chuckled a low, wicked sound. She undid his belt, his pants, and pushed them over his hips. Again she rubbed her body against his. They both sighed at the pleasure.

Her hands slid around him, moving over his throat and chest, his belly, and then boldly lower to caress his sex. "Ah-huh," she said in triumph. "It's not a gun, but I knew you had something here."

Cole groaned as she stroked his erection.

"You can move now."

"I can't. My pants are around my ankles. I'll fall on my face."

"Then back up a little."

Cole did as he was told and she slipped between his body and the wall.

"Now what?" he asked, more than willing to prolong the delicious game.

"Now I've got you locked up," she said as her mouth delivered wet, hot, open-mouthed kisses to his neck and chest. "And you'll never be free again."

"I know," he said as he raised her from the floor

and loved her until the ecstasy turned to fire and seared them both in the flame.

They had just come from the bath. The door had been left open. Damp towels were spread all over the floor, absorbing the water that had, in their playfulness and then deep loving need, been spilled.

"How did you think of that?"

"Think of what?" she asked as she stretched out comfortably and then placed her hands under her head.

"Searching me, stripping me, putting me under arrest?"

She watched his head dip toward her nakedness and his lips sip at the tip of her breast. She laughed a wicked sound. "Just brilliant, I suppose.

"Are you hungry?"

"Can we eat in bed?"

"Why?"

"I'm too tired to get up."

"Shall I feed you?"

"God, that would be heaven. A naked lady sitting on my bed, feeding me. Who could ask for more?"

"I can't sit here naked while I'm feeding you."

"Please? It would make everything taste better."

Emy laughed as she left the bed, returning with two plates. On the bed again, she sat opposite him and put a piece of cheese into his mouth. "Do you always manage to get your own way?"

"I try."

"And when you smile it usually works?"

Cole only shrugged in response.

Emy rolled her eyes toward the ceiling. "Oh, this marriage is going to be something."

"Why?"

"Because both of us like to get our own way. How do you think we will solve that problem?"

"I reckon one of us will have to give in."

"*Oui.* I wonder which one?"

"You, of course."

"Me? All the time?"

"Sure." Cole chewed on a piece of roasted chicken. "You're the wife. It's your job to give in." He said the words with absolute certainty, never imagining there might be another way.

Emy didn't respond, but looked at him for a silent moment before she said instead, "Oh, I forgot the wine."

It seemed to Cole that it took less than a heartbeat and she was standing at his side with the wine in her hands. Suddenly she dumped both the bottle and the cooler it sat in, a cooler filled with cold water, upon his chest. Cole gasped a curse and jumped to his feet as cold water soaked not only his body, but the bed as well, while the bottle of wine went unnoticed as it emptied itself upon the bed.

"Oh, I'm sorry," she said with as little emotion as possible. She grabbed her nightdress, quickly pulled it on, and sat on her side of the bed. The dry side.

After Cole finished cleaning up the mess and realized he wasn't going to be sleeping in a dry bed tonight, he looked at his wife, who was now covered as primly as a schoolmarm, the picture of demure innocence. He sat, ignoring the clammy feel of the sheet beneath him, trying to figure out how he could restore the loving moments he had so expertly managed to destroy. He cleared his throat and shifted, the movement telling clearly he was uncomfortable.

Nothing.

He made a sound that might have been a laugh. Sort of.

Nothing.

He tried another tactic, hoping to restore her sense of humor with an amusing story. "Hawk arrested a drunk today."

Emy shot him a blank look and returned her attention to her meal.

"The man insists he's Jesus Christ."

Still nothing.

"So Hawk asked him, if he's Jesus, why does he have to buy his whiskey? Why not get a jug of water and . . ." Cole's voice dwindled down to silence. He sighed, knowing that he wasn't making the least bit of an impression. There was no hope for it. The stubborn woman wasn't about to respond until he said the right words. "You know, Emy, I've been thinking."

"Have you?" She glanced again in his direction, but her real attention seemed to be on the piece of chicken she was nibbling at. "About what?"

"Maybe we could both give in."

Her eyes widened in mock surprise, as if she had never imagined such a happening. "Both of us? How?"

"Well"—he shrugged—"like if something was real

304

important to you, I could say 'no problem' and you could do the same."

"I wonder why I didn't think of that?"

"I don't know." There wasn't a doubt in his mind that he was going to have to watch himself. This woman was no weak-willed little miss, but a force to be reckoned with, and he wasn't stupid enough to play around with a temper like hers, not if he wanted a measure of peace in his life. He sighed in resignation. "It probably would have kept my side of the bed dry if you had."

"You can share mine," she said generously.

"Thank you."

Emy bit her lip, trying to hold back her laughter. "I love you."

The words squeezed at his heart. Cole wondered if he'd ever get used to hearing them. "I'm glad. If you didn't, you probably would have stabbed me instead of just dumping cold water and wine all over me."

Emy laughed. "I wasn't that upset."

"The next time I say something stupid, you could remind me of tonight. It would give me time to apologize before you do me bodily harm."

Emy nodded. "That's a good idea."

"Can I move over to your side of the bed now?"

"Anytime."

"It's going to be a tight fit," he said as he moved over and stretched out.

Emy sat on the edge. "Well, we could sleep side by side or I could sleep on you."

"I like the last one best."

"I wouldn't be too heavy?"

"Not if you took off that nightdress."

Emy glanced at the article in question. It was plain cotton and had been washed so many times, it was nearly transparent. She fingered the material as she said, "It does weigh a lot."

"You're a strong woman. It would probably crush me."

Emy laughed as she pulled it over her head and flung it to the floor.

He took her by the waist and lifted her to lay upon him. He sighed with pleasure at the feel of her soft, warm skin against his. "This is good. This is real good."

Emy felt the thickening of his body against hers. "Do you think we'll be able to sleep like this?"

"After a little bit."

Her hand reached between them, her fingers measuring the length and thickness of his erection. And the more she measured, the more thickness and length she found to explore. Emy gave the slightest shake of her head and said in supposed innocence, "After a bit, maybe. But it's not very little, Cole."

They both laughed as he nuzzled his face with a hungry growl into her neck.

"We could sleep in one of the guest rooms tonight," Cole offered. "We'd have more room on a dry bed."

"I'm too tired to get up. Besides, I love hairy pillows." She smoothed down the chest hair that was tickling her nose.

"And I love a blanket of naked ladies."

"Ladies?"

"Lady," he instantly corrected himself.

"Better."

She listened with a smile to his low chuckle of pleasure. "Who's going to put out the candle?"

"Leave it, it will burn out."

There was a moment of silence before she asked, "Cole, how did Jason save your life?"

"A few years ago I was riding through Texas. The northern part is real pretty. Lots of grass and cattle. There had been some trouble with rustlers.

"I saw a campfire and stopped, thinking the men around it were just a bunch of hands working the range. They were friendly enough until one of them slipped up and they realized I had to know who they were.

"The next thing I knew they had a rope around my neck and were dragging me toward a tree."

Emy gasped, her arms coming around him, holding him tightly. "God!"

He smoothed her hair back in a comforting gesture. "I'm here, so things must have turned out all right." Cole tried to laugh off what had been one of the most terrifying moments of his life.

"What happened?"

"They pushed me onto my horse and threw the rope over a tree branch. When they hit my horse, I hung there for a second before the branch broke.

"No!" she said as she moved up to examine his throat. She touched it so lovingly that Cole wasn't sorry the whole thing had happened.

"The next thing I knew, they were dragging me up and throwing the rope over another branch." Emy moaned her horror and held him even more tightly.

"They were pretty much interested in killing me and forgot to keep guard. Jason and a bunch of cowhands came upon us just before they got me on the horse again. With my hands tied at my back I was pretty much helpless. All I could do was hug the ground and wait for the gunfire to end.

"Three of them got away, but the rest were killed."

"Promise me you won't ride anywhere alone again."

"Sweetheart, that won't . . ."

She gave him a little shake as if to insist. "Promise me, Cole."

"You mean I might come across some dark little woman with flashing eyes, get her drunk, almost have my way with her, and then while I was trying to find her, get shot by her father, who was robbing me?"

"Oh, God." She rubbed her face against his chest. "I'll never be able to live that down." And then, as if it just dawned on her, she raised her gaze to his and asked, "You were trying to find me?"

"Of course. Did you think I would simply let you walk out of my life?"

"Why?"

Cole laughed. "Good question. I was trying to figure out why myself, when your father and Anton stepped out of the alley."

Emy moaned. The sound mingled her desperate embarrassment with horror. "That was so awful. I just about died when I saw you lying there, bleeding all over the place, knowing it was all my fault.

"Do you think you can ever forgive us for that?"

Cole sighed as he hugged her tightly against him.

"Ask me again in about fifty years."

Suddenly she asked with some surprise, "Jason was a cowboy?" She realized only when she said the words how the man walked and talked. Being a cowboy explained why he didn't sound like any servant she'd ever seen.

"Yeah. Why?"

"I didn't know there were any black cowboys."

"Sure there are. Lots probably."

"So how did he come to work for you?"

Cole shrugged. "He was tired of working the range. Guess he figured anything was better than the loneliness, so he asked if I wouldn't mind, he'd ride along with me for a while.

"When I settled here, he did too. Tried his hand at marshaling for a bit, but he didn't like it much. Said he was tired of riding, of seeing the worst side of life. Wanted to settle down. When he found out I was looking for someone to help out around here, he insisted on doing it. He pretty much runs this place. Sometimes I find myself asking if he wouldn't mind if I did something or other." Cole chuckled a soft sound. "He tells everybody that he works for me, but the truth is, he does what he pleases and I pay him for it."

"He showed me the house today."

Cole's hand squeezed her backside. "I showed you the house."

"I know, but I couldn't take it all in the first time. It was too much. Anyway, I didn't notice either of you mention his room."

"He doesn't live in the house. There's a small house out back that borders on the street behind my property. He bought it from me and lives there with Betty, his wife."

"Why didn't I meet her?"

"She's going to have a baby, so Jason won't let her work anymore."

"A baby! That's wonderful."

"It will be more wonderful when you're the one who's having a baby."

This time the mention of a baby didn't send Emy into a tizzy. She wasn't the least bit shocked, but knew only a deep sense of anticipation. "How many do you think we'll have?"

He placed his hands to each side of her hips. "Judging by the width of you, a dozen shouldn't be much of a chore."

Emy slapped at his hands and laughed. "That's easy for you to say, since I'll be the one having them." She shot him a look of surprise. "A dozen? That's quite a lot, don't you think?"

"What do you say if we start with one?"

"I'd say that sounds like a very good idea."

"I have a lot of good ideas."

"I know."

"Should I show you one more?"

"How many do you have?"

"Ideas?"

She nodded.

"Oh, a couple of dozen, maybe."

"And you want to show me all of them?"

Cole only grinned for an answer.

"Then I guess we'd better get started."

Chapter Sixteen

Kit sashayed down the narrow cobblestone sidewalk in a most unladylike fashion, catching the eye of every male she passed. She smiled at one man and then another until still another caught her eye. To Kit's way of thinking, New Orleans was much like a giant candy bowl filled with all kinds of confectionery yet to sample.

Above her head she twirled a frilly parasol, knowing the movement brought her to the attention of a dozen or more males. She listened as they called out good day to the pretty lady. God, but she loved New Orleans. Loved it like she'd never loved anything in her life.

The city radiated energy even as it offered all manner of delights. The smell and sounds were an aphrodisiac and caused her blood to race with excitement. It was another world, a world where something was always happening, something exciting and new.

Papa and Anton had gone to work at one of the

hundred restaurants that had made this city so famous. Emy was redecorating her new home. Grandmère as often as not, now that Cole had replaced the stairs, was either working in her garden, or sitting with Emy as she sewed. Servants took care of the cleaning of their rooms. Another cooked and brought them their meals.

For the first time in her life, there were no eggs to gather, no chickens to feed, no cows to milk. Everyone was busy with their own lives. No one had the time to tell her what to do.

She had the afternoon free again and had every intention of visiting with Mr. Henri, the perfumer. From the first she had enjoyed these visits, enjoyed them most especially if Mrs. Henri wasn't about and her husband could dedicate some time to his newest client. It was during these visits that Kit learned the places where perfume could be best applied.

At first she did the applying, but it wasn't long before Mr. Henri took over that chore. Kit liked that best of all. After most visits he would give her a little bottle of the sacred liquid. Kit smiled a secret smile, for she was slowly collecting quite an array of lovely perfumes.

Kit wondered if there wasn't a man or two in this city who owned a dress shop. She'd ask around today. She certainly could use a few new dresses and some frilly underthings. She hadn't worn underthings since moving there, since Emy no longer shared the same room, since she was allowed a measure of privacy. Still, she thought she might start again if they were pretty enough.

Kit smiled as she stepped into the small fragrance

shop. Mr. Henri was busy with a client. Kit suddenly realized she didn't know his first name, and realized as well that she wasn't interested in finding out. It wasn't a name that she wanted from this man. It was sex, pure and simple. Kit waited, and while she waited she took delight in the few samples he had on display.

The bell over the door rang as the woman left at last. Mr. Henri grinned at the beautiful girl with the wicked, wicked eyes. "Can I help you, mademoiselle?"

"*Oui.* I was interested in some perfume."

"Something exotic, perhaps?"

"Ah, exotic, *oui.* I'd like to try that."

Henri knew there were quite a few things this girl was willing to try, and he was all too willing to let her try them on him. "Why not step into the back room? I have something special you might enjoy."

Kit followed him into the back, never noticing the long table with bowls set out for mixing, the array of fancy bottles, the shelves of large containers holding rich scents and oils. She wasn't there to look at perfumes, nor watch their delicate creation. She was there for one purpose only, and now that she'd finally had a taste of it, she couldn't get enough.

"Let me smell it," she said as he offered her a small bottle.

He ran it quickly under her nose. "You know the best place to wear it, don't you?"

Since coming to New Orleans, she had finally disposed of her wretched virginity. A cobbler had done the trick. And never had she enjoyed herself or her new shoes more. Kit knew the fun of playing dumb. Men seemed to enjoy themselves when showing a girl certain things. She blinked in supposed confusion. "I don't remember. Where?"

"Let me show you," he said as he moved the neckline of her dress a bit lower. "If you put a drop here—" His perfumed finger moved into the deeper cleavage, pressing at her softness as he wiggled his finger between her breasts.

"No, I'm afraid this won't do."

Kit's eyes were shining with laughter. It was the same game they played the last time. "What should I do?"

"I'm afraid you'll have to open your dress."

Kit instantly obeyed even as she said, "Oh, dear. Do you think I should?"

Her breasts fell free of the garment and the man was obviously delighted at what he saw. Kit delighted in it as well, but she enjoyed it even more when he ran perfumed fingers over the lush white globes. She closed her eyes and sighed with the pleasure. It was lovely. Just lovely. Especially when he rubbed perfumed oil into her nipples. They both watched as the tips budded like pretty rose flowers.

"Are you sure this is where a lady wears her perfume?"

Mr. Henri grinned. "Here and other places."

He knew she wasn't wearing anything under that dress. At least she hadn't worn anything the last three times she'd showed up at his place.

"Show me where," she said even as she raised her skirt, allowing him full view of the most intimate parts of her lush young body.

Kit moaned at the unbearable pleasure and then

sighed with relief, her body trembling as a result of these last few lusty moments. She found herself having a bit of a problem adjusting her clothing. It certainly was getting better every time she indulged. She wondered what it would be like in a month's time.

The trouble was, Mr. Henri was terrified that his wife was going to walk in at any minute. After he finished his business, a very delightful business he couldn't help but admit, he couldn't get her out of his shop fast enough.

Without another word spoken between them, she managed the adjustment of her bodice. There had to be a better way. It was wonderful, but over too soon. Kit would have enjoyed it more, she thought, if it lasted longer, quite a bit longer, in fact.

A few seconds of him pumping into her brought a great measure of satisfaction to be sure, but it wasn't enough. She didn't want a few minutes of strained pleasure with him, always worrying if his wife might happen to walk in. She wanted a hell of a lot more than that.

Kit smiled as he stuffed his limp member into his trousers and smiled again when she clutched another bottle of perfume in her hand. Kit and Mr. Henri wished each other a pleasant day as she left the shop. Kit couldn't hold back her laugh as his wife walked in just as she left.

Charles Briggs was a man of business. The only problem being, most of his business was illegal, the rest immoral. He dabbled a bit in stolen jewelry. He smuggled Irish whiskey right under the noses of government agents, and he owned two gaming houses. But his greatest love, and most profitable venture, was women. The fact was, Mr. Briggs sampled all his products firsthand. It was only after he began to get bored with a particular lady that he sent her on to others. Sometimes to friends, sometimes to business acquaintances, but mostly he sent them to one of the four little houses that stood near his gambling establishments.

Mr. Briggs was a handsome man. He was tall and blond with startling blue eyes. And Mr. Briggs worked on those very good looks, using them to his best advantage.

He stepped out of the jewelry shop. On his arm was a young girl, no more than fourteen, who was nearly beside herself with joy at the almost worthless trinket he'd just bought her. She didn't know, of course, that the elaborately styled pin was made of glass rather than diamonds. Mr. Gladstone knew which items to show him when there was a lady on his arm and which to show when he shopped for himself.

Ruby was her name. At least it was the name he'd given her. It matched her hair. Charles thought it quite brilliant of him to name the woman after her hair. Considering the lushness of her form, she'd bring him in a good penny and then some, he was sure. All he had to do was get her to understand that a woman in love would do anything for her man.

Kit shoved the perfume into her pocket and came to a sudden stop. The most handsome gentleman she'd ever seen in her life, more handsome even than Hawk, was helping a lady into a closed carriage.

Over the lady's head, Charles's gaze locked on Kit.

At first glance he knew her for a low-class whore. Oddly enough, she looked familiar. He knew he hadn't been with her. It had been years since his tastes had run to back alleys. No, he'd never seen her before, but she reminded him of someone. Who? Charles shrugged aside the question as his glance swept over the scuffed shoes, the frilly parasol that matched nothing, the black lace evening gloves that not only were out of place before evening but had holes in them, the less-than-clean and obviously wrinkled dress.

But what really caught his attention was the fact that the little beauty looked as if she'd just come from a good toss. Her lips were swollen, or were they always that full? No. There were whisker burns around her mouth. Charles almost laughed. If he knew one thing, he knew whores. The low cut of her dress allowed him to view much of her gleaming white breasts. Her waist was very small. Charles liked what he saw, liked it very much indeed.

He studied her for a moment. She needed the right clothes and hairstyle, as well as a bath, no doubt, but if she were pox free, he imagined this one could amount to something. This one just might become a star, and he would use her until she realized she could do it on her own.

Charles spoke a few words to Ruby. He was terribly sorry, but he had a business appointment he'd only just remembered. He'd see her back at the apartment later this evening. Even as he said the words, Charles wondered if he'd bother. Perhaps he'd send her to Macy right off. Macy could see to it that the girl was placed where she belonged.

Charles walked to the small woman and gave her his most devastating smile. Kit, loving nothing more than the attention she got from men, grinned in return.

"Hello," he said.

Kit, rather than taking offense at his boldness and the fact that he dared to speak to her without being properly introduced, thought his voice deep and mellow, simply beautiful. "Hello," she said in return.

"Did you ever imagine that two souls might be destined to meet? Destined for all eternity?" They were the very same words he used at every introduction. Pretty, but the fact was, Charles was wasting his time. There was no need for poetic nonsense when it came to this girl. Kit, coarser than most, liked things straight out in the open. She didn't have much patience when it came to trying to decipher the meaning behind a man's words.

She shrugged, wondering if her first impression had proven false. She thought she detected a certain look in the man's eye. Now that he was talking about souls and that sort of rubbish, she was fast losing interest. "I don't think much about souls." She was looking to her left and then her right, wondering if there wasn't someone a bit more interesting she could attract.

"Why?"

"Because my family, especially my sister, has been trying to save mine for as long as I can remember."

Charles threw his head back and laughed with delight. Kit thought he was beautiful. She didn't notice the flatness in his eyes, nor the lines between nose and mouth that debauchery had deepened. She

318

didn't see the slight loosening of flesh around his eyes and along a once-firm jaw. What she did notice was his diamond stickpin and the two rings on his fingers. His clothes were beautifully tailored. Vaguely she wondered how much money he had. And then she found herself wondering if she could get her hands on just a bit of it.

"And have you been trying to lose it?"

That look was definitely back. Kit decided the man was more interesting than she'd first thought. She batted her lashes, knowing what it did to a man, and returned coyly, "One can only try one's best, monsieur."

Charles chuckled and offered her his arm. "My name is Charles Briggs."

"Kit Du Maurier."

"Kit, I think we have some talking to do."

She looked at him with some surprise and then frowned. "Talking?" Her tone told clearly she wasn't much interested in his suggestion.

"That and much more."

Charles signaled for a carriage. A moment later he was helping her inside. They sat across from each other. He watched her closely while she took in the luxury of the leather seats, the curtains, the fur lap rugs.

"I've never ridden in a closed carriage before." At that moment Charles could almost believe her to be an innocent. Perhaps she was, he reconsidered, in some things.

"How many other things have you never done?"

Kit blinked at the question. "I don't know what you mean."

There was nothing for it but to ask straight out, or never know the truth of the matter. "Have you had your first man yet?"

"Of course." God, she felt so sophisticated, so womanly, being able to say that. She loved it.

"How many?"

"Two. First the cobbler, Mr. Tomas, and then Mr. Henri, the perfumer."

Charles believed her. She was too exuberant, too obviously proud of her accomplishments to not be telling him the truth. He nodded. Only two men. There was a very good chance she wasn't diseased yet. And if she listened to him, she never would be.

"The first thing you'll have to learn is not to be so honest. And the next is to keep the identity of your men a secret. Never tell anyone their names."

Kit's eyes were wide as she took in his words, nodding as if a schoolgirl learning her first lesson.

"Now, I have a certain project in mind."

"What kind?"

"Well, it involves you."

Kit smiled. "Does it? Doing what?"

"I'll be showing you presently. It all depends, of course, on what you look like under that dress."

"Should I show you?"

Charles was amazed. He couldn't remember the last time one of his girls had been so cooperative, so willing to do as he asked. Usually it took a bit of pressure, sometimes even a lash or two of his whip before they agreed. "You could."

Kit felt not the least bit of indecision as she lowered her dress, exposing her breasts to his view. To her mind her body was simply a means to finding

320

satisfaction. Morals never entered her mind.

Charles nodded. "Very nice." An understatement, to be sure. She had beautiful breasts, quite the most beautiful he'd ever seen, and he'd seen plenty. "I'd ask you to show me the rest, but we're almost at my place."

Kit shrugged, knowing not a trace of modesty. She might as well have been discussing the weather and offering him a look at the sky. "It will take only a minute." She raised her skirt as easily as she might have adjusted her ratty gloves.

Charles forced back his grin. Damn, but he was a lucky bastard. She was a natural, knowing not the least restraint. Still, he'd have to teach her some. He couldn't have his best flaunting everything without getting paid to do it. "It looks very good," he said clinically. "I think we can do business."

Kit smoothed her clothes into place and then looked out the window, marveling at the passing scenery as if she were a young, innocent girl who hadn't just exposed herself to a virtual stranger. Charles had seen almost everything in his twenty-nine years, but he hadn't ever come across a woman so natural in her nakedness, nor one who could turn her sexuality on and off at a moment's notice. She was a breath of fresh air. But best of all, she could make him a fortune. Still, he thought that he might keep this one mostly for himself, except for special occasions, of course. He imagined that they would get on very well. Very well indeed.

Charles helped her from the carriage, paid the driver, and escorted her into the most beautiful house Kit had ever seen. It was one of his bordellos, but even had she known, she wouldn't have cared. There were walls of mirrors and red velvet as well. The rugs and drapery were red, even the top of the bar was red. She'd never thought to see anything so wonderful in her life.

Charles handed his gloves, hat, and a walking stick to the servant at the door. He whispered to the man something Kit did not hear and then escorted her up the wide, gleaming stairway.

In his room, a room bigger than the entire apartment she shared with her grandmother, father, and brother, he asked if she wanted a drink.

Kit shook her head. "Thank you, but I don't like the taste of drink."

Charles grinned. This woman needed no false courage. She was a purely sexual creature who knew what she wanted without the aid of artificial stimuli. Good. "The doctor will be with us shortly."

"Are you ill?"

"No. He's coming to examine you."

Kit frowned, finding that notion an odd one. "Why?"

"Because I want to make sure you're not—" Charles stopped to reword his thoughts. It wouldn't do to insult the girl. "I just want to make sure you're well."

"I am."

"Let's let the doctor have a look just to make sure, shall we?"

Kit shrugged. She didn't care. What she cared about was this room and the beautiful things in it. Someday she wanted a room just like this one.

There were golden cherubs holding long red velvet

curtains at the head of the bed. There were crystal decanters and matching glasses sitting on silver trays. There were gold-trimmed mirrors and pure white satin chairs. On a small table beside one of those chairs stood a picture of a naked lady. The pose left nothing at all to the imagination. Kit raised her eyes to Charles's knowing grin.

"Do you like it?"

"Very much," Kit said in response while wondering if she could have a picture like this of herself.

There was a knock on the door, and a man entered. His jacket and trousers were of the best material and fit his thin frame perfectly. Kit might not have known the cost, but she knew expensive clothing when she saw it. Everything in this place was expensive. She felt dowdy when comparing her best dress to the riches found here.

"I have business downstairs," Charles said. "I'll be back soon."

The doctor examined her with hardly a word spoken between them. The moment he was finished, he left, again without so much as a good day. A few minutes later a maid came with a tray of food. She also drew Kit a bath. Kit thought it the most luxurious thing in the world to bathe during the day and in a golden tub big enough for two. After her bath her hair was brushed until it glowed. Finally she was dressed in a diaphanous gown of black net, the prettiest thing she'd ever worn.

Kit, alone at last, stood before the mirror and laughed, unable to understand why anyone would bother wearing something like this. Certainly it hid nothing.

The fact of the matter was that after years of being forced to play the demure miss, of never having a minute's privacy because she shared a room with Emy and Grandmère, Kit wasn't about to cover herself now that she didn't have to.

She threw the lovely garment over a chair and laid on the bed and grinned as she looked her body over in the mirror above.

It was almost an hour before Charles finally returned, only to find his newest girl half asleep, and very, very naked indeed.

He kissed her mouth awake and then kissed everywhere else.

Sometime later Kit stretched, and while yawning said, "That was very good."

Charles frowned just a bit, but figured with all that natural talent, he could afford to tutor her some on proper manners. The first being to yawn in a delicate fashion, as if she were a lady.

"Every other time I did it, I had to rush. I knew I was missing something."

The second lesson would cover never comparing her men. "Why were you rushing?"

"Because both the men had wives and were scared they'd be back before we were finished."

Charles's lips thinned in distaste, his mind picturing a back-alley whore. Actually, his first impression. It was a good thing he found her when he did. There was no telling what she might have become if allowed to continue on with her present course. "You won't be doing that again."

"Why not? Mr. Henri might have been quick about it, but he had a big—"

"Because," Charles interrupted, not in the least interested in the size of certain parts of the man's anatomy, "I want you to move in here. You don't need more than one man."

Kit laughed at the absurdity of that notion. First of all, there was no way she was going to be satisfied with just one man. Not with the hundreds this city had to offer.

Granted, Charlie here made her feel things the other two hadn't, but she'd had only three so far. It was ridiculous to think she should settle for one when there were so many left to sample. Especially Hawk. She didn't know how, but she was going to have that man one day. Still, Charlie didn't have to know that. What she did was her own business. "I can't move in here. My family would go crazy."

She smiled at what she considered great sophistication, and said, "I almost had two at one time." Kit was under the delusion that she would have, but for her sister's untimely interruption, bedded both Hawk and Cole in the barn.

"Did you?" Charles answered without much thought. He was wondering if her family would prove to be a problem. Most likely not, judging by the looks of her. No decent family would let a young girl dress like she did, or roam the streets of this city unchaperoned.

Kit nodded proudly. "My stupid brother-in-law and Hawk. Only my sister walked in and ruined everything."

Charles was instantly alert. "Hawk?" He knew very well who Hawk was. Everyone in New Orleans knew the deputy, but . . . "Who the hell is your brother-in-law?"

"You've probably heard of him. He's the marshal."

Charles stifled a curse. He realized now why she had looked so familiar. He'd seen the marshal's beautiful wife. He should have known from the first. The two women looked remarkably alike.

For the first time in his life, Charles didn't know what to think. He had been about to insist that she stay the night, that she stay permanently, in fact, that he groom her into the perfect courtesan, that she eventually be put in charge of his girls, but there was no way he was going to get the marshal all riled up.

"How close are you and your brother-in-law?"

"Close?" Kit laughed at the absurdity. "We could have been very close, but my sister—"

"That's not what I'm asking."

Kit shrugged. "We tolerate each other."

There was something here, something he couldn't quite put his finger on. All right, so maybe he couldn't have her in the way he'd originally intended, but there had to be something he could work out, something more than an occasional afternoon of lusty pleasure.

Charles tried to concentrate, but at the moment could come up with nothing. He didn't give up hope. Charles was a patient man. He knew something would come to him. Some way he could use her. In the meantime . . . He grinned as he reached for a breast.

*   *   *

Hours later he was rollicking upon the same bed with yet another lusty lovely when it suddenly came to him. Kit was part of the marshal's family. How easy would it be for her to get certain pieces of information known only to the marshal and his deputy? How much did she hear in passing conversation?

Charles laughed as his thoughts became more clear. The marshal would know when certain shipments were brought into New Orleans. All Charles had to do was convince Kit it would be in her best interest if she passed that information along. He moved automatically, and without much thought pressed his body into the whore. Without a doubt there were great riches to be gained with the help of a certain little miss.

Grandmère and Emy sat beneath the tree in the courtyard. It was cool. The once-uncomfortable iron chairs now sported dark green padded cushions. The chairs could now be used at length with no ill effects. The two women talked as Emy sewed.

"Things are good here," Grandmère said, enjoying the cool damp air that was filled with an array of flowering scents as well as the sweet minty drink.

Emy smiled, for her grandmother seemed more rational of late, more her old self. It looked as if she were growing accustomed to her new surroundings and for that Emy could only thank the good Lord.

"Better than I ever hoped."

"You've been sewing a lot."

"I made new drapes for the sitting rooms. Now

I've got to start on the bedroom."

"And then?"

She shrugged. "I'm sure I'll find something else that needs sewing."

"Baby clothes?"

Emy raised her gaze from her work to her grandmother's wise eyes and laughed with the pure joy of simply being alive. How many more blessings did God have in store? "I never could keep anything from you."

"Did you tell Cole yet?"

"Tell him what?" Cole asked, suddenly behind his wife. He was getting better at understanding. Sometimes it didn't matter how fast Emy spoke, he could understand most of what was said. He reached down and planted a short kiss on her cheek.

Without missing a beat, for she wanted very much to tell him this particular bit of news in private, she said, "Not tell, ask. I was going to ask if you wanted anything in particular for dinner?"

Cole shrugged and leaned against the tree. He took a sip from her glass as he watched her closely. She didn't lie often, not since she came here, in fact, but he always knew when she did. Something happened to her left eye when she lied. The lid quivered just as if a nerve or muscle were upset at the deception. Cole figured he could wait until later before finding out what she was hiding.

"How come you're home so early?"

"I just stopped by for a minute. Had to get a few papers I left behind this morning." He tapped his chest, indicating the papers were in that pocket.

They kissed and he was gone. Emy heard his horse

328

trot down the street.

"He didn't believe you."

"I know."

"He knows about your eye."

Emy sighed even as a smile curved her lips. "I thought he might. It doesn't sit well to know you have not a speck of mystery. That your husband knows your every secret. Do you think I'll ever be able to control it?"

"I think it's probably best not to try."

Emy laughed, imagining how happy Cole was going to be tonight. "Come with me to Betty's. We're having lunch."

"You two don't want some old woman sitting there, listening to girl talk."

"You're right, I don't. But I want *you* there."

"And Anton loves the work. Papa can hardly get him out of the place. When he's not cooking, he's shining tables, mirrors, and floors until they glow."

They sat across from each other, finishing the last of their evening meal. "It was a stroke of luck, don't you think? Imagine Old Man Butler dying and his sons selling out like that. Amazing that they didn't even want a down payment."

"It wasn't luck at all," Emy said in all confidence. "It was my prayers."

Cole frowned. "You were praying for Butler to die?"

Emy, in a particularly good mood on this night, thought his question was remarkably amusing. "Of course I wasn't praying for the man to die. I was praying that Papa and Anton would find something they both liked to do. And cooking is what they like most of all."

"You prayed for that, did you?" It didn't take a genius to know Cole didn't believe in prayers. Both his voice and expression spoke of his disbelief. "What else do you pray for?"

"I pray for many things."

"Like what?" he asked as he sipped a glass of white wine.

"I pray for you, and for Hawk."

Cole knew a niggling sense of jealousy. "Why Hawk?"

"Because he might have to protect you someday. I want to make sure he's perfectly healthy so he can do a good job of it."

Cole grinned. "I'm sure Hawk will be happy to hear of your concern."

"You're not going to tell him, are you?"

"No. It'll be our secret." Cole couldn't help but wonder how many other secrets this woman hid from him. "Who else do you pray for?"

"Grandmère, of course."

Cole couldn't miss the softening of her voice when she spoke of her grandmother.

"And Kit."

"Your prayers might have found Jacques and Anton their restaurant, but I doubt that they're working on that score."

"What do you mean?"

"I mean she has new shoes and stinks to high heaven of perfume. How do you imagine she got them?"

Emy's mouth dropped open in shock. "She stole a

pair of shoes? And perfume?" Her eyes were wide with fear. "Oh, Cole, I'll watch her. I promise I won't let her out of my sight again."

Cole took Emy's hand in a soothing gesture. "Sweetheart," he began, knowing the truth of it was going to be even more of a shock. "She didn't steal the shoes and perfume."

Emy frowned. "Then how did she get them? She has no money." She thought for just a second and suddenly gasped. "No! She stole something from the house and sold it?" Emy's cheeks grew redder than fire. Too late, her hands came to cover her embarrassment. "Oh, my God, Cole. I'm so sorry. What did she take? I'll buy it back with the money I make from my sewing."

He looked at her for a moment before he said very simply, "I love you."

That brought her whirling thoughts to an instant stop. Her brow creased into a puzzled frown. "I know. But what has that to do with anything?"

It was then that Cole decided to allow her to believe Kit was stealing. It was better than the truth. Most anything was better than that particular truth. "It doesn't. I just wanted you to know it."

Emy smiled. "You're not angry, are you?" Her cheeks were only now returning to normal color. "I mean about Kit."

"No. I'm not angry."

"I'm going to pray harder." She nodded in her enthusiasm. "You'll see. She'll change. I know prayers can make her change."

Cole wondered if it was possible to love a woman more than he loved Emy.

*   *   *

It was dark. They had stepped into the garden before retiring to their room. Fireflies flashed their merry light as they scurried from tree to bush to vine. Cole's arm was around his wife's waist. He sighed as he positioned her so that he could snuggle her back to his chest.

"I can't begin to tell you how much I love it here."

"What is it you love the most?"

"After you, you mean?"

Cole chuckled a soft sound. "You're a smart lady. That was exactly the right answer."

"You'll always be my first love."

Cole grunted a sound of approval.

"I lied to you today."

Cole nodded. "I know."

"Grandmère said it was the eye again. I wish I could stop doing that."

"Why? Do you want to lie to me?"

"Well, no, not really, but a woman is hardly mysterious if she can't keep a secret or two, and I can't keep any if my eye twitches like that."

"Are you keeping a secret?"

Emy turned in his arms and bit her lips together as she nodded.

"But you're going to tell me, right?"

She couldn't hold back a soft giggle as she teased him. "If I told you, it wouldn't be a secret, would it?"

"You told your grandmother."

"No, I didn't. She guessed."

"Should I guess as well?"

"You'll never do it," she said in all confidence.

332

"Is it the fact that you're going to have a baby?"

Emy had been leaning against him, her arms around his neck. Now she stiffened, released his neck, and took a step back. "Cole! For God's sake," she reprimanded him unhappily. "I was waiting all night for the right moment to tell you. I can't have any fun with you at all."

"Sweetheart, the truth is, you already had fun with me, otherwise you wouldn't be having a baby."

Emy giggled as she stepped back into his arms. "You wretch. How did you know?"

"Well, since my wife thought to keep me in the dark, I had to find other means of—"

She gave him a little shake. "How?"

"We've made love almost every night since we've been married. Am I right?"

"So?"

"So, we've been here almost two months and you haven't gotten your monthly—"

"Oh," came out a soft moan, "don't. Please."

Cole smiled at her obvious discomfort. "It's a normal happening, isn't it?"

"Maybe, but it's not for a man to talk about." She buried her face in his chest and finished with, "Men aren't supposed to even know about it."

"Why?"

"I don't know. The Sisters in school always told us to never speak about it. To never go near a boy on certain days, or he'd know."

Cole shook his head in disbelief, amazed at how some could take so normal an occurrence and twist it into a shameful taboo.

"Do you think all men know?"

"I'm afraid they do, sweetheart."

It took Emy a moment to digest this information. "Then why did they tell us that? Why did they make it seem somehow wrong?"

Cole shook his head. "It's not that they purposely misled. I think they were just innocents themselves."

She leaned back and narrowed her gaze into a warning glare. "You're not implying that I'm an innocent, are you?"

Cole couldn't hold back his smile. Obviously she didn't want to be labeled as such, but there wasn't a doubt in Cole's mind, despite the things they had done together, that this woman was an innocent in the truest sense of the word. "I wouldn't think of it, sweetheart."

"Because I'm not."

"I love you."

"I'm serious, Cole. I don't want to be an innocent. It's so boring."

"Do you think so?"

"Don't you?"

"Nope."

"You mean you wouldn't rather if I were a bit more experienced?"

"Absolutely not!"

"Then what's going to happen when I am?"

"What do you mean?"

Emy shot him a look of impatience. "Cole, I can't stay an innocent. Not after being married. Does that mean you won't want me after—"

Cole pulled her tighter against him and smiled as he nuzzled his face into the warmth of her neck. "Sweetheart, there's never going to be a time when I won't want you."

She made a tsking sound. "You have me all confused."

"I think we're talking about different degrees of innocence here. Let's just say you're perfect just as you are."

"Perfect, huh?"

"Perfect."

Emy nodded. "Just as long as I'm not innocent. I think I could grow to like the idea of being perfect."

Cole laughed as he gathered her into his arms. "Good. Let's go to bed."

"And work on getting rid of some of that innocence?"

Cole glanced at his wife's hopeful expression. "My thoughts exactly."

Chapter Seventeen

Kit sighed as she lay beside Charles, her gaze upon their temporarily satiated bodies reflected in the mirror above. "When can I get a picture?"

Charles wondered what she was going to do with it once she got the damn thing. She'd mentioned it at least three times this week alone. "Suppose your father should find it?"

"He won't. He's almost never home anymore. Grandmère is the only one who might, but she's half blind and wouldn't know what to make of it if she could see it."

Charles laughed at the thought. "You mean she doesn't know what a naked woman looks like?"

"She hasn't been naked, except for bathing, in years." Kit watched in admiration as she ran her hands over her lush body. "Besides, her body and mine are hardly the same."

"When are you going to get me the information?"

"I don't understand what you want it for. What

difference can it make to you when any ship comes into port."

"I already told you why. I'm expecting new gaming tables. I don't want them to get lost at the docks."

Kit nodded. "I know that. What I don't know is what's the big secret?"

"The marshal's office is always notified when a shipment is coming in, especially when it's an expensive shipment, which most are. A few deputies are usually stationed around the docks, watching for any trouble."

"So? What has that got to do with you?"

"So do you think the marshal is going to care if someone takes my equipment?"

"It's his job to care."

"I just want to make sure. It won't hurt matters to hire my own men. Besides, I don't want any competition to find out."

Kit didn't know who his competition was, nor was she interested in finding out.

"All right. I'll get you the information. I promise."

"And I'll get you your picture."

Kit laughed. "I get the picture when you get the information, is that it?"

Charles grinned. There was nothing like a woman who knew the score.

"I'll invite myself to dinner tonight. Maybe I can find out something then."

"Good. And I'll have the camera ready tomorrow."

*   *   *

"What's the matter with you?" Kit scowled at her hovering sister. "You're following me everywhere I go."

"Nothing is the matter. Is there a particular reason you want to be alone?" Emy asked as she took a small figurine from Kit's hand and replaced it upon her husband's desk.

"Who said I wanted to be alone?" Kit shot her sister a look that was clearly puzzled. "God, Emy, since you got yourself pregnant, there's no talking to you."

Emy shot her sister a hard look. She hated the word *pregnant*. A lady never stated the fact so crudely. Always it was said that she was in a family way, or expecting. Besides, it was hardly correct that she had gotten herself pregnant. Emy almost said as much, but decided the less said on that matter, especially to this girl, the better.

"Having a baby has nothing to do with how I'm acting."

"Yeah, then what does?"

"The fact that you stole something from this house and won't be doing it again."

"Are you crazy? There's nothing in this house that I want. What would I steal?" The fact of the matter was, over the years Kit had lied on such a regular basis that Emy didn't recognize the truth when she heard it. Besides, Cole had professed the girl guilty of stealing, and she had no reason to doubt his word.

"I don't know what it was."

"That makes sense, doesn't it?" Kit was many things, but a thief was not one of them. Despite her

338

innocence on that score, she felt no anger, but merely shrugged off the accusation as nonsensical, beliving her sister's odd behavior a result of her condition. "You know I stole something but you don't know what it was. Then how do you know I stole it?"

"Where did you get those shoes, the perfume, and that new dress?"

If she thought the dress and perfume were something, Kit wondered what Emy would say if she saw the silk and lace chemise and drawers under the dress. The stockings as well. Kit was almost tempted to show her, but stopped herself at the last second. She didn't need the questions that would surely come from that. "None of your business."

"It's my business when you're stealing from my husband."

"For your information, I work for everything I get." Well, she did, sort of. It just so happened that she could hardly consider doing what she loved most in the world work. The fact that Charles gave her things was hardly important. The truth was, she loved it and would have done it all for nothing.

Emy narrowed her gaze, looking at her sister with some real doubt. "Where?"

"At the perfumery. Mr. Henri lets me sweep out the place." Kit gave a mental shrug at the lie. She hadn't been back to Mr. Henri's in weeks and she wouldn't have swept out his place if he begged her.

Emy didn't believe her for a minute. There was no way that her sister would do that kind of work. Emy had had to threaten, beg, and plead just to get her to do the smallest chores while living at home. "Why don't you work with Papa and Anton?"

"In a restaurant?" It was obvious that Kit couldn't be more amazed at the question. "I'd end up smelling like garlic, or onions."

"Heaven forbid," Emy returned with some real disgust. "Maybe even some honest sweat?"

"Sweat's all right." Kit chuckled a mysterious sound that caused her sister a puzzled and curious glance. Kit instantly hid her wicked thoughts behind a sweet smile. Honesty was one thing, stupidity quite another. Marriage hadn't loosened Emy up at all. The fact of the matter was, since marrying Cole, she had grown more prim and proper than ever. And with Cole behind her sister, being pressed into a convent became a distinct possibility if Emy even suspected what she was about.

Emy watched the flash of a smile and sighed. There was no sense trying to understand this girl. The fact of the matter was, she didn't have the time or the patience. "Come into the kitchen. I have to start dinner."

Kit wasn't interested in hot, smelly kitchens. "I thought you had a cook."

"Today is Becky's day off."

Kit sighed, knowing if she didn't linger for a bit, she wouldn't get any information at all, and if she wanted that picture and the new dress he'd promised her, she'd better get Charles something. Kit followed her sister out of the house and into the large kitchen.

Just as she knew it would be, it was hot. The fire in the stove, a fire that was rarely allowed to go out since it usually took too long to start another, made it almost impossible to breathe. Kit watched her sister lift the lid on a pot. From the scent of it, Kit knew she was making gumbo. "Invite me to dinner," she said, and watched as Emy shot her a peculiar look.

"You know I love gumbo." Kit knew a moment of satisfaction at Emy's nod.

Kit watched her sister clean the kitchen. The more she saw of married life, the more she was sure that it wasn't for her. There was no way she was going to cook like this for any man. She laughed at the thought.

"What are you laughing at?"

"Nothing," she said as she bit into a piece of crusty bread.

Emy wondered what her sister was about. Since when did she want to eat here? Since when did she want to come here at all? What, she wondered, was Kit up to?

She might not ever know, but one thing was for certain. This girl wasn't going to steal even a crumb from Cole's house. Not if Emy could help it.

"Go get Grandmère. If you're eating here, there's no sense in her eating alone."

Cole was quiet during dinner, shooting his wife one odd look after another, quieter still when he realized his sister-in-law was particularly interested in the happenings at the docks. He couldn't for the life of him imagine why. And then it hit him. She was looking to go into business, he thought. Perhaps she realized what she was practically giving away for nothing could make her a rich woman.

Well, if it was riches she was looking for, she had better get to it. He knew from personal experience, his mother being at one time the highest-paid whore in all of San Francisco, that a woman's looks didn't last long in her profession. And Cole knew for a fact that she was in that profession. Her afternoon visits to Charlie Briggs were never concealed. Anyone could see the comings and goings. Cole often spotted her coming from the whorehouse while making his rounds. It was a sure bet she wasn't going there to dust his picture frames.

The fact was, Cole didn't give a damn if she whored for the entire state. All he cared about was if she should become diseased. If that happened, then he'd have to cut off any association between the two sisters. He knew it would hurt her, but there was no way that he was going to chance his wife to his sister-in-law's depraved indulgences.

Emy handed her husband three dollars. She backed up a few feet and put her hands behind her back.

Cole frowned at the money and put it on the bed as he removed his other boot, getting ready for bed. He nodded toward the three bills and asked, "What's this for?"

"You said Kit stole something from the house, but I forgot to ask you what it was." She couldn't look at him, but kept her gaze to the floor, mortified at being forced to mention so dishonorable an act. "Because I didn't know, I couldn't buy it back. Here's the money. You do it."

Cole had never actually said that Kit stole something, but had allowed his wife to believe it rather than tell her the truth. Now he didn't know what the hell to do. He didn't want to take her money. She worked long hours over her sewing, only to gain almost nothing for her efforts. No doubt she'd completed an entire dress that very afternoon. And yet he knew she'd never rest until she believed the debt paid.

He reached for the bills as he came to his feet. "You don't have to do this."

Emy raised her gaze from the floor and nodded. "I do."

Cole knew nothing would be accomplished in arguing with her. He pocketed the money, figuring he'd get it into her purse later.

"Come over here."

Emy did as she was told and sighed her happiness as he took her in his arms. Emy pressed her face to his chest. "I'm so embarrassed. My family—" She breathed a deep, shuddering sigh, not knowing how to go on.

"There's no need. Your family got a little off the track, but they're fine now. It's just Kit that needs . . . I'm not sure I know what she needs."

"Prayers."

Cole smiled as he breathed in her clean scent and hugged her tightly against him. "Yes, sweetheart. Prayers."

*　　*　　*

"What the hell do you want here?" Hawk scowled as he looked up from the papers on his desk.

"I thought maybe you might be lonely."

"You thought wrong."

Kit sat opposite him and smiled at yet another scowl. "You know, Hawk, I think you're afraid of me."

Hawk laughed. "You might be right. Fact is, you scare the hell out of me."

"Why?"

"Because I like your sister very much."

Kit shrugged at the statement. "So. I don't care if you're making—"

"I'm not. Only a little whore like you would think that I might be. Cole is my best friend."

"And you wouldn't do anything against Cole," Kit said with childish sarcasm. "So what has all that got to do with me?"

"It's got to do with this. Your sister thinks you're a good girl. Just a little wild, but basically good. How the hell could I look at her if I did the things you want?"

"The things we both want."

Hawk didn't bother to deny her correction. He might be disgusted with her, but his body didn't seem to know any better. He wanted her, all right.

Kit shrugged. "So don't look at her."

"Most whores have some ethics, know some sense of morals."

"And you've had your share, I suppose, so you

344

know that for a fact."

Hawk didn't respond.

"Well, what I want to know is, what good are morals? Where do they get you? Nowhere," she answered her own question. "Except to learn to be humble. And you know what humble is? An excuse to do without."

Hawk still didn't respond. There was no sense arguing with her kind of mentality. She could never understand the decency of her sister. Some people were simply born lacking, and she was one of them.

"Well, not me. I'm going to get everything I've ever wanted."

"Except me."

"Maybe, maybe not." She shrugged, and both of them knew it didn't really matter to her one way or the other.

"What the hell is going on?"

Cole sipped a cup of strong black coffee, put his feet on his desk, and watched his friend study the busy street through the office window. He'd just come in. Usually Cole and Hawk worked the same shift. But since Jake Collins's wife got sick, Hawk and Cole saw each other only when one was starting and the other finishing a shift. They were talking about Kit and her unexpected visit during Hawk's shift. "I only wish I knew. She was at the house last night, acting as sweet as could be. It took me a while, but I finally realized she was asking all kinds of questions about the docks.

"What did she ask you?"

"Nothing. I thought at first all she wanted was to get into my pants, but I was wrong. Just before she left I figured out it wasn't me she wanted at all. What I can't figure out is what she's up to."

Cole sighed. He wished to hell that the little brat wasn't part of his family. He didn't want or need problems. "I reckon we'll know eventually."

"Yeah. Well, I've got to make my rounds. And then I'm going to bed. I'll see you tonight."

Cole nodded as his deputy walked out of the small office.

Kit shook her head. "I didn't get anything."

"Nothing at all?"

"No word about your tables."

"Then what?"

"Only that a shipment of silks are due to arrive Friday night aboard the merchant *Eastern Star*."

"Is that it?" Charles hoped his voice portrayed just the right amount of disappointment. It did. "Is that all you could get?"

"I couldn't ask any more questions. Cole was starting to give me odd looks."

"All right," Charles shrugged as if dissatisfied. He didn't want this one to get any ideas. She wasn't as stupid as he would have liked.

Silk was good. The fact was, silk was real good. He could almost double his fortunes if he could get his hands on an entire shipload of the stuff.

Tonight he'd send word to one of his people to

346

watch for the *Eastern Star*. Once they saw in which warehouse the silk was stored, it would be nothing to load it up and take it away.

"So? What about the picture?"

Charles smiled as he watched her take off her clothes. Usually she was naked within ten seconds of entering this room. Today proved no different. "Leave the stockings on," he said. "The stockings and these shoes." He handed her a pair of red satin high heels. Tiny pieces of glass had formed a shining flower at the toe. Kit could hardly believe it. These shoes were even more pretty than those the cobbler had made especially for her. They were the most beautiful shoes she'd ever seen.

"Oh, Charles, they're beautiful. Can I keep them?"

Charles nodded. "Once you get me the information about the right ship, I'll get you a dress to match."

"And silk underwear." Kit had come to know the luxury of silk against skin. She no longer limited herself to doing without, but had gained an appetite for the best.

"And silk underwear," he promised.

Charles spent the next half hour positioning her in every pose imaginable. He figured for being such a good girl, she deserved her choice of pictures.

It was the Monday after the *Philadelphia* made port and the day after the warehouse had been emptied, the third robbery in as many weeks. Cole frowned. He'd been marshal for more than a year, and during that whole time New Orleans had never suffered such a rash of robberies. Cole figured it was obvious that someone was watching the docks, noting when a ship came in and where the cargo was stored. That narrowed the list of suspects down to only a couple of thousand each day. There was no other answer. None, at least, that he was willing to consider. Still, he couldn't shake the feeling of approaching doom.

He didn't want to think the things he was thinking. His wife wasn't playing him for a fool again. Her family wasn't behind this. It had to be something else, someone else. Then why was he besieged with this almost devastating feeling of distrust. Cole knew from experience to trust his instincts. Only this time he couldn't figure his instincts out.

Something was wrong. The problem was, he had the feeling he knew what it was. There was something somewhere that just didn't fit.

Cole left his office, knowing the best way to find a solution to any problem was to take a long walk. He hadn't a doubt that he would find an answer to these questions the minute he put his mind to something else.

He walked along the dock, listening to the hawkers calling out the price of their wares. They sold to the private sector as well as wholesalers, who would ship much of what they bought north. They sold everything from cotton and rice to Jamaican rum and China tea.

He watched as children ran to the dock's edge

while frantic mothers called out to be careful. He watched as a ship made port and stevedores began the arduous task of unloading the hold.

And then he saw her. Just a simple whore, stumbling home after a hard night's work. She was diseased. Most of the dockside whores were, but it wasn't disease that had brought him his answer. It was the fact that she was a whore, dark and small, a woman who had once been pretty, just like the one who had sat across from his table, asking questions about ships and their cargoes.

Everything was suddenly and perfectly clear. She had done it for Emy. Emy probably figured Cole would get suspicious if she asked. Who would suspect a fifteen-year-old old? No one.

God damn his wife and her family. They had done it to him again. Jesus, was he never going to learn that a sweet mouth could hold the most bitter lies?

Cole walked the short distance to Jacques's Place. He opened the door and took in the white-linen-covered tables, the shining floors, the fragrant smells of garlic and shrimp. The place wasn't open for business yet, wouldn't be until noon, but he could hear his father- and brother-in-law in the back, arguing over something.

Cole hated what he was doing; still, it wasn't about to stop him. Spying wasn't the way he usually went about things, but he was going to know the truth. It didn't matter how he came across it.

They were yelling at each other. He didn't hope to find any information involving them. He didn't hope to be proven right. He simply wanted to find out who was behind the robberies. But their argument wasn't over stolen whiskey and silks, but the amount of garlic Anton had bought at the open market.

He insisted it was enough. Jacques insisted otherwise.

"Do you always fight like this?"

Both men spun around in surprise. They hadn't heard Cole come in. Both grinned even as Jacques shoved a cup of coffee and a confectionery treat into Cole's hands.

"We're not fighting," Anton said. "He always yells like this when he doesn't get his way."

Cole smiled, but his smile held none of the humor he should have known. He hadn't a doubt that these two were involved. Emy couldn't have done this alone. The robberies were always accomplished under the cover of darkness, and he kept her more than busy when it was dark.

God, how she must have hated that. He smiled again in self-derision. Poor Emy had to act out the loving and dutiful wife in order to attain her means. How long, he wondered, would it have gone on? How long before she and her family had enough and stole away like the lying thieves they were into the night?

Cole grunted at his thoughts, his hosts believing the sound enjoyment of the cake. There was no way that he was going to let them get away with it this time. It didn't matter that he'd likely be the one to suffer most of all. It didn't matter that it would probably kill him when he watched his own wife get arrested. He wouldn't do it himself, but he wouldn't stop Hawk from doing his job.

"Things going well?" he asked around a bite of sugared cake.

Both men smiled, for Cole spoke in almost flawless French, accent and all. "You're starting to sound like us."

He nodded. "It's living with Emy." When his wife was excited, and she often was, about anything, from seeing a snake in her garden to finding the right piece of lace for the baby's blanket, she spoke in French. It would have been hard not to pick it up.

The two men went back to their cooking in preparation for the noon hour, occasionally glancing at their guest and silently wondering why Cole leaned against a wall, watching their every move. They spoke every so often, but got little but a grunt or nod as a response. Finally, his nerves a bit shaken, Jacques asked, "Is something the matter?"

"No. I just thought I'd stop by. Haven't had a chance to see much of you lately."

"Come tonight for dinner."

Cole nodded. He leaned away from the wall and cleared his throat. He couldn't just leave without hinting that they just might have something to worry about. "There is something."

Both men looked in his direction.

"There've been three warehouses robbed in the past three weeks. You wouldn't have heard anything about it, would you?"

Both men gave silent groans. They knew Cole would mention the robberies. They knew as well that he would talk to them about it, that they would immediately be suspect. The trouble was, there was no way to prove their innocence. They could deny involvement, but why should Cole believe them? He wouldn't, of course. Not after the things they had done.

"We heard," Anton said. "Everyone has been talking about it."

Cole nodded. He didn't want to accuse them. Not yet. Not until he had some solid proof. "It was lucky, I mean the way you got this place."

Both men smiled and nodded their agreement.

"Very lucky," Cole repeated. "Most would have had to come up with a down payment at least."

"Both of Mr. Butler's sons are doctors. They wanted only to rid themselves of the place."

"I see." Cole put down the coffee and unfinished cake. "Yeah, well, I've got to go. Maybe I'll bring Emy in tonight."

Both men curved their lips into thin smiles, never realizing the smiles did not reach their eyes, but Cole did. He looked at them for a hard moment before he turned and walked out.

Both men watched him leave and sighed in relief. Each knew one thing for a fact. As long as they couldn't prove it, they were guilty in his eyes.

Cole felt his heart dry up and die. It was the last time, of course. How many hearts did a man have? He knew it was her. Maybe he couldn't prove it, but he knew it for a fact. Three times he had mentioned a

352

ship and its cargo. Three times that cargo had been stolen.

"I stopped by to see your father and brother today."

Emy was just finishing the last of the dress. It was the prettiest thing she'd ever made, and she wished she could keep it for herself. "Did you? Why?"

"No reason. I was in the area."

Emy frowned and shot him a puzzled look as she bit the end of the thread. "Cole, you're in the area every day and you've never stopped before."

"I never had the time before."

She nodded as she came to her feet and held the dress before her. "Look, isn't this pretty?"

"Very nice. Is it yours?"

She blinked her surprise. "Mine?! What would I do with a dress like this? It's a ball gown."

"You could wear it tonight. We're going to dinner at your father's place."

"Are we?" She smiled. God, but this woman was beautiful. That was how she tricked him, of course. She dazzled him with her beauty and then made every kind of fool of him.

"How nice. I don't think we've ever been out to dinner before. Except for Baton Rouge when we—"

Cole wasn't listening. He cut her off with, "Who's the dress for, if it's not yours?"

"One of Mrs. Warren's friends. The material is so delicate, I'll have to press it before I—"

Cole's mouth tightened. "You don't know her name and yet you've made her a dress?"

"Of course I know her name, darling. Mrs.

Schofield." Emy watched his eyes darken and narrow as they appeared to examine her. She felt a chill of apprehension. "What's the matter with you?"

"Nothing."

"Are you tired?"

"I said nothing was the matter."

He was tired, that was true. Jason was right when telling her that Cole got a little cantankerous when tired. She smiled and touched his shoulder. "Perhaps we should go another night."

It was amazing, he thought. It didn't matter what she did to him. He loved her. No doubt there was something lacking in his character, what little character he possessed. His mouth hardened as he shook off her hand. "I spend every goddamned night here with you. Why can't we go out tonight? Have you got something better in mind?"

Cole had promised himself that he wouldn't react to his silent charges. He didn't want to tip his hand. He had to wait to get the proof he needed, and yet he couldn't seem to stop himself from reacting to her supposed concern. Jesus, he didn't know if he could live through the pain a second time.

"No," she said, her voice just tight enough to let him know he'd hurt her feelings. Cole knew enough about women and their bags of tricks. "I haven't anything better to do. I'll be ready in a few minutes." She didn't look at him again before she left the room.

If she thought that look was supposed to make him feel guilty, she could think again. If a man couldn't raise his voice once in a while, and do it in his own house, then that was just too damn bad.

Cole poured himself a drink as he waited. A half hour later Emy stepped into the room, dressed in her Sunday best. Cole had by this time downed three hefty drinks. On an empty stomach he was feeling no pain. Unless you counted the one that was squeezing the life out of his heart. "You took your sweet time."

Emy placed her shawl upon a chair. Her smile was tight, her eyes bright with unshed tears. "I don't know what's gotten into you, but I'm not going anywhere while you're in this mood."

Cole laughed. "You don't think so?"

"Cole, what is the matter?"

"You want me to carry you, is that it?"

"Will you tell me? Please?"

"All right. You don't want to go? That's fine with me. I'll see you later." He slammed the door behind him as he walked out.

Chapter Eighteen

Cole leaned his back into the upholstered chair and wondered what the hell he was doing there. He hadn't seen Beverly since he came back to town. Since he'd gone and done the stupidest thing he'd ever done in his life. Since he'd gotten himself married.

What he should have done was taken a ride to Eleanor's, only the thought of seeing her again, of feeling her soft body pressing anxiously against his, made him feel oddly disgusted. Cole had gone to see her the day after he got back to town. To say she was a mite upset was to put it mildly, but she'd apparently realized little could be done about the fact that Emy was already his wife. That scene had been bad enough, but what was worse was when she had calmed down and more than hinted at the possibility of remaining friends, perhaps even more than friends.

What was truly amazing was the fact that before his marriage he'd practically had to beg to be allowed to touch her. Now that he wasn't interested, she had just about thrown herself at him.

Who the hell could understand women? Cole squirmed in his chair. No, he wasn't interested in Eleanor. He didn't want a lover. A lover wouldn't solve even half his problems. All that was likely to do was make him suffer more.

Bev was a good sort and didn't deserve the mood he presently found himself in. But he could think of one particular lady who deserved this mood. Emy deserved more than just a mood and was, if he had anything to say about it, going to get every damn thing that was coming to her.

If she thought because he had forgiven her once . . . If she thought because she was his wife . . . He shook his head. There was no way she was going to get away with it this time. Not a chance in hell.

"Exactly what are you doing here, Cole?"

Cole had almost forgotten the woman's presence. He looked up from his drink and tried to smile. "Drinking."

"I can see that. What I meant was, why?"

Cole didn't answer her directly but said instead, "I didn't have anywhere else to go." He did, of course, he just didn't have anywhere else he wanted to go.

"How about going home to your wife?"

"Ah, yeah." He shrugged, trying for nonchalance. "Maybe later."

Beverly sat across from him, wearing hardly anything at all. Her near-naked state made not the least impression. Right now Cole was too upset to even notice. Well, that wasn't exactly true, he supposed. He'd have to be dead not to notice that her breasts were covered in only a thin piece of gauze and that the contraption she wore covered her to her hips but left her legs bare.

He emptied his glass and filled it again. The fact was, he simply wasn't interested. Not even with old Bev. He wasn't interested in any woman tonight. He cursed his wife because his disinterest was all her fault. He didn't want Beverly. He didn't want Eleanor and, most of all, he didn't want Emy.

"This is costing you five dollars an hour."

"I don't care."

"You want some friendly advice?"

"No."

"All right. What do you want, then?"

"I want you to come over here and kiss me."

Beverly smiled and came to kneel between his knees. She rested her face against his chest for a moment, her hand covering the soft bulge between his legs, but pulled back when she felt no reaction on his part.

Lost in his thoughts, he didn't seem to notice that she was even there. All he did was continue on with his drinking. She watched him for a moment before she leaned back and sighed, "Cole, you don't want this. I work hard enough for money. Don't make me start something that's going to take hours to finish."

Cole seemed to suddenly notice her position. He shrugged and took another long swallow. "It was a stupid idea anyway."

"What's stupid is that you want one woman but have come to another."

"Don't pick on me, Bev. I need a friend tonight."

"You need more than a friend. You need your wife."

Cole shook his head. "I used to need her." He gave a dismal sigh.

Beverly poured herself a drink. She didn't usually drink while working, but figured she could relax this once since she had a half hour to kill. She sat across from him again. "But you don't now?"

He shook his head.

Beverly laughed at the obvious lie. "You love her."

He looked at his long-time friend for a minute. "So what? I'll get over it."

"What did she do?"

"Nothing."

"Has she gotten herself another man?"

Cole almost wished she had. At least he could deal with something like that. At least he imagined he could deal with something like that. In dealing with it, he meant that he'd kill the bastard and maybe his wife along with him. Cole sighed and shook his head. "No."

"So, as I see it, here's your problem." Beverly held up one finger. "She loves you." She raised another finger. "And you love her." Beverly nodded. "I can understand why you're upset."

Cole raised his gaze to her amused expression. "I could have stayed home if I wanted sarcasm."

Beverly laughed. It had been a long time since she'd seen a man who had it this bad. "Cole, go home and talk to her. You're no good like this."

He shook his head. "She'll only lie to me." Cole knew she'd lie. He didn't have to be bashed over the head to know when he was being used, when he was being taken for a fool. She'd lie to him, all right, only this time he wasn't going to give her the chance. This time he wouldn't be taken in by her magic. This time . . . Christ. This time losing her was going to kill him.

Beverly sighed at her friend's obvious suffering. Still, she had confidence that although it might take a while, things would work out all right. After all, the man's wife wasn't stupid, and a smart woman could usually keep her man under some measure of control.

Cole was obviously crazy about his wife and she, because Beverly had seen them together and knew a thing or two about a certain look in a woman's eyes, loved the man to madness in return.

So something had gone wrong. Why wasn't he home? Why wasn't he talking to his wife instead of sitting there, drinking himself to oblivion?

Damn, why did men have to be such babies? Some were better than others, perhaps, but almost all were big, sweet, slightly ridiculous babies stumbling through life without the vaguest idea of what was going on. If they didn't understand something, they simply shrugged it aside, especially if that something was about a woman. Beverly shook her head. Here was a good man and even he couldn't get it to work, which was exactly the reason that she'd never allowed herself to fall in love.

If a decent sort like Cole couldn't make it, none of the men she knew were likely to do much better.

"You'd better go. Your time is almost up."

"I'll pay you for another hour. Just let me sit here."

"Sit here if you want. I'll use another room."

Six hours later, which just happened to be the crack of dawn, Cole weaved his way down the stairs and handed the madam thirty-five dollars. It was most of an entire month's salary and he didn't give a damn.

He staggered to his horse.

Emy stood at the wide doorway to her room and watched the first glimmer of sunlight in the east. Soon it burned off the morning mist, rising higher in the sky until a red ball gleamed soft pink light over the entire city. It was a beautiful sight. From her balcony she could see over the rooftops to the blue waters of Lake Pontchartrain. The sun glistened on those waters, creating dancing lights of red and pink.

Emy might have smiled at the colors if her heart hadn't been so heavy, if tears hadn't blurred her vision.

Why was he so angry with her? What had she done? She could think of nothing. What did he suspect her of doing? It was almost as if he couldn't stand the sight of her and was looking for an excuse to get away for a few hours. But those few hours had turned into an entire night.

Why had he done it? Why had he left like that? Why had he stayed out all night? Emy knew he had spent the night at the office. She almost felt sorry for the pain he was sure to know, for his back always ached if he didn't get a few hours on a reasonably soft bed. She would have felt sorry for him if it hadn't been his own fault. She would have felt sorry for him if she hadn't just seen him ride through the courtyard straight into the sitting room downstairs.

Emy gasped. Her drapes! What was the matter with him? What in the world possessed the man to bring his horse into the house?

Emy almost flew down the stairs. "What are you doing?"

Cole grinned and weaved dangerously in his saddle. "It's a good thing the ceilings are high, isn't it?" He slurred most of the words.

Emy frowned. "What's the matter? Are you hurt?" The fact of the matter was, Emy had never seen anyone drunk before and she didn't at first recognize the obvious signs.

"What's the matter? Are you hurt?" He mimicked her in disgust. "Emy, always the sweet, innocent Emy." He sneered in hatred and then laughed that his ridicule should have brought about a shiver. He pointed a finger in her direction, almost. "That's good. That's very good."

Cole almost fell off the horse trying to dismount and then yelled at the animal as he gave it a mighty shove. "Get out. Get the hell out!"

Jason walked in just then. He had been in the kitchen, supervising the morning meal, when he'd heard the commotion. He shot the lady of the house a sharp, inquisitive look and asked, "What's going on?" only to receive a wide-eyed stare along with a slow blink of confusion for an answer.

"I'm drunk, Jason. I suppose you'll have plenty to say about that."

"Mostly I mind my own business, Cole. And how much a man drinks is surely his own problem. Won't

362

be my head threatening to explode when I wake up."

"Shut up and get me another drink."

Emy was easily as dumbfounded as she looked. She couldn't seem to move from the doorway, but stood still, watching the drunkard, a man she hardly recognized as her husband, bang into the sitting room's tables. He knocked a candle to its side and a glass bowl of potpourri spilled all over the floor. She couldn't imagine what to do.

"He'll be all right," Jason said to Emy's worried expression. "After a few hours of sleep, he'll be fine."

Jason pulled Cole over his shoulder and mounted the steps to the second floor. He dumped the man on his bed. Jason was pulling off his boots when Emy said from the doorway, "That's all right, Jason, I'll take care of it."

Jason was about to argue with her. He wasn't ignorant of the lip rouge that was all over the front of Cole's shirt, and figured Emy would only know some real sorrow if allowed to see it. Still, it wasn't his right, or his business, to interfere between a man and his woman. Whatever the problem was, whatever Cole had done, it was up to Cole to straighten it out. Jason nodded and left the room.

Emy finished the job of pulling off his boots and started on his trousers. She didn't get far. Her gaze was drawn to the lip rouge. She leaned closer, for just a second imagining he had hurt himself and the red smear was a trace of blood.

But when she leaned closer, she caught the slightest whiff of something. Emy wrinkled her nose, for the scent was none too clean as it mingled unwashed bodies and musky perfume.

Emy stood for a moment over the sleeping man. Pain ripped into her chest, but she blinked away the tears. It wasn't until the pain began to ease that the anger began.

Emy had no notion of what she was about to do. She didn't think, but acted solely on impulse. She never knew she moved. She didn't know how it happened. Suddenly she had the water pitcher in her hands. In the next second it lay in pieces all around Cole's head. She didn't remember throwing it, but Cole would remember the pain in his head for some days to come.

"My sister's not living with him anymore. How can I get the information?" Kit was no fool, she knew there was more to this than just gambling tables. Still, it didn't matter to her the man's motives. She enjoyed playing dumb. Men just loved their women stupid. But stupid women didn't accumulate the fine trappings she was gathering together, nor a bank account that was turning into a tidy little sum.

In a couple of years, if things kept going the way they were, she just might have enough to give this man some competition. Maybe, just maybe, she'd start her own place.

"If anything, that should give you more of a chance to get the information. Surely your poor brother-in-law could use a bit of consoling. He has to be upset."

"From what I hear, he's drunk most of the time."

Charlie grinned. "Better yet. He won't even remember telling you."

Kit might have heard that Cole was drunk most of the time, but it wasn't true. He hadn't taken a drink in almost two weeks, since he woke up with a headache that could have killed a horse, his head bleeding from the blow his wife had obviously delivered.

He spent every night sitting alone in the dark, watching through the trees the lights in the rooms above the garage, knowing his wife was there, waiting for morning, for the endless night to be done, for his life to begin again.

He existed only for work. He didn't sleep, he didn't eat, he didn't care.

Cole heard the sounds of her footsteps. All the servants were gone for the day. For two weeks now they had left the moment he came in from work. He knew it was her. He knew she came during the day for clothes and her sewing things, but she was gone long before he came home.

She probably thought he was out.

He waited for her to come all the way inside before he struck a match. "What the hell are you doing here?"

Kit gave a startled cry and then laughed as he lit a candle. "I thought you were in bed. What are you doing here in the dark?"

Christ. It was a good thing he wasn't in bed. Cole hadn't a doubt this one would have joined him there. And if she had, there was no telling what might have happened. More than half asleep, Cole could easily have turned to her and taken her, thinking she was Emy.

"The question, I think, is what are you doing here in the dark?"

Kit shrugged aside his question as nonsense. They both knew what she was doing there. "Emy has been gone for a couple of weeks now. If you really wanted her, you would have brought her back." Kit smiled. "There's no reason why we can't enjoy ourselves, is there?"

As she spoke, she began to undress. She didn't stop until she stood before him in her underwear.

She was walking toward him when Cole came to his feet. She never saw the cold look in his eyes as she reached a hand to his shoulder. He shuddered and she smiled. "That's what I thought." Only she thought wrong. His shudder was born of disgust, not the longing she'd imagined.

Cole had had just about all he could take. He'd had more than he could take. "Wait here, I'll be right back."

A minute or so later he was pounding on the door to the apartment. Emy opened it, obviously surprised to find him standing there. The seething anger that had been kept alive these past weeks suddenly disappeared at his shocking words. "Your little whore of a sister is at my place. I want her off my property for good, you understand?" He reached for her arm and promised, "The next time I see her, I'll arrest her for trespassing."

Emy shuddered at the terrible word he'd called her sister. In that one word he had somehow discredited her entire family, and Emy couldn't defend them, for their actions had been inexcusable. She bit her lips together, knowing only shame. Unable to look him in the eye, she gave a silent nod.

"God"—he sneered into her stony expression, her beautiful face—"I can't tell you how sick I am of your family."

Emy was in her robe and nightdress, but didn't wait to change. She slipped out of the apartment as fast as she could. The disgust in his voice was almost palpable. Emy had no defense against it. She couldn't bear any more.

Cole was about to follow her, when his gaze was suddenly upon the old lady who rocked her chair back and forth before the open door to the terrace. "We should talk, you and I."

Cole didn't want to hear anything this woman had to say. "I think it's time for all of you to leave," he said bluntly. He knew the old lady was innocent of the happenings in her family, of the lies and deceit, but he didn't want her there. He didn't want any of them there.

The old lady nodded. She'd known since the night Emy had come to the apartment that they wouldn't be welcome there much longer. Emy knew it as well, and had gotten them rooms in the city. They were due to move in a few days. "We will go soon, but Emy carries your child."

Cole almost smiled. Did she think he had forgotten the most important thing in his life? Yes, he'd been immersed in misery, but no amount of suffering could have caused him to forget his child. He hadn't meant that Emy would be leaving, at least not quite yet.

"She'll stay until the baby comes."

"I'll say my piece and be done with it."

Cole obviously didn't want to hear it, but the lady went on. "She's a good girl who loves hard. But she has pride, maybe too much pride.

"You know what it's like. You, too, have pride. Sometimes it's hard when two love this much. You're afraid. You shouldn't be. She won't hurt you."

Cole laughed out loud at the prediction, a prediction that was not only wrong, but came months too late. "You mean she won't tear my heart out?"

"You did that. You did it with your accusations, accusations she couldn't answer because you never said what they were."

Cole shook his head and walked out the door. The woman didn't know. She couldn't understand because she wasn't involved in the deceit. There was no sense in explaining. She'd never believe Emy capable of the things she'd done. It ripped his guts out to believe it himself.

Emy stepped into the dimly lit room to find her sister lounging upon the sitting room sofa. Kit was naked. Her eyes were closed, one leg was raised at the knee, her hands were beneath her head and her back arched in what was meant to be a seductive pose. Emy imagined it probably was, only Kit was wasting all that seduction on the wrong person.

A soft smile touched the corner of her mouth. Kit knew the pretty picture she made. She wondered how long he'd stand there, looking, before he said something. "Where did you go?"

It was obvious at one glance that the girl was totally at ease in this state of undress. Emy suddenly realized where the fancy clothes, shoes, and perfume had come from. She shuddered at the horror of it all. No wonder Cole thought the worst of them. They were the worst.

Kit finally opened her eyes to the silence and found, not Cole, but Emy looming above her.

She scrambled to her feet and reached for her dress. "What are you doing here?"

"Cole asked me to get rid of you, but he didn't say how. Perhaps I'll just kill you and be done with the problem."

Kit glanced toward the door to find her brother-in-law just coming into the room. "Why?" she asked, truly unable to believe that the man, that any man would refuse what she had to offer. She looked into his eyes and shrugged at the hard gleam found there. So, all was finished. Too bad. They might have had themselves a few good times. Still, he could have simply told her to leave. He didn't have to involve her sister.

Kit didn't understand why Cole had brought Emy into it, but Emy and Cole both knew the truth of the matter. He'd been protecting her, and this was his subtle way of telling her what he thought of her entire family, of telling her that the days of protection were at an end.

Kit figured she owed the spineless son of a bitch at least a parting shot. "Wasn't I good enough? Didn't we enjoy the things we did to each other?"

Cole looked from one sister to the other. He didn't give a good God damn if Emy believed her or not.

He didn't say a word, but simply shook his head and walked outside.

Suddenly Emy slapped her. Hard. The blow knocked Kit back to the couch. "Get dressed."

Cole waited in the courtyard, grunting his satisfaction at every slap he heard. Emy's low voice could be heard over Kit's pitiful wails. Another slap and then another. Good. As far as Cole was concerned, Emy couldn't hit her enough.

It was very dark. The moon was completely overcast by low, heavy clouds. Lightning flashed in the distance, and an occasional rolling crash of thunder promised the rain would soon come.

He felt the first heavy drop as the girl ran from his house. She was only half dressed, but apparently considered the storm an enviable alternative to the punishment suffered at her sister's hands.

Cole knew no fear for her. She might be only fifteen, but she'd find her own brand of security and safety on the streets of the city. What, after all, could happen to her? She had nothing to steal. And if a man had it in mind to enjoy her body for a few hours, whether it be in a small room rented for that purpose or the lesser privacy of a dark alley, he'd only be pleasantly surprised at her full cooperation.

Cole wondered how it had happened that a girl like Kit could be Emy's sister. Surely the two couldn't be more opposite. And then he laughed as he realized the way of his thoughts, for they weren't opposite at all. One was totally lacking in morality, but Kit's immorality had only to do with the flesh.

370

Was Emy any better clothed in her deceit? At least Kit was honest. At least a man knew where he stood with a woman like her. He wouldn't be promised heaven, only to find himself in hell.

He watched as she ran from the courtyard. Good riddance. Now all he had to do was rid himself of the rest of the brood.

He watched her come from the house and move toward him. It was raining hard now. Neither seemed to notice. "She shouldn't bother you again."

Cole nodded.

She started to pass him, when he grabbed her arm. "We've got to talk."

Emy shook her head. "I wanted to do that from the beginning. It's too late now."

"Why, because you thought I was with another woman?"

"Thought?" In a flash the anger came again, the seething rage that had built almost to madness these past two weeks, the anger that had known no outlet until that minute. She slapped him. He reached for her, but she evaded his hold. Her hand had already tightened into a fist. She punched him in the stomach and knew a moment of satisfaction at his grunt. She tried to run, only this time he managed to grab her. Her teeth gritted in anger as he took both her hands and pushed them behind her back. "I hate you." She kicked him with slippered feet. "I can't tell you . . . my God, I hate you."

"Do you? That's tough. Shut up and be still."

"What do you want? I got rid of her for you, now let me go."

"Not yet." He pulled her against him and spoke

371

close to her ear, his voice almost lost as the pouring rain grew into a roar.

"Cole, you want us out of here. That's fine. Let me go and none of us will ever bother you again."

"You're going to have my baby, remember? You're not going anywhere until you have it." He felt his body's unwanted response at her closeness and shoved her back. There was no way that he was going to allow this. No way that he'd fall under her spell again. If she knew what was good for her, she'd keep her distance. He raised his voice. "Then I don't care if I never see you again."

Emy knew he meant every word he said. She'd never seen him so cold, so uncaring. And the worst of it was, he had the power to do exactly as he said. The fear she knew stole her breath. She was afraid, yes, but more than afraid, she knew a sense of determination. There was no way that he was going to separate her from her baby. She'd die before she allowed that to happen.

"If I weren't having a baby, you'd want me gone from here?"

"You couldn't get out fast enough."

Above the rain and crashing thunder, they screamed at each other.

"You can let me go, then, because I'm not having a baby." Now all she had to do was to come up with a reasonable excuse as to why that should be. "What happened was, ah . . . I fell. I lost the baby because of the fall."

Cole knew different. Didn't her grandmother just mention the baby? He laughed. "Take your hand away from your eye, Emy."

"No." She shrugged. "It's not what you think. It's the rain. It's running into my eyes."

"Let's go inside."

She shook her head, never releasing her eye. "Grandmère is alone. I've got to go back."

He grinned. It was only then that he realized he hadn't laughed or smiled in more than two weeks. "I don't believe you."

Emy was a deeply religious woman. She knew all was in God's hands. Still, she couldn't control the shiver of superstitious fear. She couldn't insist on the death of her infant. Talking like this brought on an ominous feeling of foreboding. It was almost as if she were wishing the baby to die.

"All right, I didn't lose the baby," she quickly amended. And then after a moment's pause thought of another route. "But it's not yours. I slept with a man before you."

Her eyelid continued to twitch.

Cole shook his head. He grabbed her shoulders and raised her to his height. "You were a virgin the first time. I know that for a fact."

"No, I wasn't." She shook her head.

"A man knows these things, Emy. You were."

"It was after that first night. That's what I mean. It was after."

He put her gently to the ground. He didn't believe her, but even the thought of her with another caused him almost terrifying anger. He was actually afraid to touch her. "Why don't you tell me about it?"

She shook her head. "No."

He gave her a hard shake even as he repeated almost gently, "Why don't you tell me about it."

"Fine! I will," she snapped in return, and then bit her lip and looked down at her feet. "Sometimes, after you've fallen asleep, I walk in the garden. Sometimes I met him there."

"Emy, don't play games." His voice was low, an obvious warning. "Saying things like that could be very dangerous." Cole felt the need to kill, even knowing she'd just made the whole thing up. No man had ever touched her. No man ever would. She belonged to him. Cole shook himself from the thought. No. He didn't want her. All he wanted was the baby. His baby.

It might have been a warning, but it wasn't a warning she was about to heed. "Could it? Suppose I don't care if it's dangerous or not? Suppose I—"

"Shut up and get into the house."

The rain was coming in torrents now. They were both screaming above the roar and drenched to the skin, but Emy didn't care if they drowned. No, that wasn't true. She would have liked nothing better than to see him drown.

She ignored his order and tried to pass him. Again he stopped her. She shoved against him, knocking herself back a few steps. "It's dangerous for me to say I slept with someone, but all right for you to actually do it?" She sneered, "Go to hell!"

"I haven't been with anyone else since I've met you."

"That's why there was lip rouge all over your shirt?"

"I forgot about the lip rouge you women wear." Cole knew in an instant, at the narrowing of her eyes, in fact, that he'd admitted to too much.

"Not all women, Cole. Whores wear lip rouge."

"Emy, if I slept with her, I would have taken my shirt off."

Emy's laughter was hard, filled with disbelief. "Why? You haven't always taken your shirt off with me. Sometimes we've both left most of our clothes on. Remember?"

Remember? How the hell could he ever forget?

Cole knew a moment's frustration. He ran his hand through his hair while wondering how he could convince her of the truth. "I was just talking to her."

Emy laughed at the absurdity. He'd gone to visit with a whore just to talk? "What was the matter? Was she hard of hearing?"

Cole frowned. "What? Why?"

"What other reason could there be for her to lean so close, while you were *just talking?!*" As she said the last two words she stomped on his foot, praying that every ounce of her ninety-two pounds would cause him unbearable pain. It didn't. Her soft slippers could hardly have hurt him even if he were barefoot. What caused him a gasp was how her body had just rubbed against his. He'd felt a crashing moment of delighted surprise and then she was suddenly gone. Already outside the courtyard, Cole sneered at her attempted escape. There was no way this little bitch was going to get away from him. He might as well let her know the truth of the matter right off.

Emy moaned at the sudden weight that crashed into her back and sent her to her knees. A second later she was spun around as Cole took the blow of hitting against the ground. His arms were around

375

her, sprawled upon the wet grass as she lay upon him. She tried to get up, but he never eased his hold.

And then he spun her to her back just as if she were nearly weightless and straddled her hips. She punched his chest, only to find her hands captured in his.

"You're so worried about the baby, but you knock me around as if I'm nothing."

Cole knew she wasn't hurt. Yes, she'd fallen to her knees, but that had been an accident. He'd tried to pick her up, but had slipped on the wet grass. The two of them had gone down together, but almost none of his weight had landed on her. He'd made sure of that.

"You *are* nothing." It was an out-and-out lie. He'd never meant anything less in his life, for even in his anger he knew she was everything. Everything and more. "You said yourself it's not my baby, right?"

"Right." Because of the rain, Emy narrowed her gaze. But despite her glare came the flicker of her lid and still she refused to give an inch.

"So why should I care what happens to it?"

She didn't care that he didn't care. So Emy could only blame what happened next on this extremely intense confrontation. It was all simply too much for a woman in her condition. That was the only reason a sob slipped from her throat. She hadn't even known it was about to come.

Cole's eyes widened at the sound. Instantly he was filled with dread. Had he really been too rough? Had he hurt her? "Are you all right? Are you hurt?"

"I'm fine," she said, but her throat was tight with unexplained tears and the words were hardly more than a whisper. Cole couldn't hear over the pouring rain.

"Are you? Answer me, dammit! Are you all right?"

She gasped as his hand ran over her stomach and down her legs.

He heard her gasp, felt the stiffening of her body. "It hurts? Jesus, don't tell me it hurts." He released her hands and pulled her nightdress up. His hands were moving over her legs, checking for broken bones, almost praying he'd find one, for the alternative was not to be borne. She couldn't be in pain because of the baby. She couldn't lose this baby because he was a clumsy fool. Oh, God, please, no.

Kneeling at her side, leaning over her, his face only inches from hers, he took her hand in his again, brought it to his mouth, and kissed it gently. "Emy, sweetheart, listen to me. I don't want you to be afraid. I'll take care of you." He kissed her hand again, never realizing he did it. "I'll always take care of you. Just show me where it hurts."

It was beyond Emy's power to resist. She loved this man no matter his faults, no matter that she couldn't understand the things he'd done, no matter his silent accusations that never permitted her an explanation. She loved him despite the hurt he'd brought her. She loved him like she'd never love another.

It no longer mattered that she show herself strong and able to withstand his abuse. Strength had accomplished nothing. What was needed now, at this moment, was softness, both in body and soul.

So she took his hand and placed it on the part of

her that hurt, on the part of her that hadn't stopped hurting for weeks.

"Here," she said as she parted the robe she wore and held his hand to her breast. "It hurts here."

"Did I crack a rib?" Cole was almost beside himself with panic. He knew the pain of a broken rib. She was going to have a baby and he'd just broken her rib. It didn't matter that it had been an accident. It mattered only that he had been too rough. How the hell could he have done this to his own wife? "Jesus, God, I'm sorry. I'm so sorry, Emy."

"Cole," she said as she pressed him harder to her softness.

Lightning flashed, and Cole's eyes narrowed at what he saw. Her face wasn't contorted with pain. Her breathing was hard, yes, but she wasn't gasping in discomfort. "Cole," she said again, and at the sound of her voice, her soft, pain-free voice, Cole suddenly realized he was wrong. She wasn't hurting, at least not hurting in the manner he had imagined. He watched as she spread the robe apart. He watched as the thin fabric beneath became transparent from the rain. He watched as his heart turned to thunder in his chest, and she pulled the nightdress to her hips, watched as she took his hand and lowered it to her stomach and then lower still to the source of incredible heat. Her eyes held to his and her eyelid didn't flicker once. "Here," she said as she placed it where she wanted it most to be. "It hurts here."

Chapter Nineteen

Cole drew in a shuddering breath, knowing all was lost. There were certain things a man was helpless against. It wasn't simply the fact that his body ached for a woman. He'd already refused others and their offers. The truth was, no matter how his body might yearn for release, he didn't want just any woman.

He whispered a prayer to a God he wasn't sure he believed in, asking to be saved from the weakness, saved from the pain of wanting his own wife, for his body knew what it wanted no matter what his mind might claim.

She wasn't holding him to her and yet he couldn't take his hand away. The warmth of her called to him, taunted him to deny himself the pleasure, and he didn't have the strength to stop. He'd be sorry, he knew. This wasn't what he wanted, but there was no way he could refuse. The fires of hell couldn't have stopped what was to come.

With his free hand Cole reached for the neckline

of her nightdress and pulled, tearing the thin fabric to its hem. She lay there, exposed to the night, exposed to the warm rain, exposed to his hot gaze. He couldn't stop his hands from moving over the sweet temptation. Her breasts gleamed, her skin creamy soft grew softer still, smoother now that it was wet. He swore he would stop, just a minute more, but knew in his heart all was lost as he luxuriated in her. How could he have forgotten the sweet heaven of her softness? Damn her soul. She was in his blood. He burned for her, lived only to touch her, and there was nothing he could do to stop the need.

He watched his hand move, saw the contrast of dark skin and sweet, honeyed cream, and knew that he was going to make love to his wife, there in the open, in the rain, on the grass-covered drive to the carriage house.

In the flashes of lightning she saw the dark look of hunger and knew he couldn't win out against the need they both knew. He wanted her. He might not want to want her, to need her, or even to love her, but he was as helpless in his wants as she.

He'd said he hadn't been with another. Had he told her the truth? Had he held to his vows? At that moment and perhaps only for that moment, she didn't care. All she knew was she loved this man and couldn't keep herself from reaching out to him.

Her hands moved to his shirt. Buttons popped as the fabric parted. She moaned a soft sound of satisfaction as her hands found hard muscle and warm skin. God, had a man ever felt like this? Had she ever known such pleasure in only a touch?

She rested her weight on one elbow and reached her mouth to the beckoning bliss. Her tongue gathered in the moisture, luxuriated in the warmth, the hardness, the feel of his chest and belly. She loved the scratchy hair, the smooth muscles that rippled helplessly in response to the touch of her mouth. And then that wasn't enough. His trousers were open and her hand cool from the rain was against the blazing heat of his body.

Cole couldn't stop the guttural groan, nor his hips from pushing forward. No matter what she was, no matter what she did, with this one woman he was helpless but to respond.

Cole felt the wall around his heart crumble to dust and blow away at the whisper of her hot breath against his skin. He was weak, almost eager to experience more of the pain. He'd never been so vulnerable to her magic. He loved her. It was as simple and as complex as that. She filled his soul with madness and he loved her beyond reason, beyond his very life.

He knew a sense of helpless frustration as he watched his sex lengthen in her hand. It grew hard from a gentle touch and then pulsed with blood, thickened with need at her soft kiss. God in heaven, he couldn't hold back the groan as her mouth touched and nuzzled and then accepted him into the heat, loving him to madness. Her tongue slid over him and sipped at the dew of his passion, and Cole knew he was lost forever.

He was less than a man. In her arms nothing mattered. Not courage, or honor, or ethics. Not integrity, not even honesty. All that mattered was this woman and his need to keep her with him forever. All that nonsense about her staying until the baby came was simply that. He'd never let her go. Nothing mattered but the ecstasy that was her touch, the bliss he could find only in her mouth.

He'd been born for her use. It didn't matter, the things she'd done. It didn't matter what she continued to do. Nothing mattered but that he'd be allowed to sample this piece of heaven. Nothing mattered but to love her, no matter the pain, until the day he died.

"Emy." It was a beseeching cry, a wail of agony as he lost everything that was dear to him in order to gain this woman. His body shuddered against the desperate need. His hips pressed forward as she took him deeper into madness, into heaven and beyond.

He threw his head back, welcoming the rain, thankful for the coolness that masked hot tears. His hands reached for her face, bringing her up his body to kneel before him. He couldn't let her go. His hands held her cheeks, pulling her face closer, closer to his. "I love you, Emy," he said, his eyes shining with the depth of the emotion. "I love you more than my soul."

"Cole," she said.

He shook his head. "Don't say anything. Just love me. Just love me a little."

Cole groaned as his mouth slashed hard across her softness. He heard the startled intake of breath and knew he was too rough, but he couldn't hold back. He'd wanted her for so long, loved her for so long, it was beyond his power to gentle his touch, to control the need.

But Cole wasn't alone in his need. Emy might have known a startled moment as she realized the urgency of his wanting, but her body and hands told him hers was equally as great.

She gasped at the coming together of their mouths and then groaned her pleasure as that gasp drew in his scent, his taste, the deliciousness of his mouth.

She rubbed her breasts against him, and they both murmured their pleasure. And then he reached for her, his hand between her thighs, his fingers slipping easily into her heat. "Cole," she groaned as her body curled helplessly toward his and he drove his fingers with devastating effects into her warmth.

He couldn't bear this. He wanted this more than he wanted his life, and it wasn't enough. It wasn't nearly enough. He waited for the first aching waves of her release to ease before he pushed her again to the grass and covered her body with his. Hovering above her, he replaced his hand with the surging force of his body.

"Emy," he cried out as his body slid into the burning heat of hers. Bliss. God Almighty, had anything ever felt this good? He murmured again her name, a mindless chant as he pushed himself forward and then forward again.

Hearts thundered, hands reached greedily for more of the pleasure. They knew nothing but a wanting so desperate, it blotted out all but the ceaseless driving beat of two straining bodies.

How had he lived through these past weeks? How had he managed without her? Without knowing again and again the heaven that was her body? She was wet, but the wetness felt good against him. It caused her silkiness to become slick, it lessened the friction of hard against soft of smooth against rough but brought even more pleasure as wet rubbed deliciously against silky wet.

His hands came to the sides of her face and he pushed back wet tendrils of black hair, smoothed the rain from her eyes, and placed himself so she was at least partly protected from the heavy downpour.

Flashes of lightning lit up the sky, and he saw the hunger, the dark, burning need in her eyes. Her lips parted as she strained for every breath, her face open, vulnerable to the passion that blazed between them.

He wouldn't forget this. For the rest of his life he'd remember this moment of love so pure and giving, it brought tears to both their eyes.

He felt her body tighten and her hips strain toward his. A low, steady groan that was a mindless chant of building euphoria escaped her parted lips even as muscles began to tighten around his sex. She was almost there, ready to suffer the magic again, and he was helpless but to drive deeper into her softness, urging them both toward the ecstasy.

He heard her cry and prayed it wasn't pain she knew, for he hadn't the ability to stop now. Not now, perhaps not ever.

But it wasn't pain she suffered in that mindless cry. He knew it in the spasms that came to suck him deeper into the madness. He knew it in his own cry. He knew it as his body stiffened and his soul and hers collided in the darkness of near-death and then rose together into the blinding light.

There followed a moment of silence, of gasping

breaths, of trembling hearts, of silent promises that told of eternal love.

It was only after her heart returned to its normal rhythm that Emy thought to soften the intensity with a touch of irreverent humor. It was either that, or burst into a bout of tears, for the depth of emotion she suffered could never be explained in mere words. "Tomorrow there will be a permanent indentation of my rear in this driveway. Everyone for miles around will come to look at the phemomenon and wonder how it could possibly have come about."

"Ass in the grass?"

Emy shot his deliciously naughty smile a look of censure. "I wouldn't have put it quite so . . ."

"Truthfully?"

"Bluntly."

Cole grinned. God, it felt good to talk to her again, to tease her about nothing. He'd missed their conversations, sometimes serious, sometimes only playful nonsense, her delectable sense of humor, almost as much as he'd missed her body. "You think I'm being blunt? Sweetheart, I hate to tell you, but if a man should come across it, he'll know right off the cause, or at least he'll think he knows."

"A man's mind tends to run along those lines, does it?"

Cole laughed. "Are you trying to get me to admit that we're all a bunch of dirty dogs?"

"Not at all." Hardly a second went by before she shot him an inquisitive glance and asked, "Are you?"

"I'll never tell."

"Why?"

"Because if you knew the way men think, you'd

probably never stop hitting me."

"That's an admission in itself, isn't it?"

"Don't touch me."

Emy shrugged as much as she was able, considering Cole's weight still lay largely upon her. "If that's what you want."

"No, I mean, don't hit me. You can touch me all you want."

She smiled at the immediate correction. "All I want?"

He nodded.

"Anytime I want?"

"Except when we're in church." Since they had come to New Orleans, Cole had found himself escorting her to Mass most every Sunday. He'd once thought religion hogwash, a man-made setting up of rules fashioned to keep folks on the straight and narrow. He wasn't sure he didn't still. But there was something more. Something besides the rules and regulations set down from past generations. When he sat beside her and listened to the hymns of praise, he thought perhaps, just perhaps, there might be something behind this religion business.

Emy giggled at the picture his words brought to mind and then suddenly frowned. "Now you've done it. Now I won't be able to walk into church without thinking about touching you. My face will be red for most of the Mass."

"Well, if it means that much to you, I'll let you touch me in church."

"You beast."

"I love you." He smiled, his hand wiping the rain from her face. He pressed his hips to hers and moaned a low sound of appreciation. "I need you again."

"Well, I need a towel and a blanket."

Cole came to his knees and gathered her against him. "No, you don't. You need a soft bed and me."

Quickly he adjusted his clothing, and carried her into the house, to their room, to the bed she hadn't shared in more than two weeks. He threw her ruined nightdress and robe to the floor even as he carelessly discarded his shirt, pants, and boots and then joined her beneath the sheet.

Huddled together against the chill, he covered them both with the summer quilt until their bodies dried, until the shivering stopped, until the heat came again, until the need caused them to push all covering away.

He didn't kiss her. Not this time. This time wasn't meant for lost reasonings, but to sample every texture, to absorb every moment that his body was joined to hers. He took her hands in his as she reached for him. "Don't touch me.

"This time I want to see you. I want to watch your body as mine moves into you. I want to watch you bite your lip and listen to you gasp. This time I just want to feel."

"You want to keep your reasoning while I lose mine?"

"For as long as I can. For as long as I can keep the magic away."

Emy smiled and forced back the low groan at the pleasure he was causing her. "Magic. That's a good word for this."

"It's the only word. You're a sorceress, a wicked

witch that cast her spell upon this poor, unsuspecting male. I knew it that first night on the
Princess. But even then it was too late. I knew I'd
never be free of you. That I'd always, always want
you."

"Wicked?" Emy seemed to enjoy that thought
very much. "Am I?"

He smiled, his attention momentarily on her
breasts, which were moving with every thrust of his
body. Lovely. "What?"

"I asked if you thought I was truly wicked." She
shuddered as she accepted a powerful thrust.

"It's best, I think, if you never know the whole of
it."

His mouth lowered to her swaying breast. She
moaned softly at the pleasure. "You said we
shouldn't touch."

"I won't touch you. I just need a little taste."

"Tell me about her."

"Who?" Cole snuggled his face into the warmth of
Emy's neck and breathed a sigh of pure happiness at
the feel of her body against his.

"The lady . . . I mean woman you went to see."

"When?" And then realizing the way of her
thoughts, he quickly added, "Oh, she was nothing,
Emy."

"Everyone is something, Cole."

"I mean nothing to me. She was just a woman I
knew. I won't be seeing her again."

"And?"

"What happened?"

Emy nodded.

"We talked."

"About what?"

"About why I was wasting my money, sitting there drinking."

"How was that a waste of money?"

"She charges by the hour, and I wasn't using her services."

"I think I'm getting angry again."

Cole's arms tightened around her. "I swear to God you have no reason. I never touched her. All I could think about was you."

"Will we talk about it?"

Cole's eyes were dark with longing, happiness, and pain. He nodded. "Tomorrow, sweetheart. We'll talk then."

It was hours later, for Cole and Emy had made love again and again. She was exhausted and had just drifted off to sleep. Cole, on the other hand, couldn't get enough. He couldn't believe she was back. That they would work this mess out, that somehow everything would be good again.

"Cole," she murmured more than half asleep. "Stop it."

"I'm not doing anything."

"Then there's another man in our bed and he won't take his hands off me."

"Should I tell him to leave?"

"*Oui.* But tell him to come back tomorrow."

He smacked her rear. "Ow! You beast." She swung wildly behind her, contacting by accident with his nose. Cole groaned and held his fingers to one side as if to contain the ache. "You hit my nose."

Emy tried to turn around, but Cole had moved over her, his weight pressing her into the bed. "I'll probably bleed all over the sheets."

"You deserved it."

"No, I didn't."

"You hit me."

"That was only a tap."

"I'll probably have a mark for a week from your 'tap.'"

"Let's look and see."

Emy giggled at the degree of enthusiasm in that suggestion. "No. I want to go to sleep."

"How can you want to sleep when we're in bed?"

"Where else would I sleep?"

Cole ignored her question. He rolled just a bit to his side, bringing her with him so he could get his hand beneath her. And then he proceeded to move that hand very nicely indeed over all he could reach. "Now, let's get back to what we were doing."

"I wasn't doing anything. I was almost asleep."

"You were awake enough to ask me to tell the guy to come back tomorrow."

Cole smiled at Emy's chuckle.

"It was the wrong thing to say."

Her face was still pressed into her pillow. "I've already figured that out. What was I supposed to say?"

"You were supposed to tell me that you aren't interested in another man. That you never could be."

"I didn't think I was. It's just that he touched me very nicely."

"You liked what he was doing?"

"Mmm, very much. It was something like what

you're doing now."

"Then why did you want me to stop?"

"You mean that was you?"

"Emy," he warned her.

Emy's laughter turned into a gasp as the arm that was around her waist raised her hips toward him. Cole wasn't about to let this particular opportunity pass him by.

Chapter Twenty

Emy's eyes were shining when she left the house the next morning. She entered the apartment above the carriage house, not at all surprised to find her grandmother sitting on the terrace with a strong cup of black coffee in her hands.

"Good morning." Emy joined her grandmother and poured herself a cup.

Grandmère's dark eyes crinkled at the corners. "So, *chérie*. I see that you and your man have found each other again."

Emy's dark eyes held a soft, secret light. She couldn't hold back her laughter, for the pure joy of it.

"Did you talk?"

"Some."

"But not about the things that need to be spoken of?"

Emy knew she meant the estrangement and Cole's still-unknown reasons behind it. "Not all of it."

"Talk to your papa."

"Why?"

"I think he knows something."

"What?"

The old lady shook her head. "I saw in his eyes. Last night when he came home and I told him where you were. I saw the relief and something more."

How could her father be behind Cole's strange actions? Emy couldn't imagine that anything he might have done would have caused Cole such anger as to estrange himself from her. It didn't make sense.

Last night they had been too hungry for each other, too in need to chance the pleasure of the night with questions. Emy had been content to wait until today, but that was as far as her patience was likely to stretch. She'd find out today what had gone wrong. She'd know today what had been behind Cole's anger and whether or not her father was involved.

Emy stepped into the busy café and sighed, knowing she'd have to wait just a bit longer before knowing the whole of it. It was the noon hour and the café was nearly filled to overflowing with loud, hungry patrons. There was no way she could talk to her father while this crowd needed tending. She made her way into the kitchen and without being asked began to help.

Two hours later Emy sat at a table and watched her father fill her plate with Creole shrimp. "It's too much."

"You need it. The baby needs it."

Emy smiled and took a bite of succulent shrimp.

Her eyes widened with surprise even as they began to tear. Instantly she pushed a chunk of bread into her mouth, hoping to ease the burning. "The baby will likely come out holding a torch if I eat enough of this."

"Don't you like it?"

Emy laughed at the expectant look in her father's eyes. "It's delicious. Do you warn your patrons to say an Our Father before their first bite?"

Jacques shook his head. "It's not that hot. You've probably grown a little sensitive in your condition."

Emy smiled at her father's supposition. Most of her family, especially her father, treated her as if she were somehow afflicted with some mysterious disease. Emy could only thank the Lord that Cole didn't feel the same way. If anything, he was a little rough in his eagerness. Emy forced back her laugh, for she enjoyed every minute of it.

"I wanted to talk to you, Papa."

Jacques only nodded. He'd known the questions would eventually come. "About Cole."

"*Oui*. You know something. Tell me."

"I know only that he suspects us."

Emy looked at her father with some real confusion. "Suspects you? Of what?"

"Of the warehouse robberies."

Emy gasped. "How? Why should he . . . ?"

"I don't know. But I saw the look in his eyes. He thinks we're behind it."

"And if you're involved, I must be as well," Emy said with a touch of despair. She shook her head. "Why didn't you say something before."

"I thought he must have told you."

Emy breathed a sigh as her mind tried to work out the puzzle. Why should Cole suspect her and her family? No doubt because of their past criminal tendencies. Still, there had been other crimes, and he hadn't accused her of them. Emy was at a loss to understand why he should accuse now.

"I'm going to talk to him." Emy came to her feet and looked at her father for a moment. "I can tell him he's wrong, can't I? I can tell him that you and Anton had . . ."

". . . nothing to do with it. I swear on your mother's grave."

Emy nodded and left the café. She knew her father spoke the truth. Now all she had to do was convince Cole of it.

Emy preened before the shaving mirror. Propped up against the wall over the small table holding a bowl and pitcher of water, the mirror was used by the marshal or his deputy when they spent endless hours on the job. She took off her bonnet and smoothed her black hair, sliding a loose pin into place. She stepped back and tried to see her dress. The mirror was too small. She brushed her skirt and tucked her blouse into its high waistband.

"Is all that for me?"

Emy spun around, her eyes first wide with fright and then filled with laughter. "You're not suppose to scare a lady in my delicate condition."

"Delicate, huh? You didn't act delicate when I was trying to leave the house for work this morning."

Emy examined the tip of her shoe, feeling her cheeks warm at the memory. "I was only trying to get your attention."

"Yeah, standing at the door, waving good-bye naked, is bound to get a man's attention, all right."

"I wasn't naked."

Cole grinned. His eyes darkened as he remembered the sight of her coming down the stairs from their room into the courtyard, her open robe flowing behind her. "The front of you was."

"Well, I had to wear something, the servants . . ."

"I'm not complaining."

Emy smiled as she looked up into hungry eyes. "I'm not either."

"Not even when I pushed you against the wall in the courtyard and had my way with you?"

"I was just a little worried about the servants."

"I told you they don't come that early."

"But you do." Emy laughed out loud at what she'd just said. Lord, but she couldn't imagine how she'd grown so bold.

Cole bit his lower lip and smiled. His mustache tipped. God, she loved him. "You're being very wicked today. Why?"

"I don't know. Sometimes when I look at you, I feel wicked."

"Do you?"

She nodded.

"Would you like to step into the back room?"

"You mean it's my turn to get arrested."

Cole nodded. "And searched."

"But I'm not hiding anything."

"We'll see."

Emy stepped into the storeroom and smiled as Cole shut and locked the door.

"You're on duty."

"I'm performing my duty."

"You mean performing is your duty."

Another smile. "You're very bad today." He pulled her close to him, allowing her to rest against him while he rested against an old desk. He spread his thighs so her hips fit nicely within his. "Now, let's see. What have we here?" he asked as he opened her blouse. "Very pretty," he said as a fingertip ran over the smooth mounds of modestly covered flesh. "But are they legal?"

"Is this?" she asked as she cupped her hand over his arousal.

"Ah, probably not. You'd better keep it covered." Cole held her hand in place until he was sure she got the idea.

Emy laughed.

He pulled her chemise lower and exposed her breasts to his view. He played with the soft flesh for a moment, delighting in the pleasure of being able to touch her, to kiss her as he pleased. "I think it would be a brilliant piece of strategy on my part to keep you pregnant."

The word was becoming a bit more palatable. This time Emy didn't object to its use. "Why?"

He cupped the soft flesh in each hand and pressed them together. "Because these are already bigger. Imagine what they'll look like after the baby's born."

"You won't be able to do this after she's born."

397

"She?" Cole hadn't thought about the possibility of having a daughter. "I was thinking about a boy."

"Were you? Well, I think a girl would be better."

"You might be right." Cole smiled at the thought of a little girl who looked exactly like her mother. He gathered her closer and rubbed his cheeks into her softness. "Don't you think she'll want to share?"

"Babies are often greedy."

"I can probably talk her into it."

"You could probably talk a rock into it."

They held each other for a moment before Emy said, "Do you think married people are supposed to enjoy this sort of thing quite so much?"

Cole laughed. "I think married people, especially the two married people in this room, are supposed to enjoy it most of all."

"Don't you think it's—"

"Too good to be good?"

She smiled into his dark eyes. "I love you."

"Good, because I'd hate to do this to a lady who didn't love me."

Emy grunted a laugh. "But you could probably force yourself."

"Before I met you I could."

"And now?"

"Nothing feels so good as the woman you love in your arms. You're not looking at a stupid man, Emy. I told you once before, I don't settle for second best."

"Does that mean you won't be visiting your lady friends again?"

"I have no lady friends."

"Cole?"

"Never. I promise. Never."

Emy took a deep breath and smiled. "Are we going to make love?"

"I hadn't planned on it, but if you keep breathing like that, we might."

Emy laughed at his playful leer. "No, sweetheart. I have someone coming to the office in about—"

"Marshal," a man's voice called out from the other side of the locked door.

"Damn." Cole quickly adjusted her clothing. "That's Peterson. He's early."

"He's going to know what we were doing."

Cole smiled at the growing color in his wife's cheeks. "You can go out the back door and walk around the front."

Emy nodded. "I have to talk to you."

"As soon as Peterson leaves."

Emy waited, sitting herself in a chair that had been placed outside the marshal's office. Ten minutes later Mr. Peterson walked out.

"That was fast."

"Yeah, Peterson is expecting a shipment of—" The sentence came to a sudden stop as he realized who he was talking to.

Emy breathed a deep sigh, reading clearly the distrust in his eyes. "*Oui.* That's what I wanted to talk to you about."

"Sit down."

Emy obeyed and sat across from him.

"Tell me what's on your mind."

"Papa thinks that you think . . ." She shook her head and began again. "Do you think my family is involved in the warehouse robberies?"

"I'm afraid I do." Cole didn't say it, but she knew

by the look in his eyes his suspicions didn't stop there.

"You think I'm involved as well." It was less a question than a statement of fact.

Cole didn't respond.

"You do, don't you?" Emy came to her feet and began to pace the small office. "If that's the case, how can you say you love me?"

"What do you mean, say I love you? I do love you."

"But you think I'm a thief."

"I never said that." Cole breathed a sigh as his fingers played with a pencil on his desk. "What I think is, your loyalties are a bit misplaced."

"That's a ridiculous thing to say."

"Why?"

"Because I'm hardly the simpleton you'd like to make me out to be."

"Meaning?"

"Meaning I know right from wrong. And my loyalties are with you."

Cole leaned back in his chair and sighed her name.

"Why blame them?"

"For nearly a month your sister has been to dinner every Sunday."

"So?"

"Do you remember the conversations?"

Emy imagined that to be the most ridiculous question of all. How was she supposed to remember something like that? "Do you?"

He nodded. "Each time she questioned me about the ships and their cargo."

Emy gasped. "She didn't! I would have remembered something like that."

"All right. *Questioned* is a bit strong. Let's just say it was mentioned in passing."

"And that's your proof?" Emy couldn't conceal her amazement.

"If I had proof, they would already be in jail and we wouldn't be having this conversation."

"So, according to you, if Kit asks a question, my father and brother must be guilty."

"Why do you think she was so interested?"

"Couldn't she have told someone else?"

"She could have. I never said she wasn't a suspect."

"I don't know about Kit, but my father and brother didn't do it. I swear."

"You can't know that."

"I do know it and I'll prove it."

Cole frowned. "What do you mean, you'll prove it?"

"I'll find out who's doing it."

"Jesus! Are you crazy?" He almost jumped to his feet and came around the desk. "Don't even think about it. There's no way that I'd let you . . ." He took her by the shoulders and gave her a little shake. "Take it out of your mind!"

"Fine."

Cole's dark eyes narrowed in disbelief. "And I'm supposed to believe you'll listen to me?"

"I said fine, didn't I?"

"But you didn't say you'd keep out of it."

"I told you I would."

Cole groaned as he watched her eye begin to twitch. "Oh, God," he said as he pulled her hard against him. "Every time I think things are going to be great, something else happens."

"Nothing is going to happen." The words were muffled since he held her face hard against his chest.

"You're right about that. Nothing is going to happen because I'm not letting you out of my sight."

"I was only going to watch the docks."

"Is that all?" he asked with no little sarcasm. "Just watch the docks? What about the lowlife that hangs around them? Were you going to watch them too?"

"What lowlife?"

"Pickpockets, dockside whores, drunks, thieves, every kind of criminal imaginable, including hijackers. How would you like to wake up on a ship on your way to a harem?"

Emy's surprise couldn't have been more obvious. She pulled back and looked into his angry expression with huge, rounded eyes. "How come they look so normal?"

"The people you see in the daytime are not the same as at night."

"You don't go there alone, do you?"

Cole laughed in disbelief. That she should be afraid for him and yet think nothing of putting herself in danger was just about the most ridiculous thing he'd ever imagined. "I know most of them. They wouldn't hurt me."

"So why should they hurt me?"

"Because they're not afraid of you," Cole thundered. He breathed a long, weary sigh as he gathered her close to him again. "Swear you won't get involved in this."

402

"Cole, I won't get hurt."

His arms tightened around her. "Swear it!"

"All right. I swear."

He pulled back and looked her in the eye, his gaze filled with suspicion. "What are you swearing to exactly?"

"I swear I won't go near the docks."

Cole looked at her for a moment before he relaxed his hard expression into a smile. "You can tell your family they don't have to move."

Emy shot him a look of annoyance. "Until the next time you're angry, you mean?" She shook her head. "I've already found them rooms."

"I don't want your grandmother far from you."

Emy shot him a puzzled frown.

"For one thing, she'll want to be with you when the baby comes. And if she should take ill, you would have to travel to see to her care."

"She's as healthy as a—"

"Emy!"

Emy pushed herself out of his arms, having had quite enough of his orders. "I'll tell them."

Cole smiled as he watched her gather her things together. She glared at that smile. "Do you always have to get your way?"

"Only on important matters."

"I'll see you at home."

"No kiss good-bye?"

"I'm not in the mood to kiss you right now." Emy slammed the door to his low laughter.

Emy walked through the huge open market, a

403

basket on her arm. She'd already walked by most of the fruits and vegetables she'd come for, never seeing the neat displays. Her mind was hardly on shopping.

Pauline, the young girl that helped Becky in the kitchen, shot her one odd look after an other. Emy never noticed.

She couldn't get her mind off her conversation with Cole. Was Kit the culprit behind the robberies? Could it be that the girl was in league with the thieves?

There was only one way to find out. Emy was going to see her. She was going to get to the bottom of this before her father and brother suffered for it.

Emy suddenly turned to the girl who walked a few steps behind her. She shoved a few bills into her hand as well as the basket. "I've got to go. Finish this for me, will you?"

Finish? They hadn't begun. The girl's big black eyes widened in surprise. She'd never shopped for the house before. "What should I get?"

"I don't care. Whatever you think . . ." Emy hadn't finished the sentence before she was swallowed up by the milling crowd, on her way to see her grandmother, her only thought being, perhaps Grandmère would know where Kit spent her days.

Emy waved down an open carriage. It was the fastest way to get home, and now that she'd decided what should be done, she didn't want to waste a minute.

Emy almost missed her and probably would have if it hadn't been for the red dress. The color was so bright and so out of place in the middle of the day, Emy couldn't help but notice the small, dark-haired woman who laughed at something a man called out and then walked into the building. The carriage went by before Emy realized the woman with the red dress and redder lips was her sister. She called to the driver to stop, paid his fee, and stepped down.

Emy bit her lip, not at all sure she wanted to see Kit now. She was dressed as if she were a lady of the night. Emy wrinkled her nose at the thought. She had no misgivings about the fact that Kit had taken a lover. What else could have accounted for her many absences and the money spent on perfume and dresses? Perhaps she should send Cole to see her. Perhaps she should wait.

Emy shook her head. No. Kit hadn't come home last night. No doubt she'd stayed the night in this very building. She'd see her now. There was no telling when she'd get another chance.

Emy raised her hand, ready to knock on the huge ornately carved oak door. "What are you doing?"

Emy gasped at the deep voice sounding close to her ear. She spun around and held her hand to her chest as if to ease the pounding of her heart. "Jason! You scared me half to death."

"It's better, I think, than Cole beating you half to death."

Emy wondered why Cole should care if she spoke to her sister. Granted, he might not relish the idea of his wife visiting Kit's lover's lodgings, but she wasn't all too thrilled about visiting them herself.

She felt a mixture of both confusion and annoyance. The very idea that Cole would dare to raise his hand to her did not sit well at all. She was about to say, oh, he would, would he? when she

405

noticed the look of real concern in Jason's eyes. "What's the matter with you?"

"Do you know what kind of a place this is?"

"No. Why?"

Jason sighed. How was he supposed to tell a lady that she was unwittingly about to enter a whorehouse. "What do you want in there?"

"My sister. I need to talk to her."

"Kit's not in there."

"I just saw her go in."

Damn! He should have known. The girl looked to be a wild one. Still, she was only fifteen. He wouldn't have imagined she'd be at her business so young. Jason cursed and then, realizing what he'd said, apologized. "I'm sorry."

"What's the matter with you?" Emy asked again. "Are you all right?"

"I'm fine." He ran his finger inside his collar as if suddenly realizing it was too tight. "Why don't you go home and I'll send Kit along directly."

Emy smiled. It was obvious the man felt a degree of discomfort. What Emy couldn't figure out was why. "Something is the matter. Tell me what it is."

There was no way to approach the truth with any discretion. There was no way but to come right out with it. "Emy, this place is a bordello."

Emy's eyes met his, and her cheeks grew dark with embarrassment. She hadn't imagined, although she should have. No decent woman wore that color red. No decent woman painted her lips, or smiled as men called out lurid remarks to her.

Emy appeared to pay close attention to the tips of her shoes peeking from beneath her skirt as she asked, "Could you get her to come out?"

Jason nodded. "I can try."

Emy stepped to the side of the door and waited as Jason knocked. A black man almost as impeccably dressed as Jason answered. "Sorry, we don't cater to men of color here. Go to—"

Jason interrupted with, "Tell Miss Kit her sister is waiting to see her."

The man looked out the door to his left, noticed Emy, nodded, and shut the door.

Kit laughed at Big George. "My sister? Here?"

"Outside."

Kit might have been lacking in any sense of morality. Still, she wasn't all bad. Indeed, she was more forgiving than most. She harbored no ill feelings toward her sister for the slaps she'd taken the night before. She imagined Emy had merely been jealous. The fact was, jealousy simply wasn't an emotion Kit could understand. She'd never loved a man, or wanted one particular man enough to care who else he slept with.

"Tell her to come in."

George shook his head. "I don't think . . . there's a black man with her. Mr. Briggs won't like it."

Kit shrugged. "So tell him to stay outside."

Jason shook his head as George held the door wide. "Don't go in there alone."

"I'll be all right. Don't worry."

"Jesus, Cole will kill me."

"Nothing will happen."

"If you're not out in ten minutes, I'm going to get him."

"Fifteen." Emy wasn't sure how long this conversation was going to take.

"Fifteen," Jason agreed.

Chapter Twenty-one

Emy tried not to notice the mostly naked women, but there were so many of them. Good Lord, how could they lounge around in garments so thin that nothing was left to the imagination? They talked and laughed among themselves in easy camaraderie while sipping from cups of coffee, just as if they weren't exposed at all. Emy had never seen anything like it. Emy had never imagined anything like it.

She was ushered up the wide stairs, thankful to leave the chattering women behind. Perhaps her cheeks would soon return to their normal color, now that she wasn't forced to try to ignore so many pairs of naked breasts and thighs.

The hallway's walls and ceiling, like downstairs, were papered in white and gold. A red rug ran its length, and at least a dozen shining mahogany doors lead to, Emy presumed, private rooms. The man stopped at one of the many doors and knocked. Everything looked so expensive. She'd never seen wood polished to this particular gleam, nor felt her shoes sink into rugs so thick.

Emy had always imagined the wages of sin to be slightly less luxurious. She hadn't thought that so much could be gained by doing wrong.

Emy gasped as Kit answered the door, for she had wrapped a robe around her but had neglected to secure it properly until far too late. Emy cringed at the sight of her sister's nakedness, mortified that Kit could so casually expose herself, even though the man at her side seemed to notice nothing amiss as she quickly gathered the edges of her robe together.

"Come on in," Kit said as she turned and walked back into the room.

Kit sat herself before a table and mirror as Emy moved slowly into the gaudily decorated room. Tassels covered just about everything in the room, including the little chair Kit sat upon. Figurines, pictures, vases, and jars of potpourri dotted every available surface. The rugs were red, as were the chairs, the velvet drapes, and bed cover, but none of the considerable if tasteless adornments, not even the mirrors that covered most of one wall and the ceiling over the bed, would register until sometime later. Her attention was solely focused on her sister and what Emy considered a most shameful display. All she could feel was humiliation.

"Kit, how can you walk around like that? The man saw—"

"Oh, that's just Big George. It doesn't matter. Besides, he's seen just about everything there is to see."

Kit finished brushing her hair, and to Emy's absolute shock began to apply rouge to the tips of her breasts. Emy thought she'd probably gone mad. She wasn't seeing what she thought she was seeing. She wasn't standing in a bordello, watching her half-naked sister apply rouge to personal parts of her anatomy.

Emy wanted more than anything to ask Kit what she was doing, but decided at the last minute perhaps she was better off not knowing.

Emy closed her eyes and tried to hold back her mortified moan. It took her a few minutes, but she finally managed to say, "I'd like to ask you a few questions."

Apparently Kit had finished whatever it was she'd been about. She closed her robe and shrugged. "All right, so I never slept with Cole. I knew you didn't believe me. I only said it because—"

Emy might have smiled, might have, that is, if her sister's actions hadn't been a disgrace. She interrupted the last of it with "That's not why I'm here."

Through the mirror Kit shot her a puzzled look. "Then why?"

"You've been asking some questions lately about the ships coming into port. I wanted to know why."

"Charlie is waiting for gambling tables. So he asked me to watch out for them."

"Wouldn't he be notified of their arrival?"

"I don't know." Kit shrugged. "He just wanted to make sure they weren't stolen or lost."

"How long has he been waiting?"

"Oh, a couple of months, maybe."

"Kit, did you happen to mention other ships and what they were bringing in?"

Kit bit her lip, knowing that was exactly what she

had done. She wasn't sure what was behind these questions and didn't much care. She had no knowledge of the robberies, since she just about dedicated herself to only one activity and the usual conversation once in bed. She rarely ventured beyond the immediate. Still, she had suspected Charlie of ulterior motives almost from the first. "I might have said something. Why?"

"No reason." Emy had to force herself not to shout for joy. She couldn't wait to get out of there. She couldn't wait to get back to Cole and tell him all she'd learned. "I've got to go."

She turned to leave, when she was brought up short with, "Emy, wait."

Emy's hand was on the doorknob when she turned back to her sister.

"I might as well tell you now. I won't be coming home again. Probably not even for a visit." Kit shrugged as if denying any suffering on her part, but Emy knew better. The pain in her sister's eyes told clearly that this decision had not been easy to come by. "Papa wouldn't be too happy about what I'm doing."

Emy didn't respond. They both knew how their father would react to the choice Kit had made. Emy nodded.

"I just wanted to know if you and Cole are back together."

She nodded again.

"Good. You'll take care of Grandmère, won't you?"

"You don't have to ask. You know how I feel about her."

"I might be moving to Natchez. I've heard a girl can make it good there. A lot of men are willing to pay big money for a pretty woman who will . . ." Kit decided at the last second not to go into detail. Her sister might be a married woman, but Kit was positive Emy couldn't imagine what went on between some men and women. "They'll pay a good price."

Emy didn't know what to say. How could she in good conscience wish her sister luck, and yet, because she was her sister, how could she not? Emy compromised with, "I hope you'll be happy."

"It's what I want."

Kit came to Emy. The two hugged, knowing in all likelihood they wouldn't see each other again, at least not for a very long time. Emy held the girl close to her while pictures of Kit as a child came to mind. A pretty, dark-haired little girl holding to a ratty blanket while sucking on her thumb. Emotion closed her throat. She couldn't speak, and slipped out of the room as tears rolled down both their cheeks.

Emy was halfway down the stairs when a man came in the front door.

Charlie's eyes widened with shock. What the hell? "Mrs. Brackston?" he asked, clearly amazed to see her in his house.

Emy wiped the last of her tears away and glared at the man before her. Did he think her so naive as to acknowledge his presumptuous greeting? Emy knew without a doubt that this was Charlie, the very man behind the robberies who had brought blame to her and her family. Surely he had to know she wouldn't look in his direction, especially after his misuse of her sister. It never entered Emy's mind that her sister was equally at fault, that none of this would have come about if Kit hadn't been all too willing.

Charlie watched her look right through him as she walked directly out his front door. Jesus! What was she doing here?

The first thought that had come to mind upon seeing her was his damn good fortune to have the use of both sisters. It didn't take but a second before he knew she thought herself too good to even talk to him. Obviously she had come to see her sister.

What could be so important that the prim and proper Mrs. Brackston had actually entered a whorehouse?

Charlie ignored the servant who had come to his side, and headed directly for his room. He opened the door to find Kit blowing her nose into one of his snowy handkerchiefs and frowned at the liberty she constantly took with his things.

Charlie had more faults than most, but his obsession, besides women, was with cleanliness. He was meticulous with his personal articles and hated it when a woman presumed to use his combs or hairbrushes. Watching her blow her nose, he hadn't a doubt that he'd throw the handkerchief away.

He felt a moment of disgust at the sight of her, and wondered why it was that her obvious immorality, the star reason for his earlier attraction, no longer intrigued him. It was at that moment that he knew it was over between them. It hadn't taken long for the attraction to wane. Had she been more like her sister, perhaps . . . He shrugged aside the thought.

It didn't matter that Kit was an excellent companion in bed. There were others easily as good and eager. Others that were at least half as pretty, while being a damn sight more fastidious. "What did she want?"

"My sister?"

He nodded as he took off his gloves and hat.

"She came to ask a few questions, I guess."

"What kind of questions?"

"I don't know, something about the ships and their cargo."

Charlie felt a niggling sense of apprehension. His eyes narrowed as his heart began to beat just a bit harder. "What did you tell her?"

"What could I tell her? I don't know anything about them."

"Did you happen to mention the things you told me?"

Kit shrugged. "I might have. Why?"

"Stupid bitch!" Kit cried out as the flat of his hand contacted the side of her face. The blow was so hard, it knocked Kit to the floor.

She was holding the side of her face, blinking back tears of shock and pain, when she asked, "What did you do that for?"

Charlie kicked her in the stomach and snarled his revulsion as she gagged and saliva bubbled from her lips. She disgusted him. Charlie didn't think that his abuse had caused her this condition. All he could do was wonder what he'd ever seen in her. "Where was she going?"

"Oh, Jesus," Kit groaned as he kicked her again. She rolled to her stomach, bringing her hands up, too late, as she tried to protect her face from his boots.

"Was she going to her husband?"

Kit couldn't answer him. She'd never known pain like this in her life. She'd thought Emy's slaps a bit much, but those stinging insults were nothing compared to this. She was in agony. Having had the breath kicked from her, she couldn't utter more than whimpering moans in response to his questions.

Charlie paced the floor, oblivious of her agony. Suddenly he seemed to come to a decision. He was nearly out the door when he remembered her. "Don't be here when I get back."

Emy was mortified over the entire situation. She could hardly look Jason in the eye. Lord, what must he think of her and her family? Still, she saw none of the supposed censure in his dark, gentle gaze and forced a smile of sorts. "Thank you for waiting. I've got to see Cole."

"Do you want me to get you a carriage?"

Emy gave a real smile at his thoughtfulness. "No. His office is only a few blocks away."

Jason nodded. "I'll walk with you."

"Jason, I'll be fine."

Jason wasn't happy about leaving her. He didn't know why, but he felt oddly dissatisfied that she should be alone. "I'll walk with you anyway."

Emy shrugged. She couldn't stop the man from accompanying her, she supposed, even though she knew some confusion at his sudden concern.

They were a block from the office when a tough

stepped out of the alley. The man was big, but no bigger than Jason. He stood with feet spread for balance. He wore a derby, a shirt that could have been three shades whiter, with a high collar and no tie. His plaid suit was just a touch too small and had seen better days.

He invoked no fear, for many in the city dressed as he. Emy smiled and made to walk around him, when a hand suddenly reached out, held to her arm, and brought her hard up against his chest. An arm like a belt of steel held her in place.

Emy gave a startled cry of surprise to find herself clutched in a strange man's arms.

Jason, realizing his concern had been a premonition of this exact moment, reached for his gun. It had been a few years since he'd worn a sidearm, but the instinctive movement most cowboys acquire when faced with trouble had not as yet been laid to rest.

There were two problems. One being that Jason reached for a gun that wasn't there. The second being that the man he faced was not without one. Jason cursed. Regardless of the outcome, he charged the man.

The man shot Jason as easily as if he swatted away an annoying fly.

Emy's scream of horror was instantly muffled as the villain holstered his gun and covered her mouth even as he dragged her into the alley. A moment later she knew nothing but blackness as a meaty fist swung to meet her jaw.

*   *   *

As marshal, Cole was, of course, notified of every mishap within the city limits as well as out. Today proved to be no exception. A man raced into his office. "A man just got shot over on Bourbon Street!"

Cole nodded and grabbed his hat and rifle as he left the office.

He ran down one alley and made a left. He almost crashed into the small crowd of bystanders. "Move aside," he said, "let me in."

A man was lying facedown on the sidewalk, a small pool of blood gathering at his side. Cole leaned down and called for someone to fetch a doctor. It was only when he turned Jason to his back that he realized his friend had been shot. "Jesus! What the hell happened?"

Jason had blacked out immediately after the injury, and was just now coming around. He moaned in pain, but realized through the agony that Cole was kneeling beside him. "They got her."

"Take it easy. I've got a doctor coming."

"Cole, I couldn't stop him. I tried."

Cole's gaze took in the damage. Apparently Jason had been nearly on top of the man when shot. His coat was burned black with gunpowder. Whoever had done this had come damn close to killing the man. The bullet couldn't be more than four inches above his heart. It looked to be just below his shoulder. Cole could only pray it had missed a lung.

"Who did it?"

"I don't know. He grabbed Emy."

"What? Emy?! Emy was with you?"

"That's what I've been telling you, dammit! What

418

the hell are you hanging around here for?" Jason winced against the pain, his mouth tight with his suffering. "He took her into the alley."

Cole was on his feet and running before he gained his full height. He ran through the alley. Nothing. Standing on the next street, he looked both ways even as he tried to bring his emotions under control. He couldn't help her if he panicked. He'd never find her if he didn't calm down and think.

As far as he knew, Emy had no enemies. Who would have taken her? And why? Cole couldn't hold back the rising fear.

Had this been a chance abduction? Had a man simply found her appealing and taken her on a whim?

"Jesus, God, please. If you really exist, if you're there, help me!"

Hawk heard the whispered, desperate prayer and came to a sudden stop. Before returning to his rooms, he'd stopped off at a certain lady's place and to both of their delights, had been deliciously entertained for most of the morning. He was on his way home, more than ready to catch a few hours sleep before it was time to return to work. He wished Jake were back at work. He was sick of the night shift.

Hawk eyed his friend for a moment. Cole's face was ashen. He appeared weak, perhaps injured as he leaned against a wall. Hawk frowned. Since when had Cole taken up praying? "What's going on?"

Cole looked up to find Hawk at his side. The man should have been home in bed. Cole couldn't imagine why he wasn't. Unless . . .

"What are you doing here?"

"I live here." Hawk nodded toward the building Cole leaned against. "Remember? What's happening?"

"Emy's been kidnapped!"

Hawk almost laughed. "Get the hell . . ." And then he noticed the panic in Cole's eyes. "Why?"

"How the hell do I know why?" Cole grabbed him by the collar and with the strength of ten lifted him from his feet with one hand.

"Take it easy."

"Take it easy? Take it easy when they have my wife? Hawk, God, you've got to help me find her."

"I will. Just let me go." It was only then that Cole realized what he was doing. He loosened his hold and stepped back, his eyes wild with fear.

"You've got to calm down so you can think."

"I know." It was one thing to say, quite another to do. Cole wasn't sure it was possible.

"Have there been any threats?"

"No."

"What about Kit?"

It took about twenty seconds, but Cole lost that panicked look. His dark eyes narrowed as burning rage entered their depths. "What about her?"

"She's taken up with Charlie Briggs. Do you think—"

"Let's go."

Hawk had seen a lot in his life. He'd seen men die. He'd seen some beg for help and whimper in their last moments on earth. He'd seen others brave the final darkness with a glare of hatred, but he'd never seen any man with this particular promise of death in his eyes.

Hawk felt a shiver race up his spine. He sure as hell wouldn't want to face this man. The bastard who had taken Emy wouldn't have an easy time of it.

Cole hammered his hand against the solid door. This was the third place. How the hell many did the son of a bitch own? Cole stepped back, his eyes widening with surprise to see Kit answer the door. She stepped outside, a small bag clutched tightly in her hand.

Her face was puffy and red, slightly discolored around one eye. Apparently she'd taken some abuse, but Cole couldn't find it within himself to care. All he cared about was Emy, and if Kit were responsible for his wife's abduction, he'd kill her with his bare hands.

The rifle clattered to the sidewalk as he grabbed the startled girl by the throat and shoved her up against the now-closed door. "Where is she?"

"Who?" Had the entire male population of this city gone mad? First Charlie, and now Cole. What the hell was happening?

"Take it easy," Hawk said as he touched Cole's arm.

Cole ignored him.

Kit's fearful gaze moved to the man behind Cole. She could feel Cole's fingers tightening, closing off her ability to breathe. "Stop him!" The words were hardly a croak as he exerted pressure.

"If you don't tell me where she is, I'll kill you right

here on the spot."

Kit might have been a girl of only fifteen, but she knew when death stared her in the face. Her entire body trembled as if palsied. "Cole, please. I didn't do anything."

"Where is she?"

"Who?"

"Emy, you little bitch." He gave her a hard shake, not at all concerned that her head slammed into the door. "Where is she?"

"I don't know. She was here before, but she left. I don't know where she went."

"You'd better tell me, Kit. Your life depends on it."

"All I know is she came by and asked a few questions."

"What kind of questions?"

"About the ships and their cargo."

"What did you tell her?"

"That Charlie had asked me to find out about his tables."

"And you told Charlie about the ships and what they held?" Hawk asked, realizing at last who was behind the robberies.

"Yeah, I told him. He said—"

"What happened to your face?" Hawk continued the questioning.

"Charlie hit me."

"Why?"

"How should I know? All I did was tell him what Emy wanted."

"Christ," the two men said in unison.

Cole released her and hardly noticed that she

422

slumped with relief against the door. Her fingers came to her bruised throat. "What the hell is the matter with everybody today?"

Both men ignored her question and never noticed when she picked up the dropped bag and walked toward the river. She was getting out of this city. And it couldn't be too soon as far as she was concerned.

Cole shot Hawk another look. The panic was returning. He couldn't control it. They both knew who had her and why. What they didn't know was how they were going to find her. "Tell me," he urged his friend. "What? What should I do?" Cole was clearly losing it.

"I don't know. Let me think."

Hawk spoke his thoughts aloud. "What would I do if I were Charlie?"

"He probably knows by now that his man shot Jason."

Hawk cursed, hearing this for the first time. "Is he dead?"

"No. He looks bad, but I think . . . He's got to figure Jason told me what happened."

"That means he's already hiding."

"Would he keep her a prisoner in one of his places?" Cole asked, his tone oddly hopeful.

"No." Hawk shook his head. "Too dangerous. She might escape and he'd have to know that we'd find them easily enough."

"He'd get rid of her." Cole's voice was pure agony. He'd known the truth of it even before his first hopeful suggestion.

"Right, but how?"

Cole groaned. He didn't want to think of this. He didn't want to explore the hundred ways there were to kill a woman. He didn't want to think about the suffering, the fear Emy had to know before the end.

"He wouldn't kill her."

Cole thought he might collapse at the confidence in that statement and found he had to lean against a wall for support or see himself sprawled upon the sidewalk in relief. Hawk believed what he'd just said. It hadn't been said simply to ease Cole's fears. It was obvious in the man's tone and the look of concentration on his face. It took an effort to control himself, for Cole was as close to sobbing as any man had a right to be. "Why not?" He could hardly get the words out.

"Three reasons. First, he's not a murderer, and second, Charlie's the kind to cover his bets. Just in case he gets caught, he wouldn't want to face you after killing your wife."

"And the third?"

For a moment Hawk seemed reluctant to respond, but he figured his friend knew as well as he the truth of it. He was just saying aloud both their thoughts. "Emy is a valuable commodity. He could get big bucks for someone half as beautiful." Hawk watched Cole's eyes harden as the panic lessened and the rage came again. He went on. "If there's one thing Charlie knows, it's women and their value. There's no telling how much he could get for an innocent like Emy." Hawk shook his head and said in all confidence, "No, he won't hurt her."

"He's a dead man."

"We've got to find him first."

Cole had never felt so calm. He was finally thinking and one of his thoughts was how Charlie Briggs was going to die. "Contact the harbor master. Tell him *nothing,* not a ship, not even a canoe leaves these docks for any destination until I personally okay it. Then get over to the river and make sure of the same. I don't care about schedules. No paddle steamers move out to the river until I say so."

"Right. What are you going to do?"

"We need roadblocks. I'm going to get some men together and close off every road, lane, and path from this city."

Hawk grinned. "We're going to get him."

"You're right about that. Let's just hope we get him in time."

Both men knew what was at stake. There was a good chance that Emy might suffer at the hands of the whoremonger. There were innumerable things he could do to her that wouldn't involve her death. But Cole couldn't think about that now. He wouldn't think of it until he had his hands on Charlie Briggs's throat.

Chapter Twenty-two

Emy moaned at the pain in her head. She couldn't remember ever having a headache so bad. Mentally she tried to locate the exact origins. It was then she realized it wasn't only her head that hurt. It was her jaw as well. She tried to raise her hand to comfort the afflicted area and found herself unable to move.

Suddenly she stiffened. She remembered.

Emy kept her eyes closed. She didn't know where she was, but she was sure someone was there with her. Someone was watching her.

She heard a low chuckle, a man's silky, strangely obscene laugh. "I know you're awake, Mrs. Brackston."

Emy continued feigning sleep.

"I said, I *know* you're awake, Mrs. Brackston."

Emy's heart pounded in her throat. It was all she could do to remain still. But she didn't remain still for long. A hand caressed her breast, and despite the pain it caused to her head, Emy jumped.

She opened her eyes and kicked out, barely missing the man standing over her.

Charlie Briggs laughed as he jumped back. "I should probably tie your feet." He licked his lips. "But I won't. I've got plans for us later."

He grinned, watching as her eyes widened with horror and then laughed aloud as a shudder vibrated her petite form.

"I see you understand my meaning. Perhaps you're a bit more intelligent than your stupid sister. Are you?"

Emy glared her hatred. *Intelligent enough to know my husband is going to kill you for this.* There was no way Emy could respond. Not with the gag in her mouth. She tried to push it away with her tongue, but it was held firmly in place with something that covered her mouth and tied at the back of her head. Of course she could make muffled protesting sounds, but calling for help was impossible.

"You'd feel a bit more comfortable if I took the gag away. Shall I?"

Emy narrowed her gaze as she wondered why he should suddenly be so concerned with her comfort. She felt her heart sink with despair as he answered her silent question with his next statement. "We're in the hold of a ship. No one could hear you if you screamed."

Emy's eyes widened at this piece of news. Her gaze moved beyond the man to the rafters over his head, holding a single lantern, to the ladder that stood in the center of the vaultlike room and stretched to a square cut in the ceiling, the only apparent means of escape, to the huge crates stacked just about everywhere. Having never been in the hold of a ship before, Emy couldn't be sure he spoke the truth. Still, it appeared as if he had. Emy nodded and then groaned at the pain and the wave of dizziness even that small movement caused.

She wondered if the ship had been put to sea. She noticed the lantern did not sway. Actually, she felt no movement at all, but how much movement did one feel in the bowels of a ship? Emy couldn't ask. His answer meant her sanity, if not her life. All she could do was pray they hadn't as yet left port and that she had the courage and strength to escape. "Where are you taking me?" she asked the moment she was able.

"Does it matter?" The man's smile was a horrid knowing grin of pure depravity. It sent chills down Emy's spine. How in the world was she going to get out of there? "I do hope you enjoy ocean cruises."

"You know, of course, that my husband will kill you for this."

"My thoughts exactly, which is why he won't be finding us."

"He'll find us. He won't give up until he does."

Charlie tossed off a goodly amount of amber liquid in a short glass, the fear in his eyes unmistakable even in this meager light.

"And when he does"—Emy congratulated herself on her confident laugh. She wished she felt half as confident as she sounded—"I wouldn't want to be you."

"Shut up. I don't want to hear about your husband."

Emy laughed again, pouncing on the man's

obvious fear. "Don't you? Wouldn't you like to know your future?" She allowed a sly grin, praying she looked as assured as she sounded. "I could tell you what it is."

"If you don't shut up, I'll gag you again." Charlie nodded at her silence. He knew his threat would do the trick. "The fact is, we'll be gone from here in less than a quarter of an hour. He'll never find you. Not where we're going."

Emy felt a wave of relief. Inadvertently, he'd just told her that they hadn't left port. For the first time since awakening, Emy felt escape a real possibility. Without asking permission, she came to a sitting position and looked around. She had been reclining on two wooden trunks. No wonder her head hurt like it did. After the abuse she'd taken to her jaw, a bed of wood hardly soothed. "Why are you doing this?"

"Simple, really. I couldn't allow you to tell your husband about my business interests. The moment I found out you knew, I sent word out that you were to be stopped. The truth is, you were supposed to die, but the fool who found you delivered you into my hands instead."

"And you're no murderer."

Emy thanked the Lord that she was able to keep her voice flat, totally without emotion. And then she almost cried with relief at his reluctant shrug of agreement. Charlie would never know what that shrug meant to her.

"No, I'm not. What I am is a man who works with what he's got. And I figure the fates sent you to me for a purpose." Another grinning leer. "Sweetling, you're going to make me a rich man."

I'm going to make you a dead one, in any case.

Charlie laughed at the narrowing of her eyes. She was a beauty, this one. He almost couldn't wait to see what she looked like without all those clothes. But he would. He'd wait until the ship was put out to sea. Only then would he be able to relax. Only then could he enjoy that body as it was meant to be enjoyed.

Charlie had known he'd one day leave New Orleans. The fact that he'd been forced into leaving sooner than he had planned hardly mattered, nor did it matter the fortune he'd left behind. Despite his hurried escape, he was a rich man. A smile curved his handsome mouth as his gaze fell to the two bags against the wall. He'd stopped at the bank before boarding this ship and paid the captain handsomely to keep his presence a secret. No, it didn't matter what he had been forced to leave behind. Not as long as he had all that money.

Once they reached England, he'd set up business again. And this woman would be his star attraction. Charlie hadn't a doubt that after a few weeks spent sharing his bed, she'd do everything she was told. He hadn't met a woman yet that he couldn't convince, one way or another, to see to his way of thinking.

She'd be his lady whore. Damn, with that special touch of elegance and innocence, he'd have to beat the men away.

Cole walked into the café. It didn't take but a second for both the Du Maurier men to know something was seriously wrong.

"The baby," Jacques said, and then sighed with dramatic flare as was his way when Cole shook his head.

"She's all right?" Anton inquired, knowing if it wasn't the baby, then it was Emy that had caused the man this worried expression.

"I hope to God."

"What happened?"

"She's been kidnapped."

Both men spoke at once. Cole put his hand up, refusing their questions. This wasn't the time for talk. This was the time for action. "I need your help."

They continued on, speaking quickly as they bombarded him with questions.

He brought them at last to silence with "Every minute we waste could chance his getting away."

"Who?"

"Charlie Briggs has her."

Both men gasped in horror. Jacques clutched his chest and Cole wasn't sure if the man wasn't about to have some sort of attack. Both knew of the man and what his taking Emy would entail.

"Easy, now." Cole couldn't believe he was actually comforting another. "We'll find her." He directed his next words to Anton. "I want you to gather some men. We need to close off this city." His mouth tightened and his eyes narrowed with suppressed rage. "And I mean every road, every goddamned path, every possible means to get out. Unless the man can fly, we'll have him soon enough."

It didn't take but a few minutes. More than a dozen men gathered in the café, listening to the orders given. Cole nodded in satisfaction as he watched them hurry to their assigned posts, ready to see to this business. Soon, he promised himself. Soon he'd have her with him again. There was no way he'd allow anything less.

Cole had no doubt that if Briggs was still in the city, in the city he would remain. He wouldn't let himself think of the possibility that the man might have already left. He hadn't, Cole swore. Please God, there hadn't been enough time.

Cole left the café and rode like a madman toward the docks. He imagined Briggs would think a ship the most expedient means of escape. Only no ship was leaving this city before being thoroughly searched. And then searched again.

Emy watched Charlie check his watch. He'd done it innumerable times in what Emy supposed to be less than a quarter of an hour. He was obviously nervous. If his drinking and pacing were anything to go by, he was very nervous indeed.

There was no telling how long she had. Minutes, seconds perhaps. How was she supposed to get out of there?

"Can you untie my hands?"

Charlie shot her a sharp look. Apparently his mind had been elsewhere and her voice had brought him back to the immediate problem. Why the hell hadn't they set sail?

"You can stay like that for a bit."

"They hurt. I am losing feeling in them."

"If you're losing feeling, how can they hurt?"

Emy frowned. "Please?"

"Maybe later."

"Can I stand up?"

"Why, are your legs losing feeling as well?" he asked, his tone telling clearly of his irritation.

"No. I need to . . ." She bit her lip, trying to appear uneasy. Whether true or not, she certainly would have been embarrassed at the mention of so delicate a subject, but Emy knew none of her usual modesty and quite honestly amazed herself at the ability to ask, "Is there a chamber pot I could use?"

Charlie scowled. "Now?"

Emy squirmed as if uncomfortable and gave him her most pleading look. "I really have to . . ."

Damn, but women were an annoyance. Except for one thing, they were useless creatures. Even after enjoying their bodies, he often found them disgusting with face paint smeared and stale breath, as well as body odor. Generally he knew them to be nothing but trouble.

And this one, despite her refined manners and ladylike ways, was no exception. He should refuse her request. If he had any sense, he'd tell her to do what she had to do in her clothes. But the fact was, Charlie had specific plans for her and the thought of her soiling her clothes left him disgusted.

"I saw a bucket the next level up. There's nothing down here."

Emy was almost beside herself with joy, but fought to keep her smile at bay, knowing to show any excitement might very well mean her plans to escape would be lost.

She exaggerated a small groan of discomfort as he

helped her to her feet. Best, she thought, if he believed her weaker than she truly was. Perhaps he'd let down his guard. Perhaps she might make good an escape.

"Are you going to untie my hands?"

"No."

"Then how can I . . . ?" She glanced his way. Emy had no doubt that tied or not, she could somehow climb a ladder and make good her escape, but did he imagine her capable of seeing to her personal needs while bound?

"I'll help you."

The fact of the matter was, even if she had to use the chamber pot, she would have died before allowing a man, and a strange man at that, to help. She said nothing, but limped along as he guided her toward the ladder. She was a little stiff, but soon felt the strength return to her legs.

At the base of the ladder Charles seemed to hesitate, unsure of how to get the two of them up its steep incline. Finally he stepped back and nodded. "Go on."

"I'll fall with my hands bound."

"No, you won't. Just stand in front of me."

Emy did as she was told. It was slow going since she either had to hook her jaw over each rung or lean her full weight against the man behind her. Twice she stepped on her skirt, but finally watched as Charlie shoved aside the trapdoor overhead. She gained another four steps and rolled forward, crying out in indignation as Charlie's hands came to her assistance by cradling her derriere in a most familiar fashion.

His chuckle of amusement hardly registered before she gave a reflexive kick. Kicking had been her intent from the moment she placed her foot upon the first rung. The fact of the matter was, she couldn't have been more pleased to hear his laughter instantly cut off. She wouldn't know for some minutes that the heel of her booted foot had landed smack in the middle of his face.

Charlie saw stars as blood gushed from a possible broken nose. He almost fell as one hand reached for the injury.

Gutter words bellowed out behind her, careless of the fact that he was disclosing his so-far-hidden position. He had forgotten to gag her again, and Emy joined his cries of pain with her own desperate screams for help.

Charlie grabbed her foot, and Emy's terror increased tenfold. She knew, of course, who he was and exactly his intent, but grabbing her foot as she tried to crawl forward in the dark sent shivers of terror through her even as it gave her more strength than she had ever imagined herself capable of.

She kicked him again, screaming louder than ever. Her heart thundered as he loosened his hold. She shuddered at the thought of him somewhere behind her. She crawled farther from Charlie's searching hands. *God, if only there were some light!* Emy had no idea where she was or where she was going. She couldn't see a thing.

She came up on her knees and then struggled to her feet and started to run. A moment later she realized the folly of that action as she ran right into the side of the ship.

She groaned a soft sound of pain. It took a few seconds to realize what she'd done. She turned and leaned weakly against the curved wall, trying to regain her senses.

Her eyes had to adjust to the darkness. The square in the floor allowed only a meager portion of the dim light from below, but Emy could easily see Charlie clear the opening. He stepped into the darkness and Emy bit her lip, knowing his shadowing form melted as did hers into the blackness.

She wanted to cry out for help, but knew any sound on her part would only give away her position. What she had to do was find her way out of there. Apparently they were still in the hold. Idly she wondered how many levels there were. How much more would she have to climb before finding her way to freedom?

She stood perfectly still and tried to control her breathing. Something touched her foot. Good God, please not a rat! Emy would never have believed it, but she managed to stay in place and keep her scream of horror at bay as the rodent nuzzled the hem of her skirt. It moved off to her unequaled relief. She knew it had been a rat. An uncontrollable shiver ripped through her body. What else could it have been?

Her heart pounded in her ears. Could he hear it? Was he standing only inches from her side, playing a game, waiting for her to move or cry out?

Emy jumped, almost banging her sorely bruised head against the wall at the sound of his voice. She hadn't realized he'd moved. If she judged correctly, he was standing about ten feet to her left. "You might as well give it up. I'm standing in front of the ladder. You're not going anywhere."

Emy felt her hopes die an instant death. There was no way to get out of there without passing him, and there was no way she could pass him. Emy figured her best bet, her only hope, in fact, was to make her presence known. She didn't know how far below the deck they were, or if her cries for help would carry even to the floor above, but on the outside chance that someone would hear, that a brave soul would come to her assistance, she moved to her right and cried out, a continuous scream for help. She cried out until Charlie's body pressed up against hers and his hand closed over her mouth.

"Bitch," he grunted as she bit him.

Emy moaned at the blow he delivered to her face. Her head snapped to one side and then snapped again as he hit her once more.

Seven ships bobbed upon the gently flowing waters, their personnel and passengers waiting impatiently to be allowed to set out to sea. As the minutes ticked by, each captain knew he wouldn't be making his schedule, for the changing tide would soon see to it that he spent another night in the port of New Orleans.

Captain Miller, of the merchant *Sea Sprite*, was a decent sort. He didn't take much to a man misusing a woman. And it was clear to see that the woman below had been misused. Fact was, she looked unconscious, possibly from a beating, not exhausted and recuperating from an accident as the man claimed.

Still, it was hardly any of his business how a man treated his wife. Miller glanced down at his desk, his mind's eye seeing the many bills that were pushed into a secret compartment under the first drawer. He imagined he'd be able to buy his wife and the newest baby something real nice with that roll of bills.

A knock sounded on his cabin door. "Enter," he called out as his gaze moved again to his timepiece. "Have they allowed us . . . ?"

"I'm afraid not, captain."

Miller sighed, eyeing the big man who had stepped into the cabin. Except for his sidearm, he was dressed as a gentleman, but the look in his dark eyes promised not the least bit of gentleness. Miller caught the gleam of a badge almost hidden by his coat. "Marshal, if we don't leave now, we'll have to wait until morning."

"Then you'll wait." Cole offered no apology for detaining the ship. He didn't give a damn who was inconvenienced. All he cared about was finding Emy. "I'm looking for my wife, captain."

"So, I've heard, marshal. I'm afraid I haven't seen your wife."

"And you know what she looks like?"

"Ah, well no, actually, I don't."

"Then how can you say you haven't seen her?"

"Because I've been working since early this morning and no woman has come aboard this ship."

Cole caught the trace of strain in the last half of that sentence. He shot the captain a dark, hard look. "No woman, you say?"

The captain didn't answer, and for some reason

couldn't quite bring himself to meet the marshal's gaze. "None."

He was lying. Cole had been a lawman long enough to know when he heard a lie. It took more restraint than Cole realized he possessed not to leap across the desk and choke the truth out of him. "Captain, I advise you to tell me the truth. If I find out that you were involved in this kidnapping . . ."

"Kidnapping!" The captain jumped to his feet in alarm. "What the hell are you talking about?"

Cole hadn't a doubt that the man had been unaware, until that moment, of the truth. "I thought you knew. My wife has been taken against her will."

"Good God, man, are you serious?"

"Very serious, captain."

It couldn't be, of course. Mr. Smith was no kidnapper. The woman was his wife. Wasn't she?

Then why was he sworn to secrecy? Why was Mr. Smith so desperate to leave port unnoticed? He'd tried to keep out of it. He'd tried to mind his own business, but there were certain things a man couldn't let go by. "One question."

Cole nodded.

"Can you think of one reason why a man would pay me not to tell anyone he's on board."

"Any legitimate reason, you mean?" Cole could hardly talk, his heart pounded so hard with hope.

"Any reason."

"Is he alone?"

"No."

"A woman?"

Miller nodded.

"It could be they're eloping."

Miller shook his head. "He claims she's already his wife."

"Well then, why don't we ask him?"

"Good idea," Captain Miller came from around his desk and started toward the door. "I should have done that from the first."

Cole followed the man down a flight of stairs to the next level. The companionway held a dozen or more doors. The captain stopped before one of them and knocked.

No answer.

He knocked again and Cole, losing what little patience he possessed, opened the door and stepped into an empty room. "They're not here."

Captain Miller nodded while wondering where they could have gone off to. Surely the watch would have told him the moment his passengers had left. He stepped out to the hall and called, "Mr. Grasion."

Seconds later a man almost fell down the steps in his hurry to answer the captain's call. "Yes, sir?"

"The man and woman who took this cabin. Have you seen them?"

"No, sir."

"They didn't leave the ship?"

"No, sir."

Miller nodded. "Go back to your post."

"Yes, sir."

"And tell Mr. Walker I'd like to see him and three of the men."

"Yes, sir."

Minutes later the six of them began the search. It stood to reason that if Mr. Smith and his wife were not in their cabin and had not left the ship, they were still on board, but hiding. In the twenty-odd years since he'd first gained the title captain, Miller had never encountered anything like this.

They looked in every room, under every bed, in every closet and space that might permit a human form. Finally Miller sighed his disappointment. Apparently the man had left the ship after all. It was then that he glanced toward the door that led to the levels below.

"What's that?" Cole asked, not missing the direction of the man's gaze.

"The hold. They wouldn't have gone down there. There are no accommodations."

"They might if they were hiding."

"If she was taken against her will, she wouldn't be hiding."

"Unless that, too, is against her will."

Her knees wobbled but she fought against the blackness, fought against the pain, fought against the fear. He wasn't hitting her, but after three blows she wondered how she managed to remain on her feet.

He laughed at her soft moan of pain. "I've got better ways to quiet a woman," he whispered, his mouth horribly close to her.

His hold loosened just a bit. She tried to run, careless of the fact that she'd no doubt run into yet another wall, for what he was doing was worse than any amount of hitting. Only she couldn't move. His arms were around her, holding her to him with almost no effort. He was kissing her, and despite her obvious reluctance, he couldn't seem to stop.

Damn, but this woman was lovely. The feel of her body against his was enough to cause him to forget his intent to wait. He'd known from his first glance that she was lovely. Still, even with all the women he had known, he had never encountered one such as this. Her taste was sweet, even after hours of being gagged. Her skin smelled as fresh as if she'd just come from her bath. Charlie wondered if he was going to share her after all. Maybe, just maybe, he'd keep this one for himself.

She shoved at him with a shoulder, only to hear him laugh. Charlie figured one more slap was needed here. He wanted her just a bit more docile, and once docile he could untie her.

She grunted from yet another blow as he slammed her against a crate. Emy's head was spinning. This slap had been even fiercer than the last, and the last had almost knocked her out. She hardly noticed as he pulled the rope from her hands.

Careless of the pain he caused, he was kissing her again. Emy shuddered at the feel of his mouth against hers, at the feel of his tongue raping her mouth.

Emy forced her body to relax. There was no way she could win out against his strength. She had but one hope, and that was to catch him off guard.

Charlie sighed his enjoyment as he felt her soften against him. So she wasn't all that different from the rest after all. He hadn't been wrong. There was passion in this woman. All it took was a bit of coaxing and she would be as hot as her sister had been for his touch.

Emy waited. It was the most horrible experience of her life and yet she kept her wits about her and waited. He pressed his hips forward and reached for her hand, bringing it between their bodies. It was then that she made her move.

With every ounce of her strength, Emy shoved at him again. He stumbled back a step or two and might have stopped at that point had not the heel of his shoe caught on something, perhaps a raised floorboard. Whatever it was, it brought him off balance. He made a tiny sound of alarm as with arms flailing he tried to find his footing again. Only it didn't work.

They had been standing less than five feet from the open trapdoor. It took only a few steps on his part and suddenly, amazingly, he dropped through the opening to the floor below.

Emy's heartbeat thundered in her chest as she waited for the sounds of his footsteps on the ladder, for his head to surface again. She knew he'd come for her once more, only this time he'd be rougher than ever. She couldn't control the impulse to glance into the hole. She couldn't bear not knowing when he'd pounce again.

Cole heard the startled cry of a man just as he and Miller managed to shove aside the door to the hold. Light from three lowered lanterns poured into the darkness below, but the woman the men saw kneeling near the open hatch stayed in place. She didn't raise her head. She appeared to be looking down the hatch to the section below. Miller frowned. What the hell was she doing?

Cole was down the ladder and at her side before Miller could figure it out. He, too, glanced into the hold and then muttered, "Jesus" as he tore his wife from the gruesome sight.

Charlie lay against the ladder halfway down, his neck obviously broken, his body slumped, his head at a grotesque angle between two of the ladder's rungs.

Epilogue

"Exactly what do you think you're doing?"

Cole turned to grin at his wife. His eyes were shining with love and gratitude to see that she had come from her senseless lethargy at last. Grandmère had been right. She'd told him that all Emy needed was a few hours sleep and she'd be her old self again. Cole had never been more happy to see anyone's old self. "I was gathering a few things together."

Emy sat up in bed, moaned at the effort, and touched her fingertip to her swollen eye and pounding head. She winced and then muttered a soft curse. Cole figured he'd best watch his language from here on in, what with the baby and all. "Why? Where are you going?"

"I thought maybe I should sleep in the guest room. I didn't want to bother you."

Emy laughed a low sound of disbelief. "You didn't want to bother me? Since when?"

Cole grinned again, his dark eyes shining with happiness. God, but he loved this woman. Especially when she was sassy. "Are you trying to tell me that I bother you?"

"Trying?" She shot him a look of amazement and then winced again at the effort. "I thought I *was* telling you."

Cole bit his bottom lip, controlling the need to grab this woman and squeeze her tightly to him. "Would you mind if I held you?"

"You're asking me? Don't tell me you're turning over a new leaf."

"Not exactly. I asked only because you're so adorable and I'm afraid to touch you."

"Why?"

"Because you've suffered an injury."

"Oh, you mean my eye?" And at the tightening of his lips and dark look of anger, she admitted, "My head is killing me, but I imagine I'll survive."

"I love you," he said as he lifted her from the bed and walked to the chair by the terrace doors. He sat and nuzzled his face into the side of her neck very, very gently. "You're never going to know what it did to me to find out you were kidnapped." He shuddered at the memory, hardly able to believe she was safe in his arms at last.

She gave a sudden gasp and then groaned at the sudden movement. "Ow."

"What's the matter?"

"Jason. He was shot! Is he . . . ?"

"He's all right. He's milking it for all it's worth."

"What does that mean?"

"It means he's lying out in the sun while my servants wait on him hand and foot."

Emy smiled. "Really? He's very smart, isn't he?"

"Too smart. I ought to break his neck."

"Why?"

"For letting you walk into that whorehouse." His voice strengthened just a bit. "And I'm going to kick your ass all around this city if I ever find out that you stepped into another one. From this minute on, don't you ever, ever butt into my business. I swear, if you put yourself in danger again, I'll . . . I'll . . ."

Emy leaned back in his arms and shot him a long, hard look of warning. After a moment of silence she then paid a great deal of attention to her nails as she asked, ". . . Kick my what all around this city?"

There was just the slightest bit of hesitation before he returned with, "Well, maybe not all around the *whole* city."

She shot him another look and returned to the examination of her nails. "Where, then?"

"Well, maybe just here, in this room."

"And you plan to kick it, do you?"

"Kick it? Is that what you thought I said?"

She shot him a look from the corner of her one good eye. Cole figured his insides just melted and there hadn't been a damn thing he could have done to stop it. Despite her bruises, despite one eye almost swollen shut, she was simply the most beautiful creature he'd ever known. God, how he loved her. "You mean you didn't say kick it?"

"I wouldn't think of saying kick it."

"What was it you said, then?"

"Ah, what was it I said?" he asked, delaying his answer as long as possible. It was obvious the man was racking his brains trying to come up with something. "Ah, what I said was . . . kiss it. That's right. I said *kiss* it."

Emy had a time of it, trying to control her laughter at the more than obvious lie. "And you expect to kiss . . . ah . . . certain parts of my anatomy all around this city, or, as you say, this room?"

Cole sighed as he leaned his head back on the chair and then sighed again as Emy found his exposed throat quite irresistible. He adjusted his head so her lips might find more throat and closed his eyes at the pleasure. "Ah, sweetheart, I think I already am."